MIRROR IMAGE

OTHER BOOKS AND AUDIO BOOKS
BY CLAIR M. POULSON:

I'll Find You

Relentless

Lost and Found

Conflict of Interest

Runaway

Cover-Up

MIRROR IMAGE

a novel

CLAIR M. POULSON

Covenant Communications, Inc.

Cover image © Digital Vision/Getty Images

Cover design copyrighted 2005 by Covenant Communications, Inc.

Published by Covenant Communications, Inc.
American Fork, Utah

Printed in Canada
First Printing: August 2005

11 10 09 08 07 06 05   10 9 8 7 6 5 4 3 2 1

ISBN 1-59156-875-7

To my grandchildren, one of whom is adopted.

They bring indescribable joy to Ruth and me, as well as to their parents. Each one is so very special in his or her own way and is truly an inspiration. How grateful I am for my family.

ACKNOWLEDGMENT

The idea for this book was not my own. My good friend Joan Bird suggested to me one day that I should write a book about twins who were separated at birth. I liked the idea, and this book is the result. Thank you, Joan.

PROLOGUE

Had the cops found her before the accident, they might have accused her of being under the influence of either alcohol or drugs. She was lethargic, her eyes were red and could not focus well, and her speech was punctuated by long pauses. In time the cops would have discovered their error, since she was sober, had been for months, and for the sake of the precious life which she carried inside, was determined to remain so. She was in a lot of pain, and because of that she was worried that something was going wrong with her pregnancy. She was tired and afraid, but she was definitely sober.

The same could not necessarily be said of the man she was riding with. She suspected that he was high on something that afternoon, for he occasionally used drugs that he'd somehow managed to acquire without her knowledge. She had known him for a year, had fled her Texas home with him to escape the abuse and constant fear that dominated her life there. She'd left in spite of threats of death from her father and older brother, who hated her and feared the secrets that she carried away with her—secrets that could put the two men in prison, possibly even on death row.

This man she was now with had drifted into town one day and ordered coffee and a sandwich at the diner where the girl had worked. He'd paid attention to her, and though he was a lot older than her, she'd reciprocated. She liked how respectful he was to her; no leering, no crude remarks. She knew he thought she was twenty or twenty-one, but she didn't bother to correct him. Why ruin a good thing? He'd stayed around for a few days, and suddenly it had occurred to her that he might be the means of escape from the dreadful situation she lived with at home. So when he invited her, she left town with him, and for a time life was really good. He treated her well, and she actually fell in love with him. In Nevada, she even married him.

Now she carried his offspring. She also carried a few emotional scars from the occasional outbreaks of anger that occurred when he was under the influence of drugs or alcohol. But those times were not frequent, and they paled in comparison to what she'd gone through at home. So despite the sporadic bad times, she was glad she was with him. He'd made life bearable for her. He kept food in front of her and bought her nice things, and he promised to provide for the child after its birth. Lately he'd started talking about settling down somewhere and getting a real job. She honestly believed he loved her, and she had even shared with him the terrible secret that had caused her both to fear and to hate her father and brother. With a child she'd soon have to care for, she stubbornly closed her mind to where both his money and his drugs came from.

He had insisted that they change identities three or four times while they were together, so she seldom thought of herself under the name she'd been given at birth. But she didn't mind that, because she didn't want her brother and father ever to find her. She knew what her fate would be if they did. Still, she wished that her husband would allow her to carry ID. "You don't need it," he'd told her. "I'll take care of you." She felt some insecurity without ID, but so far it had not caused her any problems, so she didn't worry that much about it.

They had traveled the country from shore to shore a couple of times, had drifted briefly into Canada, and were now making their way through Utah on Interstate 70. Snow was falling with increasing intensity, and her husband kept mumbling about how hard it was to see. She asked him to slow down, and he did, but even then they continued on at what she considered an unsafe speed.

She didn't know what it was that suddenly appeared in the road ahead of them, partially obscured by the falling snow. She only knew it was big, it was dark, it wasn't moving, and that when they hit it, she was going to get hurt or die. She screamed because she couldn't help it, and she held her hands in a feeble protective gesture over her huge belly.

Sometime later, she became aware of activity around her. The pain she felt was intense and was not limited to just one area of her body. She was bitterly cold, but alive, and she marveled at that and prayed that her unborn child was okay. She was puzzled when she heard an officer say, "She's got to be the driver; there was nobody else in the wreck. Do you see anyone else?"

"No, but how did she get to the passenger side of the car?" a second officer said. "It doesn't seem likely that she would just bounce over there."

As the officers continued to talk, she was aware of hands touching her. She wondered where her husband was and hoped that he was okay. She didn't know what she'd ever do without him. He had his share of faults, but he was still her anchor. It didn't make sense that he wasn't in the car with her. Despite what the officers thought, he had definitely been driving their old, but very nice, gold-colored Cadillac, since she couldn't have driven it if she'd wanted to, never having learned to drive. She briefly considered that he might have been thrown from the vehicle, but then her pain suddenly intensified, and she began to cry. As she was removed from the wreckage, what concerned her even more than her own pain and injuries was the new little life she could feel squirming and kicking restlessly inside of her.

The teenage girl screamed with pain when she went into labor in the hospital. Finally, the doctor said gently to her, "We'll put you to sleep. It will all be over when you wake up."

Later, after the cesarean birth of two healthy infants, she woke up. She was once again in pain, and she was frightened. "Is my baby okay?" she asked.

"Yes, they are fine healthy boys with hair as blond as yours," a nurse said as she moved gently to the girl's side. The young mother tried to lift her head to see if she could catch a glimpse of her offspring, but it was clear that she was too weak from the surgery and the effects of the accident from earlier in the day.

"They?" the new mother asked hoarsely after laying her head back on the pillow. "Did you say they?"

"Yes, you have two healthy sons," the nurse said. "Would you like to see them?"

"Yes," the girl said. But before the nurse could get back with the twins, the girl convulsed and began to scream in agony.

The doctor began barking orders as he worked frantically. Finally he said, "She's hemorrhaging. I've got to go in again. Get her into the operating room!"

Despite the best efforts of a dedicated group of doctors and nurses, the girl died an hour later, never having seen the beautiful blond twins for whom she'd given her life.

Three days after the death of the teenage mother, a nurse working in the newborn nursery was caring for one of the orphaned twins in an adjoining room. When she went to return the little boy and care for his brother, the other twin was gone. A frantic search of the hospital didn't turn him up. It didn't take long to figure out that he'd been kidnapped. And even though the alarm went out within minutes of the discovery, the little boy was never found.

PART ONE

Sixteen years later

CHAPTER 1

One Up was the name of the horse Rafe Collings had drawn for the bareback event at the High School State Rodeo Finals. The rumor was that the big roan gelding had gotten that name because he always had "one up" on every cowboy that ever tried to ride him—they'd all been thrown. Rafe decided it might be a good idea to take a close look at the horse and size him up for himself before he had to get on One Up's famous back. He desperately wanted to make a successful ride that day.

The rodeo stock was penned directly behind the bucking chutes and the announcer's stand. When Rafe approached the fence, the big roan stepped away from the other horses and swung his head toward the boy. Rafe was only sixteen, but he was already a couple of inches over six feet. And he'd ridden horses since before he could remember. When it came to horses, fear was not something Rafe had ever experienced. If he could ride this horse, he stood a very good chance of winning the bareback championship.

Rafe stepped closer to the fence, and the big roan's eyes settled on the young man's face. The two held each other's gaze for a moment, then Rafe looked away, unsettled in a way he'd never been before with any horse. Something in that horse's eyes made Rafe's stomach do an uncomfortable twist. He'd seen that look before, but it wasn't from a horse. Recalling it now brought back the terrible memory that had plagued him since he was six. Those eyes and that look would never leave him. He'd seen them thousands of times in his dreams, dreams that brought him violently awake at night, screaming, sweating, and thrashing his bedcovers.

He tried to pull his mind from that long-ago event and continued to look the horse over. He was not an ugly horse, the way people commonly described mean broncos. Rather, he was big and well proportioned, as were so many of the horses Rafe had ridden this past rodeo season. Rafe had expected him to at least have an unsightly Roman nose, but his head was exactly the right size for his body. The nose was straight and the jawline clean. The only thing that detracted from One Up's appearance was that look in his eyes—the look of a hardened killer.

Rafe couldn't shake that look even as he settled down on the gelding's back in the chute an hour later. He wished he hadn't decided to look at the horse before riding him, for it was proving to be unnerving. It could cost him the championship.

Rafe had never thought of horses as evil. They were mean sometimes, and often very stubborn, but never, in his estimation, were they evil. He revised his thinking now, for that look One Up had given him was the same look he'd seen in the eyes of the man who'd murdered his mother in the bank where she'd been working ten years before.

Rafe had never forgotten that look—or the face that had delivered it. As he'd done with One Up an hour ago, Rafe and his mother's killer had locked eyes for a long and terrible moment. The man had swung his pistol toward him, held it there for a moment, and said, "You didn't see anything, kid. You ever say you did, and I'll hunt you down and do what I just did to the lady. Do you understand me, boy?"

Frozen with fear, Rafe had nodded. The killer had left the bank with his loot, and Rafe had run to his mother, but the last breath of life had already rattled out of her. There he'd sat, alone with his mother's body, sobbing uncontrollably until the other teller returned from lunch a few minutes later. Fear had so overtaken him that he never told anyone that he'd seen the man, let alone that he'd seen him shoot his mother after she handed him the money he demanded. He let everyone believe that he'd come into the bank and found her lying there behind the counter. It had seemed the only safe thing to do.

Now Rafe let go of the rigging and climbed off the horse. He had to give himself a moment to settle down, to steel himself. He silently vowed he would not let that hated man ruin his chances today.

"Hey, Rafe, you drew him, you gotta either ride him or forfeit," one of the cowboys that had been helping him said. "He's a mean one, but you're up to it if anybody is."

Rafe nodded, gritted his teeth, and said, "Just give me a second here. I aim to ride him all right."

He had drawn the roan, and he would attempt to ride the roan.

One Up snorted and kicked, rearing up and coming back down violently, his hooves ringing on the steel walls of the bucking chute. The announcer said, "Give him just a moment, folks. Rafe Collings will be ready momentarily. This horse, One Up, he's a tough horse if I ever saw one, and I've seen a lot of mighty good bucking stock in my day."

The crowd cheered in response, but Rafe heard none of this. He was remembering his mother's killer, and at that moment the strangest thing happened, a miracle, really. The fear of the killer that had plagued him for ten long years faded away, replaced by something that surprised Rafe. Fear was replaced by the desire to bring his mother's killer to justice, to defeat the man who had taken so much from him and his father. He didn't have any idea how he could ever do it, but he resolved at that moment that he would at least try.

With that resolution, Rafe again lowered himself onto the back of the raging gelding. After a moment the horse calmed down, as if he were saving the rest of his energy for the moment the chute opened. Rafe took his time settling himself just right on the gelding's back. His father appeared above him. Rafe looked up and said, "I'm going to ride him, Dad."

"I know you are, son."

Rafe gripped the rigging, leaned back, thought about the killer's eyes, then thought about One Up's eyes. Then, his lips tight with determination, he nodded, and the gate swung wide.

The rest of the world was shut out at that moment. It was as though the whole world consisted of one teenage cowboy and a horse that had never been ridden. The big roan exploded from the chute, twisting with such power that Rafe felt like his head might fly right off his shoulders. Then One Up shot skyward, slamming Rafe so far down on his back that the brim of his black hat nearly hit the gelding's rump. When the horse came back down, all four feet hit at once. To Rafe it was like being thrown into a brick wall, the stop was so sudden. Bucking and twisting more violent than Rafe had ever experienced followed. And yet through it all, he raked his spurs high on the roan's shoulders, waved his free hand in the air, and fought to stay with the angry, powerful animal.

The roar of the crowd was deafening to all but Rafe and One Up. They were so involved in their personal battle that neither was aware of anything but the other. Rafe also didn't hear the announcer as he shouted, "I've never seen anything like it! The way that horse is bucking, it should've sent that cowboy into the stands with you folks. Hang in there, Rafe!"

Eight seconds had never lasted so long. Rafe didn't hear the bell, nor did he hear the roar of the crowd. All he could think of was riding that horse. He didn't know he'd made the ride, that he'd gone past the required time, until one of the pick-up men rode up beside the bucking horse and shouted at Rafe to get off. After that, it took three tries before he could let go of the rope and jump from the bronc and into the outstretched arms of the other cowboy. A second later he was on the ground trying to keep his feet under him after the pounding and twisting punishment he'd just endured.

He finally became aware of the shouting and clapping of the crowd and the booming voice of the announcer. "Get out of the arena, Rafe!" he heard. "That horse acts like he wants to kill you."

Rafe sprinted toward the nearest fence, aware then of thundering hooves coming his way. But he knew he was too far to make the fence before One Up reached him, so he turned, praying that one of the pick-up men would be able to head off the roan's charge. But it wasn't going to happen. So Rafe did the only thing he could; he faced the crazed horse and prayed. The horse and the young cowboy locked eyes in the instant before the horse reached him. In that fraction of time, Rafe understood that One Up meant to kill him.

At the very last second, he threw himself to one side, feeling the wind of the horse's wicked hooves as they narrowly missed his face. Then he again sprinted for the fence. One Up wasn't through, spinning like a top and continuing his deadly attack against the young cowboy who had just become the first person to ever ride him. But this time the pick-up men were there. Lariats whirled, settled around the horse's neck, and One Up did a somersault. By the time he was able to get his feet back under him, Rafe was safely across the fence. It took another five minutes for the cowboys to drag the angry roan out of the arena. The crowd never quit shouting, cheering, and whistling the entire time. And the announcer kept talking.

"That was the best ride I've seen in my life. I don't know how that young cowboy stayed on that horse, let alone kept spurring the way he did. It was amazing. That horse is crazy," he ranted. "They better retire him before he kills some cowboy."

Rafe was leaning over, his hands on his knees, trying to catch his breath, when his father, stepmother, and eight-year-old sister Stephanie ran up to him. "I'm sorry, Rafe," his dad said. "I'll never let you ride another horse like that one. I should have stopped you."

"But Dad, I rode him," Rafe cried triumphantly between deep gulps of air.

"I know you did, son, but never again. Not on a horse like that one. I swear."

Stephanie said, "You were awesome, Rafe! I can't wait to tell all my friends what you did."

Then his stepmom's arms surrounded him. She was sobbing. "Oh, Rafe," she said, "I've never been so frightened in my life. I thought that horse was going to kill you."

He straightened up, wiped his brow, and said, "Yeah, but I got one up on him, didn't I?" He smiled at his folks. "Think that was good enough to win the bareback championship?" he asked.

* * *

The news of young Rafe Collings's championship ride that Saturday afternoon spread beyond his hometown of Ephraim. It spread beyond his home state of Utah. His picture and the story of his ride appeared in newspapers in several western states. The story was told of a young cowboy of amazing skill and courage who rode a horse that no professional cowboy, let alone a young amateur, had ever ridden before.

In an expensive hotel room in a neighboring state, a man stared through hardened killer eyes at the picture of the teenage cowboy. He knew he'd seen that young man before, many years before, right there in the boy's hometown. He read the article, then he stared at the picture again. He didn't like the boy's determination. It was unlikely that he was a threat, but he had to do something to make sure the boy kept his mouth shut.

He threw down the article, found a pen and a piece of paper, and wrote a short note.

* * *

In another neighboring state, several heads were bent over the same picture in the sports page of another newspaper. "You've been holding out on us, Greg," a pretty young woman said. "You didn't tell us you had a twin brother."

Greg Ralston was shaking his head. "I don't," he said. "You all know that. But I've got to admit, that guy resembles me a lot."

"No, he doesn't resemble you," one of his friends said emphatically, "he looks exactly like you. Put a big black cowboy hat like that on your head, and there goes Rafe Collings. Look, his hair is even blond and curly like yours. He just wears it a little shorter, that's all."

Greg pushed the newspaper away. "Just a coincidence," he said, then he grinned. "They say that everyone has someone somewhere in the world that is almost a match. Well, it looks like I've found mine."

But is it really a coincidence? Greg wondered. His parents had always been vague about the details surrounding his birth. Now that he thought about it, it did seem odd that he was so tall while they were so short, and that he was so blond while they were both dark-haired. Sure, his mom looked like a blond, but he knew she bleached it. He'd tried many times to find the resemblance between them and him that he could see with his friends and their parents. But it wasn't there, and there was nothing about his talents or personality that seemed to come from either one of them. He'd even asked them once, after a particularly bad argument, if they had adopted him. That had made them as angry as he'd ever seen them. They had seemed almost too defensive to him. But they had insisted that he wasn't an adopted child, and had forbidden him to bring up the subject ever again.

He hadn't, and he'd even tried to believe them; but now, with this picture, he was again filled with doubt. *Could I have a brother?* he asked himself. Had his parents lied to him all these years? And if so, why? He knew other kids who were adopted, and he saw nothing wrong with that. So why, if he was adopted, didn't they simply admit it?

He resolved to ask them about it again that evening, knowing that it would make them angry. But he didn't care. He wanted to know the truth, and deep down he felt that they were hiding something. He felt that he deserved to know what it was.

* * *

"Here are some more letters for you, Rafe," Glenda Collings said when Rafe came in the door of their ranch house one afternoon several days following the rodeo. "You'd think you'd won an Olympic medal the way people are fussing over you."

"Thanks, Mom," he said as he accepted the latest letters. Already, he'd had over twenty of them. "They'll stop coming pretty soon. In fact, these will probably be the last ones."

She grinned at him. "Except for the ones from the girls," she teased. "Hey, your dad said to tell you he'd be late tonight. He drove that yearling bull down to Richfield. That guy that was here looking at him last week decided he wanted to buy him, and your dad didn't want to give him another chance to change his mind."

"Wish I'd been able to go with him," Rafe said, for he always enjoyed doing things with his father, especially when it involved their ranching operation.

"He also said that he thinks he's found a good stud to breed that paint mare of yours to," Glenda added.

"That's awesome. Maybe he'll tell me about it when he gets home," Rafe said. "I'd sure like to get a really good colt out of her."

After visiting with Glenda for a couple of minutes, Rafe went to his bedroom. He loved his stepmother. She'd never totally filled the void that the death of his mother had created, but she'd made him feel like he belonged to her, and he was grateful for that. In a way he was lucky, he guessed, because he had two mothers who each held a special place in his heart.

And he had another mother he would never know.

But from the day his dad had told him that he was adopted, it had never seriously bothered him. Oh yes, he wished he knew more about the young girl who died after having twin boys. And he would always wonder what happened to the brother that had disappeared from the hospital nursery. But Rafe knew that he was where he belonged. This was his family. And, strangely, people were always telling him how much he resembled his father.

He threw the letters on his bed and went straight to his computer. He'd decided that if he was going to do something about the man who'd killed his mother, he needed to get started. Anyway, the letters were all about the same. It was fun reading them at first, but now he'd grown bored with it. He opened WordPerfect and began to type. As he typed, he began to sweat, and several times he had to get up and walk around to calm himself. Ever since his experience with One Up and his decision to try at last to do something about the man that had killed his mother, he'd been having vivid nightmares. The fear he thought he'd finally licked that day came back every night in the wee hours and disturbed his sleep. But the nightmares only made him more determined than ever to finally tell the truth about what he'd seen that terrible day. Two hours later, as he read what he'd written, he was satisfied.

Everything he could remember of that horrible afternoon was finally in print. He'd started with the short walk of less than two blocks from his grandparents' house in Ephraim to the bank where his mother worked three days a week. His grandmother had made cookies, and he'd wrapped one in a napkin, shoved it in his pocket, and walked to the bank to give it to his mother. One of the things he couldn't remember was what happened to the cookie. But he did remember clearly, even after ten years, the details of the horrendous event he'd witnessed. And for the first time since it happened he was determined to let others know what he had seen.

When he finally printed off the pages, saved the document, and shut off his computer, he turned to the latest batch of letters he'd tossed aside earlier. His stepmom was right—the first two he opened were from girls. The letters he'd received from girls were all alike, full of immature chatter from young women who had nothing better to do than write to boys they'd never met and probably never would.

He threw them down, sifted through the others, then stopped at one that was remarkably different from the rest. Rafe's name was printed neatly in block letters on the plain white envelope, and there were no hearts or drawings of cowboy hats to personalize it. It was addressed to him at General Delivery, Ephraim, Utah, and had no return address. That was one of the advantages of living in a rural area; you got your mail whether the address was complete or not.

He opened the envelope and pulled out a single sheet of paper. He felt the color drain from his face as he read:

Don't think I've forgotten you. And don't think I won't do to you what I did to your mother if you open your mouth. All this fame might make you think you're brave. Don't even try to be, or you'll be dead. Destroy this letter as soon as you've read it. No one but you had better ever lay eyes on it.

It was unsigned, but Rafe knew exactly who it was from, and cold dread filled his heart. Slowly, he dropped the letter onto his bed, then picked up the pages he'd just printed. He tore each sheet into tiny pieces and threw them into his wastebasket. Then he put the threatening note back in the envelope and, contrary to the instructions it contained, he buried it beneath his socks in the middle drawer of his dresser.

CHAPTER 2

The rodeo championship was history. Rafe was gradually settling back into a normal routine. Except for one thing. The letter from the man who had murdered his mother was still stuffed beneath his socks in a drawer. Occasionally, he pulled it out and read through it. Then he'd go to his computer and read what he'd written about the murder. He even refined that document a little from time to time as he remembered more details. But then he'd do nothing more, for the fear that had faded when he'd settled onto the back of the roan had returned as strong as it had ever been. His resolve to do something about that terrible man had been seriously eroded—but it was not completely gone.

Someday, he promised himself. *Even someday soon.* But as the days passed he didn't get around to it, and he knew why. He lacked the courage. He read and reread the account of Helaman and his stripling warriors in the Book of Mormon. Then he would pray for the kind of courage those young men had, those boys who were probably about his age who had risked their lives in the most dangerous of circumstances and, because of their unwavering faith, had survived.

Then Rafe would think of his family. He loved his little sister and had always been fiercely protective of her. And there were his father and stepmother to consider. Would his seeking justice for his mother's killer put the three people he loved most in danger? And the affirmative answer he always imagined was all it took to keep him from doing anything more about the things he remembered.

Whenever Rafe would think about the killer, he'd try to get his mind on something else. Often he would read the scriptures. He kept them on the nightstand beside his bed where he could even read them in the middle of the night when nightmares awoke him and he didn't feel like trying to fall asleep again. Without those scriptures, Rafe wasn't sure how he would have dealt with the horrors that plagued him. He would have liked to talk to someone about his fears, but there was no way he could do it without revealing what he'd seen, and he wasn't ready to do that. So he relied on those scriptures and frequent prayers to keep him going.

One Friday evening, Rafe and a couple of his closest friends, both priests in his ward, took three girls to a movie. After it was over, the six of them stopped at the local Subway and bought sandwiches. As they sat eating, a man Rafe had never seen before came in. Rafe judged him to be about fifty. His hair was thin but long and straggly, and he was very tall, probably six feet and six or seven inches. He had a three or four days' growth of beard on his face. His hands appeared unwashed, and his fingernails were black with grime.

Rafe wouldn't have paid much more attention to him had the man not brought his sandwich to a table near where he and his friends were eating. Rafe's date and the other girls all wrinkled their noses at the unpleasant odor that came from that neighboring table. It also bothered Rafe, and the thought crossed his mind that he could go over and ask the man to move. But he didn't, since he was polite, as were his buddies. So the six young people ate rapidly, their meal not tasting as good as it had because of the body odor coming from the next table.

Several times, Rafe got the uncomfortable feeling that he was being stared at, and he glanced at the stranger. Each time their eyes met, and for a reason he couldn't fathom, Rafe would be unable to break that contact for several nervous seconds. Finally, the tall man would smile and look down. Rafe was disturbed as much by the smile as by the way the man was staring at him. It was a superior smile. It was almost as if the man was trying to tell him something, but Rafe couldn't imagine what.

The young people left as soon as they could, and outside, they laughed nervously about the stranger, and the girls held their stomachs and pretended to throw up. It was one of the girls who finally looked at Rafe and asked, "Do you know that man?"

Taken aback, Rafe said, "I've never seen that guy before in my life. What makes you think something like that?"

"Well," she said, "it was just that he kept looking at you, and several times you looked at him. And he smiled at you too. So I just wondered."

Rafe's date chipped in. "I noticed that too. Are you sure he isn't someone you met at a rodeo or something?"

Rafe chuckled at that. "Are you kidding? He looks like an old alcoholic or addict to me. It looked to me like he was drunk or high on something. Did you see how glazed his eyes were?"

"Not really," she said. "I didn't look at his eyes much. It was you he kept looking at. It was weird, Rafe."

"That must be his car," one of the other guys said, pointing to a ten- or twelve-year-old dark green Cadillac. "I've never seen it around here before."

They walked past it, and someone said, "It has Iowa license plates."

Rafe looked down and saw that it did indeed. Not that people from Iowa didn't drive through Utah on occasion, especially this time of year—Utah hosted a lot of tourists in the summertime. But this guy didn't look like a tourist.

Another of his friends added, "Looks like the guy lives out of his car. It's full of clothes and junk. I'll bet it stinks in there. He must not shower very often."

They walked on past, heading for their car. Their interest in the man faded, and Rafe didn't think about him again until the next day when he and his father drove into town and stopped to fill the truck with gas. The green Cadillac was parked across the street. The man from the night before was sitting in it, and Rafe got the uncomfortable feeling that the guy was watching him, much like he'd done at Subway.

After finishing their business in town, Rafe and his father started home. They rode in silence for several minutes, listening to a CD. Then suddenly Rafe's dad said, "You're awfully quiet, Rafe. Is something bothering you?"

Not sure how to answer that, Rafe took a moment before saying, "Nah, I was just thinking about something." He was thinking about the tall, disheveled stranger in the Cadillac, and not feeling good about it.

"Must be something serious," Lenny Collings said to his son. "Care to talk about it?"

Rafe just shrugged, then changed the subject. He felt foolish for being nervous over a stranger he'd never seen until the night before and probably would never see again.

* * *

Summer passed, and soon Rafe's junior year of high school was in full swing. By now he had forgotten all about the tall man and the dark green Cadillac. But he didn't forget about his desire to tell someone everything he knew about his mother's murder. The nightmares continued. And he began to hate the killer almost as much for the fear he felt in his own heart as he did for what the man had done to his mother. Slowly, the resolve that the bronc One Up had instilled in him faded away, and he was disgusted with himself for his lack of courage. However, he finally told himself that the man would never be found, not after all this time, and it would only put him and his family in danger if he said anything.

The threatening letter remained buried beneath his abundantly full drawer of socks, and he finally quit pulling up the document he'd typed on his computer, the one where he detailed the murder of his mother. But he didn't delete it. He just pushed it out of his mind.

* * *

In a filthy little house on a remote and run-down farm in the western part of Texas, two men had been catching up on lost time. Harley Tuft had just been released that morning after a ten-month stint in a Texas jail for his second drunk driving conviction, and his son Deke had been filling him in on whatever he wanted to know. "I see you kept the newspapers like I told you to," Harley said as he reached for his fourth bottle of beer.

"Of course, but I don't know why you want them."

"I always read the papers," Harley said gruffly. "Can't figure why you don't."

"Never liked to read much," Deke said as he got up and went in search of the papers. "There's an awful big stack here," he shouted from another room. "Do you want the old ones first or the new ones?"

"Start me with the newer ones," his father said.

Several days passed before Harley got to one that caused him alarm. It was late afternoon, their chores were done, and both men were already drinking heavily. "Deke, come look at this," Harley shouted over the noise of the television.

"Give me a minute," Deke said gruffly. "I want to see the rest of this show."

"Right now!" his father ordered. Something in Harley's tone got Deke's attention, and he left the TV and walked over to the table where Harley was reading.

"Look at this," he said, plopping a finger down on the picture of a young cowboy from Utah. "Looks just like you did at that age," Harley drawled. "I mean almost exactly like you did."

Deke couldn't deny it. "What of it?" he said.

"Could be Stella's kid, don't you think?" Harley asked. "If she had a baby not too many months after leaving Texas, that baby would be about sixteen or seventeen now. Same as this here boy."

Deke stared closer at the picture, and he realized with a jolt that his father was right. Deke had hoped that after all these years his sister would never surface again, that something had happened to her, and that she and the stranger she'd run away with were no longer a threat to him and his father. But this picture of a young Utah cowboy sowed seeds of doubt, and it caused his gut to churn uncomfortably.

"What if Stella and that tall fella she run off with are alive somewhere? And what if they decide to talk?" Harley asked.

Deke felt a chill course through him. "Can't let that happen," he said.

"It's a long shot, I know, but maybe this young man," Harley said, stabbing a finger on Rafe's picture again, "could lead us to them."

They had both been angry when Harley's sixteen-year-old daughter, Deke's sister, had suddenly left with a man in his late twenties who had been passing through their little town. When she left, she took dangerous knowledge with her. At first Harley had assumed it would only be a matter of days before the stupid girl came crying home. As days turned into weeks, Harley had rationalized that she undoubtedly met with an early death—what else could she expect, running off with that loser drug addict, anyway? But now Harley had to consider other alternatives. "Maybe you ought to take a little trip up to Utah," Harley suggested. "If Stella and that guy she run off with are still around, we'll need to do something about it."

"Don't you want to come?" Deke asked.

"No, not now. I got a lot more catching up to do. But you go on up there. Find out if there's any chance this here kid is Stella's boy. Then you come on back. If Stella and that druggie boyfriend of hers is up there, we'll have to go do something about them. We can't take no chance on either one of them ever talking about us. Ten months in jail almost done me in. I ain't lettin' nobody put me there for the rest of my life," Harley said, and he took another long drink from his bottle.

* * *

Another person was also concerned with old newspapers in another state many miles from Texas. "Lindsay, would you carry these old papers out to the garbage for me?" Paula Diamond called out to her fifteen-year-old daughter. "I don't know why we've collected so many."

"Sure, Mom. Can I finish getting ready first?"

"Just don't forget," Paula called. "There's quite a pile of them. We've collected them for months it looks like."

Lindsay continued brushing her long dark hair. It soon glistened like polished ebony. She examined herself in the mirror and dabbed on a touch more eye shadow. Greg would never notice her, she was sure, but she wanted to look just right at the basketball game that night, just in case he looked up from the court and saw her in the stands. Too young to date, she could only dream of the tall blond ballplayer.

Deep in her heart, she knew it would never be anything but a dream because he wasn't even a member of the Church, and she had not only promised her parents that she'd never date anyone who couldn't take his bride to the temple, but she'd promised herself that as well. She'd written it in ink in her diary. To Lindsay, that was binding.

But Lindsay could still dream.

Satisfied that she looked the best she could, she put on a jacket to ward off the late November cold and went in search of the newspapers. She picked up a huge armload and headed for the door with them. But as she opened the door, the papers slipped from her arms and landed in a disorderly mess at her feet. She impatiently kicked them aside and opened the door before kneeling to pick them up again. "Stupid newspapers," she fumed under her breath. "And why do I have to deal with them, anyway? It's not like I ever read them."

She stopped short, gaping. There beneath her lay a color picture of Greg Ralston! Only it couldn't be Greg; he didn't wear a black cowboy hat, or any cowboy hat for that matter. But it was his face. She picked up the paper and stared at the picture. Then she read the caption beneath the picture and the headline that accompanied it. The boy's name was Rafe Collings, and he was a champion high school rodeo cowboy from Utah. She could hardly tear her face from the picture. Finally, she laid the paper aside so she could give it further attention later, gathered up the rest of the pile, and carried it to the garbage.

She took out all the rest of the papers as well before she again picked up the sports section she'd set aside and carried it to the privacy of her room. After taking off her jacket, she read the entire article. She was impressed that this guy who looked like Greg Ralston had accomplished the impossible. Five months ago, Rafe Collings had ridden a horse that even professional rodeo cowboys had never been able to ride. She finished every word on the front page of the section and turned to the next page where it was continued. There was another picture of the cowboy there, only he didn't have a hat on in this one, and his hair was a little shorter, but just as curly and definitely as blond as Greg's.

She stared at the picture, her heart fluttering. At last she tore her eyes away and finished the article. Then she read the whole thing again. She clipped the article and the pictures out of the paper and stuck them inside her journal as an idea began to form in her head.

Rafe Collings was from Ephraim, Utah, right there in Mormon country. Maybe he was a member of the Church.

Finally, Lindsay looked at her watch. Her friends would be here to pick her up any moment to go to the basketball game. She checked herself in the mirror, brushed her dark hair once more, and left her bedroom. She had been thinking about her idea, and it became more than an idea; it became a plan, one she was determined to carry out. She'd do it tonight after she got home from the game.

Greg Ralston played exceptionally well that night. A junior on the varsity team, he was the hero of the basketball game. But as Lindsay watched him, she found herself thinking about another boy, one who lived in Utah, far to the south of her Idaho home. And she wondered how two guys, clearly about the same age who lived so far apart, could look so much alike.

* * *

He had come to watch the people as much as to watch the ball game. A few years out of high school, he worked odd jobs, spent hours on his computer, and took pictures of everything. He drove his parents crazy because he kept flip-flopping on where he'd go to college, and whether or not he'd go on a mission. He had no intention of moving out yet. It was cheaper to live at home, and, besides, the idea of being on his own sort of scared him. He watched as the people filed in to see the game. One girl in particular caught his eye. She had long, shining black hair, expressive brown eyes, and was willowy, yet athletic looking. He judged her to be about fifteen. He waited until she and the girls with her had found a place to sit, then he crowded in not far away. As the evening progressed, he glanced frequently at her, wondering what her name was.

He found out when one of her friends shouted, "Lindsay, did you see that shot Greg just made?"

Even as she answered, "Of course I did," he tucked her name away in his head. He also took a closer look at the ballplayers. Before long he'd figured out which one was Greg. He couldn't help but notice how Lindsay seemed to be watching Greg. Her expression of innocent admiration made his fingers itch to photograph her, but he restrained himself. If his parents saw the photo, they'd think he was obsessed or something. Really, though, he just liked to watch and record the world around him, especially the people. Moments like this were beautiful.

When the game was over, he trailed behind Lindsay and her friends until they were outside, then he moved away and headed across the parking lot to his car. He liked to come to these games, since no one ever seemed to pay any attention to him, but he could almost always find someone that kept his artistic eye occupied for the whole evening. Maybe he'd spot Lindsay at the next game, he thought as he drove slowly home. She certainly was a pretty girl.

* * *

Shortly after Rafe and Stephanie had left for school one Monday morning in late November, Glenda Collings went to work on the laundry. Later in the day, as she opened Rafe's drawer to put his newly folded socks away, she realized that he had more socks than would fit in the drawer. She decided to sort through them and get rid of the ones that were no longer any good. She began pulling the socks from the drawer and placing them on his bed, good ones in one pile, worn ones in another. She was surprised to see an envelope at the bottom of the drawer. Curious, she pulled it out and looked at it.

She assumed that it must be a letter from some girl, perhaps one of the many who had written to Rafe following the championship ride that had brought him so much attention. She couldn't help but smile as she wondered if a girl had caught his interest. He had read a few of the letters to her before, and most were very silly. This one must have been more serious for him to have hidden it. But what if it was too serious? Mentally asking Rafe's forgiveness, Glenda decided to read this letter for herself. When she extracted the single sheet of paper from the envelope and read through it, her heart convulsed with terror. The letter was short, so it only took a moment to read it twice, and when she'd finished, her hands were shaking badly. She loved Rafe as much as she did her own daughter, Stephanie. She'd raised him as her own from the time she'd married his father, just over a year following the death of Rafe's mother.

The man who had murdered Rafe's mother had never been found, and this letter was from that man! Tears spilled from Glenda's eyes, and with the note in her hand, she fled the house in search of her husband. She found him in the barn sitting at his workbench where he was working on a braided halter to give to Rafe for Christmas.

"Lenny," she cried. "You've got to look at this!"

The alarm in his wife's voice caused Lenny to drop the halter and jump up from his workbench. She was holding the letter out at arm's length, and the single sheet of paper was shaking as if a wind was blowing through the barn. Lenny took it from her hand and read. She watched his face as it slowly lost its color. He didn't take his eyes off the paper for two or three minutes. When he did, the look on his face made her tears flow again. Lenny was a brave man, but that note had thrown fear into him, unmistakable fear. Her heart went out to him, and she wanted to take him in her arms. But she didn't, for he was standing stiffly, his arms locked in front of him holding the paper. She stood and watched him, shivering from the cold, her heart aching, and fright constricting her throat.

At length, the tension seemed to drain from his muscular body, and Lenny slowly sat back down at his workbench, pushed the unfinished halter aside, laid the note in front of him, and dropped his head into his hands. Helplessly, Glenda watched as his broad shoulders shook. She couldn't be positive, but she was fairly certain that he was reliving the terrible thing that had happened to him when Rafe was just a little boy. Glenda knew that Lenny loved her, but she also knew that he loved his first wife just as much, and that had always been okay with her. But now, as she watched grief pour from her husband, she wondered how he'd ever been able to forget enough to love again. And she loved him all the more because he had been able to do so.

Finally, she wiped her eyes, then reached out with a trembling hand and touched his hunched shoulder. Lenny stirred, and then he slowly rose to his feet, leaving the terrible note, the note that was so short and yet said so much, lying on his workbench. He took Glenda in his arms, as if she were the one who needed comforting, and he held her close. Then he said simply, "Rafe saw him kill her. He got there in time to see it happen, not after, like we've always believed. But he's never dared say so. The murderer must have threatened him."

He broke down and cried like Glenda had never seen him cry before. She held him, cried with him, and wondered what the world now held in store for them, and for their son.

Several minutes later, with the envelope and the note in hand, Lenny and Glenda climbed in the truck and headed for town. Lenny talked as he drove, and Glenda listened quietly. "Rafe saw it, Glenda. I know he did. And that man threatened Rafe. He scared an innocent little boy out of his mind, scared him so badly that he's never uttered a word about what he must have seen. What kind of monster would do a thing like that to a child?"

Glenda didn't respond. She knew Lenny wasn't asking for a response. He drove in silence for a mile or two, then he said, "This guy must have seen Rafe's picture when he got all that publicity over riding that crazy horse. I wonder if he's written like this to Rafe before or if this is the first time."

He was silent again, then he said, "Glenda, one day early in the summer when Rafe and I were coming home from town, he was unusually quiet. I asked him if something was the matter. He said everything was okay, but I got the uneasy feeling that there was something he wasn't telling me, something he didn't want to talk about. It must have been this letter."

"He's had it for months," she said, picking up the envelope and examining the date stamped on the front. "It was postmarked right after the rodeo finals. And it was mailed in Cheyenne."

"This guy must still be on the loose out there." Lenny paused and shook his head. "Oh, the poor kid, this must be eating him up inside," he said. "You know, now that I think about it, he's seemed quite withdrawn lately. Has it seemed that way to you?"

"Well, yes, in a way. But I guess I didn't think much of it," she answered. "I know he's been working hard to keep his grades up."

Lenny looked at the time on his watch. "It'll be a while before school's out. Let's go talk to the police chief first, then we can drive over to Manti and find Rafe. If school isn't over by then, we'll get him out of class."

"I hope Rafe won't be angry with me for snooping," Glenda said.

Lenny looked over at her. "You were just doing his laundry and getting rid of old socks," he said. "What's to be mad about?"

"But it was obvious he was trying to hide the letter."

"I wonder if he reads it occasionally," Lenny mused. "He didn't throw it away like the writer ordered him to, so he must have been planning to do something about it. Maybe he was even hoping you'd find it."

A car was coming toward them, and Glenda watched as it passed. She didn't remember ever seeing that car before, an older green Cadillac with Nevada plates. And why would it be driving in the direction of their ranch? she wondered.

Quit it! she ordered herself silently. There are always strangers on this road, and it wasn't as if it led exclusively to their ranch. She was just frightened and jumpy. She needed to get in control of herself before she saw Rafe.

Chief Johnson took the letter very seriously. "I know that this has been handled a lot, but we'll process it for prints anyway. You can keep a copy if you like."

Lenny and Glenda looked at each other. "I guess we should keep a copy," Lenny said.

"I think it would be good if I could talk to Rafe," the chief said. "And even though this is several months old, we must take this threat seriously. I wasn't chief when your wife was murdered, Lenny, but I was the first officer on the scene. I was the one who tore your little boy's arms from around his dead mother's neck. This guy, this killer, has no conscience."

Lenny nodded and said, "I remember that you were there. So does Rafe. You've always been a hero to him. He was excited when they made you police chief."

"Rafe's a good kid. Would you like to bring him here, or would you like me to come out to your house later?"

"Do you mind coming out to our place?"

"Not at all. I'll bring a detective by later this afternoon."

As they got in their truck, Glenda said, "Lenny, let's go over to the elementary and get Stephanie before we go to Manti."

She didn't explain why. She didn't need to, and Lenny nodded in understanding. They both wanted their children close to them while they sorted through the fears they were facing.

* * *

The dark green Cadillac stopped at the ranch that the driver already knew belonged to the family of Rafe Collings. He'd been relieved when he passed Lenny and Glenda Collings a few minutes earlier, presumably on their way to Ephraim. Now he could take his time and have a look around, see if he could find anything in the house that would answer the questions in his mind. He'd considered doing it several months ago but hadn't. He didn't intend to delay again. There was something he felt he had to know.

Pulling on a pair of thin gloves, he left his car parked out of sight of the passing road and walked to the house. It was locked, but that was not a problem for a man of his skill. Within a couple of minutes, he was inside, the door pushed shut behind him. And he began to search, very methodically and very thoroughly.

CHAPTER 3

"Rafe Collings, would you come to the administrative office, please?"

Rafe looked up from his desk, surprised to hear his name called over the intercom. He couldn't imagine why he would be needed at the office. He closed his book and stepped up to the teacher's desk. She smiled. "I heard it," she said. "Go ahead."

He spotted his dad in the hallway outside the office door, and Rafe knew instantly that something was terribly wrong. He hadn't seen his father look like he did at that moment since the murder of his mother. He walked rapidly, and his dad met him partway. "I've checked you out for the rest of the afternoon," Lenny said, his voice breaking.

"Dad, what's wrong?" Rafe demanded. "Is Stephanie okay? And Mom?" All sorts of terrible scenarios were thundering through his head.

"They're fine. They're outside in the truck."

"What's the matter then? I know something's happened," Rafe insisted.

"We'll talk in a minute," Lenny promised. "We're parked by your truck."

As they approached their pickups in the parking lot of Manti High School, Rafe began to panic. His stepmother looked frightened, and she was holding Stephanie tightly in her arms. Rafe wasn't sure what was happening, but he was beginning to suspect that it had to do with him—that he was somehow responsible for the fear he could see in the faces of his family.

When they reached their parked trucks, Lenny said, "Glenda, why don't you and Steph bring my truck. I'll ride with Rafe."

That was all that was said until they were on their way to Ephraim. Then Rafe asked again, "Dad, what's happening? I can't stand this anymore."

Lenny looked at him and then said, "Glenda cleaned out your sock drawer today."

He suddenly felt faint and could almost feel the color fading from his face. For a moment he didn't say anything, but he knew that his father could tell that he was fighting to control his emotions and that he was afraid. And he knew that his father, whose face still betrayed a heavy heart, was waiting for him to say something.

When Rafe was finally able to speak, he stared at his hands and said very softly, his voice trembling slightly, "She found the letter. I'm sorry. I've been wanting to say something about it."

"Why didn't you?" his father asked gently.

"I was afraid," Rafe said truthfully. "Not just for me, but for the rest of you too."

"You saw more than you've ever told, didn't you?" Lenny asked.

Rafe nodded, and he felt that horrible coldness descend upon him that came every time he thought about what had happened to his mother, about what he'd seen that fateful day. "I've wanted to say something for a long time," he said after a moment's silence. "This summer I even wrote everything down that I could remember. It's on the computer at home."

* * *

The green Cadillac left the Collingses' yard and took the long way back to Ephraim. The driver didn't want to risk being seen again on the road between the ranch and the town. He didn't want to take a chance of meeting any of the family right now. The only thing he'd taken from the house was knowledge. But it was enough.

* * *

Chief Johnson and a detective came out to the house as promised. Rafe printed a copy of the statement he'd written and refined back in the summer. Then, as the officers questioned him, he remembered a few more minor details. It was well after dark before the officers left, leaving a caution to the family.

"Let's keep this thing under wraps," Chief Johnson said. "Nobody but you folks and the police need to know about this right now. The last thing we want is for it to get to the press. Obviously, this guy, whoever he is, reads the papers or watches the news. As long as he doesn't know that you've finally told your story, Rafe, he probably won't make any moves against you. But if he were to somehow figure out that we now know that you saw him that day . . . well, you know what that could mean. We simply can't take that chance."

Lenny and Glenda nodded their heads. Rafe simply recalled that afternoon so many years ago, and that was more than enough to convince him to follow the chief's advice.

Later, as he was getting ready for bed, Rafe stopped what he was doing and studied his room. Something wasn't right. He couldn't imagine what. He slowly looked over everything in the room. Finally he realized what was bothering him. It was his scriptures. They weren't on the nightstand where he always kept them. They were now on his desk, and he knew that he hadn't put them there.

His mother must have searched his room after finding the note from the killer and inadvertently moved his scriptures. He couldn't blame her if she had searched the room, and it didn't make him angry, but he still felt unsettled, so he went downstairs to his folks' bedroom. The door was closed, but he could hear the hum of their voices inside, so he knew they weren't asleep. He tapped lightly on the door.

His father opened it a moment later. "What is it, son? Did you think of something else we should know?" he asked, his voice strained and tired.

"No, but I just wondered about something. It doesn't matter, and I'm not mad at all, but did Mom look through my room after she found the note?" he asked.

Glenda appeared at the doorway beside her husband. "No, I just read the note when I found it then ran in search of your father. I went back in there while you were talking to the officers and finished sorting your socks, but that's all I did. Why do you ask?"

"Somebody else has been in my room," Rafe said quietly.

"Are you certain?" his dad asked in alarm.

"Oh yeah," Rafe said, his voice shaking. "There's no doubt about it. I always keep my scriptures on my nightstand, and now they're on my desk. I know I didn't move them."

"Maybe it was Stephanie," Glenda suggested. But when questioned moments later, the drowsy little girl assured them she hadn't even been in Rafe's room that day.

The sheriff and one of his deputies came to the house along with Chief Johnson late that night. They soon concluded that not only had Rafe's room been searched, but so had the rest of the house.

"Do you have any idea who it could have been?" the sheriff asked. He'd been briefed on what Rafe had revealed about his mother's murder, and he was as concerned as the rest of them. "Could the man who wrote you that letter be in town? I know it was months ago that he wrote it, but I still wonder."

That was the very thought that was disturbing Rafe and his family. Glenda thought of something. "When we were driving into town after finding the letter, someone in a car I didn't recognize passed us, coming this way. I think it was a Cadillac. It was green, and it had Nevada plates on it, but I know that probably doesn't mean—"

Rafe's heart had begun to thud. "Was it dark green?" he asked, interrupting her.

"Yes, and probably ten or fifteen years old," Glenda said.

"Why do you ask?" the sheriff wanted to know.

"Is there something else you haven't told us, son?" Lenny asked.

Rafe nodded. "I didn't think it was important, but not long after the rodeo finals there was this guy in town. He ate at Subway one night when several of my friends and I were there," he said. "He kept looking at me and smiling kind of strange like. He hadn't shaved for days, and he smelled like he hadn't showered for a while."

"You think this guy was the one driving the car your mom saw today?" Chief Johnson asked.

"Well, after we left Subway, we saw a car I hadn't seen before. It was a dark green Cadillac at least ten years old. The next day, while Dad and I were gassing up, I saw it across the street. This guy in it looked like he was watching me," Rafe said. "But I haven't seen it since, so it's probably nothing. Anyway, it didn't have Nevada plates."

"Were they Utah ones?" the sheriff asked.

"No, it had Iowa plates."

"Are you sure?" Lenny asked.

"Yes, I'm sure. My friends and I talked about it and how it wouldn't be unusual that time of year for a car to be in town with Iowa plates. But we also talked about the fact that this guy didn't look like a tourist," Rafe said.

"Do you remember what he looked like?" Chief Johnson asked.

"Oh yeah. Like I said, he was dirty and hadn't shaved. He was also really tall."

"How tall?" the sheriff asked.

"Oh, at least six foot six. Probably more."

"Could it have been the man who killed your mother?" the chief asked.

"No," Rafe said flatly. "It wasn't him. That guy wasn't nearly that tall. And I'd know that monster if I saw him again."

"But it's been a long time, Rafe, and you were young then," the chief said. "And he may have changed a lot."

"I'll know that man if I ever see him," Rafe reiterated firmly. "Believe me, the guy we saw at Subway was too old and a lot taller."

"But you said he kept staring at you," the sheriff said. "You said the other kids noticed it too."

"That's right, he did, but I'd never seen him before."

"So, assuming this is the guy who searched the house, what was he looking for?"

Rafe sighed. "I wish I knew."

* * *

The car that cruised slowly past the short lane that led to Lenny Collings's house a few nights later was not an old green Cadillac. It was much older than the Cadillac. It was a silver Honda with numerous dents and a lot of rust on it. And it didn't have its head-lights on. Deke Tuft pulled off the road and walked back toward the lane. He'd made a few discreet inquiries in town, and he knew that this was the place he was looking for.

However, he couldn't be sure there was anything or anyone of interest to him here; it required a closer look. He crept up the lane, past the row of tall poplars that lined it, and drew up short when he came within view of the yard. There were numerous lights on in the house, and a dog began to bark. A man came outside, called to the dog, and patted his head for a few moments.

Not wanting to attract attention, and not knowing how long the family would be up, Deke worked his way back the way he'd approached, got in the dented Honda, and drove away, his lights still turned off. He'd learned a lot already in town. It didn't appear that Rafe was being raised by Stella, if she even was his mother. There was only the unusual family resemblance that kept him interested. And if by some slim chance Rafe was Stella's son, he might find something in the house to indicate it. He'd wait for a few hours and then go back there, after the family was sleeping soundly.

* * *

Lenny had slept with a gun resting on the nightstand every night since their house had been searched. Actually, he wasn't really sleeping this night. He was in bed, but he tossed and turned restlessly, wide awake and fully aware of the close proximity of his pistol. Fear for his family, especially his son, was intense, and it made it hard for him to sleep. He prayed a lot that night as he lay in bed and wondered what the future held. After all these years, he'd almost come to accept what had happened that day in the bank. He'd managed to go on living despite it, and he'd actually found joy in life again. But these last few days it was on his mind constantly. It was like it had only happened a few days earlier. All the grief and turmoil he'd felt so long ago had descended upon him with nearly the same intensity he'd felt then. And he couldn't rid himself of the sorrow and worry that now plagued him.

He was also puzzled. He could understand how a man as evil as the one who'd killed his first wife might come back to silence a witness. What he couldn't understand was what interest the man in the green Cadillac had in Rafe, if he had any—for Lenny was convinced that he was not the killer. Lenny believed his son and trusted the boy's memory. And no one had seen the man or his car since he'd passed them on the road the day Glenda found the letter in Rafe's room. He also wasn't sure it was the same man who'd searched their home the day the letter was found, and Lenny especially couldn't imagine what that man or any other would have been searching for in their house. It was beyond belief that someone would search the house and not take anything. Yet there didn't appear to be anything missing, certainly nothing of value. If he hadn't taken anything, then what was he searching for? Information, maybe? But about what? He had no idea.

The dog barked just as a terrible thought, one he hadn't been able to shake over the past few days, again entered Lenny's restless mind. What if the man in the Cadillac had been hired by his wife's killer? The dog barked again.

"Lenny," Glenda said, sitting up in bed and grabbing his arm tightly. "The dog's barking again, like he was earlier."

"I heard it. Probably just a raccoon running around. He calmed right down when I went out earlier, but I'll go check again," he told her, trying to sound calm, even though he was anything but that. For some reason, the sound of the dog's barking was different, and it caused fear to grip him. He told himself that he was being unreasonable.

"Be careful," Glenda said.

"I'll lock the door behind me. Don't come outside," he warned.

With his pistol in his hand, Lenny unlocked the front door.

"Where are you going?" Rafe asked from the darkness behind him.

"Skip's barking again," Lenny said. "I'm sure it's nothing, but we can't be too careful."

"Yeah, I heard him. He sounds upset. I'm coming with you, Dad," Rafe said. "Let me get a gun. It could be a raccoon, and we don't want it to get the chickens."

Lenny thought about telling the boy to stay, but he knew Rafe would insist, and there wasn't time to argue, so he said, "There's probably nobody out there, just a coon, like you say, but we'll be real careful anyway. Get a flashlight too."

A minute later, Rafe was at the door, his 16-gauge shotgun in one hand, a flashlight in the other.

"Let's keep the flashlight off for now," Lenny said as they stepped out into the darkness. There was only a thin sliver of moon, and the stars shone brightly. A faint breeze stirred the frigid night.

The two of them slipped silently along the front of the house, stopping every so often to listen. If it weren't for the racket that the dog was making, it would be a normal, peaceful night. Lenny was afraid that something unusual was upsetting old Skip. He prayed for a raccoon or even a skunk, but he had a feeling that wasn't what Skip was barking at. *Maybe there's a cougar,* he thought. Anything would be better than a burglar prowling around.

Rafe and Lenny stayed close together as they left the proximity of the house. They tried to keep to the shrubs and trees that lined the yard, to stay as much out of sight as possible, as they made their way to the corrals where the dog continued to create a fuss. His barking turned to fierce growling, and Lenny felt the hair on his neck rise. Rafe touched his arm but said nothing. Skip was not a mean dog, just a cow dog, a black and white Border collie. Barking was common, but Skip seldom made the kind of ominous and threatening sounds he was making now. The father-and-son team continued to inch closer to where Skip was, not at all sure what to expect.

The growling stopped abruptly, and the little Border collie once more began to bark. There was the sound of a scuffle, then the dog yelped as if in pain. There was a grunt, and the sound of something thudding hard. Skip yelped once more, weakly this time, then he was silent. Lenny's soft heart was bleeding, for he was almost certain his dog had been badly hurt. He was equally certain there was someone, not something, beside the barn where the last sounds had come from.

Lenny grabbed Rafe's arm to make certain the boy didn't do anything rash; he knew that the young man also loved their gentle dog. The two of them hunkered down beside a fence and listened intently. But whoever had silenced the dog was not making any noise. Lenny feared what would happen if that person somehow reached the house without them knowing it. He decided it was time to take stronger measures. He whispered into his son's ear, then he pointed his pistol into the dirt a few feet away and pulled the trigger.

Flames shot out of the barrel, and the sound echoed through the night. He and Rafe immediately scurried back up the fence, then again hunched down and listened. There was the distinct sound of someone running away from the barn, in the opposite direction of the house, toward the county road. The shot had gotten the desired results. Lenny and Rafe then raced to their garage, jumped in Lenny's pickup, started it up, backed out of the garage, and sped up the lane.

When they reached the county road, there were taillights streaking away to the west. The vehicle was too far up the road to bother chasing it, and they had no idea what kind it might be. Whoever had been in their yard had left in a hurry, and Lenny hoped the intruder wouldn't be a further threat that night. They turned and hurried home.

"I'll make sure that Glenda and Steph are okay; you check old Skip," Lenny said to Rafe.

There were many thoughts running through Rafe's mind as he jogged, his flashlight illuminating the way to the barn. He swung around the side, slowed down, and began looking for Skip. In his mind, he tried to sort through all of the strange and frightening things that were happening. He was afraid that he and his family were in danger, but he had no idea what could be done about it, what anyone could do to make them safer.

His troubled thoughts turned only to Skip when he spotted the dog's forlorn form lying on the ground near the back of the barn. Rafe knelt down, laid his shotgun on the ground, and gently cradled the dog's head in his hands. Despite himself, he couldn't stop the tears. The faithful old dog was dead, the latest victim of violence brought against the Collings family.

* * *

Chief Johnson shook his head in discouragement. The threatening sheet of paper and the envelope that young Rafe Collings had received had been handled so many times and by so many people that getting useful fingerprints off of them had been fruitless. Sheriff Stone rose to his feet and walked restlessly about the chief's office. He was equally discouraged. They were both exhausted, as were several of their officers. They had both responded to the call from a very worried Lenny Collings. They now had some photos of tire tracks and footprints, one dead dog, and a terrified family, but nothing else.

Although a number of people remembered seeing a tall man of about fifty and an older green Cadillac around town a few days earlier, no one remembered seeing him recently. There were discrepancies over the state that the car's license plates came from. Some witnesses said Iowa, others said Nevada. One woman swore the plates were from Oregon. None of them knew the license numbers.

The authorities in Cheyenne were of no help, either. Even though the letter had been mailed there, it was months ago and impossible to trace who had been responsible for it. There were just a lot of dead ends—and a lot of fear.

CHAPTER 4

The police insisted that they inspect any suspicious piece of mail Rafe received for the next few weeks. He didn't think it mattered, since he hadn't received any letters for quite a while and didn't expect to. He wished he'd never received any after his famous ride, for he couldn't help but wonder if all the problems facing him and his family were somehow related to that threatening letter.

When Rafe went to the mailbox on Wednesday, he was surprised to see that he actually had received a letter. Fortunately, Rafe couldn't see anything suspicious about it at all. The return address was clear enough—it came from Pocatello, Idaho, and bore a feminine name. Rafe's address was simply written as Ephraim, UT 84627. The handwriting was very neat. Rafe opened the letter with relief, but with very little interest.

What he found inside the envelope was very puzzling. There was a two-page letter from a girl of fifteen. It wasn't mushy, and it only gave, and sought, seemingly innocent information. However, the three newspaper pictures that had also been enclosed caused Rafe to do a double take and then stare in utter amazement.

They were different poses of a young man the writer identified as Greg Ralston. Rafe was stunned as he looked at the pictures. Except for the style of clothes and the length of the blond hair, he could have been staring at photographs of himself. He considered the facts. His birth mother had died when he was born, and she had never been identified; he had a twin brother, but that baby had disappeared from the hospital and had never been tracked down.

Now this. But surely the picture he was looking at couldn't be his brother. It was just too crazy. After all, these were just newspaper clippings. The only color one was a basketball action shot, and the other two appeared to be from the school paper and were too grainy to be reliable. And in spite of his own height, he was terrible at basketball. He dismissed the whole thing as a coincidence and focused on the letter's author instead.

Rafe liked the girl's name. Lindsay Diamond. It had a pleasant ring to it. And he found himself interested in reading what she had to say. She mentioned in the letter the surprise she'd felt at seeing the picture of him in a newspaper she'd nearly thrown away. Rafe's photo bore a striking resemblance to a guy she knew at her school, Greg Ralston. She said that Greg played high school basketball and that he was really good. She also told Rafe a little about herself, including such things as her favorite color, which was blue, and her favorite food, which was pizza. She mentioned an older brother who had already graduated from high school and was serving an LDS mission. She even told Rafe her birth date, and then asked him what his was. She also asked him to tell her a little about himself.

After reading the letter over again and looking at the pictures of Greg Ralston, he put everything back in the envelope. He thought briefly about answering the letter, but wasn't sure he should. Lindsay sounded like a really nice girl, but she was young, barely fifteen, and he had more than enough going on in his life right now. So, after debating with himself for a moment, he dropped the envelope into a desk drawer. Maybe he'd write her later, just to be polite. He had no intention of bothering his father or his stepmom with this incredible coincidence, and it certainly wasn't anything that would interest the police. They all had enough things to worry about right now.

The rest of the week, the police kept a close watch around the Collingses' ranch. They escorted the kids to and from school, and they kept a sharp lookout for the Cadillac or any other suspicious cars. By Saturday, the surveillance was relaxed, and on Sunday it was dropped altogether.

The family, trying to act normal so they wouldn't attract attention from other ward members, attended church on Sunday like they always did. They didn't notice an old Honda that passed them on the highway along with a lot of other cars.

When they got home after their meetings, they nervously checked the house when they went in. To everyone's relief, everything seemed to be in order, and they were able to eat a fairly relaxed dinner.

That evening, Rafe was in his room reading the *New Era*. He laid the magazine on his desk and opened the drawer where he usually kept some gum and pulled out a stick. He replaced the package and began to shut the drawer, but stopped and opened it again. *Where is the letter from Lindsay Diamond?* he wondered. He was sure this was where he put it. *Maybe I'm just being paranoid.*

He stood staring for a minute or two, trying to remember having done anything else with that envelope; he was almost certain he hadn't touched it again. He quickly shuffled through each desk drawer, and even his dresser, but the envelope was gone. He remembered wanting to look at the pictures and read the letter again. But he'd resisted, thinking that his life was already complicated enough. He didn't need a pen pal right now, and he didn't need the stress of trying to figure out whether Greg Ralston was his twin.

Rafe supposed it was possible that his dad or stepmother had taken the envelope out just to make sure it wasn't something that the cops might like to look at. He didn't really like them going through his things, but he knew they were just concerned about him. That was probably what had happened, he told himself, and he went back to reading the *New Era*.

However, he'd only read part of a page before he stopped again. His mind was not on his reading; he was still thinking about the missing envelope. Surely, if one of his folks had taken it, they'd have said something, since the amazing likeness of the guy in the pictures to himself was not something either of them would be likely to just shrug off the way he had. But if they didn't take it, then who did? And why? He felt his skin prickle.

Rafe again put his magazine down and got off the bed. He looked his room over very carefully, but he concluded at last that if someone had broken in again, the telltale signs were not present. *Maybe the man was more careful this time,* he told himself. He laughed nervously at the thought. The more he thought about it, he wasn't so sure he had put away the letter. *I must've left it on the desk, then accidentally thrown it out when I cleaned my room yesterday. I really need to loosen up! Too bad about the letter, though; I did want to write back eventually.*

He went back to his reading and tried to force the matter from his mind. And gradually, over the next few days, he thought less and less about it, and life seemed to return to some sense of normality for him and his family.

* * *

Lindsay had checked the mail every day, hoping for a reply from Rafe Collings. She just couldn't keep him, or his puzzling resemblance to Greg Ralston, off her mind. She really wanted to know what his birthday was. She had managed to find out what Greg's was, and if the two guys happened to have the same birthday, that would just be too much. And she also secretly hoped that she could strike up some kind of ongoing correspondence with him. It would be fun— and harmless, she figured.

When she hadn't received a reply by Friday, she felt a very keen disappointment. She told herself she was just a silly girl with an even sillier crush, but it didn't help. When her friend Stacy called and said that her dad was taking her to the game that night and that she'd like her to go with them, Lindsay decided she'd do it. After all, she did like to watch Greg play basketball. He was not only cute, but he was an exceptionally good player. She'd heard that he was already getting letters of interest from colleges around the country.

Stacy and her dad had been late picking her up because of a flat tire, and the gym was already packed by the time they got there. The area where they usually sat with other students was filled to capacity, so they were forced to search for seats elsewhere. There was just enough space for the three of them about a dozen rows up, between a mother of one of the ballplayers and a blond man of about forty she'd never seen before. Their seats were on the opposite side of the basketball court from where they usually sat, and she ended up next to the blond guy who looked about her dad's age. He smelled like he hadn't showered for a few days, and he had a scraggly, unkempt beard. It wasn't starting out to be a very fun night, she decided gloomily.

Greg played very well, and their team was soon up by fifteen points. She cheered loudly, thinking maybe the evening might turn out after all. Just then, the guy beside her poked her in the ribs and said, rather harshly, "You're too loud. I came to watch the game, not listen to some brat scream."

She couldn't believe it. Nothing like that had ever happened before, and she was always loud during ball games. Everyone was. After that, Lindsay paid more attention to the blond man, and it seemed to her like he was very nervous. He never cheered or even seemed interested in the score, and yet he was watching the game intently. Soon Greg hit a three-point shot and was fouled. She cheered, forgetting the man beside her for a moment.

"I said to shut up," the blond man growled fiercely.

From the other side of her and one row back, sitting right behind her friend, someone said, "Hey mister, you don't need to give her a hard time. It is a ball game, you know."

Lindsay looked back. A twenty-year-old guy holding a camera smiled shyly at her. "Thanks," she said, returning his smile.

His smile grew broader, but it was short-lived, for the blond man also looked back, his eyes narrowed to slits. "Mind your own business," he said in a threatening tone of voice.

Embarrassed for him, Lindsay looked forward again and hardly cheered after that. She wished she'd stayed home. How was she to know she'd have to sit by some old guy who didn't know how to have fun. He didn't even have the sense to unzip his heavy coat. Even though it was quite cold outside, it was hot in the gym, and she was sitting on her coat. When he eventually zipped the coat open, she feared he would take it off and hoped it didn't release even more bad odor. She was already feeling nauseated from the smell, and didn't know if she could stand it if it got worse.

The coat didn't come off. Instead, the fellow reached into an inside pocket and brought out an envelope. She tried not to watch him, and looked back at the game. Greg made another long three-point shot, and she almost cheered, but then she remembered the guy beside her and kept quiet.

Stacy leaned over and said, "Did you miss that, Lindsay? Greg just made a great shot and you didn't even cheer."

Not wanting to be overheard, she spoke directly into Stacy's ear. "This creepy guy beside me, he told me to be quiet."

Her friend looked over at the man like she hadn't seen him before, nodded, and said, "Was that who made that rude remark a little while ago? I didn't realize he was talking to you. That's awful."

The crowd let out a collective groan as the opposing team made a three-point shot, and Lindsay's friend turned her attention back to the game. A moment later, Lindsay glanced the blond man's way again. He had a picture of Greg in his hand, and he was looking at it very closely. Then he peeled another one from beneath it, and Lindsay had to choke back a scream.

She knew those pictures!

They were exactly like the ones she'd sent to Rafe Collings in Utah.

When the man finally pulled a third one from beneath the other two, Lindsay felt sick. It was the third one she'd sent to Rafe. She was definitely sick. It wasn't possible, it was just a coincidence that he happened to have the same three pictures that she'd sent to Rafe, she tried to tell herself.

Just like it's a coincidence that Rafe and Greg look alike, a little voice inside her head whispered. She had to get out of there. She had to find a rest room. She was afraid if she didn't that she really would throw up.

But she forced herself to sit still. She wanted to know why this man had photos of Greg. She tried to watch the game, but she couldn't get into it again at all, even though Greg was all over the floor, both defensively and making point after point on offense. Her eyes kept shifting sideways to the man beside her, who still held the pictures. Then his hand went back into his coat and he pulled the envelope out and put the pictures back inside. As he lifted it back toward his coat, the front of the envelope was briefly exposed to her view.

Lindsay, without warning, threw up all over the back of the woman who was seated in front of her, splashing on Stacy and the blond man.

* * *

If it wasn't for his aversion to attracting unwanted attention, Deke would have smacked the little girl when she threw up. He'd never seen such a brat in his life, except for his sister, Stella. Screaming like a maniac during the game, and then suddenly getting sick and not even having the brains to go to a rest room when she had to heave was almost more than he could stand. And what really infuriated him, he thought as he opened the door to his dented, rusted silver Honda, was the fact that some of the nasty, smelly substance got on him! It had taken him five minutes in the rest room to clean himself up.

But to a degree, despite fate sitting him next to an impossible brat, Deke had enjoyed a successful evening. The girl who'd written the letter he'd taken from Rafe's house had mentioned that Greg was a high school basketball player. And he'd gone to the game that night hoping to see him. And he had seen him, and he was convinced that Rafe Collings and Greg Ralston were brothers. There was just no other explanation for the way they looked so exactly alike. And their resemblance to him when he was their age was way too much. The question he had now was why they were not being raised in the same family. He'd already pretty well convinced himself when he was in the Collingses' house that Rafe was adopted. Now what he needed to find out was if Greg was still living with Stella.

Deke felt compelled to find her and the man she'd run away with, and he had to make sure they would keep their mouths shut forever. He'd planned to follow Greg home that night, but then the black-haired brat had thrown up everywhere. When he returned from cleaning up, the game was over and he couldn't find Greg. That meant he had to find some other way to figure out where Greg lived. He'd tried the phone book that afternoon and made some calls to people listed under the last name Ralston, but none of them had a son named Greg.

Then he realized that there was still a way to find out where he lived. After all, Deke had the address of a girl who seemed to like both Greg and Rafe. It was on the envelope in his pocket, the one he'd taken from Rafe's desk drawer on Sunday morning. Yes, that's what he'd do. Lindsay Diamond, whoever she was, could tell him where to find Greg.

* * *

The guy who had sat behind Lindsay's friend had actually come to the game to watch the ballplayers for once. He had a brand-new camera that took fantastic close-ups and action shots—he just couldn't resist. He also snuck in a few of Lindsay. He'd been tempted to knock the head off the blond man she was sitting beside, and he'd even said something to the guy, winning a smile from Lindsay for his efforts. No one had the right to talk to girls like that, he'd thought with anger as the game continued. He dreamed about how impressed Lindsay and her friend would be if he took the next step to rid Lindsay of her tormenter by delivering a few well-placed punches to his face.

But he'd done nothing more, for the other man was not only over twice his age, but he was also a whole lot bigger. Really, he'd surprised himself even saying something to the brute. He'd always been so painfully shy that he preferred to blend into his surroundings. And he never talked to strangers unless absolutely necessary. *And this was necessary,* he told himself. *Sometimes you just have to open your mouth.* Suddenly he realized that his bishop was right; he had more inner strength than he ever gave himself credit for.

The young photographer left the game early and drove straight to his bishop's house. He was finally ready to get serious about going on a mission.

* * *

Lindsay's mother felt her daughter's forehead again. "If your father wasn't out of town, he could give you a blessing. You must have the flu. But you don't seem to have a fever," she said. "Could it have been something you ate?"

"Maybe," Lindsay said, knowing full well that she wasn't being honest, but so embarrassed over what had happened that she just couldn't tell anyone why she'd *really* thrown up. It was the most horrible thing that had ever happened to her. Oh, the lady in front of her had been really sweet about it all. Everyone, including Stacy's dad, had shown nothing but concern for her, and several people had pitched in to help clean up the mess.

It overwhelmed her to think what all the kids would be saying when word spread of the incident, and she knew it would spread.

She'd just die before she ever told anyone about sending those pictures of Greg to Rafe. It would be as unthinkable as passing her personal diary around for everyone to read. If anyone ever found out what really happened, what had actually made her sick, she was sure she couldn't continue to live in Pocatello. She would have to move.

Lindsay kept thinking about the smelly man with the stringy blond hair that had the pictures she'd sent to Rafe. She didn't know what had happened to him after she got sick. He certainly hadn't helped clean up. She hoped she would never see him again. And yet she couldn't help but wonder who he was and why he had Rafe's letter and the pictures of Greg. Then she had a thought. Maybe he was someone that Rafe had sent up here to look at Greg in person, to try to assess whether or not they could be related.

That seemed logical enough. It would explain how the guy had gotten the pictures. Yet it didn't satisfy her. She couldn't imagine a guy who was as nice as she imagined Rafe to be, as nice as the article she'd read in the paper had said he was, having anything to do with someone as creepy as the man she'd sat next to at the ball game.

Lindsay went to bed early after her mother left to go visit an elderly lady in the ward who was homebound and had called earlier about needing help getting ready for bed. "I won't be gone too long," her mother had promised. "And I'll check on you when I get home." Lindsay laid there for several minutes wishing she'd never written that letter or sent those pictures of Greg to Rafe.

* * *

Deke inspected himself in the mirror after he finished showering, shaved off two weeks of beard, and combed his hair. He'd put on the only spare pants and shirt he'd brought with him, and decided that he looked presentable. He didn't want to frighten this Lindsay Diamond, if he found her at home that night, for he needed to get Greg's address from her.

Deke splashed on a healthy dose of aftershave, something he didn't ordinarily use, and then put his coat on and left the motel. The coat didn't look very good, but he could leave it in the car when he got to the house where Lindsay Diamond lived. He knew from the map he'd studied earlier that it was a fairly short drive. And it shouldn't take him long once he got there to obtain the information he needed. Then it was off to the home of Greg Ralston, and most likely that of Deke's traitorous sister, Stella.

CHAPTER 5

Lindsay heard the doorbell ring, but she ignored it. It rang again, followed by a persistent knocking on the door. She wished her mother hadn't gone, but since she had, and since Lindsay wasn't really ill, she climbed out of bed, slipped into a robe, and headed barefoot toward the front door. Whoever was there must need help, she reasoned. Probably a neighbor.

She opened the door and stared at the man who was standing there. He looked very familiar, but she couldn't place where she might have seen him before.

"You must be Lindsay Diamond," the man said politely as Lindsay began to regret opening the door. There was something about this guy that bothered her. For one thing, he wasn't wearing a coat, and it was a very cold night. And he smelled strongly of cheap aftershave. His blond hair was combed straight back, and there was a spot of blood on his cheek where he must have cut himself shaving. She didn't think that most men shaved at night, but he was obviously very freshly shaved. Those thoughts flashed quickly through Lindsay's mind as the stranger inspected her far too closely.

Suddenly he nodded his head like he'd figured something out. Then he rolled his eyes. "Well, are you Lindsay or not?" he asked sharply.

In that moment, Lindsay recognized the man, and her eyes widened in fear. He was the creepy guy who had the letter she'd sent to Rafe. She screamed, but the scream was cut off as the blond man clamped a hand over her mouth and pulled her tightly against him. Then he hurriedly half dragged, half carried her to an old car that was parked with the motor running in the driveway only a few feet from the door. He shoved her in and said, "I have a gun, and I'll use it if you scream or try anything. I only need some information from you, and then I'll let you go." From somewhere, he had come up with a pistol as he spoke and the barrel gleamed dangerously under the dome light that went out when he pulled the door shut behind him.

A little voice in her head spoke to her. *Don't believe him. He'll never let you go.*

Lindsay believed that voice. She also believed the man would use the gun if she gave him any reason to. She had to get away, but she also had to stay calm, to do what he asked until she could find the opportunity to escape. She had a feeling that her life depended on her getting away from him. So she began praying as he backed the car recklessly into the street and drove away.

"Remember, don't try screaming again," her captor reminded her.

It was all she could do not to scream when her mother's car passed them only a few blocks from the house. She was surprised that she'd been able to control the scream, but she knew it would have only made things worse. She tried to concentrate on what was happening to her, and she forced herself to be alert to every move the horrible man made. And she wondered what he wanted from her, and why he'd come to her house.

They'd only driven a few more blocks when she found out. The kidnapper said, "Tell me what Greg Ralston's mother looks like."

"What?" Clearly she'd been taken by a raving lunatic.

"You heard me."

She wracked her brain and remembered seeing Greg at the last game with a couple that must have been his parents. "Um . . . she's very blond, thin, and not very tall, I guess."

"How old?"

"I don't know."

"Guess."

Lindsay had no idea. The woman seemed younger than her own mom, but that's all she could figure. "Maybe thirty-something?"

"Fine, now tell me where Greg Ralston lives."

The relative calmness she'd been feeling fled in that instant and panic set in. Lindsay had no idea where Greg lived. She'd never even talked to him. But if she told this volatile man that, he might kill her right here and now. She didn't know what to do, so she did nothing, hoping and praying that she could think of something before it was too late.

It was starting to snow, and for two or three more minutes they continued on. Then the man suddenly pulled off the street they were on and into a very dark alley. He stopped the car and then said, "I asked you where Greg Ralston lives. Tell me now!"

He turned on the interior light of the car. She didn't look at him. She was afraid to look at him, so she faced the passenger window and the snow that was falling beyond it.

"Look at me, Lindsay. We are going to come to an understanding, and you will tell me where Greg lives."

She knew she had to say something, but she was slow in doing so, and he suddenly grabbed her long hair and pulled her toward him. He then forced her head around until he was glaring directly into her eyes.

"I ought to break your little neck for throwing up on me," he said, waving the gun in her face with his other hand. "Tell me where Greg Ralston lives."

"I . . . I don't know his address," she stammered.

His face twisted with rage, and Lindsay knew real fear then. With the speed of a striking rattler, he let go of her hair and struck her face with terrible force. The blow snapped her head back and threw her against the window on the far side of the car. "If you want to live, you're going to have to earn it," he said. "Take us to Greg's, and don't you hesitate one more second."

"Okay, okay," she cried in desperation. "I'll show you where he lives. It's past my house, the other direction from the way we came just now." She was buying time, and that was all. She was desperate to get away.

He turned the car while she watched for a chance to swing her door open and leap out. She could feel blood pouring from her nose, and her lip felt like it had been cut. She could taste blood in her mouth. The falling snow was increasing in intensity, and it was beginning to accumulate on the pavement. The car slipped as they climbed a hill, and for a moment her abductor was forced to concentrate on his driving. Lindsay didn't hesitate. She grabbed the door handle, opened the door, and tried to jump. But his hand, the one that had held a gun in it just a moment before, shot out and grabbed a fistful of long black hair. He snapped her back until she rammed into his solid body.

The car was sliding sideways, and she was certain they were going to crash, but somehow he got it straightened out without losing his grip on her hair. The door she'd opened slammed shut of its own accord, and she was once again trapped in the car with him. Her bravery began to evaporate, and tears poured from her eyes, mixing with blood as it spilled down her cheeks.

"Heavenly Father," she cried aloud, "please help me."

"Ain't no God interested in helping a brat like you," he scoffed as he slowed down and pulled onto a side road where there were no houses in sight for quite some distance.

He was wrong, for though she was terrorized, though she was in pain, and though she was crying, she was also, with God's help, able to think. She knew he must have dropped the gun when he grabbed for her hair, because his other hand was on the steering wheel. She was feeling around for it now, and suddenly her hand felt it on the seat beside her. She grabbed it, and when he got the car stopped and shoved her upright, she eased it around her body, saying nothing.

"Try something like that again, and both you and that boyfriend of yours will get it. You got that?" he shouted.

Again he turned on the interior light. And she slid against the door and produced the gun in a trembling hand. "I'll shoot if you don't let me go," she said, her voice breaking badly.

His eyes grew wide. But he said, "You ain't got the guts to kill me. They'd put you away for life. It'd be murder."

Lindsay was pretty sure that wasn't true under the circumstances, so she held the gun as steady as she could, and with her free hand she opened the door. She backed out, holding the gun in front of her. But when her bare feet hit the snow-covered pavement, they slid out from under her, and she fell hard into the snow. The gun was knocked from her hand, and she was aware of it sliding beneath the car. She scrambled on her hands and knees for the far side of the road. She could hear her assailant getting out of the car. She glanced back just once before she managed to get her bare feet under her and run into the trees beside the road. It looked like he was searching for the gun, and she continued to flee, her robe flapping open, the cold air chilling her to the bone through her pajamas.

She fell repeatedly, but ignoring the pain, she continued on. Once, she heard the gun fire, then a curse. But she didn't stop. The snow was falling very hard now, and she thanked God that it was, for it had to be almost impossible for him to see her.

For several minutes she continued blindly on. At last she reached a house, ran up to the front door, and began ringing the doorbell. "Coming," she could hear a man shout from inside, and she literally fell into his arms when the door opened.

The beating, the cold, the barefoot run in the snow, and the terror had taken its toll. All Lindsay managed to say before she passed out in his arms was, "He kidnapped me. He wants to kill me."

She didn't regain consciousness until around noon. When she did, she had very little to say. The trauma had been so intense that she couldn't remember what had happened. The last thing she could recall was her mother leaving the house that evening. Her mother told her that the door to the house had been left open. A neighbor said she'd heard the tires of a car screeching in the street. But Lindsay couldn't remember a thing. Her family, her friends, and the police could only speculate.

* * *

Deke's father cursed at him on the phone when he called from somewhere in Utah. "Go back and find him. You've got to make sure Stella don't ever say nothing."

"I can't go back," Deke said. "The cops are lookin' for me."

"You fool, you shouldn't have ever grabbed that girl," Harley told him.

"What else could I do? She recognized me, and she screamed," Deke said. "We'll have to wait and try again after things have cooled down. We've made it without Stella talking this many years, what's a little more time gonna hurt?"

Harley didn't like it, but there was no way Deke was going to go back to Pocatello and face prison time. So Deke continued toward

Texas, taking back roads much of the time and constantly looking over his shoulder for cops.

* * *

Rafe drove to town alone late on Saturday afternoon. "I can't just sit around waiting to see what happens," he told his dad. "I've got to get on with my life. We all do."

Lenny had finally relented, but he insisted that Rafe carry a gun with him. So Rafe drove to Ephraim, the Manti radio station dispatching the latest country music into his truck. He was feeling as relaxed as he'd been for quite some time.

Until the national news came on.

It told of a fifteen-year-old girl in Pocatello, Idaho, who had been kidnapped the evening before. "The girl is so traumatized that she's unable to remember what she went through. It's unclear how she even managed to get free. She's been identified as fifteen-year-old Lindsay Diamond of Pocatello."

Rafe pulled over and stopped his truck. His hands were shaking, and he felt a chill spread over him. This couldn't be just another coincidence. He remembered that name only too well. The letter with her address had disappeared from his room. And now something terrible had happened to her. It made no sense, but Rafe couldn't help thinking that her abduction and his recent troubles in Ephraim were directly related. And Greg, the guy who looked like him, must be connected. There might be some evil force at work here, he considered, that was separate and apart from the murder of his mother. He just didn't know what it was or if he even wanted to.

It took several minutes for Rafe to get control of his emotions and think things through. He turned around, drove home, and confided in his folks, who immediately called the sheriff. He in turn talked to the police in Pocatello, but it didn't help. Lindsay remembered nothing, Rafe was told. She'd said nothing about a letter, and her parents wouldn't let her talk to the police for a while, since it just seemed to upset her further. The best the police could do was look for an older green Cadillac with Nevada, Iowa, or Oregon plates.

Rafe felt helpless, and he worried about Lindsay, but the sheriff told him there was nothing more he could do.

* * *

Winter passed. With spring, and its attendant grass, leaves, and flowers, came new calves, new lambs, new colts, and lots of work on the ranch. Rafe's schoolwork didn't let up, either. Gradually things returned to something that resembled normal. No more threatening letters came, no more late night visits to the ranch by unwelcome trespassers occurred. It was almost as if none of it had ever happened—except that it had, and Rafe and his family could not forget.

One day in early April, Rafe opened the mailbox and found a letter addressed to him at General Delivery, Ephraim, Utah 84627. There was no name on the front of the envelope where a return address in Pocatello, Idaho, was printed. But the neat, feminine handwriting looked familiar.

Rafe waited until he was alone in his room to open the letter. As he had hoped, it was from Lindsay. She began by reintroducing herself and asking if he had received a letter from her four months ago. She briefly explained what was in the letter and that she figured it had been stolen from him, but she didn't know if that was before or after it had arrived at his house. She said that she thought that he might have heard about what happened to her, and that she hoped he hadn't worried about it.

He looked up from the letter and thought back over the past months. He'd worried all right, and he'd asked the police chief to check and see if anything more had happened. Chief Johnson called his counterpart in Pocatello, but all he learned was that Lindsay was recovering but still couldn't remember any details of what had happened that fateful night when she was taken from her home.

Rafe began reading again. Lindsay wrote that she was gradually beginning to remember some things, but she was afraid to tell the police because if they caught the kidnapper, she'd have to face him at a trial, and she didn't think she could handle that. She said that the kidnapping had to do with Greg Ralston, and that Greg and his family had moved as soon as the ball season was over. She had no idea where he'd gone. Her father had been offered a promotion in another state, and they would soon be moving, so she couldn't see what good it would do to stir things up by telling the police when neither she nor Greg would be in Pocatello anyway. She said she had originally decided that she wasn't going to tell anyone what she was remembering, but had thought about Rafe and decided that he had a right to know, since she now remembered seeing the kidnapper with the letter she'd sent to Rafe.

She wrote in some detail of the man who had abducted her, of how she'd seen the letter and pictures at the ball game. She said that he looked different when he came to her house later that night, and that she didn't think he'd initially intended to kidnap her, that it was only Greg he was trying to find. She was still fuzzy about how she'd escaped from him, but she gave the Lord the credit.

Rafe again looked away from the letter. Now he knew that somebody had in fact stolen that envelope and all that it contained, and that the person who'd done it was not the tall man in the green Cadillac. That man probably had nothing to do with any of the trouble, he reasoned. It was some blond man of about forty or so, it seemed, who had been in their house. And that man had an interest in him and Greg Ralston, his supposed twin. For the first time, Rafe began to seriously consider the fact that Greg really might be his twin brother, and that someone, for some reason, wanted to know more about them. Maybe that person had lost interest now. He hoped so; for whoever it was, he was not a nice person.

Rafe began to read again. Lindsay had suddenly remembered a piece of information she had tracked down not long after she sent the first letter: Greg's birth date. Rafe felt his mouth go dry. They not only looked alike, but they also shared the same date of birth. That was not a likely coincidence.

Finally, Lindsay told Rafe that she'd love to hear from him if he felt like writing. She said she'd let him know her new address when she got one, but that the address on the envelope would get her mail to her for some time to come. She closed by saying that if he didn't want to write to her, she'd understand, and promised not to bother him again if he didn't. Under her signature, she'd added a postscript, asking him to please destroy the letter when he'd read it and not to tell anyone what she'd told him. She added that if he would keep her address in a safe place, she'd like that very much.

When he finished reading, Rafe put the letter down and thought for a long time. Then he booted up his computer and typed a short note.

Lindsay,

Thanks for writing. I'm sorry for all the trouble you had. I did receive the letter you sent. It was stolen from my room the Sunday after it came while my family and I were at church. I suppose you're probably right about keeping these things between us. Since the guy who might be my brother has moved, there's no point in stirring things up. And I'm glad you're moving, and hope you stay safe. I do wish I knew more about Greg. I am adopted, and my twin brother was stolen from the hospital when our birth mother died. Since my birthday and Greg's are the same, it's pretty obvious that he's probably my brother. I'll write again sometime.

Rafe Collings

It was short, but it was all he was up to right now. Maybe later he could tell her more, he thought. He printed the letter, put it in an envelope, and mailed it at the post office in Ephraim the next time he was in town. He didn't want to risk anyone seeing Lindsay's letter to him, so he tore it in tiny pieces and carried it to the big garbage barrel outside. But he kept her address tucked away in his scriptures.

A couple of weeks later, Rafe received another letter from Lindsay. There was no return address on the envelope, and Glenda gave Rafe a funny look when she handed it to him. "Must be from a girl," she said, and Rafe just grinned at her and said nothing. The letter was short and didn't tell him much new; mostly she just thanked him for responding. But when he looked at the photograph of herself that she'd enclosed, he was impressed. She was pretty enough to be a model, but he would never have guessed it from her friendly and unpretentious letters. He hid the photo in his favorite mystery novel on his bookshelf and occasionally looked at it. They began a regular correspondence which they maintained even after she and her family moved to Michigan.

Given Lindsay's age, and the sheer distance between them, Rafe found it easy to keep the relationship platonic. It wasn't long, though, before he had to admit to himself that he hoped he and Lindsay would be more than just friends in the future.

* * *

Harley and Deke Tuft eventually got new tires on their old black Ford Bronco and drove it to Pocatello. But when they drove by Lindsay's house, there was a For Sale sign in the yard. The house was empty. They didn't know if that was good or bad; they just didn't want her to be a threat to Deke. They didn't like people who were threats, people whose memories could send them to prison.

They made a few discreet inquiries around town, but it seemed that both Greg Ralston's family and Lindsay Diamond's had moved. Nobody seemed to know where they'd gone. "Deke," Harley said after jamming a chew of tobacco under his lip, "I can't believe we lost Greg. We was so close and you messed it up. I got a feeling that he's with his ma and her fella, and that they keep on moving around just so we won't ever find them."

"Maybe Rafe—" Deke began.

"Forget Rafe. He don't know nothing. Looks to me like Stella kept the one kid and gave the other one away. Maybe someday we'll get another lead on Greg, then we'll find him and his ma, and that tall guy too, if he's still with them. Till then, I guess we'll just have to hope she keeps her mouth shut."

They talked for a minute about Lindsay, but they decided that if she'd left Pocatello, she probably wasn't a threat. It wasn't worth worrying about anymore, Harley pointed out. "She's running scared, that little gal is. She ain't a problem."

"I hope yer right, Pa," Deke said.

The old Bronco headed for Texas.

PART TWO

Five years later

CHAPTER 6

Twenty-two-year-old Rafe Collings plopped his diploma down on his dresser. Now that he'd graduated from Snow College with an associate's degree, the pressure was on to make a decision as to what he should do with the rest of his life. He'd served a mission between his two years of college. He'd done a little calf-roping in rodeos, and even made some money at it. He'd given up bareback riding after his championship ride in high school. But he missed it, and he thought about trying his hand at that again. After all, he'd been pretty good at it. But he was a lot taller and bigger now; it would be more difficult to compete. So after some debate with himself, he left the broncos alone.

The offer was there to help his father with the ranch, even to expand the operation if he wanted to get more involved. However, his folks were encouraging him to go on to Utah State University in Logan and earn a bachelor's degree in agriculture or animal science before pursuing a career as a rancher and farmer. That idea was appealing to Rafe because he enjoyed working the soil and he loved animals. But he'd drug his feet and had failed to apply to any four-year college, including USU. He knew it might be too late now for the coming semester, especially if he was to get help with expenses by being awarded a scholarship, since he hadn't applied for one.

No one understood his reluctance to move ahead with his education right now, but Rafe knew that there was something else he wanted to do, something else he needed to get done. And he'd been reminded of it when he stepped into the bank an hour after graduation. He could never go into the bank without remembering the murder of his mother. And with that reminder this afternoon, he also recalled his desire to someday, somehow, bring the murderer to justice, and time was moving on. The longer he waited to actively begin the pursuit, the harder it would be.

Rafe looked at himself in the mirror. He was six-five now and weighed 220 pounds. He was not a bad-looking fellow, he guessed. At least plenty of girls were always flocking around him. And though he dated, he hadn't gotten serious with anyone, nor had he forgotten Lindsay Diamond.

They had finally met in person shortly after he graduated from high school. Her family had come to Utah when her brother got married in the Salt Lake Temple. Rafe had driven up and spent an entire Saturday with her. That same summer, her family had moved again, and this time they were closer to Utah. He took her out then and a couple more times when she came to Salt Lake and visited her brother. And he'd written to her for the first part of his mission. There was no denying that they were falling in love. She was then and continued to be the girl of his dreams.

She'd suggested early in his mission that her writing to him might prove a distraction to him. So she suggested that they take up their correspondence after he got home. But when he wrote to the last address he had for her after his release, the letter came back stamped undeliverable. And he never got a letter from her. So now he didn't even know where she was. He wondered if she was married. He assumed that she might be, for that would explain why she didn't write to him after his two years were over.

Rafe tried to push Lindsay gently from his mind. Maybe it was just as well. He didn't think it would be fair to get too involved with anyone at this point anyway. As he concentrated on what he wanted to do next in life, he would very likely be putting his life in danger. An idea had been on his mind for some time now, but he'd never mentioned it to anyone. He had done some research, and he knew that it would take time.

With sudden resolution, Rafe's decision was made, and he strode from the room. It was time to do what had to be done, and he was going to start the process no later than tomorrow. Rafe found his father in the equipment shed changing the oil in one of their tractors. This was not going to be easy, but Rafe had to do it.

He entered the shed quite silently. "Hey, Dad," he said, startling his father.

"Hey, son, what's up?" Lenny asked with a grin as he wiped a greasy hand on a rag.

"Not much. I, uh, well . . ." Rafe said awkwardly, not sure how to begin.

Lenny made it a little easier. "You have something on your mind, don't you?" he asked. "Well, let's sit down and talk about it. Maybe I can help."

They found a couple of old folding chairs and sat facing each other. Rafe thought about how much he loved his father. He couldn't have asked for a better dad, and the thought of disappointing him now was very difficult for Rafe. He was certain that his father would be disappointed with the decision he'd made.

Rafe still didn't know how to start, and stuttered for a moment before Lenny made a move to put him more at ease. "Son," he began, "if this is about your future, you need to know that your mother and I will support you in whatever you decide to do. You know I'd love to have you working here alongside of me, and that offer stands, but if there's something else you'd rather do, then you have my blessing. You have your life to live, and I understand that."

"Thanks, Dad." Rafe relaxed a little. "I hope you don't sell the ranch, because someday I might want to come back, but for now, I want to pursue something else."

"Great," Lenny said. "I'll be working right here as long as the Lord's willing. There's nothing else that I want to do. Glenda loves it here as well. And if and when you do want to come help, it's here. So, what will you be doing?"

Rafe wasn't surprised at the look of concern on his father's face when he said, "I'm going to be a private investigator."

There was a long moment of silence. When Lenny spoke, his voice suddenly sounded tired and old, and there was a sadness there that tore at Rafe's heartstrings. "This is not what I expected, Rafe, but I can't go back on my word. You have my blessing. But what brought this on?"

Rafe looked at the toes of his boots for a long time. Finally he looked up, prepared with his answer. But before he could speak, his father said, "You want to find your mother's killer, don't you?"

"How did you know?"

"Just makes sense," Lenny said. "I'm right, aren't I?"

"Yes," Rafe admitted. "But I think I'd enjoy the work, anyway. You know how I enjoy mysteries. I'm going to give it a try. I've been looking into what I have to do to get licensed. It's not going to be easy, but I'm going to get started right away. I'll have to move to a larger area. Whenever I can, I'd like to come back here and help out on the ranch."

"You're welcome anytime, of course. But be careful, Rafe," Lenny said as he stood and embraced his only son. "Stay close to the Lord. And don't take unnecessary risks. I'd ask you how you plan to begin the search for your mother's killer, but I'm not sure I want to know."

"I haven't got that far anyway," Rafe admitted. "I've got a lot to learn first. I'm sure it'll take quite a while to get a license. But I want to get started now on whatever training and experience I need."

* * *

Thorndike Stanbury was a bear of a man. A retired Los Angeles detective turned private investigator, he'd traded the mild climate, heavy population, and thick smog of LA for the relative quiet but harsher climate of Provo, Utah. In his midsixties, Thorndike worked hard every day, but found himself getting behind. What he needed, he finally realized, was to hire some help.

The ad he'd put in the paper had specified that he wanted someone with experience, integrity, and motivation. The young man seated across the desk from him now didn't fit the first of those three criteria; he had no experience at all. What he wanted was to work as an apprentice until he could get his license. On the other hand, he was more motivated and brighter than any of the half dozen other men and women he'd interviewed. And it remained to be seen if he was honest, but Thorndike had a feeling the young man would measure up in that respect. He already knew he'd served an LDS mission and that he was an Eagle Scout. But was that enough to justify hiring him? He thought not.

"I'll work hard and I'll take whatever assignments you give me," Rafe said as Thorndike slowly shook his head.

"I'm sure you would," Thorndike said. "But I need someone who can deal with seedy people. Many of my investigations involve less-than-desirable folks and some very dangerous ones. I'm really looking for someone who has a police background, someone who has dealt with the kind of people you'd come across in this business."

"Like the man who murdered my mother?" Rafe asked.

Thorndike saw something in the young man's eyes at that rather shocking question, and he found himself wanting to know more. "Tell me about your mother, Rafe."

"No, you're a busy man, and I don't want to waste your time," Rafe said.

"You are interested in getting a job, aren't you?" Thorndike asked.

"Yes, but I don't have experience. Maybe I'll look into law enforcement. I could do that for a few years, at least until I get enough experience to get a job like this one."

"Please, let's talk. Tell me about what happened."

Rafe did as he was asked, and Thorndike listened as the story of a little boy witnessing a horrendous crime unfolded. Finally, he asked, "Did they ever arrest the man who did this to your mother?"

Rafe shook his head.

"He threatened you, and you didn't dare tell the cops what you'd witnessed?"

"That's right. At least not for a long time," Rafe said. "Not until I was seventeen."

"And why did you tell them then?" he asked.

Rafe grinned awkwardly and said, "Because my stepmother found a letter the killer sent reminding me that I better not say anything about what I'd seen."

"After, what, ten or eleven years?" Thorndike asked. "I've never heard of such a thing happening. In this letter, did it say why he was giving you that reminder?"

Again Rafe shook his head. "But it might have been because he learned something about me that made him think I wasn't afraid anymore."

"And what could he have read that might have made him think that?" Thorndike asked. "I get the feeling that there's a lot more to your story than what you just told me. I'd like to hear it."

Hear it he did. When Rafe had finally finished, Thorndike said, "You've had some tough times. But things are okay now? This girl from Idaho, she hasn't heard anything more from whoever the blond guy was, the one you say couldn't have been the killer."

"That's right. At least she hadn't the last time I heard from her."

"Which was?"

"About three years ago, just a few weeks into my mission."

"And you haven't seen the guy with the green Cadillac, the one you called the tall man, for several years either?" Thorndike asked.

"Nope," Rafe said.

"You have no idea how the blond guy, the tall man, and the killer might be connected, or if they even are?" he asked.

"That's right," Rafe said. "I haven't a clue."

"And you've never heard from this Greg Ralston, the young fellow you think may be your brother?"

"I have no idea where he is or if he really is my brother," Rafe answered. "I would like to meet him someday, though. I'd like to know for sure, I guess."

"Still ride bucking horses in the rodeo?" Thorndike asked.

Rafe grinned. "No. But where did that come from?" he asked.

"Just wondered. You don't seem like the kind of young man who would give up easily. Why don't you still ride? Sounds like you were very good."

"I rope instead," Rafe said. "I'm too tall to make a good bronc rider anymore."

Thorndike nodded his head. "You are tall." He was thoughtful for a moment. Rafe sat quietly, his eyes dropping to where he held his hands folded on his lap. Thorndike felt drawn to this young man, and he was intrigued by his story. Finally he said, "If you were here asking me to work for you, to investigate your mother's death, or to find your brother, or to try to figure out who the tall man and the blond man are, I'd take the job. Sounds both interesting and challenging."

"Thanks, but I can't afford to pay you."

"So instead, you want to learn the business so you can solve those mysteries yourself?" Thorndike asked shrewdly.

Rafe looked him in the eye when he answered. "I didn't tell you everything about riding that bronc called One Up. When I looked into his eyes before I rode him, I knew I'd seen that look before."

Thorndike interrupted. "In the eyes of your mother's killer?"

Rafe nodded. "That's right, and when I was settling down on his back to ride him, I made a promise to myself. You're right, Mr. Stanbury. I want to find that man someday." Rafe stood up. "I'm sorry to have wasted your time."

Thorndike didn't move. He waited until Rafe reached for the door handle, then he said, "Do you want the job or not?"

Rafe faced him, looking puzzled.

"Well, do you? I'm offering it to you," the burly investigator said with a smile.

"If you're sure, I'll take it," Rafe said. "And I won't let you down."

"A lot of the work is very boring and mundane," Thorndike warned.

"I'll do whatever you ask me to do."

"And you won't bellyache over the drab work we do?"

"You have my word."

"Good, because there's a lot of boring stuff that I'm behind on. Later, when we get caught up on the work, and if you would accept my help, maybe we can solve the mystery of your past together."

"That would be great, but how?" Rafe asked, his face brightening.

"Be patient, my boy. You'll learn all that in time," the old detective said. "Now, when can you begin?"

"Is today too early, Mr. Stanbury?" Rafe asked.

"That'll work. And, oh, Rafe . . . my friends call me Thorn."

* * *

The little bar was dingy and poorly lit. No one knew for sure what had caused the fight, but when it was over, one man lay dead on the floor. By the time the cops arrived, the patrons involved had left the bar and scattered. The lone bartender reported that the customers in the altercation were all strangers to him. None of them had been a regular customer. He didn't think any of them had ever been in the bar before, at least not on his shift. He wasn't even sure who'd been in the fight. So all he and the handful of regulars who were there could do was describe the people who'd been there that evening. The officers spent a couple of hours interrogating them, eliciting as much information as they could.

Suddenly, one of the patrons remembered having recognized one man. "He was quite tall and very blond," the man reported. "If you watched the NBA draft earlier this year, you'll have seen him. And he's been on the local sports page here lately. He was the player taken in the first round by the Dallas Mavericks. A point guard, as I recall."

"Do you remember his name?" Detective Rett Vancott asked, suddenly very interested.

"Not at the moment, but it'll come back to me. It's been a rather traumatic night here," he said. "I've never seen anybody die before."

"I understand, but from what you've told me, it sounds to me like you're talking about Greg Ralston," Vancott said, thinking that an NBA player like Ralston would probably be a good witness, since it would hurt his career if he didn't cooperate fully with the police.

"Yeah, that's him," the witness said. "He's a really blond guy, and he was drafted from some little college somewhere. Yeah, I'm sure that was him. It was Greg Ralston that was here tonight. And I think he might have been in the fight. Yeah, I'm pretty sure he was."

That, along with the murder weapon—a three-inch pocketknife—and fingerprints from a number of glasses and bottles, was all the investigators had to begin with in their search for a killer.

After more interrogation, the bartender remembered something he thought might be of help to the cops. Yes, he was quite certain, he told Sergeant Bill Latner and his partner Detective Vancott, that the guy the patron had described had been carrying a pocketknife in a sheath on his belt when he came into the bar that evening. When pressed on how he remembered a detail like that with so many customers milling around in the little bar, he explained that it was because he always looked for weapons, that he didn't want anyone getting hurt on his shift.

"Didn't work too well," Detective Vancott said with a chuckle.

"Guess not," the bartender agreed.

* * *

The green Cadillac was getting older but it was still running well. And the man who drove it was hurting for money. He'd spent the past several days trying to figure out how he was going to be able to get money from the new millionaire basketball player, Greg Ralston. He'd tried every scheme he could think of during his life, except getting a real job, to come up with money to live on and support his on-again, off-again drug habit over the years. He recognized that he was getting too old to keep making a living the way he'd been doing all these years.

What this called for, he decided when he read about Greg signing with the Mavericks down in Texas, was a big score, something that would bring a lot of money. Then he could kick back in some quiet place and relax for a few years.

When he read the article about Greg's look-alike, Rafe Collings, becoming an apprentice to a private investigator, an idea began to form in his conniving mind. He was certain that Greg and Rafe were twins. Yes, he thought greedily, there was a way to make money from the knowledge he possessed. All he needed was a couple hundred thousand dollars or so and he'd be satisfied for a few years. And Greg could afford to help him out. But Rafe might have to be the one to convince Greg. After all, he'd seen plenty of TV programs showing how strong the bond between twins.

The key was Rafe's younger half-sister, Stephanie Collings. The man who'd had almost as many identities over the years as he'd had birthdays began to form a plan. It would work. It had to work. Unless he made some money in the next few weeks, he'd be broke.

* * *

Deke had tried a kidnapping once, and he'd failed miserably. It still made him angry to think about it. If Lindsay and her family hadn't moved, he'd have gotten his revenge, but they had. Now he had another kidnapping in mind, but this one he was going to plan out. And he wouldn't be working alone. He had his old pa to help. They would be sure of every step, they promised each other. They had too much to lose if they messed it up.

But they didn't want to take too much time, for Greg Ralston was in Dallas now, too close to them for comfort. His presence here could mean that his mother might be close by, and that was too good an opportunity to pass up. They needed to find out for sure where Stella was so they could silence her forever. And it might be necessary to silence Greg Ralston and his twin brother, Rafe Collings. Who could ever know what their mother might have told them if she'd had contact with them? And they had to assume that she had, for they couldn't take any chances. They had to act decisively, and they couldn't waste too much time before they did so.

The most effective way to find out what they wanted to know about the boys' mother was to force the twins to talk—especially Greg, since they were pretty sure he had been raised by Stella. But to do that, there had to be leverage. Deke wished Greg had a wife or something. But the more he thought about it, the more he realized that Rafe's little sister was even better. After all, it was Rafe's stupid pen pal that had ruined his plans years ago. Now Rafe would have a little trouble of his own to deal with. And surely Greg would tell them what they needed to know when his twin's innocent little sister went missing. Deke knew exactly where to find her. He cursed his luck that the engine on the Bronco had thrown a rod. It would take him a few weeks to get it running again. But after that, with a little good luck for a change . . .

* * *

Kerry Sundolf, as the man was now known, carried the large package that he'd picked up at the post office that afternoon into his beautiful and expensive new home in Portland, Oregon. He removed the bundle of newspapers it contained and piled them by the recliner in his family room. He didn't have a family yet, but his marriage to a beautiful young woman was set for the weekend. Someday maybe he'd even have a kid or two, he figured, and pass on his rather good genes.

Kerry was a successful businessman now who kept one eye on his thriving business and one eye on his lucrative past. The newspapers, although each was fairly current, pertained to his life before he'd settled in Portland and taken the name of Kerry Sundolf.

Some of the papers were from small towns, others from large cities. He had current subscriptions to each of them, although they were in a variety of false names and were delivered initially to a post office box in Cheyenne, Wyoming. Every couple of weeks he had a former associate collect them, box them up, and forward them to another post office box in Portland under another assumed name, of course. His only interest in perusing the papers was to see if anything was ever mentioned that might be an indication that the police in the various areas where the papers were published had made any progress in identifying him or even if they were still interested in him. His life of crime was more or less over now, but he considered himself a cautious man and kept track of those locations where he'd committed his more serious crimes. Using part of the large amount of money he amassed over the years from various crimes he'd committed, he established a legitimate business in Portland. He was gaining a good reputation as an honest, dedicated citizen, and he wasn't about to let anyone from his past upset his current status.

It was a couple of hours after he arrived home before Kerry sat down, turned on the television, and began skimming through the large stack of papers. As usual, nothing alarmed him. Even the picture of Rafe Collings didn't cause him undue stress, for he was used to seeing something in the local paper from Sanpete County, Utah, about Rafe or his family from time to time. But the caption beneath the picture provoked a double take. He read it carefully a second time, then read the short accompanying article. He scowled; then he swore; then he threw the paper on the floor.

The man who had killed Rafe Collings's mother knew exactly why Rafe was training to become a private investigator. But it wasn't going to work. Rafe had been warned twice now. He'd send him one more note. After that, if Rafe didn't leave the past alone, the young would-be detective would never know what hit him.

* * *

"There's a movie I want to see. Melly says she can go tonight. We were wondering if you'd like to come too," Cybil Prescott said to her roommate.

Lindsay Diamond groaned, and she looked crestfallen. Before she could say anything, Cybil chuckled and said, "I know, you'd like to, but you have a date. Lucky you."

Cybil dated more than Lindsay, but it just happened that no one had asked her out for a couple of weeks. She often wondered why Lindsay didn't seem that interested in guys. Several times she'd asked her if there was someone in her past that she couldn't forget. Lindsay had never admitted that was the case, but Cybil was pretty sure there must be someone.

Lindsay smiled at her roommate. "I do have a date. But I have an idea. I can pretend to be sick, and when Bob comes, you can tell him I'm a bit under the weather, and that I asked you to take my place."

"You're not serious," Cybil said.

She was surprised when Lindsay responded, "I honestly don't feel all that good. It's mostly because I really don't care for this guy. But he's nice enough and he keeps asking. He's in one of my classes, and I . . . well, I just didn't feel like I should give him one of my usual excuses. He seems kind of shy."

"Is he cute?" Cybil asked as Melly entered the apartment.

"Is who cute?" Melly asked.

"Bob," Cybil answered brightly.

"Bob who?"

"I don't know. What's his last name, Lindsay?"

"Staw. His name's Bob Staw," Lindsay said.

"What about him?" Melly asked.

"Lindsay's trying to pawn off her date for tonight on me," Cybil answered. "I'm just trying to decide if I want to let her or not."

"Wait a minute," Melly protested. "I thought the three of us were going to go together."

"That's what I thought, but Lindsay has a date."

"So, the two of us can still go, can't we?"

"Sure, why not?" Cybil answered. "In fact, we could go as a three-some, me and you and Bob Staw. If he's cute, that is. So, Lindsay, is he?"

Lindsay shrugged. "You guys might think so."

"That didn't sound very enthusiastic," Melly said.

"I'm not. He seems like an okay guy, just different. And he must be at least twenty-five."

"I don't have a problem with that," Cybil said. "Tell you what, Lindsay, we'll wait here until he comes tonight. You stay in the bedroom when he knocks. Then if Melly and I approve of him, we'll make an excuse for you and see if he'll let us fill in. If we don't like the looks of him, then you're stuck."

"Hey guys, thanks for the offer, but I wasn't really serious. I can't do that to Bob. I told him I'd go, and I will. I just don't look forward to it, that's all," Lindsay said.

"Is he a returned missionary?" Melly asked. "If he's an undergrad student at BYU and is older, like you say, he must be an RM."

"I don't know if he is or not. I don't really know him that well. I do know that he's not my type."

* * *

It was a long evening. Bob seemed to want to know all about her, but he wasn't so free with information about himself. He seemed nice enough, and he was a gentleman, but he definitely wasn't her type. She felt like she had to do all the talking and quickly became bored of listening to herself. To her surprise, when he walked her to the door later, he asked her out again. She tried to say no, but it came out yes. As soon as the door closed behind her, and he was on his way back to his car, Lindsay groaned.

She'd never admitted it to her roommates, but Cybil was right. Even though she'd only actually gone out with Rafe a few times, and even though she was the one who quit writing him on his mission, she had never gotten over him and had hoped to renew their relationship after he came home. But it hadn't happened. She'd written to him, but he hadn't answered. She assumed that his feelings had changed over the course of his mission. Unfortunately, other guys just didn't measure up to Rafe. If only she could forget him and get on with her life, she thought as she braced herself for the questions she knew Melly and Cybil would have for her when she walked through the front door.

CHAPTER 7

Rafe found himself enjoying his work very much. Some of the assignments, although boring, were new to Rafe, and so they didn't seem so bad. And Thorn was a great teacher. From time to time they worked together on things, and he always took the time to explain what they were doing and why. The two soon became fast friends.

Rafe sensed that Thorn was thinking a lot about Rafe's past, for he occasionally asked Rafe a question or two about the murder or his family. Before long, Rafe was sure that his boss had gained every bit of information it was possible for him to supply. But he never said a word about why he was asking, until one day late in the summer when he said, "I have a friend in the Los Angeles Police Department who is a police artist. He's as good as they come in drawing pictures of faces as other people describe them. I'd like to know what this killer looks like."

"What killer?" Rafe asked. Up to that point their conversation had been about the background check they'd been doing on some employees of a business that was suffering an unusual amount of theft of light equipment.

"Your mother's killer," Thorn clarified.

"Oh, well, like I told you before, he had brown—" Rafe began.

Thorn cut him off with a chuckle. "I remember what you've told me about him, but if we get a good police artist to listen to your description, then maybe we could come up with a fairly close likeness of the guy. It would be helpful."

Rafe was skeptical. "Five years ago we tried to do a computer sketch, but it didn't really look right. I don't think the guy that was doing it was an expert, though. Can they really make it that recognizable?"

"Oh yeah, especially Tom. He's the best I've ever seen."

"But Thorn," Rafe began. "It's been a long time since I saw him. Even if we can manage to get a fairly good picture of him as he looked when I saw him, he'll look a lot different now."

Thorn chuckled. "Once we get a good likeness, it can be age-enhanced on the computer. Tom has all the tools he needs. He can add beards, short, long, full, whatever. And he can change the hair—the color, the thickness, the style, and so on."

"Must be expensive," Rafe said, thinking that it was a good idea, but way too much for him to spend right now.

"Could be," Thorn agreed. "But Tom will do it for me on his own time. He has his own equipment; and most importantly of all, he owes me."

"He owes you?"

"Yeah, I saved his skin a couple of years back. He was accused of a pretty serious crime, and the LAPD was ready to dump him. He called me, I got to the bottom of it, proved that it was all an attempt by the family of a guy he managed to help put away to smear him, to ruin his career. By then, he'd spent a ton on lawyers and had lost a lot of wages because he'd been suspended. So I told him that I'd work for future help when I needed it. Now I need it."

"Actually, I need it, Thorn," Rafe reminded him.

"Same difference. I need to go to LA in a week or two. Maybe you could go with me, help me get finished quicker down there, then we can see what Tom can do for us."

"Once we get the pictures, then what?"

"Let me worry about that. I'll see that they get in the hands of the right people around the country. It's a starting place, that's all. But it could pay off big in the end."

* * *

Greg Ralston was arrested a few days later for the murder that had occurred in a west-side Dallas bar. The police felt very confident that they had the right man. After all, his pocketknife was the murder weapon, and among the prints on the knife, some of Greg's were found. And his prints were also all over one of the glasses in the bar.

His arrest was national news in the sporting world. Rafe, who was watching the sports news while he read a mystery novel, sat stunned that evening. He was stunned for two reasons; first because of Greg's tragic arrest, but also because he was a newly drafted member of the Dallas Mavericks. Rafe remembered that Lindsay Diamond had told him that Greg was a really good basketball player in high school—but the NBA? It seemed unreal.

The piece showed several pictures of Greg, then there was a brief interview with a man who claimed to be his agent, Jim Hanks. Hanks said that Greg was innocent, that even though he'd been in the bar earlier that evening, he was not there when the murder occurred. Next there was an attorney who had already agreed to defend Greg who said that he would prove his innocence and that he was requesting a bail hearing. "We'll get Greg out of jail while we fight these bogus charges," the lawyer said.

Rafe was sick over what he heard. Even though he'd never met Greg, he was almost certain he was his missing brother and he'd hoped to meet him someday. And he was afraid that Greg might actually be guilty. It all seemed like a terrible nightmare.

It was one of three nightmares that evening. Rafe pulled on a pair of latex gloves and again picked up the envelope that had been waiting in his mailbox when he got home. He read it through once more. How did his mother's killer know that he was training to be a private investigator? He folded the unsigned, threatening note back in the envelope.

The third nightmare was a call from Rafe's father. Rafe could tell he was upset the moment he heard his voice. "Dad, what's wrong?" he asked.

"I got a letter today," he said.

Rafe's stomach twisted. "So did I."

"Yeah, I forwarded one on to you yesterday. It worried me only because there wasn't a return address. The one I got today looked about the same, but it was addressed to me," Lenny said.

"What did it say?" Rafe asked, scared to death of what he might hear.

"It said that I should encourage you not to start looking for him. It didn't say who *him* was, but I'm sure he knew that I would know. Anyway, he said that if you tried to find him, that something might happen to both . . . or to one of your family members." Lenny didn't say anything else.

Rafe asked, "Was that all it said?"

"That was more than enough," Lenny said.

"You guys be careful," Rafe admonished his father. "I honestly haven't done a thing about looking for the guy. I can't figure how he knows what I'm doing now, but he does. It's like he keeps track of me all the time or something."

"It's sinister," Lenny said. "And I don't need to tell you that he's dangerous."

* * *

"Lindsay, I thought you said one date with Bob Staw was enough," Melly said with a wicked grin. "But now you tell us you have a date with him tonight."

"I guess I just don't like to hurt people's feelings," Lindsay said with a groan. "Bob really isn't my kind of guy. Believe me, he isn't. I just don't know how to get rid of him without hurting his feelings."

"I think he's kind of cute," Melly said. "Why don't you give him a chance?"

"I guess that's what I'm doing," Lindsay said morosely. "But I refuse to go out with him every night, or even every week."

Melly just smiled. Bob seemed nice to her, and he was certainly cute enough. Lindsay just might learn to like him, she thought.

"I hope he doesn't keep me out too late tonight," Lindsay said. "After my classes in the morning, I'll be starting my new job at the bank tomorrow."

"Yeah, I know." It was Melly's turn to be morose. "I wish I could find a good job. So does Cybil. You're really lucky, you know. You have a great new job and a boyfriend."

"A date," Lindsay said firmly. "Bob is not a boyfriend."

* * *

"You look a little down this morning, Rafe," his boss said as he walked into the office a little before eight. "You must have seen the news last night."

"Yeah, I did," Rafe agreed as he pulled on a pair of latex gloves and then retrieved the killer's letter from an inside pocket of his jacket.

"Was that your brother, the ballplayer who was arrested for murder in Dallas?" Thorn asked.

Rafe nodded. "What do you think? Did you see the pictures of him?"

"I did indeed, and I'd bet dollars to donuts that he's your twin," Thorn said. "So much for searching for him. What have you got there?"

"He's watching me, Thorn," Rafe said, shaking the letter. "My mother's killer is watching me. My dad forwarded this letter to me. He got one like it yesterday, only his threatens my family too."

Thorn shook his head. "We'll try getting prints off this, although I suspect that it'll be a waste of our time."

Before touching the envelope, the older man also pulled on gloves, then he took the letter from Rafe's hands and read it. When he'd finished, he asked the very question that had been running through Rafe's mind all night long. "How did he know you were working for me?"

Rafe shrugged, for he knew Thorn didn't expect an answer, he was just getting his sharp mind focused.

"Was this mentioned in any newspapers that you know of?" Thorn asked.

"My local paper, but I don't know of any other ones."

Thorn looked very thoughtful for a moment, then he said, "This moves the timetable up, my boy. This guy needs to be found."

"But I don't want to do anything that will be dangerous for my family," Rafe said as he remembered all that he'd put them through when he was still in high school. "So what will we do?"

"I'm thinking on it," Thorn said. "Now, back to this guy in Dallas. He is most likely your long-lost twin brother. I suppose you'll be wanting to talk to him, even if he is in some pretty deep trouble."

"But Greg swears he didn't do it," Rafe responded defensively.

"They always do. In this case, I hope you're right, but it sounds like the cops think they have a pretty good case. We'll follow it closely, see what happens. If you'll follow up on the Smith matter today, I'll see if I can get us a part-time secretary. You and I can't keep up the book work ourselves. I listed the job several days ago. I'll see what kind of interviews I can arrange today. And tomorrow morning, I think we might go to Los Angeles. I'll get a flight for both of us and make arrangements to meet Tom and get that drawing done. You can go tomorrow, can't you?"

"Oh yeah," Rafe responded.

"No hot dates or anything the next two or three nights?"

"No dates at all," Rafe said. "I haven't been on a date in, well, months, I guess."

* * *

The job at the bank was great. Lindsay's roommates had been a little jealous, but when she got home from work that evening, Cybil Prescott had exciting news.

"I have a job!" she cried with delight when Lindsay came in.

"Wow, that was fast. You didn't even have any leads when you went to class this morning," Lindsay said.

"I went to Workforce Services at eleven. They had a new listing. I applied and got hired right away," she said, bubbling with excitement. "And you won't believe this job. I'm going to be working as a part-time secretary for a detective agency."

"Sounds exciting," Lindsay said sincerely. "I wonder how Melly did today. I hope she's as lucky as us."

"I hope so, too," Cybil agreed. "Oh, I just can't wait until Thursday. My boss wants me to start then, and he wants me to begin setting up a better filing system for him, to answer his phones, to call back when people leave messages when either I or one of the two detectives aren't in. And I'll be doing all the billing."

"Sounds interesting," Lindsay said as she began to rummage through the refrigerator for leftovers. "You say there are two detectives in the agency?"

"Yeah. The boss, his name is Thorndike Stanbury. He's a retired cop, and tries to come across as a tough guy, but I think he's really kind of a softy. The other guy is not actually a licensed investigator, he's what Mr. Stanbury called an apprentice."

"I see," Lindsay responded, only half listening now.

"I met the other guy. Wow! What a guy he is. He's really cute. And get this, Lindsay. He's single, he's a returned missionary, he's a hunk, and he's really tall. Must be six-five or something."

"Great. Sounds like you got really lucky." Cybil was always meeting amazing guys.

Cybil wasn't through yet. "You know what? I've been thinking ever since he came into the office right after I was hired that maybe it's fate. You know, maybe he and I are meant to end up together. He's just the perfect guy for me."

"Kind of early to tell that, isn't it?" Lindsay asked. That was also typical of Cybil. She thought every man she met was the right one.

"You might be right," Cybil said with a chuckle as she brushed a lock of her light blond hair out of her face.

"You don't even really know him," Lindsay added.

"Except what Mr. Stanbury told me. He says that Rafe has had a tough life, but that he's really determined to be a good detective. I could go to work tomorrow, except that he and Rafe have to fly to LA. It has something to do with the murder of Rafe's mother."

Lindsay felt the blood drain from her head and her knees suddenly felt like jelly. It took her a long moment to reply again. Finally she asked, "That wouldn't be Rafe Collings, would it?"

"Yeah, how did you know that?" Cybil asked. "He says he's only been in Provo for about three months. He's from Ephraim. He's been to Snow College. He's a cowboy. He—"

"I know, Cybil," Lindsay broke in. "He rides bareback broncs and lives on a ranch."

"Not anymore. I mean, he lives here in Provo now."

"Does he still wear his blond hair quite short?" Lindsay asked.

Cybil turned to Lindsay. "How do you know him?"

Just then the door opened and Melly came in carrying a copy of the *Deseret Morning News* and her purse. "I bought a paper," she said. "I thought maybe we could look in there for jobs, Cybil."

Lindsay and Cybil looked at each other quickly—but not quickly enough.

Melly was a very smart young woman. "Cybil, did you get a job today?" she asked.

Cybil nodded, and Melly just sighed and said she needed to do some homework. After Melly went to her room, Lindsay picked up the paper and said, "I'm afraid she's discouraged. Maybe you and I can help her." She opened the paper and began thumbing through. "I'll find the want ads," she said. Suddenly she gasped and dropped all but one section of the paper.

"What's the matter?" Cybil asked, alarmed.

Lindsay didn't answer. First, news that Rafe was right here in Provo, then this. She was too stunned to speak. The first boy she'd ever had a serious crush on was staring up at her from the front page of the sports section of the paper. Of course, he wasn't a boy anymore, and he wasn't smiling like he always used to do when she knew him in Pocatello. What she was reading was shocking in two ways. First, she couldn't believe Greg Ralston was in the NBA. But even harder to believe was that he'd been arrested for stabbing a man to death in a Dallas bar!

She dropped the paper, and Cybil picked it up and shrieked. "Lindsay, Rafe's picture's in here, only it can't be him," she said.

"It's not him," Lindsay managed to say.

"If that isn't Rafe, who is it?"

"It's Greg," Lindsay said weakly. She had to get out of there. She had to do something physical to keep from going nuts. "I'm going out for a run," she told Cybil in a strangled voice. "I'll be back in a little while."

Cybil gave her a strange look, then began reading the article. When Lindsay returned from her bedroom in shorts, a T-shirt, and running shoes, she said, "Hey, wait up. Do you know anything about this guy? You were right. His name's Greg. But he sure looks like Rafe."

Lindsay couldn't talk about it other than to say, "They're brothers." Then she was out the door.

* * *

Dempsey Guthrie was waiting outside Lindsay's apartment. His heart leaped when he saw her. She was such a pretty girl. Someday, he intended to claim her for his own. But for now he was content to watch her, to revel in her beauty.

She began running, and Dempsey's heart raced after her. Her glistening locks of wavy black hair bounced on her back and shoulders, and her long tan legs flashed in the receding sunlight. As he watched her, he pictured her perfect face, every feature of which he'd memorized. In fact, he'd memorized everything he'd ever learned about Lindsay Diamond. She was indeed a beauty. She was also very smart. Her grades at the university were almost perfect. She worked at a bank now. Dempsey knew that, for he'd followed her there earlier today. And he'd followed her home when she got off work.

He followed her again now for a ways on foot, but he couldn't keep up with her. Cigarettes, booze, and drugs had slowed him down over the years. But he was pretty sure she'd come back this way, so he slowed to a methodical walk and thought about how it would be someday. He was right about her return, for a figure soon appeared on the trail. It was almost dark, but he was certain it was her. When she was almost to him, he ducked his head so she couldn't see him. He didn't want Lindsay to see his face, not yet anyway. When she passed, he recognized the tantalizing smell of her perfume. He turned and watched her until she was so far away he almost couldn't see her anymore.

He walked back the way they'd come. He hung around outside her apartment for a long time, just thinking about her. He stayed in the shadows so he wouldn't be noticed. A couple of times, he caught a glimpse of her through her partially open living room blinds. Then she disappeared. He finally went home to get some sleep. It was a fairly short drive and didn't take too long. He'd be back in the morning. He couldn't wait to see Lindsay again.

* * *

Lindsay couldn't sleep that night. By morning, she felt like she'd been drugged or hit by a truck or something. Greg Ralston was a murderer, or at least he was accused of it. It was the most shocking thing she'd ever read. It was enough of a surprise to find that he was in the NBA, but a killer? And Rafe, who had never answered her letter, was right here in Provo, and he was still single. It was all too much for her to absorb.

"Better do something about your eyes," Cybil said as the two of them passed in their small kitchen. "They're really red this morning."

"I didn't sleep well," Lindsay said.

"I need to tell Rafe about his brother. I wonder if he already knows," Cybil said.

"I don't know if that's such a good idea," Lindsay told her. "He doesn't know his brother, and he has enough to worry about without having to be concerned about that."

"How do you know him? Rafe, I mean. You keep avoiding my question. You've never mentioned him before, but I can tell you must know him. Is he a friend of yours?" Cybil pressed.

"He used to be," Lindsay said morosely. "But when you see him on Thursday, just say Lindsay says hi. But please don't mention Greg."

Lindsay did what she could for her eyes, but she'd spent much of the night crying. She just hadn't been able to help herself. At twenty to eight, she left for campus, just in time to make her eight o'clock class.

* * *

Dempsey watched Lindsay all the way to her car. And he followed her until she pulled into one of the parking lots at BYU. He'd have pulled in there and watched her walk to the door, but with so many people around, he didn't want to attract attention, so he left. He'd watch for her at the bank where she worked that afternoon. He was reasonably sure he knew what time she'd be there. He'd soon have her new routine down perfectly.

* * *

The work in LA didn't take long, and it was pretty clear that Thorn hadn't needed Rafe's help on the case he was working. But Rafe was grateful that he brought him along, for the police artist was everything his boss had told him he was and more.

By ten o'clock at night on the second day in Los Angeles, Tom had reproduced the face that had haunted Rafe for so many years.

Then, as the computer printed out a number of variations that altered the picture for age, hairstyle, and so on, Rafe was able to recognize the face each time. "It's the eyes," he said to Tom and Thorn. "I always knew I'd recognize his eyes."

"You have an amazing memory," Tom told him. "I've never had anyone who could do so well after so many years." He turned to Thorn. "What are you going to do with these now that you have them?"

"Get them out to as many police agencies as I can as soon as possible," Thorn said. "But I want to make it clear that they are not to be posted anywhere that the public might see them. In fact, I think I'll mark the posters as being for police eyes only, with instructions that they not be posted."

"That's good," Rafe said with some relief. He'd been both glad and worried over what Thorn was doing. What would the killer do if he found out he was being looked for before he was found? Of course, he knew the answer. It was in the notes that had been sent to him and to his father. He still wondered if it was a mistake letting Thorn forge ahead. He prayed that it wasn't.

"I'll help you get the poster made and distributed," Tom offered.

Before they left LA, Rafe e-mailed copies of the poster containing the pictures of the killer to his family and told them what was being done. He told them that it was very unlikely that the killer would know about the pictures being sent to police agencies across the country, but he still reminded them to be very cautious.

CHAPTER 8

Rafe looked up from his desk and into the lobby as the new secretary walked in early Thursday afternoon. He hoped she was as smart as she was attractive, because she certainly was that.

Rafe worked on a report at his desk in the tiny office his boss had given him off to the right of the lobby. He could hear the chatter as Thorn gave Cybil a complete rundown of his office, how it was set up, and how he would like her to change a few things.

Shortly before noon, Rafe had finished the report and he entered the lobby. "What's next?" he asked his boss as he smiled at Cybil, whose face went red.

"I need you to make a couple of visits this afternoon for Super Computers." Thorn had been hired to look into the backgrounds of several men who were seeking a very sensitive position with the computer firm. "I've arranged an interview with a former employer of one of the applicants in a few minutes. I'd like you to do the interview. Here's the address. Then see the next fellow on this list." He handed Rafe a copy of the names and addresses of the men who were being considered for the job. "If there's time, you might also look up the next guy. We don't want to miss anything, Rafe, so take your time and be very thorough. While you do that, if you don't mind, I'll see if I can find a way to contact your brother's agent or his attorney. I know you'll feel better about things when you've had a chance to meet him, talk to him, and sort things out for yourself. I'll see if that's going to be possible."

"Thanks, Thorn," he said as he shrugged into his jacket.

Cybil squirmed at her newly assigned desk. "Greg Ralston is your brother?" she asked.

"I think so," he answered.

"I saw his picture in the paper. My roommate, Lindsay, recognized him," Cybil revealed. "Oh, I almost forgot. She said to tell you hi."

Rafe was stunned. His knees felt weak. A lump formed in his throat. He knew only one Lindsay who also knew Greg. A day didn't go by that he didn't think of her—and wonder why she'd never written to him.

"Are you all right, Rafe?" Cybil asked. "You don't look like you feel too good."

"You know Lindsay Diamond?" he asked weakly.

"Yes, she's my roommate," she responded.

So she was still single. Why hadn't she written to him? he wondered sadly. She had his Ephraim address. "Where is she right now?" he asked numbly.

Cybil looked at her watch. "At work. Why?"

"I'd like to talk to her."

"You would?" she asked, suspicion in her voice.

"Yes, I would," he answered. "About Greg."

"Okay, then I'll call her for you. She gets off at six and—" she began.

"No, just tell me where she works," Rafe interrupted. "I'll meet her there when she gets off." He didn't know if that was a good thing to do, but he needed to know if in fact she no longer cared for him the way he cared for her. If she didn't, and he assumed that was the case, then maybe he could finally get her out of his system.

"Rafe," Thorn said later, having listened to the entire exchange and waiting until Cybil was out of earshot. "Is this the girl who was kidnapped?"

"Yeah. Sounds like she's right here in Provo," Rafe said.

"And she knew your brother, of course?"

"Yeah, sort of," Rafe said. "Why do you ask?"

"Just wondered," he said, and turned to go into his private office.

A few hours later, with the bank's address and the description of Lindsay's car in his head, Rafe drove toward the bank. During the course of the afternoon, he'd conjured up the image of a young girl of seventeen, the age she was when he saw her last. The age she was in the picture he'd torn up a few weeks after he'd gotten home from his mission. She was pretty back then, and he'd kicked himself a hundred times for not keeping the picture. He wondered what Lindsay looked like now.

Rafe drove by the office on his way to the bank. Both Cybil and Thorn were gone. It was five thirty; Lindsay would be off work at six. He laid the notes he'd made that afternoon on his desk, and left. It was only after he'd climbed into his pickup in the small parking lot beside the office that he noticed a large car slowly disappearing around the corner half a block away. Unless he was seeing things, it was a very old Cadillac, dark green in color with a number of rust spots. But he had so much on his mind right now that it didn't register why that might be important.

Once Rafe had driven to the bank where Lindsay worked, it only took a moment to spot Lindsay's red Dodge Stratus that Cybil had described. Rafe thought about going inside the bank to talk to Lindsay, but he decided against that. He didn't want to disturb her until she was off work, and that shouldn't be too long if Cybil was right about her hours. Anyway, the moment he met her would be awkward, and he was hesitant now that he was so close. He was suddenly feeling foolish. Just because she'd told Cybil to tell him hi, that didn't mean she wanted to see him. She probably didn't.

He started up his truck, put it in gear, then sat there with his foot on the brake. *Oh, what could it hurt?* he thought. He shut the truck off. He'd thought of her almost every day for too many years. The least he could do was talk to her now that she was this close. Then, if that was the end of it, so be it.

As Rafe waited in his truck for Lindsay to come out, he was alert and watchful. Ever since the pictures of his mother's killer had been sent to police departments across the county, he worried about what the man might do if he saw one of them. That was very unlikely, given the instructions that were printed right on the poster. But who knew? He could be a cop. Stranger things had happened. He didn't want the man to surprise him, so he kept a close eye out most of the time.

Not that there was much to see in this parking lot. In his short career working for a private investigator, Rafe had learned how slowly time drags during stakeouts. Not that this was a stakeout, but it was similar, even though it promised to be short in duration. He kept glancing at his watch. Only ten minutes had passed before he watched another car pull up and park near him. Actually, several had entered the parking lot since he'd been here, but in every other case, the driver had parked and then entered the bank, each coming out again after a short time. This car, a very old Jeep Wagoneer, had a lone occupant in it, a man with a baseball cap that he was wearing backward. He didn't exit his vehicle. Instead he slumped down in his seat and watched the bank entrance closest to where Lindsay's Stratus was parked.

Another five minutes passed, and the man remained seated in the car, watching the bank, much like Rafe was doing himself. Rafe chided himself for watching the man so suspiciously, since it was very likely that his wife or someone else was expecting him to be there to provide a ride. That was the most logical explanation Rafe could think of.

At six o'clock, people no longer entered the bank, but several came out. Rafe assumed that, like Lindsay, they were employees. None of them were of interest to Rafe until a particularly attractive young woman with long black hair came out. It was Lindsay, and she was even prettier than he'd remembered. His heart began beating rapidly. For a moment, all he could do was stare. Then he realized that she'd be in her car and gone before he got a chance to speak with her, so he opened his door and got out.

As Rafe walked toward Lindsay, he took one more look at the man in the old Wagoneer, and he realized the guy was watching Lindsay very intently as she walked toward her car. The guy made no move to get out, nor did he look at anything else. He was staring, and it gave Rafe an uneasy feeling. He stopped and watched for a moment. Then, again, he realized that he was going to miss Lindsay if he didn't hurry, so he walked rapidly toward her car.

She had the door unlocked and was reaching for the door handle when he said, "Hi, Lindsay."

She turned, a slight look of alarm on her face, but it was almost instantly replaced by a look of total shock. Then she began to smile, a smile that enhanced her already attractive face. It almost took Rafe's breath away. Her skin was smooth, the color of honey. Her teeth were dazzling white; her eyes, dark brown and sparkling. She was slightly taller than when he'd seen her last.

When she spoke, her voice was mellow and sweet but deep for a woman, just the way he remembered. "Rafe? Rafe Collings?" she cried out in apparent delight.

"Hi," he said again. He was suddenly feeling very awkward.

"I can't believe it's you," she said as she stepped toward him, her car keys dangling from one hand, her purse in the other. "My roommate told me you were working in Provo now, but I still can't believe it's you. It's so good to see you again, Rafe."

She stepped so close to him that he could smell the sweetness of her perfume, and he self-consciously shuffled back a half step, but she stepped quickly toward him and threw her arms around him, hugging him fiercely. His heart raced. But then, as quickly as she'd stepped close she stepped back. She looked him over for a moment, like she was inspecting him. Then she said, "Thanks for looking me up. I've thought about you a lot, and I've missed you."

"I've missed you too," he said.

"How was your mission?" she asked.

"It was great. And I enjoyed another year at Snow College. Gee, it's been so long," he said. He couldn't take his eyes off her face. But he had to. He wasn't being very watchful. He looked quickly around, and felt a shock run through him when his eyes came across the Jeep Wagoneer. The driver was still slouched in the seat, and he was looking in their direction, and although Rafe couldn't see his face very well, he'd have sworn that the fellow's lips were drawn back like a mad dog.

Instinctively, he stepped to his left, blocking the man's view of Lindsay, and said, "Do you have a minute or two? I'd really like to talk to you."

"Sure," she said with a smile. "Rafe, you look so good."

"Thanks, so do you. Ah, would you mind if maybe . . ." Rafe stopped midsentence. Many people would never believe it, but he was by nature a fairly reserved man. He was uncomfortable in settings like this.

Lindsay nodded her head, her dark hair falling partially over her face. She swept it back gracefully with the hand that held her keys, giving him a minute to organize his thoughts. "Are you terribly busy?" he asked. "Could I buy you something to eat?"

"Dinner would be great," she said.

"Really? Then maybe, ah, maybe you could come with me. I'll bring you back to your car later," he suggested. "If your car is okay here, that is."

"It's fine. And I'd like that," she said. "I'll lock my car and we can go. Do you have a place in mind?"

He had not thought that far ahead, so he said, "No. Why don't you suggest someplace?"

* * *

Dempsey watched as Lindsay got in the truck with the tall, blond young man, and hatred seethed through him, hot and thick. When they drove away he didn't follow. He would wait. And he would think about her and what his next move would be. He would also think about *him*. He had to do something about that man before things got out of hand.

* * *

Rafe had introduced the topic of Greg Ralston. It seemed safer than talking about themselves. And it seemed to help put Lindsay at ease—Rafe could tell that she was as nervous as he was.

"Greg was always a good guy," Lindsay said. "In fact, he was a little shy, I was told, sort of like . . ." She stopped herself, thinking that Rafe might consider her rude.

"Like me?" he asked unexpectedly.

"Yeah, sort of," she said. "But it's like I told you before; I never really knew Greg. He was older than me, and I was too young to date. Anyway, he wasn't LDS, and even if I'd been sixteen, I still wouldn't have gone out with him."

Rafe's eyes rested on her face, and her smooth honey-colored skin took on a slightly red tone. He said nothing, just watched her for a moment, enjoying what he saw.

"Like he'd have ever asked me," she said. "Greg was very popular. And I was too young. Anyway, it's you I've thought about all these years, Rafe."

"I'm sure you've thought about him too," Rafe said, trying to sidestep her comment for now. "And you knew him. Can you believe he'd be capable of killing someone?" Rafe was looking deeply into the dark brown of Lindsay's eyes, and he felt a little dizzy.

"No, I can't imagine it. Of course, I hadn't heard anything since I told you he'd left Pocatello. I guess he could have changed."

"Yeah, I guess. I've wanted to meet him for years now, but I didn't even know how to begin to find him. Maybe if I'd read the sports page more I might have seen him mentioned. He must have played college ball somewhere. But I've never really been into basketball. But now that I know where he is, I want to meet him, even if he is in trouble."

"That would be great, Rafe. But I can't believe this about him. I can't imagine that he'd ever hurt anyone intentionally."

Their meals arrived, and nothing more was said about Greg as they ate. They talked about other things for a little while, but then they drifted into silence. Rafe was aware of her watching him now, and he realized that he'd withdrawn a little. He couldn't help himself. He kept looking around the restaurant.

"Rafe, are you looking for someone?" Lindsay asked.

"Yes, I'm looking for the man that killed my mother."

"But he wouldn't be in here," she said.

"He could be anywhere, Lindsay," he said. "He might know that I'm after him by now."

"Are you?" she asked.

"With my boss's help, yes," he said. Then he explained about the pictures the police artist had created, and how they'd now been sent to police departments nationwide.

"But surely he wouldn't know that," she said doubtfully. "Not if they weren't posted in public places."

"I hope that's right, but for some reason, he seems to know a lot about me," he said. "Recently, I got another anonymous letter. It was from him. Somehow, he found out that I'm working for a private detective, and he told me that I better not even think of looking for him."

"Rafe," Lindsay said, and the color drained from her face. "That's awful."

"That's not the worst," he said. "He also sent a letter to my family and threatened them."

"Oh, Rafe!" Lindsay exclaimed.

"He knows I can put him away for the rest of his life, that I could testify against him if he were arrested. He could be anywhere, Lindsay," he said. "And I have to remember that. I need to see him before he sees me. If I don't, he could win. And he's not interested in only seeing me go to jail."

Lindsay shivered. "I'm sorry," she said. "You be careful. And I hope you can see Greg."

"I've got to. We may not be at all alike, but it appears that he is my brother, and I want to get to know him. I only regret that I haven't gotten to know him sooner. Maybe I could have . . ." He didn't finish his thought. He was going to say that maybe things would have been better for Greg, that maybe he wouldn't be facing murder charges. But he just kept silent.

They talked a little longer. Then Rafe said, "I better get you back to your car. Thanks for talking with me."

"Thank you," she said. "I can't believe how good it's been to see you again. I've really enjoyed talking with you. I hope Greg will be all right. And I hope you and your boss will find that other man. I'll be praying for you, for all of you."

"Thanks, Lindsay," he said as he dropped a tip on the table. "That will be a lot of help."

During most of the short ride back to the bank, they didn't say much. Rafe felt like an idiot. He knew he'd made a bad impression on Lindsay, something he hadn't wanted to do from the moment he saw her come out of the bank. He couldn't help it that he was so absorbed in his past and worried about the dangers that might be out there, but he was afraid he'd appeared foolish to her. As he pulled into the parking lot, for some reason he looked for the Wagoneer. He was relieved when it wasn't there.

Lindsay hopped out of the car before he could get out and open the door for her. "Thanks, Rafe," she said with what seemed to him was a sad smile. "It's been great seeing you."

"Yeah, same here," he said. He wanted to tell her he'd like to take her out formally sometime when he didn't have so much going on, but he didn't. He wasn't sure how to go about it without seeming like even more of a fool.

"Rafe, why didn't you answer my letter?" she suddenly asked, a hurt look in those dark brown eyes of hers.

"What letter? When?"

"You know, the one I sent right after your mission."

He was stunned. He hadn't received a letter. And then he remembered, and he wanted to scream. The post office had delivered what was left of an envelope in a plastic bag. The envelope had been badly torn, the return address was missing. There was no stamp, nor was there any letter, just his address typed on the front and a note from the postal department. They'd apologized that the letter had been somehow destroyed, and hoped that it hadn't caused him any problems. "I didn't get it," he said lamely.

"Really?" she asked. "I thought maybe . . ." She turned away, her eyes glistening.

"Really," he said desperately. "I did get what was left of a damaged envelope. Maybe that was it."

"Maybe," she said doubtfully, but she didn't turn to face him again. As he watched her walk to her car and get in, he felt a strange emptiness inside, like he'd just lost the most important thing in the world. And he feared that he had.

Unbidden, and totally unexpected, a memory rushed into Rafe's troubled mind as he drove home. It was about a man in a dark green Cadillac—one that looked just like the one he'd seen turning off the street a half block from his office when he'd been leaving to go meet Lindsay. Beads of sweat gathered on his brow. He turned and drove back toward the office. But of course he couldn't find the green Cadillac.

I'll see it again, he told himself, and that thought left him a little shaken. But not as shaken as he felt from his parting with Lindsay. It had felt so final. She didn't seem to have believed him about the destroyed letter. And yet he could think of no other reason why he wouldn't have received the letter she'd written him.

And the postal department hoped it hadn't caused me any inconvenience.

CHAPTER 9

Lindsay was later than usual, but Dempsey had been waiting when she got home. At least she'd gotten rid of the blond guy. He hoped she'd go for a run again tonight. He liked to watch her when she was running. But even though he waited for a long time, she failed to come out of the apartment. Disappointed, he crept up to the window and tried to peek in. Luckily, the blinds weren't completely drawn. Lindsay was sitting on the sofa, a book on her lap and papers spread out on both sides of her. But she didn't seem to be studying. She was just staring at the TV.

Which was turned off.

He watched her for an hour. He crept away only when she left the room.

* * *

When Rafe went to get in his truck the next morning, he noticed a note under the windshield wiper. He pulled it out, got in his truck, and then smoothed out the note. The handwriting was sloppy and it was hard to read. Slowly, he began working his way through it. It read,

Rafe,

You've never met me, but I need your help. I've been down on my luck lately and I need some money bad. Your brother, Greg Ralston, is very rich now that he's in the NBA. I was hoping you could get him to maybe lend me a couple hundred thousand. That's all I'll need.

Rafe looked up from the paper in confusion. Someone wanted Rafe to persuade Greg to lend a lot of money to someone neither one of them even knew! That was absurd. Why would anyone expect that Greg would be willing to do that? And why should Rafe even ask him to? He felt his hands trembling and he looked away from the paper for a moment. *What could this really be about?* he wondered.

He looked down again and resumed reading.

In case you wonder what's in it for you, all I can say is, consider Stephanie and the guy you call your father and the woman you claim as your mother. You wouldn't want something to happen to one of them, would you? Talk to Greg. I'm sure you can make him help me.

Then came the most shocking part of the entire note. It was signed, *Dad.*

Feeling like a hundred pounds was on his shoulders, Rafe picked up the phone and called home. He told his father about the note and his suspicion about the tall man in the green Cadillac. After reading the note to his father, he said, "Don't let Stephanie go anywhere without you guys. I'm sorry about the trouble, but I'm so worried."

"We'll just keep her here at home," Lenny promised. "And we'll watch for the green Cadillac."

When Rafe reached the office, he hurried inside hoping to get to talk to Thorn right away, but Cybil stopped him. "Good morning, Rafe," she said. "Did you get to talk to Lindsay yesterday?"

"I did," he said. "Didn't she tell you that?"

"No, she came home late and she seemed upset. She said she wasn't hungry and wanted to do her homework. Melly and I went to a movie. When we got back, she was still in her room. She didn't even say a word to me or Melly," Cybil said.

"Melly?" he asked.

"Our other roommate," Cybil told him. "So, what did you say to upset her?"

"I don't know," Rafe said. "I didn't mean to make her feel bad if I did."

"So you guys used to know each other?" Cybil asked. "Did you date?"

"A little," Rafe said. "But I haven't heard from her for over three years."

That drew a puzzled look from Cybil. "But, she said to tell you hi. I don't get it."

Just then, the door to Thorn's office opened. "Rafe, I thought I heard your voice. Come on in. I got a hold of Greg's agent."

Rafe was relieved. He didn't feel like answering Cybil's questions right now. Thorn shut the door when Rafe got into the boss's private office. "You look worried again," the old investigator said. "Has something else happened?"

"This was on my windshield this morning," Rafe said, handing the note to Thorn.

After reading it, Thorn said, "Do you have any idea who this might be from?"

Rafe began to shake his head, then he said, "Well, maybe sort of."

"Maybe sort of?" Thorn asked with a grin. "What does that mean?"

"Well, you remember me telling you about the green Cadillac."

"Tall man driving it?"

"Yeah, that's the one. I saw a green Cadillac yesterday. It was less than a block from here. I never even thought about it at the time because my mind was on other things."

Another grin from Thorn. "Like a certain Lindsay Diamond?"

"Yeah," Rafe admitted.

"How did that go?"

"Not so well. Anyway, I wonder if this note could be from the guy in the Cadillac," Rafe said.

"Tall man," Thorn said thoughtfully. "You and Greg are tall. He signed the note *Dad.*"

"Maybe he really is my father, my biological father," Rafe said.

"Could be."

"And he's only asking for a loan."

"That's what it says, but is that what he means? Of course, he was quite vague. And yet . . ." Thorn drifted into thought.

Rafe waited while his boss was thinking. But finally he said, "So you made contact with Greg's agent."

"Yes, I did indeed." Thorn paused, as if completing the thought Rafe had interrupted. Then he said, "Rafe, we've got to treat this note as a threat. And we've got to look at it as an attempt at extortion. The guy could actually be your father, but then again, he could be an impostor."

"That's what I was sort of thinking," Rafe said.

"Yeah, well, anyway, we better keep an eye out for the dark green Cadillac with a tall man driving it," the boss concluded. "Now, about Jim Hanks."

"Jim Hanks?" Rafe asked.

"Yes, that's the name of Greg's agent. I didn't like him, quite frankly. He seems arrogant, self-serving, and greedy. However, he also said that he can't imagine Greg killing anybody. I asked him if Greg had been drinking a lot lately. He said he didn't know, but that Greg had mentioned that his parents had recently divorced, that he hadn't heard from either of them for several weeks. Hank said that Greg mentioned to him one day that he wasn't convinced that they are really his parents. I guess they acted really crazy any time Greg brought up his birth."

"Thorn, I wonder if . . ." Rafe began, but he didn't complete the thought.

"Rafe, I think you're thinking like a real investigator here. I suspect that you're thinking the same thing I am. Say what you have on your mind."

"Well, it seems crazy, but I wonder if they stole him from the hospital," he said very slowly.

"That was my thought," Thorn said triumphantly. "The people who raised him might have wanted a baby, and simply stole Greg. Or maybe they knowingly bought the baby on the black market. Makes sense. You're going to make a really good investigator, Rafe."

"Thanks."

"I mean it. Of course, it may be that his parents just hate admitting he was adopted; they might be completely innocent themselves. Anyway, back to the present. Jim Hanks says Greg's attorney got his bond reduced enough that Greg was able to make bail. He gave me Greg's phone numbers, both to his apartment in Dallas and to his cellular phone. I think you'll be able to reach him okay, because he's supposed to stay in the area. Here, I've written them down for you." Rafe accepted the sticky note from his boss. Then Thorn said, "Go call him, Rafe. Call him right now. And if he'll agree to it, tell him that you'll go down there."

Cybil smiled at Rafe when he came out of Thorn's office. He returned her smile, although it was difficult with all the turmoil going on inside of him. But she was a nice girl, so he decided then and there that he'd be nice to her, even though she annoyed him a little.

Then his thoughts turned to Lindsay Diamond, and when that happened, he began to worry about her. He couldn't think of her without feeling like bawling. He was so afraid that he'd blown it with her. He also couldn't think of her without thinking of the Jeep Wagoneer and the creepy guy that was in it. He was probably wrong about the guy, but he couldn't help what he thought.

Rafe sat down at his desk and sighed. He needed to concentrate on the task at hand. He picked up the receiver then looked at the numbers on the sticky tab. What was so difficult about placing a simple phone call to someone, especially someone who was a blood relation? He returned the receiver to its cradle and thought about his family in Ephraim, and he felt a tug of homesickness. He missed them, he missed the ranch, and he missed the animals, especially his horses. He shook his head and picked up the phone again. If he was going to call his brother, he better get it done now.

His palms were sweaty, and his hands were shaking as he punched in each digit. The phone rang several times, and Rafe was about to put the receiver down with a sense of relief when a voice came on the other end of the line. "Hello."

"Greg Ralston, please," Rafe asked, trying to keep his voice from shaking.

"This is Greg," the voice said.

"Greg, my name's Rafe Collings. I think we're . . ." He paused. This was so hard.

"Brothers," Greg finished for him. "I saw you in the paper years ago, and your name has stuck with me ever since. But my parents say I don't have a brother."

"I see," Rafe said. "So how are you doing? I just thought I'd call and, uh, well, say hello, I guess."

Greg chuckled on the other end of the line. *He doesn't seem nervous, so why am I feeling so uneasy?* Rafe asked himself.

"I'm doing fine, I guess, for someone who's been accused of a murder he didn't commit. I can't leave the area, my whole career might be screwed up, but other than that, I guess I'm fine. So how are you?"

"I guess I've got my share of trouble too. Someone is threatening my family and me, and I, well, I learned a guy I think might be my twin brother got arrested, and well, I guess I'm okay," Rafe said, feeling like a fool, just like he knew he sounded.

Again came the chuckle on the line. "Hey, Rafe, I'm glad you called. My parents haven't been threatened or anything, but they're so messed up it's unreal. But they insist that they didn't adopt me and claim they got divorced because I don't believe them," he said.

"Uh, Greg, is that true? Do you? I mean, do you not believe them?"

"I guess I don't," Greg said. "So what about you?"

"Well, my parents definitely adopted me, and they say I had a brother, an identical twin brother, but he was taken from the hospital shortly after we were born, and our birth mother died. Nobody could ever find out what happened to the other baby. I was hoping you were that brother," Rafe said as he finally began to calm down.

There was silence so deep on the line that Rafe wondered if something had happened to their connection. But finally, he heard breathing, then Greg's voice, very soft and sounding full of emotion— no hint of a chuckle now filled the phone. "Rafe, are you sure?"

"Yeah, I'm sure. My dad never kept it secret from me. Well, I guess he did for a while. I was about eight or so when he told me. And I've wondered ever since then what happened to my brother," Rafe said.

"Wow! This is unbelievable," Greg said. "And yet it explains so much."

"Like what?" Rafe pressed, even though he thought he already knew.

"Well, for one thing, like you, I'm tall and blond. My folks are both very dark and short. And yet they've always insisted that I wasn't adopted," Greg said. "When I first learned about you, it was when you made some fancy ride in a rodeo. Kids at the school in Pocatello, where we were living at the time, showed me your picture in the paper. I went home that day and told my parents about you. They acted really strange, got angry, and told me that I wasn't adopted, if that was what I was thinking. But I didn't know what I was thinking, I just knew that having someone who looked almost exactly like me was rather strange. But they insisted that I was their natural child. I loved them, and they were good parents, so I let it go. But frankly, I've always had doubts about who I really am. Now I'm wondering if they took me from the hospital. It's a terrible thing to think, but it also makes sense. It would explain why they were so defensive when I questioned them."

"Yeah, that's true. You know, there are ways to tell for sure if we're twins. We'd have the same DNA, if we're identical, that is. I'd like to know for sure," Rafe said. "I've always wanted a brother." He couldn't believe he was talking this way, but he meant it. And he yearned now to meet Greg in person, to sit down and just talk for hours.

"Rafe, you can't mean that, not with me charged with murder," Greg said darkly.

"Maybe you're innocent, and even if not, I'd still like to meet you, Greg," he said.

"Well, that's nice. But I will tell you this. I didn't kill anyone. That's not who I am. I could never do that."

"I'm glad," Rafe said, feeling awkward again.

"The trouble is proving it," Greg told him after another moment of strained silence.

"Maybe my boss and I could help," Rafe suggested, wondering what Thorn would think about that.

"Your boss? What do you do, Rafe? How could you help?"

"My boss is a private investigator. And he's really good at what he does. I'm in training right now, so I don't know a lot, but I'd be willing to do what I could."

"Great! I don't trust people here. I'll pay you whatever it costs, Rafe. I'm not one to ask for help, but if you're really my brother, I guess now's a good time to ask. I'm sure in a rotten mess, and I think the cops, the media, even my lawyer, think I'm guilty. Would you really come down and help me?" Greg asked.

"Yes, as soon as I can arrange it. There's only one thing I ask, and that is that you level with me on every detail of what happened the night of the stabbing. You've got to be completely honest. If you hold anything back, it will just waste my time and my boss's time."

"And my money," Greg added. "You have my word. You'll only get the truth."

"Good, then answer this question for me," Rafe said.

"Whatever you need to know I'll tell you. That is, I will if I can," Greg promised, sounding very sincere to Rafe.

"Good. Did you kill that man in the bar?" Rafe asked suddenly.

"I already told you once, and I'll say it again. No, I did not. I wasn't even there when it happened."

"Your knife was," Rafe reminded him, sounding to himself like a would-be detective, not a loving brother. "So were your fingerprints."

"So I've learned. I had the knife on my belt, but someone must have taken it out of the sheath. I'll admit, I was pretty drunk that night. I don't usually drink, but that day I'd received a call from my mother. She and my dad had finalized the divorced, and I hadn't heard from either one of them since the day I signed with the Mavericks. Anyway, she called and she was angry and said it was my fault that their marriage ended. When I asked her how it was my fault, she said it was because I didn't believe them when they told me I was not adopted. She said it caused disharmony and distrust in the home. I hadn't mentioned adoption to them for years, and I think she was just angry and lashing out. But it upset me anyway, and I went to that bar and started drinking. It doesn't take much alcohol to put me over the edge. But I didn't kill anyone, Greg. I wasn't so drunk that I could have done it and not remembered. I wasn't even there when the fight occurred. I left earlier," Greg said. "I swear it."

"Give me your address," Rafe said. "I'll fly down to Dallas as soon as I can. We'll talk more then."

"You do believe me, don't you?"

"I really want to believe you. I'll see if there's anything my boss or I can do to help you. And Greg, I really do look forward to meeting you."

"Thanks, that's all I can ask," Greg said, and the two of them ended the call.

For a long time after that Rafe sat at his desk, thinking about how complicated his life had become. He hoped Greg was innocent, but he couldn't be sure. He was more convinced than ever that they were brothers, and despite all the problems, he was glad. He couldn't wait to see Greg in person, to get to know him.

He just hoped that it wouldn't turn out the way seeing Lindsay had. He certainly messed that up. And he ached at the thought.

Finally, he got up from his desk and left his office. Thorn was talking to Cybil in their little lobby. He looked up when Rafe entered. "Reach him?" he asked.

"Yeah, we talked."

"Good. Are you going down there?"

"If it's okay with you."

"I already told you it was. Cybil and I will make the arrangements."

Cybil smiled in agreement. And Rafe thought about her roommate.

"Thorn," Rafe said.

"What is it, Rafe?"

"Greg needs help proving his innocence. I told him we would help if we could. He says he can pay."

Thorn waved a meaty hand in the air. "Of course we'll help. You get on down there and see what you can learn. I'll come down if you need me to, but I want you to take the first crack at it. I can coach you by phone. Now go home and get ready to go. We'll make arrangements for either a flight tonight or tomorrow. Cybil will let you know."

The flight was arranged for the next afternoon. Rafe was to be in Dallas at nine that night. He called Greg and told him that he'd find a hotel and then come see him first thing the next morning. Greg said that he'd prefer that he come that night. "I have nothing better to do," he said with the chuckle he'd had early in the first call. "And I have plenty of room here." So it was settled. And Rafe's stomach churned in anticipation.

He was tempted to call Lindsay and tell her, but he convinced himself that she didn't care. Anyway, he knew that Cybil would tell her.

CHAPTER 10

Stephanie was an outgoing and fun fourteen-year-old. She loved the ranch, she loved her dad's animals, and she even enjoyed helping her mother in the house and in the yard. But she also liked to spend time in town with her friends. She had always loved her brother Rafe and was proud of him. They'd had very few spats growing up, and she'd never been what she would have called *furious* with him.

But she wasn't happy with him right now. Her folks wouldn't let her go anywhere without one of them being with her, and that wasn't fun. She'd had a sleepover planned at Becky's house for weeks. But when she reminded her mother that it was tonight, she was told she couldn't go because it was too dangerous.

And it was because of Rafe. First, he just couldn't leave things alone. He should have paid attention to the threats that had been made by that awful man who murdered his mother. But instead, he went and found a police artist and then sent the guy's picture to police all over the country. She didn't really believe the guy would see them, but her folks weren't taking any chances. She knew that the notes came before Rafe or his boss had done anything, but knowing that didn't help her situation now.

It also didn't help that some guy who claimed to be Rafe's father was threatening them. It was all so unfair, and it was messing up her life. Deep down, she knew that Rafe hadn't intentionally done anything to put his family in danger, but right now she was mad, and since it was mostly his fault, she fumed at Rafe.

Never in her life had Stephanie been openly disobedient to her parents, but she thought she might be justified in this case. She'd promised Becky that she would come to the party, and Becky had thrown an absolute fit when she told her she couldn't but didn't tell her why. Her parents had suggested that they not talk about the danger they were in to others, and she agreed with that. It was embarrassing. Her parents had originally given their permission, and her friend Becky couldn't understand how they could change their minds now for no reason. She told Stephanie that she'd already rented some really good movies and that they had lots of food coming.

It wasn't fair that Stephanie would miss out on all the fun. She'd be safe at Becky's house. She pestered her folks about it until after it was time for the party to start. Her dad had finally suggested firmly that she go to her room and get some homework done. There would be other sleepovers, he promised. Right now just wasn't a good time.

She'd begun to work on her homework when Becky called Stephanie's cell phone. "Everybody but you is here," Becky said. "And they're all mad that you didn't come."

"But my dad and mom—" she began.

"They don't need to know you're here," Becky said. "My brother will come pick you up. You can tell your folks you're going to be in your room. Then you can just climb out of the window and he'll meet you at the end of your lane. We'll make sure you're home before six in the morning. That way your parents won't even know you're gone."

"I don't know," Stephanie said. "I've never—"

"Are you my friend or not?" Becky broke in angrily. "Come on, you don't want to miss out. And it won't hurt a thing."

Not wanting to hurt her friend's feelings, Stephanie finally agreed.

"Good, my brother will be there by eight thirty. You just be out on the road."

Stephanie felt guilty, but she kept telling herself it wasn't her fault. Rafe's problems shouldn't be hers, and she didn't want to lose her friends over it. Anyway, her parents wouldn't even know she was gone.

She opened her bedroom door and listened to the sound of her mother and father talking in the living room. Then she shut the door, eased her window open, and climbed out onto the lawn. She was panting when she reached the road, and hoped that Becky's brother wouldn't be too long.

* * *

Lenny Collings was feeling bad for his daughter. He knew how much she'd wanted to go to Becky's and that she'd been terribly disappointed when they hadn't allowed her. But he also knew that she didn't fully understand the danger she might be in, the danger they all might be facing. He admitted to himself that she was likely just as safe at Becky's as she was at home. On the other hand, get a bunch of teenage girls together and you never knew what sort of trouble they'd get into. Usually it would be harmless, but under the circumstances . . . He paused at her bedroom door. Maybe she was still awake. If she was, he'd talk to her and help her understand how serious the situation was.

He eased the door open and stepped over to her bed. His heart leaped in his chest when he saw it was empty. He looked up. A stiff evening breeze was blowing the curtains; her window was wide open.

He told himself not to panic. He knew what had happened. It wasn't like her at all, but she must have gone to the party anyway. He looked her room over quickly, and when he couldn't see her cellular phone, he hurried to the kitchen where he dialed her number. It rang several times, but there was no answer. He remembered Stephanie saying that the slumber party she'd wanted to go to was at Becky Thornton's house. He called there, and Becky answered.

"Hi, Becky. This is Lenny Collings. I need to talk to Stephanie. Would you have her come to the phone, please?"

"Stephanie? But she's not here," Becky said. "She told me you wouldn't let her come, and I haven't seen her."

* * *

All Rafe could think about when Lenny called and told him that Stephanie was missing was the man who'd left him the note, the tall guy who drove an older-model green Cadillac. The man who was likely the one claiming to be Rafe's and Greg's father.

Rafe could hear his stepmom crying softly in the background. He had to do something, but what could he do? He was already in a rental car, leaving the Dallas airport, driving toward Greg's apartment. This visit just became harder. He absolutely had to get the money from Greg. There might be no other way to get Stephanie back. He swore to himself that if Greg would lend him the money, he'd pay every dime of it back if it took him the rest of his life.

Rafe explained to his father where he was. "I'll try to get the money," he said. "In the meantime, we better wait."

"But shouldn't I call the sheriff and tell them what's happened?" Lenny asked. "Or are you thinking we need to wait and see if we hear from this guy?"

"I think no on the police, Dad. That might make it worse. But yes on waiting to hear from this man, whoever he is. I'll be at Greg's in a few minutes. Somehow, I'll convince Greg to give me the money, loan it to me. If he has it, that is."

"You can't pay that much money back, Rafe," his father reasoned. "But the ranch is worth a lot more than that. I'll use our equity line of credit on the ranch. That's what I'll do. Tell Greg you can have the money back to him within a few days. This is our problem, not his."

"Dad, you can't do that. How could you ever pay off the loan?" Rafe protested.

"That's not even important, son. You and Stephanie and Glenda are my life. I can sell some of the ranch if I have to. I can work in the turkey plant if I can't make ends meet with a smaller place. Just tell Greg that if he has the money, I'll pay him back. And I mean that."

His father was right. Stephanie's life was worth more than any worldly possessions any of them might have. He checked his location. According to the map, he was getting close to where Greg lived. He was more nervous than ever now. Meeting his brother was getting more complicated by the hour.

Given the danger his family was now in the thick of, Rafe was glad he'd followed Thorn's advice. Not knowing what he might be getting into in Dallas, Thorn had insisted that Rafe take his pistol with him. He was fully trained and licensed to carry it. It was a small gun, a snub-nosed .38 revolver. At the airport, they naturally wouldn't allow him to carry the pistol on the plane. It took a half hour before he could convince them to check the gun and take it on the flight with the guarantee that it would be returned to him when he was ready to leave the airport in Dallas. It was now concealed beneath his sports jacket. He also had a spare holster in his right boot.

Silently he prayed that he wouldn't have to use it, and he prayed that Stephanie would be okay. When would the trouble be over? he asked himself. Or would it ever be? He tried to have faith, and to be positive, but it wasn't easy.

Then, even though it was late, Rafe called his boss. He explained to him that Stephanie was missing. "I'll head to Ephraim right now," Thorn said. "Explain to me again how to get to the ranch, and give me your dad's phone number."

Somehow, Rafe felt better knowing that Thorn would be with his folks. He felt like the thought to call him had been an answer to prayer, and he thanked the Lord. Thorn would know what to do down there.

* * *

Lindsay had been out with Bob Staw again that evening. When she got home, Cybil asked her if she'd had fun. That was easy to answer, for it took only two letters, n and o.

"Then you've got to tell him that the next time he asks you out. Say no, Lindsay. You don't have to date anyone you don't want to," Cybil said.

"I wish it was that easy, Cybil. But he's a nice guy, and I don't want to hurt his feelings. I don't know what to do," Lindsay said.

"I know what I'd do," Cybil told her. "Sometimes I think you're just too nice. You can't always be so nice."

"I know, but I can't help it," Lindsay cried. "Maybe I shouldn't have ever gone out with him the first time. He's such a gentleman, and now it's harder than ever. I don't dislike him, but I don't enjoy being with him."

"Well, you have my advice," Cybil said. "Sooner or later you'll either have to say no or else you'll have to marry him."

Lindsay shuddered, then felt guilty. Bob really was nice, but she could never marry him. She wasn't at all sure that he didn't have exactly that in mind though. That night, he'd produced a camera and asked her if he could take a few pictures of her. He'd told her he loved photography, and when he got the pictures developed, he'd give her copies. He was so sweet about it. He didn't make her feel offended when he took her picture. He made her feel pretty.

But marry him? The thought was just too much. But he was nice, and tonight she'd finally figured out where she'd seen him before. Like her, he was originally from Pocatello. She'd mentioned it to him and he'd just grinned. "I was wondering if you'd ever remember," he'd told her. Well, yes, she remembered him now, the guy with the camera at the basketball game, and she had appreciated his chivalry back then. But he still wasn't what she was looking for in a future husband.

"Hey, Lindsay, guess who flew to Dallas tonight?" Cybil suddenly said.

Lindsay's heart practically turned over in her chest. The only way she'd managed to get through the evening with Bob was to think about Rafe. Ever since seeing him again, she couldn't get him off her mind. And she felt bad about the way she'd treated him over the letter he hadn't answered. Maybe he really didn't ever receive it. And yet the way his attention kept shifting away from their conversation suggested he just wasn't interested in her anymore.

She finally answered Cybil, saying, "Must be Rafe."

"Yes, he and Greg are going to be meeting in person. Isn't that great?"

"Yes, that really is great," Lindsay said, brightening up a little.

"And Rafe and Thorn are going to try to help him beat the murder charges. Greg told Rafe that he didn't do it, and I think Rafe believes him," Cybil said.

"I believe him," Lindsay said. "There's no way Greg is a murderer. By the way, where's Melly?"

"She's in bed. She said she didn't feel well tonight, but I think she's just worried sick over not having a part-time job yet. She can only last about a month without running out of money."

"Monday, I'm going to help her," Lindsay said firmly. "I can't put if off for another day. It's the least I can do. But for now, I think I'll do what Melly did."

"Okay, but there's a good movie on the TV tonight," Cybil said.

Lindsay smiled. "I've had all the movies I can take for one night."

Later, in her bedroom, Lindsay toyed with her cellular phone. She wanted in the worst way to call Rafe. She thought she might have misjudged the situation the other night, and worried he now had the wrong impression of how she felt. How could she tell him that, though? Well, she rationalized, she at least needed to wish him luck on meeting his brother. So she really did need to call him. But she didn't have his number. Maybe she could call information, get his father's number and then call him and ask for the number to Rafe's cell phone. But she hesitated. It was getting late. And yet she felt compelled. She sat thinking about it, trying to get up her courage.

* * *

Still seething, Dempsey finally headed home. He didn't know who the guy was that Lindsay had been with tonight. But whoever he was, the guy needed to learn that Lindsay was spoken for. He'd learn that soon enough, he promised himself.

* * *

Harley and Deke Tuft were in the older-model Ford Bronco. It was black and was very rusty, with numerous dents and scratches, but Deke had finally got it running again. He'd even installed a new muffler after rebuilding the engine so they would be less likely to attract attention. The area of Dallas they were driving in that night was upscale and unfamiliar to them. They found the apartment complex they'd been searching for. "These apartments must start at a thousand a month or more," the old man said. "Our boy definitely has money to burn. Maybe before we're through with him, we'll not only know where his mother is, but we'll have ourselves some money to spend."

"Hey, is that him?" the younger man asked.

"Just getting out of that silver car beneath the street light? Looks new. Could be. He's tall. He's blond. Looks like we may be in luck, Deke. We can take him right now and not have to break into his apartment."

The two looked at each other and shared a pair of tobacco-stained grins. "I'll strike up a conversation with him," the old man said. "You know what to do when I get him distracted."

Deke nodded, and without another word, they got out of the car and walked over to where the tall young man was standing, looking at the apartment complex.

The older man walked past him, then stopped and turned back. "Hey, young fellow, maybe you can help us."

"I'm not from around here," he said.

Then his eyes opened with surprise as the younger of the two men shoved something hard and round into his ribs and said, "This is a gun, and I know how to use it."

"Hey, what are you guys up to?" Rafe asked even as he berated himself for letting his guard down.

"You're coming with us, Greg, and you're doing it quietly or you'll never live to play another day of basketball," the blond man said. "The black Bronco. You'll be getting in that. And don't try to get smart. We're in no mood for games."

* * *

Greg was puzzled. He'd been watching Rafe from his apartment window when two men had approached him as he'd stood surveying the apartments from beneath a street light. Greg couldn't be sure what had happened, but it looked like they'd talked for a moment, then Rafe had walked with them to a run-down black vehicle, got in, and rode off with them.

As he thought about the strange turn of events, Greg's puzzlement turned to alarm. He remembered Rafe saying that he and his family were in danger, but he hadn't told him any more than that. Could these two have something to do with the danger he'd mentioned? If so, Rafe could be in big trouble.

He thought about calling the police, but then he decided that would do no good. They had accused him of murder. He feared they would just figure he was up to something and ignore him. He didn't know what to do. So he did nothing but worry.

* * *

The cell phone in Rafe's pocket buzzed. "Don't answer that," he was told gruffly, and the order was punctuated by a poke in the ribs to remind him that they were armed. "Give it to me."

Rafe had no idea who these men were or what they wanted, but he recognized his luck in being mistaken for Greg. If these men, whoever they were, had realized he worked for a detective agency, they'd undoubtedly have frisked him, and that would have meant the loss of the pistol which his hand was now closing around beneath his jacket.

But he let go of it, realizing that the only way to make use of the weapon was to fire it through his jacket, and he wasn't ready to kill anyone. The very thought of it made bile rise in his throat. So he pulled out the cell phone, glanced at the number displayed, but didn't recognize it. He shut the phone off and placed it in the outstretched hand of his captor. The blond man flung it out the open window and said, "You won't be needing that."

"What's this all about?" Rafe demanded. "Where are you taking me? If it's money you want, I'll get you some. But I have things to do right now, very important things."

The old man who was up front driving said over his shoulder, "We'll be needing some money all right, but you ought to be thanking us for picking you up and taking you with us. Now you won't have to be tried for murder." He laughed at his own joke. The younger man, the one with the gun, joined in.

After their laughter had subsided, Rafe said, "If you want money from me, I'm going to need a few answers."

"You don't need nothing," the man with the gun hissed. "We are in charge here. You're going to help us, and then you're going to get us the money."

"And what happens after that?" Rafe asked, fighting hard to keep the fear he was feeling from coming out in his voice. "It sounds like you plan to kill me after that."

"That could be, unless you do everything we say."

"Sure, then you'll let me go so I can tell the cops what you've done, and since I'm a famous ballplayer, they'll go after you. Sounds likely, doesn't it?"

"You're a murderer, Greg my boy. You're through playing ball."

This was getting Rafe nowhere, but he made one more attempt. "Can't you at least tell me what this is about?"

The old man in the front seat swiveled his head around and said, "I guess we can tell you a little. It's about your mother."

That didn't make sense to Rafe. They clearly didn't know who he was or they wouldn't be calling him Greg. So they couldn't be working for the man who had killed his mother in the bank in

Ephraim. And as far as his birth mother was concerned, both his and Greg's, she was also dead. Rafe knew nothing about Greg's adoptive mother and wondered then if somehow this had to do with her.

"What about my mother?" Rafe asked, hoping to get more information from them.

"We need to talk to her, that's all," the old man said gruffly. "And you're going to help us find her."

Rafe didn't respond to that. He didn't know how to. If this had something to do with Greg's adoptive mother and he said the wrong thing, they might figure out he wasn't Greg, and the end result of that might be that he would lose his gun, his one hope of getting out of this situation alive.

"You will help, Greg. And you'll tell us everything she's ever told you about us."

With every word the old man said, Rafe was more confused. What they wanted either had to do with Greg's mom, or it had to do with the woman who'd died when he and Greg were born. And if that was the case, then the two of them clearly didn't know she'd died following their births. He continued to keep quiet, deciding that for now that was the safest course of action.

They too seemed ready to leave the subject alone for now, and they lapsed into silence. With a sick feeling in his gut, he realized now that both he and his sister were in the same predicament. He could only hope and pray that somehow she might have gotten away and that he could do the same. For unless she did, or unless he did, there was no way for him to talk to Greg and get the money it would take to buy her release. It was all Rafe could do to keep from crying. He avoided it by silently pleading with his Heavenly Father.

* * *

Lindsay was still holding the phone in her trembling hand. She'd talked with Rafe's father, and had learned that his sister was missing. Then she'd tried to call Rafe. The phone had rung several times, then it had abruptly quit. Her heart ached. It ached for Rafe, it ached for his little sister, and it ached for Rafe's parents. She dropped to her knees beside her bed, and sobbed as she prayed.

CHAPTER 11

Rafe was ushered roughly from the Bronco past a broken down, badly rusted Honda into a very run-down house. "You're home, Greg," he was told.

"Home?" he asked.

"Yes, where your real family's from. The home your dumb teenage mother ran away from with that tall, good-for-nothing drifter."

Rafe actually found some measure of relief from that statement, for now he knew his abduction wasn't about Greg's adoptive mother, but rather their biological mother.

"Your job now is to take us to your mother, my daughter," the old man said.

"And my sister," the younger man added as he pushed Rafe into a dark, smelly room that appeared to only have one door, the one through which he was entering.

Rafe was thinking quickly. All he wanted was time to get at his gun and get the upper hand on these men, these men who may well be his relatives by birth—although they didn't appear to be anyone he wanted to claim. "Why didn't you say so?" Rafe asked after turning around inside the room and facing his captors who were still on the far side of the doorway. "What are we waiting for?"

"So you do know where she is?" one of the men said.

"Of course," he answered, thinking of the cemetery in Richfield where he was told she'd been buried without so much as a name to carve on a headstone.

The old man's eyes lit up. "Is it far from here?"

"Yes, quite a ways."

"Then we'll leave in a day or so," the blond man said, the man Rafe was now trying to get used to thinking of as his uncle, the brother of his birth mother. It was not a pleasant thought. An even worse thought was that he might have descended from the older man.

"Why not now?" Rafe asked.

"Because I said so," he was informed brusquely. "Now shut yer yap." With that rude remark, the door was slammed shut in Rafe's face.

That they locked it did not come as a surprise to Rafe. But when they opened the door later the surprise would be theirs, he thought as he pulled his pistol from beneath his jacket and held it in his hand. He just prayed that he wouldn't have to shoot anyone, for he wasn't sure he could do that.

* * *

"He didn't answer it before, and now it's not ringing at all. It just goes straight to voice mail," Lenny said to Glenda. "That's not like Rafe to ignore his phone, especially with all that's been happening."

"I'm sorry, Dad," Stephanie said. "I won't ever do anything like this again. I promise. But we've got to keep trying to call Rafe. I feel terrible that he's so worried about me."

Lenny shook his head sadly as he looked at his daughter. "It was bad enough that you snuck out and went to Becky's party when you'd been told not to; but to have Becky lie for you, that's too much."

"I didn't know she was going to do that," a very humble Stephanie said. "I promise I won't ever do it again." She was really embarrassed that Rafe's boss had driven all the way down from Provo to help find her. It had been his suggestion to go to Becky's house and look for her.

After taking her back to her house, Mr. Stanbury had said to her folks, "I've just learned over the years that kids lie sometimes, even good kids." Then he'd winked at her and left.

They'd been trying to reach Rafe ever since.

* * *

She'd seen that face somewhere before. Lindsay was sure of it. It might have been recently; then again, it might not have been. But it was vaguely familiar. The face in question had a short, reddish beard. And it seemed to be watching her from behind the windshield of an old four-wheel-drive vehicle of some kind. She wasn't into cars, so she had no idea what make it was, but, like the face peering through its windshield, it seemed familiar.

Then she remembered, and she frantically picked up her pace as she did. That car had been parked at the bank when she came out the evening she had dinner with Rafe. It had been close to Rafe's pickup. She felt her skin prickle, and she hurriedly got in her car and drove off. She watched her mirror, and, as she feared, the car followed. She could see it all the way to campus, then it finally turned off when she entered the parking lot. She was still trembling when she entered the auditorium where sacrament meeting was held.

* * *

Greg's phone rang and he picked it up without taking time to look at the caller identification. He was almost certain it was Rafe explaining where he'd been all night. But the voice that spoke to him was not Rafe's, but that of an older man. "Greg Ralston?" the man asked.

"I'm Greg," he answered.

"Very good. It's a pleasure to talk with you, son. I've been waiting a long time for this," the man said.

"Who are you?" Greg demanded angrily. He didn't have time for this, he thought, wondering if the call could be from some crazy basketball fan who wanted to welcome him to the Mavericks or something.

"Don't get all riled up," the voice said. "I'm planning on telling you who I am. And when I do, I'll need a favor."

"Listen, mister, I'm very busy," Greg said.

"Just shut up and listen," the voice barked. "And don't try hanging up the phone, because I'll just call back."

Greg had very nearly done exactly that, but he changed his mind. "I'm listening," he said. "Just make it fast, please. I'm expecting a very important phone call."

"This is the most important phone call you'll be getting today," the voice said. "So pay attention. First off, I am your father and—"

"You are not my father!" Greg interrupted. "You don't think I'd know my own father's voice?"

"I didn't say your adoptive father, I said your *father*. Your birth mother died when you and Rafe were born. She was my wife."

That stopped Greg cold as he remembered what Rafe had told him.

The man said, "But I'm not dead, Greg, and I know all about you and your twin brother, Rafe. You two have done quite well for yourselves, especially you, Greg. You make your old man proud."

"I don't know you," Greg mumbled, wondering if there was any reason to believe this man.

"You don't need to know me. But you will need to send me some money."

"I don't need to do any such thing," Greg retorted hotly. "Whoever you are, you can go get a job like everyone else if you need money."

"Everyone except you, you mean?" the man said. "You don't have to work. All you'll be doing is playing ball."

"That's a job," Greg said. "It's a lot of work, but I earn my own living doing it. I'm going to hang up now."

"And jeopardize the safety of Rafe's little sister?" the voice said darkly. "Either you lend me what I need or she'll disappear, and I'll expose you for who you really are, you and your private-eye brother."

"We know who we are," Greg said boldly. "You can't intimidate me with that." Although as he spoke, terror was rushing through him.

"Maybe not, but I mean it about Stephanie Collings. Call Rafe. He'll tell you all about her. You can reach him in Provo, Utah. I'll give you a little time to do that. Then I'll make contact again. When I do, I expect you to make arrangements to deliver some money. I'll tell you where and how much. Oh, and one more thing. Don't even think about calling the cops. That will only make things worse for you, for Rafe, and for Rafe's sister."

The phone went dead before Greg could say anything more. Where was Rafe? he wondered in frustration. Why had he left with those men in that rusty black vehicle? Surely Rafe would know what to do, or at the worst, he could call his boss. They were, after all, investigators.

Greg tried Rafe's cell phone, but it was either dead or turned off. "Come on, Rafe," he said aloud. "Things are getting complicated here. Where in the world are you?"

* * *

Lindsay was scared now. She'd been kidnapped before, and all the terror of that experience came rushing back as she parked her car as close to her apartment as possible.

That man was parked out on the street. And he was watching her.

As soon as she was inside, she called Rafe's cell phone again. But it still wasn't working. Her hands were trembling, and she didn't know what to do now except offer a silent prayer and hope the guy was gone next time she came out.

* * *

The green Cadillac was gone. Parting with it had been like giving up dope. It was one of the hardest things he'd ever done, but he needed something he was certain no one would recognize him in. So the Cadillac had been replaced with an old Ford F-150 pickup, brown in color. There were so many pickups in Utah that he felt he would not draw any attention to himself if he were driving one. He assumed that would be especially true in the rural areas of Utah, like Ephraim.

To add to the effect he sought, he bought a cowboy hat, shoplifted a pair of boots in one store, and stole some Wrangler jeans and a western-cut shirt in another one. He was satisfied that he looked just like all the other cowboys in cowboy country.

* * *

Rafe had been sleeping, something he hadn't intended to do. He awoke with a start and heard the door being locked. He groaned. He'd missed a chance to get free. He stood up and walked over to the door. There was a bucket there and a plate of food and jug of water. At least he wouldn't starve, and he was certainly in need of a bathroom—that was what he guessed the bucket was for. He ate slowly. The bread tasted moldy, and the potatoes were cold, but it was food. The water at least tasted clean.

When he'd finished, he sat down again, his back against a wall, and watched the door. He checked his watch. It was a little after two o'clock.

He wondered and worried about Stephanie. He was wide awake now, and that was good, because he didn't want to fall asleep again. The hours dragged slowly by. If he was forced to spend another night in here, he wasn't sure he could stay awake. He was, after all, only human.

* * *

The stalker was still there when Lindsay went next door to do her visiting teaching. When she got home, she tried Rafe's number over and over again, with the same frustrating result each time. She didn't know who else to turn to. Maybe the police, she decided after a lot of thought. If he was there the next morning, and he followed her when she left for school, then she'd lead him to the police department.

* * *

Lenny had a Church meeting to attend, and rather than leave Stephanie and Glenda alone at the house, he took them with him. They piled into his truck, and he pulled up the lane toward the road. They had to wait for one vehicle to pass. It was a brown Ford F-150 with a temporary sticker in the rear. Lenny didn't recognize the tall cowboy driving it, but he didn't give the matter a second thought. He pulled onto the county road and headed for Ephraim, the opposite way from the F-150.

After the meeting, the three of them stopped to visit an older couple in their ward before returning home. By the time they arrived back at the ranch, it was getting dark, and Lenny had the usual evening chores to do. He escorted Glenda and Stephanie to the house, then headed for the barn. His wife called loudly from the house before he got inside. "Lenny, can you come take a phone call?"

"Can I call them back?" he shouted. "I'd really like to get the chores done."

"This is important. It's Greg Ralston," Glenda said.

Lenny's stomach took an uncomfortable twist and he hurried back to the house.

"Greg, this is Lenny Collings, Rafe's father, what can I do for you?" he asked, the moment his wife handed the phone to him.

"I'm sorry to bother you, Mr. Collings. I called information to find your number. I didn't know your first name, so you're the third person with the last name of Collings that I've called. I'm glad I finally reached the right person," Greg said.

His voice, remarkably similar to Rafe's, was strained, and Lenny wondered what could be happening. He hoped that Greg could at least tell him where Rafe was at and what he was doing. He asked, "Is Rafe with you?"

"No. That's what I'm calling about, Mr. Collings. I was hoping you could tell me where he is. I'm worried."

"So are we. He was planning to be at your place last night." Lenny was more worried than ever upon hearing that Greg didn't know where Rafe was.

"He was here," Greg said. "At least he almost was. I saw him from my window. He'd just parked his car and got out of it. It looked like he was trying to figure out which apartment was mine. I was going to go down and meet him, but then two men approached him. He talked with them for a minute, then went with them in their car. The car he'd rented is still parked where he left it, and he hasn't come back. That was twenty hours ago."

The chill that settled over Lenny was so severe that he could scarcely talk. "Oh no," was all he could get out.

"Do you think he's in some kind of trouble?" Greg asked.

"I'm afraid so," Lenny managed to say. He had to pause and clear his throat before he went on. "Are you aware of the threats made against Rafe and against us by the man who killed his mother?"

"I thought she died when Rafe and I were born, if I'm Rafe's brother," Greg said.

"No, I mean his adoptive mother," Lenny said. "My first wife."

"Oh no," Greg groaned. "Rafe didn't tell me about that."

So Lenny spent several minutes explaining it to Greg. When he'd finished, Greg asked, "Do you think his going with those men could have anything to do with that?"

Lenny said, "Yes, it could."

"I'm sorry, Mr. Collings. I had no idea. I was hoping you'd heard from him."

"And I was hoping you had."

"There's something else," Greg said, and it seemed to Lenny like the young man was hesitant. But after a short pause, he went on. "Your daughter's name is Stephanie, isn't it?"

Lenny hadn't thought he could feel worse, but he did. "Yes," he said.

"I'm sorry. I hate to make you worry more, but a man called me earlier. I'm expecting him to call back," Greg said.

"Surely it didn't have anything to do with Stephanie," Lenny said as he fought to clear his voice. He was aware of Glenda and Stephanie watching him. They could only hear one side of the conversation, but the looks on their innocent faces, the terror there, was almost more than Lenny could stand. He had to hear what else Rafe's brother had to say, and yet he dreaded it. It couldn't be good.

"It did have to do with her. The man claimed to be the biological father of Rafe and me," Greg revealed.

Lenny had to find a seat. His wife and daughter closed in on him and they sat as a tight, frightened unit on the sofa. This had to be the same man who'd left the note on Rafe's truck the day before, the man who had caused them to fear that Stephanie had been kidnapped for ransom. "What did he want?" Lenny asked, although he was certain that he knew. He must have decided to go directly to Greg to demand money.

"He said that he wants money, lots of it. He thinks I have a lot, but I don't. I will have if I get out of the mess I'm in and get to play ball, but that's all in the future. Right now I don't have very much."

"Greg, did he say what he'd do if he didn't get the money?" Lenny asked.

"He said something would happen to Stephanie," Greg said. "I thought you needed to know so you could take some precautions."

"Thank you, Greg," Lenny said as he began to gain control of his emotions. "We'll do that. Is he going to call you back?"

"That's what he told me," Greg said. "But he hasn't yet."

"Okay, here's what you do. When he calls, tell him that you can come up with some money but that you're not sure how much," Lenny began.

"But I don't have it," Greg protested.

"I realize that, but I have a ranch, and it's paid for. I'll use the equity if I have to. Anyway, tell him you can come up with it but that it will take a little time. Find out how much he wants, then call me back. But don't, whatever you do, let him know we've talked."

"Oh, don't worry. I won't tell him. I just wanted to warn you."

"Greg, you need to know that this isn't the first threat he's made. He already made a demand on Rafe."

"That doesn't surprise me. But where did he think Rafe would get the money?" Greg asked. "Private investigators can't make all that much."

"That's right. He wanted Rafe to get it from you. I guess it hasn't occurred to him that I could get money for Rafe mortgaging the ranch, or even selling part of it."

"I'd give him what he wants if I had it," Greg said, "if it would stop all the madness." Lenny was certain the young man's voice was choking up. "But I don't have it."

"I can get it," Lenny reminded him. "And if I have to, I will, for your sake and for ours."

They talked just a moment more before disconnecting. Then Lenny had to explain everything to his wife and daughter. He tried to play it all down and failed miserably. Finally he said, "We may have to mortgage the ranch, but before we give this guy money, let's go for a long trip somewhere. If he can't find us, he can't hurt us. I'll see if I can find someone to do my chores and keep the water lines moving. The hay will be okay for a while longer if we can't get things resolved and get back here soon."

"When will we leave?" Stephanie asked.

"As soon as I can get things arranged. But the three of us will be together every minute until we can get away. It may take a day or so."

"What about school, Dad? I can't miss school."

"Yes you can. And you will. Your life is what is most important," he said. "By the way, Greg's voice sounds just like Rafe's. They've got to be twins. It was almost like I was talking to Rafe."

* * *

Greg was beside himself with worry by the time the phone rang again an hour or more after his talk with Rafe's father. The feelings he'd been experiencing were strange ones. He felt a connection with Lenny, and found himself very worried about Rafe's family. It was almost like they were a part of him.

He answered the phone after several rings and recognized the voice instantly.

"It's your dad," the man said. "I suppose you've had plenty of time to think about things."

"Yes," Greg said flatly. "I've been thinking."

"Good. I've decided that a little loan for two hundred thousand will do me for now. I'm sure you could spare more, and maybe sometime I'll need to call on you again," the man said. "But that's all I'll need for now."

Greg swallowed hard then responded. "So it's just a loan you want. You'll pay it back?"

"If I can," the man said. "If I can't, I guess you can consider it a gift to your father. So, when can you have it ready for me?"

"Well, you've got to understand that it'll take me some time to come up with that much money," Greg said. "Even though I have a contract with the Mavericks, I haven't actually played yet. I get paid when I play ball."

It was silent at the other end of the line for almost a minute. Finally, the voice said, "I'll need it fairly soon. You may have to borrow some. I need the money, son."

Greg cringed, but he said, "I'll be able to get it. Call me in a week. I'll see what I can come up with by then."

"No, a week's too long. You have two days. And if you don't make a big enough effort to find me the money, just remember: I know where Rafe's family lives, and I'm very good with explosives." And with that veiled threat filling the air like sulfur, the caller disconnected.

Greg sat almost frozen for several minutes before he roused himself and made a phone call.

* * *

Lenny listened while Greg spoke. "He didn't actually say what he'd blow up, he just said he was good with explosives," Greg explained.

Lenny's wife and daughter stood close to him as if their close proximity to each other would be a protection for the evil that threatened them. Finally Lenny said, "Thanks for calling, Greg. I've already met with my bank. The money will be available in a few days. But in the meantime, for the safety of my family, we're going to go on a trip. You can call me on the cell phone if you need to, though, and I can get the money wired to wherever it needs to go, but not for a few days. You'll have to stall him when he calls again. We plan to leave first thing in the morning."

* * *

The brown pickup slowed down near the lane. The tall man was thinking about how he might best use the nitrogen fertilizer that was in the back of his truck to achieve his aims. It was very explosive when in the hands of someone who knew what to do with it, and he knew. He would only use it if Greg stalled. But if he needed to use it to make his point, he would use it. He very much wanted the money, and he believed he could get it.

CHAPTER 12

"Get up. We've got to get moving now."

Rafe shook the sleep from his eyes. He'd failed again. His best chance to get away had been snatched away because he'd fallen asleep again. As he pushed himself up from the floor, he glanced at the luminous hands on his watch. It was three in the morning. He remembered checking the time at a little after two. He must have fallen asleep shortly after that. He swayed unsteadily on his feet, and the younger of his two captors, the one claiming to be his uncle, steadied him with one hand while poking him in the ribs with the gun he held in the other one.

"Where are we going?" Rafe asked as they started toward the door in the semidarkness of the room.

"To find your mother, of course," he was told. "And if you know what's good for you, you won't be yanking us around."

"Why would I do that?" Rafe said, trying to sound callous. "I don't know what you want with my mother, but it's nothing to me."

The old man was waiting in the lighted room. His eyes were bloodshot and his face seemed unusually red. As Rafe walked near him, he could smell the odor of alcohol on his breath. The younger man had been drinking too, but he didn't smell nearly as bad as his father and seemed quite in control of his faculties.

"Have a good nap?" the old man asked.

"Not really. And it would be nice if you two would tell me your names. My mom never talked about you, so I haven't a clue what your names are."

The two looked at each other, then the old man said, "Name's Harley Tuft, and your uncle here is Deke. Don't know what your mama told you her name is, but I'm sure she lied about it. Not a trustworthy gal, that one. Her name's Stella."

"Do I have a grandma?" Rafe asked as the two men ushered him toward the front door.

The old man coughed, and the look the two gave each other was very strange. "Mean woman," Harley said. "Died of meanness years ago. Didn't Stella never say nothing to you about her? Was sure she would. The two was a lot alike."

"Nope; like I said, she didn't talk about her family at all. In fact, she and I haven't had much to do with each other," Rafe said.

Another look passed between the two men. Rafe had no idea what it could mean, but for some reason, it seemed significant. He decided he better not push his luck, for the mood of both men had soured considerably over the past minute or two, and Rafe didn't want to make them angry. They were clearly men who were not strangers to violence.

Outside, a luminous half moon shone from almost directly overhead. It gave enough light that Rafe could easily see the men, their vehicle, and the old cars and other junk that littered the yard. From somewhere behind the house, a dog barked—or bayed might be a better term, he decided as other dogs joined in. He'd listened to the dogs off and on during the long hours in the locked room. Coonhounds, he assumed. He'd heard that people liked to hunt raccoons in Texas.

Rafe reached the old Bronco, the gun still poking in his ribs. He opened the door and started to get in. "Not so fast, boy," Deke said, shoving the gun so hard into his side that he couldn't suppress a yelp of pain. "We got a long ways to go, I suppose. You'll need to have yer hands tied in case you forget yer manners."

Harley then approached. "Put yer hands back here, boy," he ordered, swaying drunkenly as he stood next to Rafe.

Rafe reluctantly obeyed, still looking for a chance to do something to overpower the two of them. Deke unwittingly created the opening he needed when he said, "Hey, Pa, better let me tie his hands. Yer a little unsteady, and we gotta make sure he can't get loose of them. We need fer them to be tight."

The pressure on Rafe's ribs eased, and Deke held the gun out to his father. *It's now or never,* Rafe told himself, and he spun, knocking the gun from the old man's hands before he ever had a good grip on it. Harley stumbled and fell backward to the ground. Rafe then hit Deke squarely in the face. Deke stepped backward, but then started forward again, cursing. As Rafe threw another punch, a much harder one than the first, he wondered if he'd made a mistake, for Deke was clearly stronger than he'd imagined. The first punch didn't seem to have hurt him much at all.

However, the second punch slowed Deke down, and Rafe took advantage by darting away from the men and running rapidly into the darkness of the trees that bordered the junky yard. He could hear one man coming after him. He assumed it was Deke. Then he heard Harley shout, "I'll get the shotguns, Deke. We'll shoot him when we find him."

Rafe had no doubt that they would do exactly that if he allowed them to get their hands on him again. As much as they wanted him alive to find Stella, it wouldn't be worth it to them if he escaped and blabbed to the police. And this house of theirs was so far away from other homes that it was very likely they'd get away with it, that no one would hear the shot. But he also knew that the advantage was his again, for he now held his little revolver in his hand. He slowed down and began to make his way through the woods as silently as he could. Then he passed through a field and entered more woods. From the sounds that were coming from behind him, it was clear that Deke wasn't sure exactly where he'd gone. Rafe was in good condition, and despite hunger and a lack of sleep, he was sure he could go until he found help.

Then he heard Deke shout, "Pa, get the dogs. We'll let them tear this fool kid to pieces, and then we'll bury what's left beside his grandma. Serve 'em both right."

Several things went through Rafe's mind. First, he wondered how many dogs there were, since if there weren't too many of them, he could probably shoot them. He also wondered if they were something other than coonhounds, something that would truly kill a man. Then he thought about the grandma. He wondered what had happened to her. From what Harley had said, it didn't sound like either her husband or her son had cared for her. He'd like to learn someday what had happened to her, he decided as he stopped to get a few gulps of air. But that could wait.

When he moved on, he changed direction and soon found himself in thick brush and trees, making it hard to get through. But he persisted even as he heard the sudden baying of the hounds start up. The sound sent chills through him, for it was more intense than when they'd made their disturbance in the yard a few minutes ago. They sounded eager and excited to Rafe, like they were ready to track down and kill something. That something would be him. He began to look for a place to make a stand. He hoped he hadn't too severely underestimated these two men.

* * *

"What time is it?" Stephanie asked when her father gently shook her shoulder.

"It's almost four thirty," Lenny said.

"Why are you waking me up so early?" she asked.

"Your mother and I have been awake all night. And we've been talking. We think we better leave now. I can make some phone calls in a few hours and get things taken care of here," he explained. "We'll take a phone book with us."

"Leave now, in the middle of the night?" Stephanie asked in dismay.

"Yes, now, sweetheart. I'm sorry, but if you'll hurry and pack a suitcase, we can get on our way."

"Where are we going?" she asked.

"Well, Rafe went to Texas. We thought as long as we had to go somewhere, maybe that would be as good as anyplace."

"Texas?" she asked. "So could we meet Greg?"

"Yes, I'm sure we can. And we'll try to find Rafe. Your mother and I have spent a lot of time on our knees, and we both feel like Rafe is alive. We might be able to help him."

Stephanie forced herself to throw back the covers. Then she climbed from the bed. She dropped groggily to her knees beside it.

"What are you doing?" Lenny asked. "We have to hurry."

"I always say my prayers when I get out of bed," Stephanie answered, "just like you taught me to do. And I especially want to pray for Rafe right now."

"I love you, Steph," Lenny said as tears filled his eyes. "You're a good girl."

"I love you too, Dad. I won't be long, I promise."

Stephanie began praying the moment she heard her father close her bedroom door. Her prayer was short but very intense and full of faith. "I'm thankful I'm safe and might get to meet Greg," she said in a reverent whisper. "And please protect Rafe. Wherever he is right now, please, please, please don't let him get hurt."

* * *

A fallen tree lay directly in front of another tree, a very large one. Behind the trees was a steep slope that ended in a huge forest of dense trees and bushes. Rafe had decided to make his stand using the fallen tree and the large one standing behind it as a fortress of sorts. Thick, stiff branches poked upward from the fallen tree. He thought he could shoot through them, but it would be very difficult for an attacking dog to get through and reach him. Then if the going got tough, he could slide down the steep slope behind him and enter the very thick foliage below. His gun was loaded. It held five rounds. In addition, there were ten more in his pocket. He had fifteen shots, and that was all. He had to make them count.

The hounds were getting closer, and the intensity of their baying increased. Rafe was certain that they knew their quarry was close. He was sure that Deke and Harley, with their shotguns, were not far behind them.

A cloud drifted overhead, hiding the moon and making it too dark to shoot very well. Rafe looked up. It was a small cloud. He prayed that it would move on quickly. A moment later the moon reappeared, and almost simultaneously, the lead dog, a large, cruel-looking black animal, rushed headlong from the scrub oak and stopped just short of the fallen tree.

This was no coonhound, Rafe decided as he pointed the pistol at the animal's head. This dog was a killer. It was no longer baying, but its fangs were exposed, with its jowls curled back, and a deep-throated, threatening growl warned Rafe that it meant business. He began to put pressure on the trigger. Yet he hesitated—not that he felt any guilt as far as shooting the dangerous animal was concerned, for it was a matter of his life or the dog's. But he didn't want to give away his position, nor the fact that he was armed, to Deke and Harley any sooner than he had to.

The dog was crashing against the limbs, intent on breaking its way through. Rafe still held off. But then a second dog came charging into the clearing, and Rafe pulled the trigger. The large black dog was stilled instantly, and the second dog, one that looked more brown in the moonlight, leaped over the body of the black one. Rafe didn't hesitate this time. The second dog died before a third appeared. After shooting it, Rafe replaced the empty cartridges with new ones and waited. The fourth and fifth dogs—the last ones, Rafe concluded when they began to growl and there was no further baying behind them—came charging into the clearing. Slowly, deliberately, Rafe eliminated one of them. Then the other one leaped and yelped as he fired. He either missed it or wounded it. But it appeared that it recognized its odds, and it fled back into the oak on the far side of the clearing.

At that moment, the dark form of a man appeared across the clearing. Rafe saw the foot-long sheet of flame that came from in front of the man even as Rafe was ducking behind the trunk of the fallen tree. As the pellets from Deke's shotgun riddled the branches from a second shot, Rafe was sliding down the hill. Within seconds, the protective trunks and branches of hundreds of small trees and a mass of bushes welcomed him into their midst. He crawled more than ran as he forced his way deeper into the cover he'd found. The shotgun fired a third time and then a fourth, but he was safe, at least for the moment. And if his luck held, he would get away. So after resting, he pushed on.

* * *

It was eight in the morning when Greg's phone rang. He'd never felt such relief when he heard the voice that was on the other end of the line. "Rafe, where have you been?" Greg asked. "It's been a day and a half. Everyone's been worried sick."

"Sorry, Greg. It's kind of a long story. Looks like you and I must attract bad luck," Rafe said.

"Yeah, your dad told me about your mom. I'm sorry. He thought your disappearance could be related to that. Are you okay? I saw you the night before last on the sidewalk in front of my apartment, and I was going to come down and get you when you suddenly left with a couple of old guys."

"That was the Tufts. They kidnapped me at gunpoint. Actually, they thought I was you, and lucky it was, if I might say so."

"Oh, Rafe, I'm sorry. But I don't know anyone by that name. What did they want me for?"

"Again, it's a long story, Greg. In a nutshell, they're blood relations of ours who seem to think you are acquainted with our birth mother. When we get together, I'll tell you all about it. But for now, I need to find a way to get back to Dallas. Then we'll see if we can figure out what to do about your situation."

"Thanks, Rafe, but there's a more serious problem," Greg began.

Rafe said, "I know, at least I do if you're talking about my sister. The guy who has her—"

Greg cut him off. "She's safe, Rafe. She was never kidnapped. She'd snuck off to a slumber party. But the guy you thought had her is still threatening. He called me yesterday. He claims to be our biological father."

"Oh, thank goodness Steph's okay. As long as everyone stays out of his road, I don't believe that guy will hurt us. But you can't imagine how I've worried about Stephanie."

"Actually, I think I'm getting some idea. You have a great family. Speaking of which, I just talked to your father. They're on their way down here as we speak."

"Why are they coming here?"

Greg chuckled, and it felt good to be able to do so. "Like you were saying a moment ago, it's a long story. Where are you at, Rafe?"

Rafe told him, and Greg said, "Good grief, that's a ways away."

"I know. I traveled every mile of it in the backseat of an old Bronco with a gun poking me in the ribs."

"I'm just relieved you're safe. Listen, I'll come get you. We can talk on the ride back. I'll be there in a couple of hours. Do you still have your cell phone? Everybody's been trying to call it."

"No, they threw it away. But I'll get another one as quick as I can. I feel naked without it. I'm calling from a pay phone now, and people are looking at me like I'm a wild man. I've been in the bushes for several hours. I'm a mess."

"I'll bring you some clothes," Greg promised. "I'm sure they'll fit." The two of them laughed at that and then he continued, "Hey, do you have enough money to call your dad? He'll be so relieved to hear from you."

"Yeah, I'm using a calling card, and I've got plenty of minutes left. I'm going to try his cell phone now. I tried the house already, and I got no answer."

"Now you know why," Greg said.

As soon as Rafe had hung up, Greg began gathering a few clothes for his brother. Then he hurried to his car, put the clothes in it, jumped in, and drove off.

He'd gone over a mile before he noticed a car that appeared to be following him. It was quite a ways back, but it made every turn he did as he headed for Interstate 45 going south. When he entered the freeway, so did the other car, a dark blue sedan, but it was too far back to be sure what make it was. It made him nervous because he was technically going out of the area the judge had told him not to leave. But his brother needed him. *His brother.* That sounded good. He kept an eye on the rearview mirror, but as he continued on, the car made no attempt to gain on him. So he eventually relaxed the best he could and drove toward where his brother waited nearly a hundred and fifty miles from Dallas.

* * *

Rafe insisted that Lenny let him talk to Stephanie. "I just want to hear your voice," he told her. "I've been so worried about you."

"I'm sorry, Rafe. I was being stupid. But I guess we're sort of even," she said, "because I've been worrying about you too."

The siblings talked for a minute or two, then Lenny took the phone again. "Rafe, you've got to be extra cautious," he said.

"Don't I know it," Rafe agreed. "It seems like Greg and I have more enemies than we can keep track of."

"I sure hope Greg's not mixed up in that murder he's accused of. He sounds like a really nice guy," Lenny said.

"Totally. I can't believe he's guilty, but until I can get with him, I don't know what we're up against. I just hope I can help, especially with all of these so-called relatives of mine swarming all over the place," Rafe said, trying to be nonchalant about it all.

"They may not be relatives at all, not any of them," Lenny said. "And even if they are, they aren't the kind of people you want anything to do with."

"Don't I know that," Rafe said.

"Hey, I've got another call coming in. Give me a few minutes and call me back," Lenny said. "But do it from another phone. I don't like the thought of you being too exposed."

"Okay. In the meantime I'll try to call Thorn. I could sure use his help," Rafe said.

He dialed the number of the office. There was no answer. He tried Thorn's cell phone. Again there was no answer, even though it rang and rang. That wasn't like Thorn. He always had his cell phone on. Well, Rafe decided, he'd just have to try again later.

As soon as he'd hung up the pay phone, Rafe moved away from it quickly. He walked a block, keeping a close eye on every side. Mostly, he was watching for the black Bronco. He wouldn't put it past Deke and Harley to come right into this town looking for him. They seemed to feel like he, or at least Greg, was a serious threat to them. And the more he'd thought about it the past few hours, the more he wondered if it could have anything to do with Harley's dead wife, his dead grandmother. The two of them had acted really strange when Rafe had mentioned her.

* * *

"Mr. Collings, it's Lindsay Diamond again. My roommate told me that Stephanie's okay. I'm so glad."

"So are we, Lindsay," Lenny said.

"I've been trying to call Rafe. I've got a problem I was hoping he could help me with, but I can't—"

Lenny cut in. "I just talked to him. He's had some trouble, but he's okay now."

"Oh, thank goodness," Lindsay said. "Maybe I can call him. What I need right now is some advice."

"Are you in some kind of trouble?" Lenny asked.

"Maybe. There's this guy, and I think he's stalking me. I'm pretty scared. He's behind me right now," Lindsay said, her voice beginning to tremble.

"Are you on foot or in a car?" Lenny asked.

"I'm in my car."

"Good. Okay, so why don't you give the police a call? Just dial 911," Lenny suggested.

"I'm actually planning to go to the police station now. I just want to talk to Rafe on my way," Lindsay said.

"Okay. He doesn't have his cell phone, but he'll be calling me in just a little while. Give me your number, and I'll have him call," Lenny told her. "But if it looks like that guy is getting too close or if he seems to be trapping you in any way, you call 911."

"Okay," Lindsay said as she looked in her rearview mirror. He was still there. Her heart was pounding rapidly. She turned from the route she usually took to campus and headed for the police station. She'd looked up the address before leaving her apartment that morning. Unless Rafe told her to do something different, she'd go there.

CHAPTER 13

The tall man in the brown Ford F-150 was getting very tired, but he couldn't pull over to sleep. He had to keep the pickup he was tailing in sight. When the Collings family had pulled onto the county road beside their ranch early that morning, it had angered him. But it hadn't been entirely unexpected. That was why he'd been watching their lane. He'd half expected them to leave.

He'd been so angry at first that he'd considered wiping all three of them out before they ever left the state, but he'd quickly cooled down. He'd never killed anyone, and he didn't want to now. It was money he was after, Greg's money, and Rafe's family was nothing more than leverage to get that money. So he was following them now, trying not to lose sight of them, but he was getting very tired. What he needed, he told himself, was a hit of something strong. He cursed. He didn't have anything in the truck. He'd had a small stash of drugs in the Cadillac, but he'd forgotten about it when he traded it in. That fact only added to his impatience now. It also frustrated him that the Collingses had the advantage of more than one driver. They'd changed drivers twice, but he had to do all the driving, and because of them he was already sleep-deprived.

He also kept watching his gas gauge. Unless he got gas very soon, he'd run out. He was relieved when they eventually pulled into a gas station. He filled up across the street from them and bought a spare can and filled that too. It was apparent that the Collingses' GMC pickup could go farther on a tank of fuel than his old Ford. If he had to, he could stop and pour the can into his tank and then catch up by driving very fast for a while. He hoped he wouldn't have to do that, but he could if it became necessary.

When the Collingses pulled out of their station, he was already waiting, and he pulled onto the street behind them. As he drove he considered his options. He'd never been this close to so much money before, and he wasn't about to let anyone cheat him out of it. After all, those sons of his owed it to him. He'd given them life, and giving something back was the least they could do, he reasoned.

* * *

Lindsay's heart nearly burst with terror when she felt the drag of the steering wheel that could only mean one thing: a flat tire. She tried to keep going, but she couldn't, so she pulled to the curb, hoping passing motorists on the busy Provo street would help her, and that the man following her would continue on.

She got half her wishes. A car stopped and a man got out and offered to help her before she could even call 911 on her cell phone.

But her good Samaritan was the stalker himself.

* * *

Rafe already had more on his mind than he could handle, and when his father told him that Lindsay Diamond needed to talk to him about someone that she thought was stalking her, he felt overwhelmed. He was a young, inexperienced, partially trained investigator, and yet the demand for his services was more than he'd ever dreamed it would be. He wasn't sure what to tell Lindsay except the very thing his father had already told her: to contact the police.

Promising to call Lenny back shortly, Rafe dialed Lindsay's number, secretly glad for a chance to hear her voice, but also worried that he would let her down. When Lindsay didn't answer his call, he felt a wave of panic wash over him. She'd suffered a kidnapping before. Surely she wasn't facing such a terrible fate again, he thought desperately. Without hesitation, he dialed the number of the Provo Police Department, a number which Thorn had insisted that he memorize the first day he worked for him. As he made the call, he continued to scan the surrounding area. The phone had only rung twice when he spotted the black Bronco. At the same time Deke, who was driving it, apparently spotted him, for he pointed in his direction and gunned the vehicle.

Rafe did the only thing he could; he dropped the phone and ran into and through the nearest building, out the back, and down an alley. Their very presence here in this town in broad daylight, after all the crimes they'd committed against him, told Rafe that they would continue after him. He was now a threat, even as they perceived that the long-dead girl they called Stella was a threat. He had to keep from letting them spot him again if he could. Yet that would be nearly impossible, since Greg couldn't pick him up if he couldn't wait for him along some street he could describe. He also had to call Greg just to give him a meeting place. Then an idea occurred to him. He could do the very thing he'd planned to tell Lindsay to do; he could go directly to the police station.

Borrowing a phone in a store which he entered by the back door from a dark alleyway, he called for a cab. When the cab arrived, he rushed out and got in it, spotting the black Bronco less than a block away. His heart beating wildly, he said to the driver, "Take me to the police station and do it quickly."

"Hey, aren't you Greg Ralston, the new Dallas Mavericks point guard?" the cabbie asked. "Looks like you've had a rough time of it."

"I'm not Greg Ralston, I'm not a ballplayer, but yes, I've had a rough time. So please hurry, if you don't mind. There are a couple of guys in a black Bronco that you won't want to have catch up with us."

The cabbie looked back at Rafe in alarm and said, "You sure look like Greg Ralston, but I'll hurry. I don't need no trouble."

They'd only gone a couple of blocks when Rafe had an idea. "You wouldn't have a cell phone I could borrow, would you? I'll make it worth your time."

"Sure thing," the cabbie said.

A minute later, Rafe was talking to the police in Provo. "I don't know where she was exactly," he said after telling them of Lindsay's suspicions. "All I know is that she was driving from her apartment and that she was most likely going to your police station. Could you just have some officers check along that route and make sure she's not in trouble there somewhere?" He gave them a description of her car and the streets she'd most likely be traveling on, then disconnected, feeling like he'd probably done nothing to help Lindsay.

He tried Lindsay's cell phone again, but there was still no answer. His next call was to Greg. He told him quickly what was happening and that he'd meet him at the police department. Greg was not at all excited about that prospect, but after a very quick explanation of the trouble he was now in, Greg reluctantly agreed. Finally, Rafe called his father back.

* * *

Harley and Deke Tuft were each blaming the other for letting Greg Ralston get away. "And now look what he's done," Harley ranted. "He's gone to the cops, and who knows what he'll tell them. This is just what we needed to avoid. You should've searched him, you idiot."

"Who ever heard of ballplayers running around with guns?" Deke countered. "Anyway, if you hadn't been so clumsy and dropped the pistol—"

"Didn't need yer help anyway. I could've tied him up just fine myself," Harley snarled.

The argument gradually died down, and the two of them began discussing what they could do now. Both feared that Greg knew something about his grandma, that his mother had shot her mouth off, and that he was now telling what he knew to the cops. All that aside, all he had to do was tell them what they'd done to him, and they might be coming after them, they realized. What they needed to do now was leave here and drive to Dallas. They would have to wait back in Dallas at Greg's apartment. When he returned, they'd make sure he didn't say anything else to anyone, then they'd skip the country. As angry as it made them, neither of them could come up with a better solution to their predicament.

* * *

Lindsay felt like a fool as the unkempt man with long red hair sticking out from under his backward baseball cap threw her spare tire in the trunk and brushed his dirty hands on his pants. She thanked him, then he said, "Better get that replaced right away." Then he got back in his old Jeep Wagoneer and drove away.

He'd been both polite and helpful. Now, as she drove to her class on campus, she wondered about the coincidences that had led her to believe he was stalking her. He hadn't made any move to hurt her, had been very polite, and had driven away like he had no interest in where she was going next. She managed to convince herself that she'd seen the last of him and wished she hadn't said anything to anyone about him. People would think she was a paranoid fool, she told herself, especially Rafe. The last thing she wanted was for Rafe to think her a fool.

There were a couple of missed calls on her cell phone that had apparently come in while the fellow had been changing her tire. She'd left the phone on the seat and had watched him change the tire from the side of the busy street. She'd heard it ring, but hadn't wanted to draw his attention away from his work by answering it. Now she wished she would have, although she didn't know who the calls had been from. The numbers were unfamiliar to her. She called the latest number listed. It rang several times before someone answered.

"Hello," a voice said.

"Hi, I'm just returning your call," Lindsay responded.

"My call?" the voice asked. "I didn't call anyone. I just heard this pay phone ringing as I walked by the phone booth, so I answered it."

Lindsay cut off the call. Who would be calling her from a phone booth? Could it possibly have been Rafe? she wondered hopefully. She decided she'd check the area code when she had a moment, but right now she was already late for class. She'd try the other number that she'd missed later, she decided.

* * *

The likeness was uncanny. Meeting for the first time in their lives, Greg and Rafe stared at one another after Rafe had jumped into Greg's car. It was like looking into one's own face. There was a long moment of awkward silence. Then Greg offered his hand to Rafe. "It's good to meet you, uh, brother," he said with a nervous chuckle. "But you need a shave, a shower, and a change of clothes."

"Sorry, it's been a long thirty-six hours or so," Rafe said with a grin as he pumped the hand of the man he was positive was his brother. "Gee, I feel like I'm looking into the mirror, except, of course, you're cleaned up and I've been in the bushes."

"Sorry about that," Greg said. "This is weird. To think that I didn't know I had a brother. But we must be, don't you think?"

"Yeah, I'd say so, Greg. Of course, I always knew . . . at least I knew there had been two of us. I just didn't know what happened to you. Nobody knew," Rafe said.

Greg's face grew hard. "I bet my parents knew. They might have even taken me right from the hospital where we were born. I wish they hadn't lied to me."

Rafe didn't know how to respond to that. He knew that even though he'd been through so much with the death of his adoptive mom, he was the lucky one. "I'm stinking up your car," he said awkwardly. "I'm sorry."

"Hey, what you went through was in my place. Don't worry about it. Anyway, I noticed a truck-stop on the edge of town as I was coming in. I think it might have showers. We'll pull in there and I'll keep a lookout for those guys while you clean up. I brought some clothes for you to change into. No need to stay dirty when you don't have to."

Rafe noticed that Greg was watching the rearview mirrors closely as they drove. "Is someone following us?" Rafe asked nervously. "The Tufts were in a black Bronco."

"We're being followed, but it's not the Tufts. It's the same car that was behind me when I left my apartment earlier. They never try to get very close. They just hang back there. I haven't even been able to get a look at who's in it," Greg said. "You'll want to hurry when we get to the truck stop."

"I'll do that," Rafe assured him.

"So what did you do in the cop shop back there?" Greg asked. "Cops aren't real high on my list right now."

"I understand, and we'll get to your problem as soon as we can," Rafe assured him. "What I did was told an officer who I was, showed him my ID, and explained about being followed by a couple of guys who'd tried to kill me."

"Who are the Tufts, anyway?" Greg asked.

"They claim to be our uncle and our grandfather," Rafe said.

"Likely story," Greg responded. "Seems everybody wants to be a relative anymore."

"Strange, isn't it? My father mentioned that the tall man, as we've come to think of him, called you," Rafe said. "Seems he wants us to believe he's our biological father."

Greg nodded. "Seems like it, all right. So what did the cops say back there?"

"Not much. I think they thought I was a nutcase. They promised they'd keep an eye out for those two who took me for a ride, but I don't think they will," Rafe explained. "The Tufts seem to think we, or at least you, might know something our birth mother might have told you that could be very dangerous to them. They want to find her too. In fact, I'd promised I'd take them to her."

Greg looked over at him. "Why would you do that? You said our mother died when we were born."

"Yeah, she did. Something went wrong when we were born, but they don't know that. I was just stalling for time, and it worked," Rafe explained. "Anyway, they seem very determined to find out what we know or what our mother might remember. At one time, they even mentioned the man who our supposed mother ran away with."

"Was he tall?" Greg asked.

"Yeah, that's the kicker. He was. And they clearly don't like him."

"So this guy who's after money, he really could be our father," Greg said.

"I suppose so. At any rate, the Tufts seem to think that Stella— that's our mother, if they're telling the truth—has some knowledge that is dangerous for them."

"Any idea what it could be about?" Greg asked.

"I've been thinking about that a lot the past few hours. I'm wondering if it could have anything to do with our, uh, our grandmother. They speak like she was dirt, and I'm guessing our mother might have known something about what happened to her and they're afraid that either she or the tall man or one of us might tip off the cops. That might not be it at all, but whatever it is, it must be bad, because they look to me like men who've been in plenty of trouble," Rafe said. "But whatever this is about, it sure does make them nervous."

"There it is, the truck-stop," Greg told him. "Yeah, it says 'showers available' on that sign. I'll cruise around out here while you go in."

"I have a better idea," Rafe countered. "I'm armed. The gun saved me once, and I'd feel better knowing we both had it to help us out of a tight spot, if we get in another one. So why don't we both go in?"

"Are you sure?" Greg asked.

"Hey, it took nearly twenty-three years to meet you, Greg. Let's not take a chance on getting separated again before we even get to know each other."

"Okay, that's what we'll do," Greg agreed.

It only took Rafe fifteen minutes to shower, shave, and put on one of Greg's shirts, a pair of his slacks, and some loafers. Greg stayed within earshot during it all, and the long-lost brothers compared a little of their life histories. After Rafe had finished dressing, he pulled his gun from the holster that had been hidden beneath his jacket. He shoved it in the waistband of the slacks, left his shirttails out to conceal it, bundled up his dirty clothes, and said, "Let's hit the road."

The two hadn't discussed the murder Greg was accused of committing, but Rafe believed already that Greg was innocent. He couldn't believe anything else. Greg seemed like a really decent guy. Rafe found that he was determined to do whatever it took to clear his brother's name. He checked himself in a mirror before leaving the shower area and was startled. Greg was standing beside him dressed very much like he now was. He'd never seen two twins who looked more alike. He was certain that they could easily pass for each other, even with those who knew them each best.

They were both alert as they left the building and hurried to the car. And they both sighed in relief when they were in it and back on the road. "Hey, can I use your phone?" Rafe asked. "There's someone I need to call back in Utah."

"What's mine is yours, Rafe," Greg said generously, and somehow, Rafe believed he was sincere.

* * *

The two officers looked at each other in amazement. "There's two of him," one of them said. "And they're up to something."

They'd been watching the car Greg had parked earlier. And they'd pulled close enough to get a good look when the two men came back out. What they'd seen had been enough to make them both gasp. There was no way to tell which one was Greg Ralston—the suspect in their murder investigation who had, without permission, driven beyond the boundaries set for him by the judge who set bail—and which one was either a twin brother or a fantastically talented disguise artist.

"They're planning to switch places," the older officer, Sergeant Bill Latner said suspiciously. "If we let them do that, the fingerprints we have will mean nothing."

"So what do we do?" Detective Rhett Vancott asked.

"There's only one thing we can do," Bill said.

Rhett nodded. "Then I guess we better do it."

* * *

Lindsay answered her cell phone. She'd just turned it back on after coming out of her class. She didn't recognize the number, but the area code seemed familiar. "Hello," she said.

"Lindsay?"

She nearly squealed with delight. "Rafe?"

"Yeah," he said. "It's good to hear your voice. Are you all right? Did you go to the police like my dad suggested?"

"Yes, I'm fine. And no, I didn't go to the police. I feel like such a fool. I'm sorry I bothered you," she said, wishing this whole embarrassing episode had never happened. She didn't want Rafe to think she was an airhead.

Rafe sounded firm when he spoke again. "Lindsay, don't take any chances. If some guy you don't know is hanging around you a lot, it could be dangerous. Did he follow you to campus again?"

"Well, not really," she said. "It looked like he was, so then I headed for the police department and I blew a tire. Of course, I had to stop. The guy I was worried about stopped and changed the tire for me. He seemed really nice and was very polite. When he finished, he told me to be sure and replace the tire real soon and then he left. I'm sure I was just imagining things. And I'm so embarrassed."

"Lindsay," Rafe said with a sternness that surprised her, "you keep your eyes open and watch for him. It's too much of a coincidence that he was right behind you when you had a flat. If he shows up again, call me on this phone. It's Greg's. I lost mine, but Greg and I'll be together for a while, and you can call on this one."

"You're with Greg Ralston?" she asked.

"Yes, I'm with my brother," he agreed.

"I can't believe it," Lindsay said. "I just knew you two were brothers clear back when I first saw your picture."

"Well, looks like you were right," he said. "You take care of yourself, Lindsay. I mean it. I'm worried about you."

"Thanks, but I don't think you need to be," she said. "I'm okay. Really."

"Lindsay," Rafe started again, the sternness back in his voice, "you watch for that guy."

"Rafe, it was nothing," she insisted.

"By the way, what was he driving?" he asked.

"It was an old four-wheel-drive thingy. I was trying to look at it while he was changing my tire," she told him. "I'm pretty sure it said Wagoneer on the side."

"Was it brown?" Rafe asked.

Rafe was right. But how could he have known? she wondered as once again she felt a tightness develop in her chest. "Yes, I think so," she answered Rafe.

"His hair's sort of red and quite long? Maybe he's wearing a ball cap on backward?"

"Yes, all of that. How did you know?"

"He was at the bank when I met you there," Rafe said. "You be careful, Lindsay. Go to the police and give them a description. If you see him again, call them immediately."

"But he seemed really nice," she said weakly.

"Don't you believe it," Rafe warned her. "You watch for him. And tell the cops what he's been doing."

"Rafe, speaking of cops, those are cops back there," Greg said, interrupting his conversation with Lindsay. "They just put a light on us."

Rafe nodded. "Lindsay, I've got to get off the phone. You call if you see that guy again."

"Okay," she said.

"Promise?"

"Yes, I promise."

"Good."

Greg was pulling to the side of the freeway as he disconnected. Rafe looked back. The car was unmarked. Could they be sure it was the police? he wondered nervously. Or could it be one of his many enemies or someone hired by them? He touched his gun and prayed.

"So, who was that on the phone?" Greg asked as he slowed down, apparently not worried at all.

"Lindsay Diamond.

"From Pocatello?"

"Yeah, that's the one."

"Wow, what a small world. I sort of knew her when I lived there. She got kidnapped by some guy."

"Yeah, like maybe Deke Tuft," Rafe said.

"You're kidding."

"I'm guessing, but, no, I'm not kidding."

"Some of the guys said she had a thing for me. She was too young then. But she was gorgeous," Greg said as he pulled to a stop.

"Still is," Rafe said.

"Hey, she must have a thing for you now," Greg said with a grin.

"I wish."

CHAPTER 14

"Yeah, it's the police," Greg said, looking into the rearview mirror as the two officers approached the car with their weapons drawn. "I recognize both of them. They're homicide detectives from Dallas."

"What did they stop us for?" Rafe asked.

"Probably because I left the Dallas area. I'm out on bond right now, and I wasn't supposed to leave Dallas or go near the area of the murder *I didn't commit.*"

"Greg, why didn't you say so? It's my fault you're here, not yours."

"Don't worry about it. What are brothers for, even if they don't know each other," Greg said as he turned toward the window and rolled it down.

One of the officers shouted from the back of the car for both of them to put their hands out of their windows and hold them there. Rafe and Greg complied. Then while one of the detectives continued to cover them from behind Greg's car, the other one approached Greg and ordered him to get out. Then he made him lie on the roadway between the two cars while he handcuffed him. Then Rafe got the same treatment.

Rafe was mad, and it was all he could do to keep from saying something that might make matters worse. Greg was quiet, not saying a thing. Finally, speaking evenly, trying to act calm and control his temper, Rafe said, "There's a pistol in my waistband. My ID is in my wallet in my back pocket, along with my permit to carry a weapon. I work for a private investigator in Utah."

"And my mother's the governor of Texas," the younger of the two detectives said snidely.

Rafe waited in silence while his gun was taken and his ID examined. Then they also checked Greg's ID. Finally, they were both ordered to their feet and told to stand in front of the detectives' car. "Which one of you is Greg Ralston?" the older detective asked.

"You just looked at my ID," Greg responded. "I'm Greg."

"But this man over here could also be Greg, and you could be the one pretending to be a private eye," the second officer reasoned. "We think you two were trying to trade places so that the fingerprints at the murder scene wouldn't match. Well, it's not going to work. We'll take you both with us now and we'll make sure who is who from the booking fingerprints. And this little trick should be enough to make the judge decide to hold whichever one of you is Ralston without bail."

"I'm here to help Greg prove his innocence. And I suppose you two can prove who you are," Rafe said. "We need to see some ID."

"The older one's Sergeant Bill Latner," Greg spoke up. "And the other one is Detective Rhett Vancott. They may not be very bright, but they really are homicide detectives."

The officers looked at one another in surprise. Then Detective Vancott said, "They've got their stories put together well, it looks like."

Rafe shook his head in disgust. Then he said, "Listen, we have some things to do. Both of our lives are in danger, and we'd rather not be out here on the side of the freeway like this."

"If we had more time, it might be interesting to hear about why and how you're in danger," Detective Vancott said with a chuckle. "But we don't have time for your games."

Sergeant Latner asked, "What were the two of you doing at the police station back there?"

"Your partner just said you don't have time to listen. And I feel like a sitting duck here," Rafe said. "Let's get off the side of this freeway before someone comes along and takes a shot at us. I've dodged enough bullets for one day."

"You'll answer my questions," the sergeant said, his face hard and his eyes boring right through Rafe. "And we aren't interested in fairy tales."

"Fine. I was taken there by a cab driver after Harley and Deke Tuft spotted me talking on a pay phone. I'd already been shot at by

Deke. He missed, but I don't care to have it happen again because he might not miss the next time," Rafe said. "The officers back there believed me about like you appear to, but that's how it is."

"Is that so?" the sergeant said.

"Bill, let's just haul them back to Dallas. I've never heard such bull," Rhett said.

"And they aren't the only ones who are after me. The man who killed my mother, my adoptive mother, when I was six, could be anywhere, and he suspects that I'm after him," Rafe said, looking the sergeant in the eye. "My boss had an LAPD artist's drawings of him sent to every major police station in the country. You should have seen one very recently."

"This is garbage," Detective Vancott said.

But Rafe saw a look of interest in the eyes of the older detective, and his anger had unexplainably abated.

"Wait a minute, Rhett. I think I'd like to hear more. I remember seeing a flyer that was from the LAPD, but it had a Utah contact number on it."

"That's it," Rafe agreed.

"And did you say Harley Tuft a moment ago?" he asked Rafe.

"Harley and Deke," Rafe said.

"Harley, was he an old man, grizzled, about six feet tall? Thin and wiry, with kind of wild gray hair?"

"That fits him," Rafe agreed.

"You must not have mentioned his name back there to the cops."

"I'm sure I did."

"Well, you must have talked to someone who was pretty green, then. Out here just about every cop would know Harley, and the other one too, I suppose. Tough nuts."

"Come on, Sarge, let's take these guys in. I'm sure they've got all kinds of stories. We don't have time to listen," Rhett insisted.

Rafe ignored the young detective. "Sergeant, in the trunk of Greg's car you'll find the clothes I changed out of at the truck stop back on the edge of town. If you cared to take the time and go to the trouble, you'd find that there are traces of dirt that will match the house the Tufts live in and the woods where I was shot at by them and where I killed their dogs. And you can even check and see that my gun's been fired. I'm quite certain that I can take you back to where the spent casings are. The dead dogs might still be there too, along with one that I either missed or just injured."

"Sergeant," Rhett said impatiently. "I've heard enough."

"But I haven't, Rhett. Rafe's right about that poster. And if you were older you'd remember Harley Tuft. He's a tough old codger and meaner than a snake," Bill said. Then he turned again to Rafe. "Why don't we go back into town and talk to some senior officers there. I think that as soon as they hear Harley Tuft's name they'll be interested in your story."

"His wild story," a very disgusted Detective Rhett Vancott said.

"What were you doing with the Tufts?" Bill asked, ignoring his partner.

"They took me at gunpoint from in front of Greg's apartment in Dallas," Rafe said. "My rental car is still there. At least I hope it is. Anyway, they mistook me for Greg."

"Now that I can believe," Rhett cut in. "Which takes me back to our original point."

Rafe ignored him again and said, "They wanted to know how to find our birth mother. I don't know why. She's dead, and Greg and I were both adopted by different families shortly after we were born. Anyway, that's a whole story of its own, and we haven't even had the chance to sort it all out because we only met a few minutes ago. Now, please, let's get off this freeway. We both have more enemies than just the Tufts."

Detective Vancott was clearly fed up and he said, "This is all lovely, gentlemen, but I think it's time my partner and I got back to taking care of why we stopped you in the first place. We do have a murder investigation going on."

"As do I," Rafe said. "My mother's."

"I remember that case now," Sergeant Latner said calmly to his young partner. "I don't know why I hadn't connected it to that poster that came from the LAPD. It was years ago, when I was working in Vegas. It was during a bank robbery in a small town in Utah. Her son was the one who found her dead."

"Actually, I saw him do it," Rafe said. "I just didn't dare say so for a long time. I recently got a note from the guy. It seems like he's keeping track of me. He could very easily be after me, so I'd like to be able to defend myself if he comes."

Sergeant Latner turned to his younger partner. "Rhett, take Greg with you back to the police department in town. I'll ride with Rafe in Greg's car. We'll sort things out when we get there."

"But we don't even know which one is—" Rhett began.

"I believe I do," Bill countered.

"They may not even be brothers. One of them could be a disguise artist," Rhett argued stubbornly.

"I doubt that. Let's go, gentlemen," the sergeant said as he took the cuffs off Rafe's wrists. "Do you mind if your brother drives your car?"

"Not at all."

"Good. Well, I'll keep the gun for now. Rhett, take Greg with you."

* * *

It was only a glimpse, and the car was quite a ways down the street, but Lindsay was quite sure it was the same old vehicle that had stopped behind her when she blew the tire. She turned into the bank, trying not to think about the car and the fellow within. But once inside, she found she was trembling. A customer she knew, Professor Fallows from the university, was just leaving. She stopped and said hi to Lindsay. Then she asked, "Are you feeling okay, Lindsay? You look kind of peaked."

"Yes, I'm fine, Professor," she said. Then she had a thought. She was actually several minutes early for work and had not yet clocked in. So she said, "Would you mind doing me a favor?"

"I'd be glad to," Professor Fallows said, looking puzzled.

"Would you just give me a ride down the street and then back to the bank?" she asked.

That drew even more of a puzzled look, but the professor said, "Of course. Is something wrong?"

"I don't know for sure, but I'd appreciate your help."

Lindsay then explained about the flat tire that morning and how she thought she'd spotted the same car parked down the street from the bank, and she told the professor that she just wondered about it. She didn't mention the other times she'd seen the man she'd come to think of as her stalker. "I don't want him to recognize me and wonder what I'm doing," she said by way of explanation for the ride.

"Lindsay, is this someone who has been harassing you?" the professor asked astutely.

Lindsay just nodded, and then she got in Professor Fallow's car.

Lindsay thought she would pass out when they drove by the old Wagoneer. They were on the far side of the street, and she kept her head turned away as much as she could, but there was no doubt about what she saw. Her benefactor said, "Lindsay, let's go to the police right now. I can tell from the look on your face that you're frightened."

"It's okay," Lindsay said, even as she was trying to tell herself that she was being foolish, that it was just another coincidence. But she wasn't convincing herself. "We can go back now. And when we go past him again, would you read the license number to me?" Lindsay asked. "I have a friend who works for a private detective agency who asked me to call him back if I saw this guy again. Maybe he can figure out who he is."

"So you have sought help?" the professor said with some relief in her voice.

Lindsay didn't even look up when they passed the Jeep Wagoneer again. She wrote the number down that the professor read off the license plate. Then Lindsay pulled her phone from her purse and began to dial. They were at the bank again when Rafe picked up.

"Rafe?"

"Yes, it's me," Rafe assured her from his location hundreds of miles away.

"Just a minute. I need to tell you something," she said. Then she turned to Professor Fallows. "Thanks for your help. I'll be fine now."

"Are you sure?" the professor asked. "I'd be glad to take you down to the police station right now."

"That won't be necessary, but thanks for helping," Lindsay said as she got out and hurried up the walk. Professor Fallows had pulled up near the door in such a way that the stalker's view would hopefully be blocked.

"Rafe," she said as she opened the bank door, "that guy's parked a block down the street from the bank."

"Okay, Lindsay," his reassuring voice said, "try to stay calm. You'll be safe in the bank." Even as he said this, he had to block the images of his mother's death from his mind. *This isn't the same,* he told himself. "Now, I'll call the Provo Police Department and get an officer down there to meet you. What time do you get off?"

"Six."

"Okay, don't you leave the bank until an officer comes in there and talks to you."

"Okay," she said. "I'm sorry to bother you, Rafe. I know you're terribly busy and I'm probably being paranoid."

"You are not being paranoid," he said. "I wish I was there where I could help you personally. But I'll get you some help. And don't you take any chances."

"I won't, Rafe. You can count on it."

"Thank you. I'll call you back later," he said, then his comforting voice was gone, and she felt alone and vulnerable in the busy, crowded bank.

* * *

"A client?" Sergeant Latner asked as soon as Rafe had disconnected.

"Yes, a very frightened one," Rafe agreed. He hadn't thought of her as a client, but he guessed that in a way she was.

"Is she being stalked?" the sergeant asked.

"I think so. And it worries me. She was kidnapped years ago up in Idaho. The connections are mind-boggling, but it was somehow related to both me and Greg, though we didn't understand it back then. But I think it could have been Deke Tuft who did it. She managed to get away, but I'd feel terrible if anything ever happened to her."

"The Tufts again," the sergeant said softly. Then he asked with just the slightest hint of suggestiveness, "So, is she more than a client?"

"No, not really, but she's a good friend and a great girl. I'm worried about her. Do you mind if I make a call to the police in Provo now?"

"No, go ahead," Bill said.

They were back at the police department where Rafe had waited earlier for Greg before he finally was able to talk to an officer he knew in Provo. He explained what was happening with Lindsay, and the officer promised that someone would meet her at the bank. Satisfied that he could do nothing more, he closed Greg's phone and put it in his pocket.

Once the name Harley Tuft came up, the veteran officers were very interested in what Rafe had to say. One of them, a Captain Stevens, was especially interested. "Harley had a daughter," he said. "She was a pretty girl, but very reserved. She worked as a waitress here in town for a while. We used to go in there for coffee when I was a young officer. She disappeared suddenly, and the rumor was that she'd run off with some guy she met in the café, a very tall fellow, as I recall."

Rafe felt that only too familiar twist in his gut at the mention of the man who could be his biological father.

"I remember that I was sure at the time that I'd seen him talking to her," the captain went on. "But no one ever filed a missing person report, so we never did anything. We assumed she was glad for the opportunity to get away from her family."

"What did he look like?" Rafe asked.

"It's been a long time, but like I just mentioned, it seems like he was a tall man, like you and your brother, maybe even a little taller. He had brown hair, as I recall. He was a lot older than the girl. Stella was her name. She couldn't have been but sixteen or seventeen at the time. He'd have been at least ten years older. She had long blond hair, about the color or yours and Greg's," he said, looking from Rafe to Greg and back again. "Blue eyes. Very pretty eyes, but I remember talking about how she always looked like she was frightened of something. She wasn't a happy girl. Harley always brought her to work, and either he or Deke picked her up. They always seemed to get angry when they saw any young men talking to her. And young men liked to do that. When she smiled she was very attractive, but we didn't see that smile too much. She was afraid of something. Her father and brother, I would assume."

"Did she have a mother at the time?" Rafe asked.

"Yes, but she never came to town. Come to think of it, I don't remember seeing her around since long before Stella left. Haven't really thought about her mother since Stella ran off," Captain Stevens said. "Why do you ask?"

"Something I overheard Deke and Harley talking about after I got away from them and they were trying to find me. For some reason, they think that Stella knew something that could be dangerous for them. They seem to also think that Greg knows too, and possibly that I do. They seem to think Stella is alive and that she raised Greg," Rafe said. "I also remember one of them saying that if they caught me again, they'd put me beside my grandma, or something to that effect."

The captain sat back with a grim look on his face. "I'd like to have a talk with those two. I think we have enough for a warrant for their arrests based on what you've told us. I believe I know a judge that will give us a search warrant as well. Maybe we'll take a drive out there as soon as we can get the warrants, if you could show us where they live. I've never actually been to their place. They say it's a little farm way off the beaten path."

Rafe thought about how long it took him to walk back to civilization. It was definitely off the beaten path. "It might take me a while, but I think I can find it," Rafe said. "But trust me, those guys will use their shotguns if they feel threatened. And they may still have at least one dog, a killer dog."

"We have shotguns too, and weapons more sophisticated than that. Yes, I think we better make a visit as soon as we can get ready," Captain Stevens said.

"The kidnapping was in Dallas," Sergeant Latner reminded him.

"We have attempted murder in our area," the captain countered with a grim smile. "Sergeant, would you and Detective Vancott like to come out there with us?"

"I wouldn't miss it," the sergeant said.

"Bill, we have a murder of our own, or have you forgotten? We have a certain Dallas Maverick here who killed a man in a bar," Rhett remarked bitingly.

"And he's with us now," the sergeant reminded his younger partner.

"But he violated the terms of his bond," Rhett said. "Just because he's someone famous doesn't mean that we let him run all over us."

"Just because he's someone famous doesn't mean he's not innocent until proven guilty. We have some work to do on that case, but for now, I'm giving him the benefit of the doubt. We're going for a ride with these men."

Rafe and Greg had a moment to confer privately before Captain Stevens took Rafe with him to help in getting the warrants. "Rafe," Greg said, "Detective Vancott is determined to pin this thing in the bar on me. I swear, I wasn't even there when the fight occurred."

"I believe you," Rafe said. "But I think the best thing we can do right now is cooperate with these officers on the Tuft thing. If nothing else, I get the feeling that it's turning Sergeant Latner in your favor. That could help a ton when Thorn and I get to digging into what happened in that bar."

"Thorn?"

"Thorndike Stanbury, my boss. I'm going to see if he'll come down and help us."

"That would be great," Greg said.

"I also think that we might learn something about our own roots here. They sound unsavory, but I'd like to know if Stella Tuft was our birth mother, wouldn't you?"

"Yes, I would," Greg agreed.

An hour later they were all headed for the Tuft farm.

* * *

At the risk of being overly paranoid, Lenny took another look across the street. The brown pickup was beginning to look familiar. And it was making him nervous. The man who was pumping gas into the truck was tall but had his back to them. It was quite a ways over there, so he couldn't really be sure of anything. At this point, though, he couldn't be too careful, he told himself.

When he'd paid for his gas and had his wife and daughter back in his own truck, he said to Glenda, "I don't want to worry you more, but would you look across the street at that brown pickup?"

She looked back where he indicated. "What about it?"

"When I pull out of here, just see what that truck does," he said.

She got a panicked look on her face and asked, "Why? Do you think it's following us?"

"I said not to worry. I'm just curious."

"Sure you are," she said with a quiver in her voice. "I know you too well, Lenny Collings. I'll watch."

"So will I, Dad," said Stephanie from the backseat.

Lenny pulled away from the station. "He's coming," Glenda said. "When I get on the freeway up here a little ways, see what he does, and remember, it probably means nothing."

Lenny had been driving south on Interstate 25 through Santa Fe, New Mexico. They'd made good time, and he hated to have anything slow them down.

"It's back there a ways, Dad," Stephanie said after they'd entered the freeway a couple of minutes later. "But it's going the same way we are."

"He might have just needed gas when we did," Lenny said, trying to sound like it was no big deal. And it probably wasn't. Except that this was the second time they'd both filled their tanks at neighboring gas stations. But he didn't mention that to Glenda and Stephanie.

As they approached Albuquerque less than an hour later, Stephanie said, "Dad, that truck is still behind us. It's quite a ways back there, but it's still there. I'm getting scared."

"Don't be," Lenny said easily. "But just to make sure, we'll take the next exit and drive around Albuquerque for a little while."

When the brown truck also took that exit, Lenny became seriously worried, and his wife and daughter were in a state of near panic. "Okay," he said, trying to stay calm. "Suppose he is following us. All we have to do is some fast driving, and we can lose him."

Taking a chance that he'd never normally take, Lenny shot through a light just as it was turning red. Then he turned left, sped for a block, and turned right. He drove for twenty minutes through the city. "We'll take another route," Lenny said. "If that guy is following us, we don't want him to figure out that we're headed for Texas, in case he finds us again and we have to do this crazy act once more."

So instead of continuing south on Interstate 25, Lenny drove east out of the city on Interstate 40.

* * *

The tall man was raging. Somehow, Lenny Collings had figured out that he was being followed. Now he couldn't find him. For lack of a better idea, he got on I-25 and drove south.

CHAPTER 15

Armed with a search warrant and arrest warrants for both Harley and Deke, the officers headed south. After five or six wrong turns, Rafe finally directed them onto the badly rutted lane that led to the run-down farm where Harley and Deke Tuft had taken him. When they got close to the yard, Captain Stevens had everyone stop. He left Rafe and Greg with a couple of officers, telling them that he couldn't take them any farther because of the danger. Then he and the rest of the police officers went on. In ten minutes the captain returned and informed them that it looked like Harley and Deke had packed a few things and left in a hurry.

Rafe asked about the dog he thought had survived, and Captain Stevens reported that they hadn't seen any dogs. He then invited Greg and Rafe to come and observe as the search proceeded.

While several officers searched the yard for evidence to back up Rafe's story, others, including Greg, followed Rafe in the direction he'd fled after overpowering the Tufts. When they reached the fallen tree where Rafe had made his stand against the killer dogs, Rafe insisted that the officers go ahead of him. They found the bodies of the dead dogs, still lying where they'd fallen. And they found the spent .38-caliber shell casings Rafe told them would be there. In addition, they found fresh empty casings left behind after being fired from a 12-gauge shotgun.

That evidence, coupled with the tracks Rafe's boots had made, convinced the officers, even the skeptical Detective Vancott, that Rafe was telling the truth. Back at the farmyard, the search intensified. As authorized by the search warrant, the officers were allowed to search for any documents or other items that might verify the fact that the Tufts had an interest in Rafe and Greg. That effectively allowed a search of the entire premises.

Rafe and Greg had been instructed to touch nothing, but they were allowed to observe the search as it progressed. "Look what we have here," Sergeant Latner said suddenly.

Rafe and Greg both joined him, as did Captain Stevens and Detective Vancott. "They seem to have collected a pretty good history of you two," Bill said as he showed them the stack of newspaper and magazine clippings he'd found on a dusty shelf in the living room.

Rafe felt weak as he and Greg were shown the papers. For such seemingly disorganized men, Harley and Deke had neatly stacked all of the articles according to the dates they'd been written. On the bottom of the stack were the oldest. There were several articles from various papers and magazines that contained the story of Rafe's bareback championship. But what hit Rafe the hardest were several articles about the kidnapping of Lindsay Diamond in Pocatello, Idaho. None of the articles about her made mention of either of the twins. But the presence of the articles in the stack with the ones of the twins convinced Rafe that he'd been right when he suspected Deke Tuft of being responsible for Lindsay's kidnapping. The envelope from Lindsay must have been taken by either him or his father. He shuddered at the thought.

"So you know this girl?" Sergeant Latner asked Rafe, pointing to a picture of Lindsay taken when she was a high school freshman.

"Yes, she's the girl I've been concerned about today," Rafe said, "the girl I talked to when we were driving here. Unless I'm badly mistaken, I'd say that Deke Tuft was the one who kidnapped her up there in Idaho. His age would be right. Harley was too old. But I suppose he may have been around at the time. Also, Lindsay, though she remembered nothing for a long time after the kidnapping, did eventually remember some things. One of them was that the man who abducted her was driving a small, silver two-door. She thought it was dented up and rusted."

"Like the one that's broken down outside," Captain Stevens said. "Very interesting."

Greg was studying the pictures of Lindsay that accompanied the article. "Is she still this cute?" he asked Rafe.

Rafe shook his head sadly. "She gorgeous, Greg. And she's also a really good person."

Greg chuckled softly. "Don't let her get away, Rafe. I have a feeling she's perfect for you."

"I don't think she thinks that," Rafe said somberly.

"Well, my advice, brother, is to go after her."

"We'll see," Rafe said, thinking he would do just that after all this craziness was taken care of. He hoped she would forgive him eventually.

"It's strange that she's connected to this. I mean, all the guys used to kid me because she had a crush on me. But that was our only connection. I never even knew where she lived," Greg said. "And what puzzles me is why Deke, if you're right about him, would have kidnapped her. That makes no sense."

"Oh, but it does. It was to get to you," Rafe said. "Clear back then, Deke and Harley must have been worried about us and what they thought we knew."

"But how would he have known that I even knew her?" Greg asked.

"She wrote me a letter when I won the bareback championship. As you can see, the Tufts knew about it. And someone stole the letter from my house," Rafe explained. "She talked about you in it and sent some pictures of you. She thought I should know I had a look-alike. The letter didn't have your address, but it did have hers."

"Dang!" Greg exclaimed. "I had no idea. It makes me sick to think about it." He was silent for a moment, then asked, "So what else is in that stack of papers, Sergeant?"

"A lot," Bill said. And one by one he showed them articles about the two of them, mostly about Greg, however. At the top of the pile, he showed them some that pertained to Greg's rise to the NBA and his arrest for the murder in the bar.

Rafe couldn't keep his mind off Lindsay as they were looking at the articles. *Could the man who was stalking her have anything to do with the Tufts?* he asked himself over and over again.

Also of interest in the Tuft's filthy living room was another collection of articles that were about unsolved crimes that had occurred outside the general area of Northeastern Texas where the men lived.

Captain Stevens speculated that maybe Deke and Harley had something to do with them, that they were crimes they'd committed. Not one article referred to crimes in their local area. In that same stack was an article relating to the arrest and conviction of Harley for drunk driving.

In an attic above the room where Rafe had been locked in darkness for many hours, there was an old wooden box. Inside the chest were things that would likely have been of interest only to a woman. It's contents were very old and they didn't appear to have been disturbed for a long time. Harley and Deke may not have even known it existed. Near the bottom of the box there was a large envelope that was filled with pictures. They included ones of Harley as a young man and a beautiful blond woman. "That was his wife, Helen," Captain Stevens told them. "I'd sure like to know what became of her."

But what caught the interest of Rafe and Greg were the pictures of two children from when they were infants to their teenage years. One was a very pretty girl who only became more striking in the pictures of her as she became older. "That's Stella," the captain said. "As you can see, she was a very pretty girl."

The other child was Deke. Even at a young age, there was a look of meanness in his eyes. But what was most disconcerting was the likeness that Rafe and Greg bore to pictures of Deke as a young teenager. The two looked at each other, and silently acknowledged that they had found their roots, undesirable though they were.

Finally, folded in a frilly apron at the very bottom of the box, they found the diary of Helen Tuft. Captain Stevens began to read it aloud, beginning with the very last entry.

I would run away from here, but I have no way to take Stella. I can't leave her here with these beasts who are my husband and my son. I am the only protection she has. If only I could drive a car, then I'd load her up and drive as far away from here as I could get. But I can't. But I fear for my life if I stay. Harley and Deke get more violent every day. Stella says I shouldn't worry, but I do. I pray every day, but I still don't know what to do. If nothing else, I'll tell Stella when she gets home tonight that she's got to run away if anything happens to me. I sure do love her. She is such a beautiful and good girl. She is the only reason why I can't wish I'd never married Harley. I hate him now, and I fear him. He poisoned Deke right from the start, so he is a monster, just like his father. I protect my sweet daughter from them when I can, but I know she gets hurt sometimes too. Oh, Stella, dear Stella, how I pray for you.

The entry was dated about eighteen months before the twins' birth. Earlier entries portrayed vividly the abuse and hatred that had gradually increased over the years toward Helen Tuft by her husband and son. Captain Stevens looked up from the diary and said to Rafe, "You thought one of them said something about burying you by your grandmother?"

"I'm sure of it," Rafe responded sadly.

"Then her bones are here somewhere. I wonder if we can find them," the captain mused. "I think it would be worth the effort. It would be interesting to know how she died."

* * *

Kerry Sundolf had left his new, young, and very pretty wife at home where she was now unpacking her things. He'd been overseas with her on their honeymoon since their wedding. After eating the breakfast she'd prepared for him that morning, he'd gone downtown to catch up on work.

He was angry when he learned that one of his employees, a man he'd trusted with an important position, had been arrested for drunk driving during the night. He was needed at work, but had not yet been bailed out of jail. "I'll go get him out," Kerry said to the manager. "Have him finish up what you need him to do, then fire him."

A few minutes later, Kerry walked into the jail, cash in hand. He was angry that he had to be bothered about such things. He walked past a bulletin board that was plastered with wanted posters without a second glance and approached the receptionist. He stated his business, gave her the cash for his employee's bail, then impatiently wandered around the waiting room. He again passed the bulletin board, glancing at it as he walked. Then he took a double take and swung toward the board. For a moment, his heart almost quit beating.

Staring back at him from near the center of the board was a flyer with pictures that bore a remarkable resemblance to him. In the main drawing, the hair was a little thicker than his and a little longer. The face was clean shaven, while Kerry was sporting a neatly trimmed beard. And the nose wasn't right. But other than that, it was too much of a resemblance to ignore. Beneath the large picture were several smaller ones. They were variations of the main drawing, differing only in the amount of hair, the way it was combed, and with different styles of beards and moustaches. At the bottom of the small poster was a line asking any officer who might have a lead as to the identity of the man pictured there to contact a phone number that followed. It had an 801 area code.

Utah.

Kerry swore to himself. He then looked back at the woman. She was talking now to an officer. Neither of them were looking in his direction. He looked at the poster again. At the very bottom was a line that read *For police eyes only—do not post.* He reached up and tore the poster from the board and stuffed it in his pocket, chuckling to himself. He wasn't meant to have seen this. Some police employee messed up by posting it there. Rafe would pay for that mess up. Then he walked back over and summoned the receptionist. "I've had something come up," he said. "Tell Joe he can find his own ride when you release him."

She nodded, and Kerry turned and left the building. He waited until he was back in his car to pull out the poster and look at it again. There was no question about it. The picture was meant to be him. A murderous rage filled him. It wasn't a perfect likeness, but it was close enough. And it was evidence that Rafe was looking for him, like he'd been warned not to.

Kerry didn't think any cop would actually recognize him from the sketch, though. He'd been very careful over the years. His only slipup had been in letting that little boy live. He had assumed the kid couldn't remember enough to be damaging, anyway. But now here was this flyer. If it hadn't been for the nose job he wisely got a few years ago, this new development could have proved disastrous. The boy was just too persistent. With a new identity, a young wife, a luxurious home, a profitable and mostly legitimate business, and a growing reputation in the Portland area, Kerry couldn't afford to let anyone disturb his new lifestyle by bringing up his crimes of the past. He was no longer on the run. He was a man of growing influence in the area. No one suspected his dark history. Rafe Collings could not and would not be allowed to upset the life he now led. This poster was Rafe's death warrant, he swore to himself. It was only a matter of when and how it could be safely carried out.

* * *

The Wagoneer had not been anywhere in sight when Lindsay, accompanied by a Provo police officer, left the bank a few minutes after six. The officer talked like he believed her about the stalker, but she had the feeling he really didn't. However, after he'd followed her safely home, he told her to call him if the guy showed up again. He gave her his personal numbers. "I don't ordinarily do this for people, but Rafe's a good friend. I'm doing it for him," he said.

Because you don't really believe me, she couldn't help but think.

Cybil and Melly were eating when Lindsay walked in. "Hey, we made enough for you," Melly called cheerfully.

"Thanks. Let me put my things away and I'll join you. It smells really good," she said.

When she joined them a moment later, Cybil was telling Melly about her day at the office. "It's a really fun job. Mr. Stanbury is a really good detective and a lot of fun to work for. I just hope he's okay."

"Why wouldn't he be?" Melly asked.

"He went home sick before noon. He looked really pale," Cybil said. "He said he probably had a touch of flu and that he'd be back tomorrow. He needs Rafe here. They've got so much work to do."

"When will Rafe be back?" Melly asked.

"I don't know, but it's really lonely in the office with him gone. When he comes back I'm going to ask him to dinner. I probably can't afford it, but I won't let him know that. I know it's bold, but I think I have to make the first move. Since I sort of work for him, I guess it could be weird for him to ask me out. But I'm pretty sure he likes me."

That wasn't what Lindsay wanted to hear, because as hard as she tried to avoid thoughts of Rafe, she simply couldn't get him off her mind. But she wasn't the kind of girl that would step in and try to steal a man from someone else. If he liked Cybil and Cybil was interested in him, then she'd just have to keep her distance from Rafe if she could. She wished now that she hadn't called him about her stalker. She was frightened, and yet she couldn't help but think that it was all in her head.

After they'd finished dinner and the dishes were done, Cybil said, "I'm going to go for a run. Would you two like to come with me?"

Melly said she would. Lindsay thought about it for a minute, then said, "I'm really tired tonight. I think I'll pass. But thanks, Cybil."

She didn't want to see that man out there, if he was out there, for she was afraid she might say something, and she didn't want Cybil to know. Cybil was no dummy. She was capable of putting two and two together, and when she did, she'd have a million questions. Lindsay didn't want to talk about that guy. She only wanted the *coincidences* to stop and for him to disappear.

Melly and Cybil were laughing as they left. "Sure you don't want to come?" Cybil asked as the door began to close.

Lindsay didn't have time to respond before it shut, but she did want to go. She hated being a coward, and she loved physical activity. Maybe she could catch them. She hurried into her room, stripped off her slacks and blouse, jumped into a pair of shorts, and pulled on a T-shirt and light jacket. She quickly laced her running shoes and rushed out, forgetting to lock the door behind her in her haste.

She raced up the walk. She thought the girls would be heading for the jogging path, and she hoped to catch up with them before they reached it. She lowered her head and began running quite rapidly. But when she reached the path, her roommates were nowhere in sight. Maybe they'd decided to just jog around some city blocks, she thought. She almost turned back. Then she stubbornly told herself that the red-haired guy had undoubtedly been scared off by the police officer earlier, and she really had nothing to worry about. So she turned onto the jogging path, slowed her pace, and tried to enjoy the brisk late-September air.

* * *

Dempsey watched her until she was out of sight on the path. She was so desirable. He wasn't sure how much longer he could stand to just watch. He wanted her, but he wasn't quite ready for her at home. But he was afraid she was getting suspicious. When that officer drove up to the bank, it really worried him. And he got angry when the two of them walked out together. He'd have to speed up his preparations. He wanted things to be just right for Lindsay when he took her to *their* home.

He knew she hadn't seen him this time. He was being more careful. He'd left the Jeep and rode his bike. He was still on his bike now. Maybe he'd just pedal back to her apartment. Perhaps he could even take a look inside. He'd watched her roommates leave, and unless he was mistaken, Lindsay hadn't taken time to lock the door when she left. He would hurry. It wouldn't pay to be caught in the apartment. Maybe he could just take a little something from her room. Just a little keepsake, something of hers to place next to him on his pillow, something to comfort him until he had her all to himself.

* * *

The tall man was pretty sure that Lenny Collings was headed for Texas. That was where the other boy was living—Greg, the one who was a ballplayer, the one with lots of money. It would be easier this way, not having to follow them. He'd just go down there, figure out where Greg lived, and wait for a chance to do something to let them all know he meant business. It was most unfair the way his boys were keeping all the wealth to themselves. They owed him! If it hadn't been for him, they wouldn't even be alive. Whether they liked it or not, he was their father.

* * *

"Pa, we left too fast," Deke was arguing. "What if the cops come to the place sometime. They might see the news stories you liked to cut out. And who knows what else they might find? We should've gotten rid of them."

"Yer worrying too much," Harley said.

"And yer not?" Deke scoffed. "They find what we put in the orchard, and they'll look for us until they find us."

"If they believe Greg, they might come after us anyway. We better just keep going," Harley argued. "The farther we are from Texas, the safer we'll be."

"I'm driving. I say we go back," Deke said as he slammed on the brakes and pulled off the road. "We'll dig Ma up and put her down in the swamp like we shoulda done in the first place. And we can get rid of all the stuff we collected on Stella's boys."

"They could be watching fer us already," Harley warned.

"What we got to lose? Some cop gets in the way, we'll finish him off and put him in the swamp too." Deke was turning around as he spoke.

"Yer a darn fool, boy," his father said.

"And yer not?" he retorted.

"Let me out," Harley demanded. "I ain't going back there. Yer crazy, boy. I ain't going to prison for nobody."

"We're in it together, Pa. Yer coming back with me. It won't take us long, and we'll work in the dark. We'll park in the south forty and walk up to the house. We got shotguns. Ain't nobody going to mess with us and live to tell about it."

Harley stared hard at him, then he slumped back in his seat. "You better not get us kilt," he warned.

Deke didn't respond. He just glared at his father and then drove.

CHAPTER 16

Cybil heard Melly cry out and turned to see her roommate on the ground behind her. She was holding her ankle. Cybil ran back to her. "Hey, what happened?" she asked.

"I twisted my ankle," Melly moaned.

"How did you do that?"

"That crack in the sidewalk," Melly said, pointing. "I didn't see it and stepped in it. This hurts really bad."

"Okay, we better head back to the apartment. I'll have to help you," Cybil said. "If it's too bad, I'll run home and get my car."

"If you help me, I'll be able to make it," Melly said with a grimace.

"Okay, but when we get there, I'll wrap it for you." Cybil was examining Melly's ankle as she spoke. It was already beginning to swell.

Fortunately, they had decided to just run in the neighborhood; and though they'd planned to keep going for another half hour or so, they were not far from the apartment at that moment. With Melly hopping on one foot while holding onto Cybil for support, they cut through one block, crossed the street, cut through another block, and turned right. Another block and a half brought them to the apartment.

Cybil grabbed the door handle and tried to turn it, but it wouldn't give. "Huh, the door's locked," she said. "Maybe Lindsay decided to go out." She fished in the pocket of her shorts for her key and unlocked the door. "Let's get you to the sofa. I'll fix an ice pack. That's getting quite swollen."

"Sounds like Lindsay's in her room," Melly said. "I wonder why she locked the door."

"Maybe we did when we left, but I don't remember doing it. Oh, well, here, sit down," Cybil instructed her.

Melly moaned in pain as she eased herself onto the sofa. "I can't believe I did this. I'm so clumsy."

"It can happen to anyone," Cybil responded in an attempt to comfort her. "I'll hurry with the ice pack."

Cybil opened the freezer and then paused. It sounded like Lindsay was opening her window. That was strange, because the temperature in the apartment was quite comfortable. *Maybe she just needs fresh air,* she thought as she pulled out a couple of trays of ice cubes. It was quiet in Lindsay's room after that, and Cybil didn't give Lindsay any more thought as she prepared the ice pack.

After applying the ice to Melly's swollen ankle, Cybil went to the bathroom and looked for something to tape the ankle with. She couldn't find anything. She might have to go to the store and buy something to wrap Melly's ankle with. Unless . . . maybe Lindsay had something. She tapped on the door to Lindsay's bedroom. When there was no response, she called out, "Lindsay, do you have anything we could use to wrap Melly's ankle? She sprained it."

There was still no answer. Lindsay must have fallen asleep, she decided. She hated to disturb her, but she also didn't want to have to buy anything if Lindsay could help out. So she took hold of the door handle and turned. Lindsay's bedroom door was locked. Getting irritated now, Cybil pounded harder on the door and shouted, "Lindsay, can you hear me? I need your help."

"I know she's in there," Melly called out from the sofa. "I could hear her moving around. There's no way she's had time to go to sleep."

Cybil reentered the living room. "Well, she's not answering, and it's quiet in there now. If she was asleep, my knocking and calling to her would have woken her up. Maybe she's mad at us for something. But I don't know what it would be. We did invite her to come running with us, but she didn't want to."

"Lindsay doesn't get mad very easily," Melly reminded her roommate. "But she was acting funny at dinner. She didn't say much when we were eating. Now that I think of it, she seemed worried or something."

"Yeah, she did," Cybil agreed.

"So do you think there's something really troubling her?" Melly asked anxiously.

"Possibly. Maybe it's bothering her that I'm attracted to Rafe," Cybil said thoughtfully. "I don't know, but she was certainly not herself at dinner. I'll go knock on her door again."

There was still no response from Lindsay's room. When Cybil again entered the living room, Melly had a funny look on her face. "I know this sounds crazy, but I thought I heard her open her window when you were getting an ice pack for me."

"Yeah, I thought the same thing," Cybil agreed. "And it's been quiet in there since then."

"Like I said, this sounds crazy," Melly went on. "But I wonder if she left . . . went out the window. Maybe she doesn't want to talk to us for some reason."

"Gee, I hadn't thought of that. I suppose you could get out of the windows in our bedrooms, but you'd have to push the screen out first," Cybil said thoughtfully. She moved purposefully toward the front door. "That would be a totally weird thing to do, but I'll just go around back and look. If nothing else, I'll be able to see if she's asleep or maybe pretending to be."

The screen to Lindsay's window was lying on the grass behind the apartment, and the window was open as wide as it would go. Surprised that Lindsay would do something like this to avoid her roommates, Cybil walked to the window, stood on her toes, and peered over the window sill.

As she expected, Lindsay was not in her room. What had they done to make Lindsay act like this? she wondered as she went back inside and informed Melly. Then, remembering that she still needed the wrapping for Melly's ankle, she grabbed her car keys. "I'll be back. I'm going to run down to the store and get something to wrap that ankle with," Cybil said. She drove to the store, quickly made her purchase, and came straight home to wrap Melly's ankle.

A few minutes later, Lindsay came in. "Hey, what happened to you?" she asked when she saw Melly on the sofa with her foot propped up.

"I sprained my ankle," Melly complained. "We should have gone on the jogging trail. I stepped in a big crack in the sidewalk, and down I went."

"I'm sorry. I left right after you guys and tried to catch up, but when I got to the jogging path I could see that you weren't there. I figured you must have decided to just run around the neighborhood, but by then I figured I wouldn't be able to find you."

Just then, Cybil came out of her bedroom and said, "What, decided to use the door this time instead of your window?"

"What are you talking about?" Lindsay asked, a look of confusion on her face.

"You know very well what I'm talking about. After we got back, you left, but you didn't use the door. I hope you can get your screen back in." Cybil had planned to say more, for she was quite irritated. But Lindsay's face was stricken and white, and Cybil thought maybe she'd said too much already.

"I left right after you did, and I used the door," Lindsay said in a weak voice as she stepped from the living room, around the corner, and down to her bedroom.

Cybil followed her. Lindsay grabbed her doorknob and twisted. "It's locked," she said.

"Didn't you lock it?" Cybil asked, confused, her anger draining away. She could tell from the look on Lindsay's face that something was terribly wrong.

"No, I didn't. In fact, I don't think I even locked the front door when I left," Lindsay admitted. "I decided just as you guys left that I wanted to go. I was hurrying, hoping I could catch up with you, and I don't think I remembered to lock the door."

"You must have," Cybil said, as she felt her skin prickle. "It was locked when we got home."

"No, I really don't think I did," Lindsay said softly. "In fact, the more I think about it, the more sure I am that I didn't. I was in a hurry to catch up with you guys. And I know I didn't lock my bedroom door. I don't think I even closed it."

"Lindsay," Cybil said, beginning to feel frightened herself, "Melly and I both heard you moving around in your room right after we got back."

The two of them had walked back into the living room and Melly spoke up. "We heard you open your window." She paused. "At least, we heard your window being opened."

"I never open my window," Lindsay said. "Cybil, the key to my room is in my room. I can't get in."

"Unless we crawl through the window," Cybil suggested.

"Let's do it," Lindsay agreed. "Then I can unlock the door from the inside."

"This is spooky," Melly said, her round face white and her eyes wide.

Cybil followed Lindsay outside. She was scared, and she rushed to get close to Lindsay. As they rounded the edge of the apartment building, the two of them walked side by side in the near darkness. When they got to the back, Lindsay spotted the screen where it lay beneath her window.

"Somebody shoved it out," she said. She approached the open window, looked in, then said with a choked voice. "Cybil. Someone's been in there. My stuff is all messed up."

"A burglar," Cybil said, shivering at the very thought. "Melly and I must have come in time that we scared him off before he got into all of our rooms. I'm sure no one was in mine. But we haven't checked Melly's room. We better do that."

"Unless I'm mistaken, he's not a burglar," Lindsay said. "He's a stalker."

"What are you talking about?" Cybil asked as a fresh chill ran all the way up her spine. She was worse than frightened now. She was wishing Rafe was in town. She'd call him and he'd come over if he were here, she thought. Maybe she should call Mr. Stanbury. But he was sick, she remembered.

"I think some guy's been stalking me," Lindsay said. "A police officer followed me home from the bank."

"You've had a stalker and you haven't mentioned it to us?" Cybil said.

"I didn't want to scare you guys."

"Let's go back inside. I'm not crawling in there," Cybil said. "Anyway, we need to call the police."

"I'll call the officer that followed me home. He's a friend of Rafe's and said I could call him anytime," Lindsay explained.

"A friend of Rafe's?" Cybil asked. "Have you talked to Rafe? We haven't been able to reach him."

"Yeah, I talked to him. When did you last try calling him?" Lindsay asked.

"Sometime this morning. Mr. Stanbury went home sick before lunch; it was before that. How did you get a hold of him?" Cybil asked.

"He called his dad from a pay phone. His dad told him I'd been trying to call to talk to him about the guy I thought was stalking me. He called me after that and told me I should call the police and told me how to get a hold of his friend at the department. The officer met me at the bank and followed me home. He said to call him if I saw the guy again," Lindsay explained.

When they were back inside the apartment, Lindsay called the officer who had escorted her home earlier. When she explained what had happened, he said, "Don't touch anything. I'm on my way, and I'll have some other officers head over as well. In the meantime, lock your doors and don't let anyone in but us."

Cybil was listening to the call on the extension, and she hung up when Lindsay did. The two girls looked at each other, then Lindsay walked over and locked the door.

"What's happening?" Melly asked.

After they told her, the three very frightened friends huddled while they waited for help to arrive.

* * *

The rental car was right where Rafe had left it. It didn't look like anyone had touched it. Greg had him move it behind the apartments where he had an extra space for visitors, then the two went inside. Greg's apartment was spacious and obviously new. Greg showed Rafe to the second bedroom, which had a bathroom attached. Rafe was totally exhausted, but he wanted to talk with Greg more before he went to bed, so he showered, put on some of his own clothes, then joined his brother in the living room, feeling nervous about staying there for even one night.

"So what do we do now?" Greg asked.

"I was thinking about that as I showered. First, I know you've got a really nice place here and all, but it might be best if we found a hotel room for the night," Rafe said.

"You're kidding, right?" Greg asked.

"No, not really. You know what my dad said a little while ago," Rafe began, referring to a call he'd made to Lenny less than an hour ago. "The tall man who claims to be our father trailed them clear to Santa Fe. At least, Dad thinks it was him. They lost him and they're taking a longer route here, but it could be that the tall man will come directly here now. If he can get your phone number, he can get your address. And I don't think we want to let him find us sleeping here."

"We can lock the doors," Greg reminded him.

"He got in our ranch house several years ago. At least, I think he did. And our doors were locked. So were the windows, and nothing was broken out. Really, Greg, I don't think we should take the chance."

"Okay, you're probably right. Let me gather up a few things, listen to the messages on my answering machine, and then we'll go."

Rafe sat on the sofa while Greg busied himself in his bedroom. He slumped down and closed his eyes. He awoke with a start when Greg said, "Rafe, you won't believe this!"

"What?" Rafe asked as he got to his feet, rubbing his eyes and wondering what was happening.

"I just talked to Jim Hanks, my agent," Greg started.

"Oh yeah, what did he want?"

"He says the Mavericks are thinking about letting me go already."

"That's crazy," Rafe said. "Why?"

"Because of the murder rap," Greg responded angrily.

"But you're not convicted of anything," Rafe said. "They can't do that."

"That's what I said. But Jim said that even though they would have to pay me the first year because of our contract, that they didn't have to let me play, nor would they renew my contract after that."

"Then play for another team," Rafe suggested.

"I said that too, but Jim said it wouldn't be easy to get anyone to sign me now."

"Even when we get you off?" Rafe asked.

"If I get off," Greg answered with a long face. "Then Jim said maybe someone else would sign me if I'm found not guilty, but not to hold my breath."

Rafe looked Greg square in the eye and said, "Greg, we are going to find a way to prove you weren't in the bar when that man died. Then we'll worry about what to do about your career. If you're as good as they say you are, you'll still play in the NBA."

"I'm glad you think so, because Jim Hanks doesn't."

"Then get another agent," Rafe suggested.

"I'll have to, because Jim just told me he wouldn't represent me anymore."

"What a jerk," Rafe said. "But believe me, Greg, we are going to get this thing straightened out. Sergeant Latner told me just before we left the Tuft house that he was going to dig deeper."

"Honestly?" Greg asked, surprised.

"Yes, that's what he said. And with his help and my boss's help, if I can find him, we'll figure out what really happened in that bar. My boss hasn't been answering his phone. He must be busy. I'll call the office first thing in the morning. Anyway, we'll find witnesses that will prove you'd left before the fight."

"But I left alone, and I came straight home. I don't think anyone saw me except the cab driver."

"Cab driver?" Rafe asked.

"Yes. I'd left my car here so I wouldn't be tempted to drive after I'd been drinking."

"And you told the police that?"

"Oh yeah, but they claim they couldn't find anyone who remembered bringing me home."

"Then they didn't look hard enough. We'll find him. And we'll also find some of the others in the bar that will admit to seeing you leave. Relax, brother. We'll get you out of this."

"I'll make it worth your time if you do," Greg said.

"You know what would make it worth my time?" Rafe asked.

"Whatever you want, I'll pay it," Greg said. "If I have it, that is."

"Not money," Greg said. "If you'll promise never to drink again, it will be pay enough for me. Of course, Mr. Stanbury will need to be paid, but all I want is for you to not drink again."

"You've got my word," Greg said without a moment's hesitation. "I haven't had a drink since I was arrested. I'm not much of a drinker anyway. I'm through with it."

Rafe clapped him on the back. "That's great, Greg. Now, let's get out of here."

* * *

"Is anything missing?" an officer asked.

"Well, my purse is here, money and all," Lindsay said as she rustled through it. Then she looked around the room, which had by now been photographed and dusted for fingerprints. "My stuffed kitten is gone!" she said suddenly.

"Your stuffed kitten?" the officer asked, raising an eyebrow. "You think someone stole your stuffed kitten? Now that's weird."

"Yes, it's gone. I've had it for years. I always keep it on my bed, right here, when I'm not sleeping," she said as she touched her pillow at the head of her bed.

"What color is it?" the officer asked.

"Yellow and white," she answered.

"Anything else missing?"

Again she looked around the room. Then she looked in the drawers of her dresser. Her heart about got caught in her throat when she realized what else had been taken. "Oh no," she moaned.

"What is it?" the officer asked.

"One of my nightgowns is gone."

"Just one?"

"Yes, I only have three, and the other two are here."

"What color is the missing one?" he asked.

"Yellow. I like yellow," she answered with a shiver.

* * *

He placed the stuffed kitten on his pillow and laid the nightgown below it. Then he smiled to himself. *This will do for now,* he thought. *But just for a little while, my kitten. Just for a little while.*

CHAPTER 17

Lenny, Glenda, and Stephanie met Rafe and Greg at their hotel the next morning. Rafe explained why they'd moved to a hotel, and Lenny agreed that it was best. As the family met Greg, there was a lot of emotion. "You look just like Rafe," Stephanie cried, and she gave him a huge hug.

Lenny and Glenda both shook his hand and told him how glad they were to meet him.

"You shouldn't be," he said. "All I've done is caused Rafe a lot of trouble."

"You're his brother," Lenny said as he felt his voice choke up. "It's great for him to be able to meet his brother."

"His brother who's in a lot of trouble," Greg said morosely.

"My brother who is going to be cleared of the charge," Rafe said with resolution. "And we'll start getting that done this morning." He was anxious to get finished here in Texas and get back to the other things he had to do. *Like making sure Lindsay is safe,* a persistent voice whispered in his head.

"What can we do to help?" Lenny asked.

Rafe smiled affectionately at his father. "You can keep yourself, Mom, and Stephanie safe," he said.

"That's why we came here, but what can we do to help while we're here?" he asked. "There's got to be something we can do that will save you some time."

Stephanie said, "Maybe we could drive through the area where Greg's apartment is and see if the guy who was following us is there."

"Not a chance," Rafe said quickly. "He'd recognize Dad's truck. Remember, he's the reason you left Ephraim. If he sees you, then you would be in a lot of danger."

"Then we won't drive the truck," she said. "We'll drive something else."

"Good idea," Lenny agreed. "We can go rent a car and leave the truck parked here at the hotel."

"No need to rent a car. You can take mine," Greg said. "I'll be going with Rafe today while we try to find a cab driver we need to talk to. I doubt if he knows what I drive, and even if he does, there are a lot of cars around like it. Just be careful that he doesn't see your faces if he happens to be hanging around."

"Sounds like a plan," Lenny said firmly.

"I don't know, Dad," Rafe said. "It worries me."

"Don't let it worry you, son. We'll take care of ourselves. I won't take any chances," he promised. "And I'd go crazy just sitting in a hotel room. You know me, I don't spend much time sitting around."

"You don't need to sit around. There are a lot of things to do in Dallas and Fort Worth. There's the zoo and museums and . . ." Rafe paused, thinking. "Hey, I know, you could go visit a cattle ranch outside of the city. You'd all enjoy that," he suggested brightly.

"Maybe later, if we have a lot of time to kill," Lenny agreed. "But for right now, I'd really like to know if that tall man shows up. And if he does, maybe we could plan a little surprise for him."

"Surprise?" Rafe asked suspiciously.

"Sure. Maybe it's time we all went on the offensive. But that can wait. Let's see if he shows up first."

Rafe still didn't feel good about his family driving in the neighborhood of Greg's apartment, although reason told him that they should be safe enough. But as he and Greg left to begin the search for the cab driver who'd driven Greg home from the bar that fateful night, little worries continued to gnaw at his stomach. He couldn't quite put his finger on what it was that made him so nervous, but somehow, he had the feeling that his dad's simple plan was flawed. But without having something more than just his feelings to go on, he knew Lenny wouldn't back down on what he was doing.

He needed Thorn's advice, he concluded and he dialed the number of the office. There was no answer. He knew that Cybil would be in a little later, that this was one of the mornings she had classes. He tried Thorn's cell phone. There was no answer. Finally, he tried his home phone. Thorn's wife answered and Rafe asked if he could speak to Thorn.

But she broke down and sobbed. "He's had a heart attack," she told him as soon as she was able to speak.

"Oh no!" Rafe said as a terrible knot formed in his stomach. "How bad is it?"

"Pretty bad. They just took him in an ambulance. I'm going to the hospital now," the distraught woman said. "I don't know what I'd do if I lost Thorn."

Rafe didn't know what he'd do, either. "Tell him I'm praying for him," he told Mrs. Stanbury.

"I will," she promised. "He thinks a lot of you. As they took him away, he said, 'I've got to get on my feet right away. Rafe needs my help.'"

"I'll manage," Rafe said hopelessly. "You tell him to just get better."

"What was that about?" a worried Greg asked when Rafe had completed his call.

"I guess we're on our own," Rafe said. "My boss had a heart attack."

* * *

"I've got to go away for a few days," Kerry told his young wife as they sat sipping cold drinks on the patio at the back of their house. "I'll need for you to stay here and take care of things while I'm gone."

"But you said we'd be together all the time," Mina said, with a tiny frown she knew he'd find irresistible.

"A figure of speech," he said, and he leaned over and gently kissed her lips. "That means that we won't get divorced or even separated. It means we'll be together whenever I'm not working or golfing or something like that and you're not with some of your lady friends. Think about it, no two people can be together every hour of every day. They'd drive each other crazy."

"I know all that," she said, running her fingers lightly over his hand on the table. "But I thought that when you had a trip to go on that I'd be able to go with you, then we could go out to dinner and find some entertainment, that kind of thing. And you wouldn't have to be alone in hotel rooms at night," she argued sweetly.

"It's nice of you to think of me," he said. "But this trip is one where there will be no leisure time. Anyway, we just got back from a very nice trip. This one is not one you'd enjoy. I'll be very, very busy. Anyway, I won't be gone long."

"Please," she begged. She loved traveling and didn't want to miss out. She was prepared to try another argument, but a dangerous look appeared in his eyes that startled her, frightened her even. She leaned back, wondering if there was a side to her husband that she didn't know.

After a minute, his face softened. "Tell you what," he began as he pulled out his wallet and extracted a credit card from it. "Take this and go do some serious shopping."

She looked down at the silvery card and saw it had her name imprinted on it. "For real?" she asked.

"Yes, of course. Have some fun. I should be back in two or three days."

Mina smiled, and he kissed her again. Then they walked into the house. He packed a small bag, and she followed him to his new silver Cadillac. She watched him drive off and kept watching until he was out of sight, then she looked at the credit card she still held in her hand. She would have a ball.

But as she walked back in the house, her new and very plush house, she couldn't shake the image of that look that had been in his eyes. She knew she hadn't imagined it, and again she felt a shiver of fright. She told herself that she should not be pushy with him again. She'd heard of wives being abused by their husbands, even pretty young women like herself. She knew nothing of his past. She promised herself that she'd be more careful from now on. She didn't want to get hurt, and she didn't want to lose access to his money.

* * *

Kerry left the new silver Cadillac in a long-term parking lot where he paid cash in advance for several days' parking. Then he took a cab to a rental car company where he rented a car under one of several aliases he'd kept just for an emergency such as this. Then he headed for Utah. He could have flown, but there was the problem of getting his gun on the plane. Anyway, he wanted this trip to be as anonymous as he could make it. Later, in another state, he'd rent another car under another name. After he'd taken care of Rafe, his last rental car would be abandoned, as would the identities he'd used on the trip. The gun he used would also vanish. Then he'd rent another car, using another name, and drive back to Portland. He hoped that he could then safely resume the life he'd set up for himself.

The only other thing that worried Kerry a bit was the pictures that must have been sent to police agencies all across the country. But there wasn't much he could do about that. Of course, not many cops knew his face. And unless someone else made a mistake, the flyer wouldn't be posted for the public to see.

* * *

Lindsay was disappointed to learn that morning from the police that whoever had been in her apartment the night before had worn gloves. The only prints the officers were able to identify had been her own, along with a few that had been left by Cybil and Melly. "We ran the license plate number you gave us," she was told by a detective. "But it comes back to someone we can't find a trace of. Even the address in Salt Lake is false. It doesn't exist."

Lindsay shivered. This was getting more frightening all the time. "What can I do to protect myself?" she asked.

The officer shrugged. "Just keep your eyes open. I wouldn't go anywhere alone if I were you. For now, I'd say the guy probably won't hurt you, but that could change in time. It often does with stalkers like this."

"But I can't have someone with me all the time," she protested. "I have school and I have a job."

"And you have your life," the officer said in a way that made her feel more vulnerable than ever. "You watch out for yourself."

Melly, who was lying on the couch with her sprained ankle propped up, said, "I'm not doing much, Lindsay. I still don't have a job and I can't very well go job hunting like this. Maybe we can sort of hang out together for a while."

"But we have our classes," Lindsay protested.

"I'll go with you to yours, and you can come to me with mine," Melly said sensibly.

"But there is my job," she said. "I don't have an excuse to stay home, and I don't want to risk losing it."

"Being stalked could be considered an excuse," the detective suggested. "Why don't you stay home?"

Lindsay shook her head. "I can't just sit around here and wait for him to come again," she said. "Anyway, he's already shown that he can get in our apartment."

"But you left the door open," he reminded her.

"He could probably get in if it were locked," Lindsay countered. "I'll be fine going to work."

"I'll ride with you, Lindsay. Isn't there a break room in the bank where I could study while I wait for you to work?" Melly asked.

"You don't have to do that," Lindsay protested.

"But I want to. I'd be glad to help you. Anyway," she said with a shiver, "I don't think I want to be home alone while you and Cybil are working."

Lindsay certainly understood that. So it was settled. When the two of them left the apartment, they both looked nervously for the brown Jeep Wagoneer, but they couldn't see it. And they also didn't spot it as they drove to campus.

* * *

Lindsay's apartment was empty again, but even though it was tempting to go in and spend more time in her room, Dempsey didn't want to take the chance of being seen by a neighbor, and that was likely to happen if he broke in while it was still light. So he got on his bike and pedaled off. Maybe he'd just go home and hold the stuffed kitten for a few hours, think about Lindsay, and look at the picture of her he'd taken from her roommate's purse and put in his wallet.

* * *

The tall man was angry that he still had to take risks like he'd taken during the night. If his sons would just give him the money he'd asked for without making him go to so much trouble, he could go to some exotic place and take it easy for a while. He wouldn't have to steal a car. He hadn't stolen cars since before he'd married Stella. But he couldn't afford to buy another one right now, nor did he want to waste the time it would take to do that. He couldn't keep driving the brown F-150 pickup he'd bought in Utah, though. He was afraid that Lenny Collings and Rafe and Greg might be watching for it down in Texas. If that was where Lenny was headed, and if Rafe was down there like he suspected. He was fairly confident that he was. After all, he'd told Rafe to talk Greg into giving him the money he needed.

He'd taken the gold-colored Toyota he was driving from a driveway that had been within walking distance of the shopping mall where he'd left the pickup. It had been easy, really, but he still knew it was risky, and he was getting too old to take risks. He'd picked the lock on the front door, found a purse in the kitchen, and had taken the keys from the purse. He'd also taken some of the cash in the purse, then he'd left as quietly as he'd entered.

He'd driven the Toyota back to the mall, transferred all of his belongings from the truck to the car, including the bags of nitrogen fertilizer, which he now hauled in the trunk. Then he'd resumed his trip to Dallas, wondering as he drove what had ever become of Stella's father and brother. He'd detested them. Stella had feared them, and for good cause. He'd been tempted at times, just for spite, to call the cops down there and tip them off over Stella's dead mother, but he'd never bothered.

* * *

Rafe was worried sick over Thorn. He needed his advice, but since it was not possible right now, he simply was doing the best he could on his own. The first thing he and Greg had done was look up the cabbie that drove Greg home that night from the bar.

"Yes, I remember you," Benny Jordan said as he looked at Greg. "I picked you up at the bar where that man got killed a few nights ago."

Rafe nodded. *So far, so good,* he thought. "Can you give us the exact time you picked him up and the time when you delivered him to his apartment?" he asked.

"My dispatcher can get that information for you," the cabbie said.

"Good, we'll go talk to your dispatcher then. And I'll need a statement from you saying that you remember giving Greg a ride home that night," Rafe told him.

"Sure, but hey, wait a minute," Benny said, pointing to Greg, "didn't they say you killed that guy yourself? I don't know if I should get involved."

"You are involved," Rafe said. "My brother wasn't even at the bar when the victim died."

"Can you prove that?" the cabbie asked.

"That's what we were hoping *you* could do," Rafe informed him. "You see, Greg couldn't have committed the murder while you were driving him home. We know what time that was, but the cops don't believe Greg. Let's go see your dispatcher right now and get those records. They'll prove that Greg couldn't have done it."

"Really?" Benny asked.

"Yes," Rafe agreed. "And then you'll be a hero for saving a member of the Dallas Mavericks from unjustly spending the rest of his life in prison."

The little fellow beamed. "You'll get me tickets to a game won't you?" he asked Greg.

Greg looked doubtfully at Rafe. Rafe gave an almost imperceptible nod of his head. Then Greg said, "Of course. You've earned them."

The cabbie, whom they had found at his apartment after a visit to the cab company's headquarters, rode with them in Rafe's rental car. Back at the company, Benny told the on-duty dispatcher what they needed. It only took a few minutes, and the information that could clear his brother of murder was in Rafe's hands. Then the cabbie sat down and wrote his statement. When that was done, Rafe said to him, "It would be worth fifty bucks if you'd come down to the police department with us right now and tell the police what you've told us. If you don't do it now, they'll be looking you up later anyway. And it might not be as convenient for you then."

Benny reluctantly agreed, and he rode with Rafe and Greg downtown. "Is Sergeant Bill Latner in?" Rafe asked after they had arrived at police headquarters.

"Who's asking?" the desk sergeant inquired while looking at Greg and Rafe over the top of his glasses.

"Rafe Collings and his brother Greg Ralston," Rafe said.

The sergeant's eyes opened wide. "Greg Ralston?" he asked in surprise.

"Yes," Rafe replied before Greg could answer.

"But you're a suspect in—" the sergeant began.

"That's what we need to talk to the detectives about. Benny Jordan here can clear him," Rafe interrupted, patting the cabbie on the shoulder.

"Just a minute. I'll see if Bill and Rhett are upstairs," the desk sergeant said.

"You'll never know how glad I am that you remember me," Greg said to Benny as they were waiting.

"How could I forget?" Benny said. "But what I can't figure out is why the cops didn't already come and talk to me about this."

"I guess they didn't think to," Rafe said. What he didn't say was that they had been so convinced that Greg was guilty that they hadn't made much effort to locate him.

"Sergeant Latner said to tell you to go on up," the desk sergeant said. He gave them directions, and they headed for the elevator.

Both Sergeant Latner and Detective Vancott met them when they got off the elevator and escorted them to the area where their cluttered desks stood next to each other amidst dozens of similar ones. "What can I do for you?" Bill asked after he'd invited the men to sit down on three chairs he and Rhett had drawn up to the desk.

Rafe came right to the point. "This is Benny Jordan," he said, pointing to the cabbie. "He was driving Greg home when your victim was stabbed in the bar."

The two officers looked at each other for a long moment, then Sergeant Latner said, "Are you sure?"

"Sure as I've ever been of anything. And we have the company records to back it up," Benny said proudly.

Two hours later, Sergeant Latner offered his hand to Rafe. "Very good work," he said. "All the charges against your brother have been dismissed by the judge. You should leave that private detective business and come join us."

"Thanks, but I'm sort of enjoying what I'm doing," Rafe said.

Sergeant Latner smiled. "Well, I've got to admit, you do it well. Your boss should be proud of you. You did what we failed to do; you cleared your brother. Now our work starts all over again. We have to find out who the real killer is." He turned to Greg and said, "I'm glad you've been cleared. I hope it hasn't caused you too much trouble."

"It only cost me my contract with the Mavericks," he said with an edge of bitterness to his voice.

"Don't they understand that even though someone is charged, that they are still considered innocent until proven guilty?" he asked.

"I guess not," Greg said. "Come on, Rafe, let's get out of here. You too, Benny. I've spent way too much time in this place lately."

"Wait," the sergeant said. "I'll call someone personally. They can't do this to you. I'll meet with your agent."

"He quit on me," Greg said.

"But if you wouldn't mind, a call to the front office of the Mavericks wouldn't hurt," Rafe told the sergeant. "In the meantime, we'll be finding Greg a new agent. He isn't through with basketball just yet."

"Anything I can do to help, I'd be glad to," the sergeant promised.

When they entered the bright Dallas sunlight, Greg seemed to feel better about the world. "Benny, thank you," he said sincerely. "I'm sorry I got a little cranky in there."

"Glad I could help," the cabbie replied. "And you certainly had the right to get angry."

"And as for you, Rafe," Greg said, "thank you is not enough. I owe everything to you."

"I didn't really do much. Anybody could have found old Benny here. It's not like he was hiding," Rafe said, grinning at the cab driver.

"But you're the one who got it done," Greg said. "I didn't even know where to begin. I owe you big time."

"You know what my fee is," Rafe said.

Benny gave Rafe a strange look. "You're charging your own brother?" he asked.

"Oh yes, we agreed on a fee earlier. And it's pretty steep," Rafe said with a grin. "Greg can't ever drink alcohol again."

"You're okay," Benny said, laughing. "Both of you guys are okay."

Rafe pulled out his wallet. He extracted a fifty dollar bill which he held out to Benny. "We had a deal with you too," he said.

"Put that away," Greg said. "I'll pay Benny." He pulled out a hundred dollar bill.

Benny shook his head and put his hands behind his back. "Never thought I'd do something like this, but I can't take money from either one of you," he said. Then he grinned. "But I do want tickets to a Mavericks game."

"But I'm not going to be with the—" Greg began.

Rafe cut his brother off. "You'll be playing somewhere," he said. "If you don't play for Dallas, you'll play against them. Benny, you'll get your tickets."

At that moment, the elusive worry that had been gnawing at Rafe came into focus. "Greg, call my dad. Tell him to stay away from your apartment."

"Sure," Greg said, pulling out his phone. "But why?"

"The tall man won't be in the truck Dad saw him in at that gas station in Santa Fe."

"Why not?" Greg asked as he dialed the number.

"For the same reason he got rid of the green Cadillac. He doesn't want to be recognized," Rafe replied.

"Your dad's not answering," Greg said, and Rafe could see that he, too, was worrying.

Rafe spun on his heels and ran back inside the police headquarters. A minute later he had the attention of Sergeant Latner. "You said to call on you if you could help," Rafe began. "I'm worried about my family." He explained quickly about the man who claimed to be the father of Greg and himself.

"Rafe, this sounds serious," the sergeant agreed. "I'll send some officers there right away."

"Thanks, we'll head there too, as soon as we drop Benny off at his apartment."

"Rhett," the sergeant called out to his young partner. "Take Benny home. I'm going to run out to Greg's apartment. I'll explain why later."

Rafe drove as fast as he could. Greg kept trying to call Lenny's cell phone. There was no answer on every attempt. Rafe had him try Glenda's number and Stephanie's, but theirs went directly to the answering service. Rafe felt sick. He prayed earnestly for his family as he drove.

CHAPTER 18

Everything seemed normal on the street in front of Greg's apartment when Rafe and Greg arrived. But Lenny Collings was still not answering his cell phone. Sergeant Latner, who had been able to make much better time than the brothers, was talking to a couple of uniformed officers in the parking lot of the apartment complex when the two of them drove up.

Upon seeing them, the sergeant signaled for them to join the little gathering of officers. Rafe was slow to get out of the car, looking around very carefully as he did so. He knew he was getting paranoid, but he also knew that he had far too many enemies out there to be otherwise, even when there were cops around. When he finally followed Greg over to the apartment, Sergeant Latner said, "Greg, let's look inside. We don't see anything out of the ordinary out here."

"That won't help," Rafe said. "No one would have been going inside Greg's apartment. If my family was here, they'd have only been driving around and watching for the truck the tall man was driving. And as I'm sure you know, it isn't in sight, and neither are my folks."

Sergeant Latner insisted that they check inside anyway. As expected, everything was undisturbed. Rafe was sick with worry. He borrowed Greg's phone and tried Lenny's cell phone again. But the call didn't go through. "What do you suggest we do now?" Greg asked.

"Let's look around and see if we can find the tall man in some other vehicle. For all we know, he could be watching us right now."

* * *

The tall man peered through the binoculars he was holding. There was no way of telling which young man was which except for the way they were dressed. It seemed reasonable to assume that Rafe was the one in a western cut jacket, dark slacks, and black cowboy boots. Trying to be patient, he continued to watch. He hoped the police officers weren't talking to his sons about him. He hoped they would soon leave and that he could finish what he'd started. But he was alarmed when the officers got in their cars and started driving toward him. He slumped down. There was nothing to worry about, he told himself. He was two blocks up the street and in a car no one would recognize. He'd even switched the plates earlier.

The marked police car turned south before it got to him, and he watched it driving very slowly away from him until it was hidden by a building. The unmarked car also pulled onto the street. Both Greg and Rafe were in it along with one officer. That was especially confusing. He hoped they weren't being arrested for something. He didn't want to see his boys go to jail. And they would be of no use to him there. The unmarked car drove in the opposite direction than the marked one had. But like the marked one, it too turned onto a side street and began slowly driving up it.

A couple of minutes later, the marked car appeared again just a block from him. He ducked out of sight and waited. When he finally looked up again, it was no longer in sight. He laid the binoculars on the seat, started the ignition, and pulled away from the curb. He would just have to come back later, he decided. Sticking around with cops snooping in the area was not a good idea, especially when he was sitting in a stolen car.

* * *

Greg's cell phone rang. Rafe watched as he studied the number displayed on it. "Anyone you know?" he asked.

Greg shook his head and answered the call. Rafe saw the look of relief on his brother's face. "Yes, he's right here," he said. "I'll let you talk to him yourself." He held the phone out to Rafe. "It's your father."

"Rafe, I thought we better check in with you guys," his father's voice said.

Rafe sighed in relief. "Dad, where are you?" he asked. "We've been worried sick."

"Why were you worried? I told you we'd be careful. And we have been. We're fine," Lenny said. "We decided not to go over to Greg's. I got to thinking that the tall man might be driving a different vehicle, one we might not recognize. When I thought of that, there was no way I was going to take a chance. So I took your suggestion."

"You went to a ranch?" Rafe asked.

"Yes, and it's been most interesting," Lenny said. "In fact, I've found a bull I want to buy. I think if you saw him that you'd agree. He's a beauty. If we can get out of this situation with the man who claims to be you boys' natural father, I plan to do just that."

"That's great, but while you've been shopping for a bull, we've been trying to call. Don't you have your cell phone with you?" Rafe asked.

Lenny laughed. "I'm afraid not. This rancher was showing me some of his best young bulls. I wanted to get closer to this one I hope to buy, so we got in the pen with them. Somehow the phone came off my belt while we were in there, and I didn't miss it until we were out. When I did, I went back in to find it, but it had been stepped on. I'll need to buy another one."

"That makes two of us," Rafe said. "But I also tried Mom's and Steph's."

"Didn't I tell you? We don't have theirs with us. In our hurry to leave home, we left both of them plugged into their chargers. Sorry son. We didn't mean to make you worry."

"It's okay, Dad," Rafe said. "I'm just glad you're all safe. Let's meet at the hotel. We have great news. The charges against Greg have been dropped. So we need to decide what to do now. We've been driving around the area where Greg lives trying—"

"That's dangerous!" Lenny cut in. "Like I said, that man might be driving a different vehicle for all we know."

"I realize that, Dad. But we're with the police. We're looking for any suspicious vehicle, but we've come up empty-handed so far. We're going to quit now, and Greg and I'll be heading back to our hotel.

Why don't you guys meet us there? Then we can decide what to do next."

The first thing both Rafe and Lenny did after they were all reunited an hour later was buy new cell phones with their old numbers programmed into them.

Rafe's rang before they ever got back to the hotel. "Rafe!" Cybil cried. "You've found your cell phone. Lindsay said you'd lost it."

The last thing he wanted to do right now was explain to Cybil what had happened to his phone. It would generate a lot of questions that he wasn't prepared to answer just yet. So he said, "Yes, I have my phone. Have you heard how Thorn's doing?"

"Not well," she said. "I just got off the phone with his wife. He's in intensive care. They say if they can get him stabilized that they'll do a bypass surgery. I'm really afraid for him."

"So am I," Rafe said.

"And there's another problem, Rafe," she said.

"What's that?" he asked.

Her answer chilled Rafe to the bone. And it created a serious dilemma. Together with Sergeant Latner, he and Greg had begun to form a plan to set a trap for the tall man, to go on the offensive as Lenny had suggested. Until the tall man was in custody and charged with something, there would be no peace for Rafe's father, step-mother, and sister. But now Rafe knew that Lindsay Diamond, who to his frustration was never far from his mind, was in even worse danger than he'd thought.

"What are you going to do?" Cybil asked. "I'm afraid to go home."

As well she should be, Rafe thought. Though it appeared that this stalker had fixated on Lindsay, he was also potentially a threat to Cybil and Melly. "I'm coming home," he said with sudden determination.

"When?"

"As soon as I can get a flight," he told her.

"Oh, Rafe. I wish you were already here," she said, and from the sound of her voice, Rafe could tell that she was in tears.

"Where are Melly and Lindsay?" he asked.

"Melly is with Lindsay," he said. "They should be at the bank by now. We're all afraid to go home."

"Okay, here's what I want you to do," he said. And he laid out a simple plan for her. After instructing her to call the bank to tell Lindsay and Melly the plan, he disconnected. A couple more calls followed. After he'd made them, he tried to convince himself that the young women would be okay in Provo until he could get back. But he didn't feel very convinced.

"Is the Diamond girl in some kind of trouble?" his father asked after he had completed all his calls.

"Yes," he said. "I need to go back to Utah. But we've also got to find the guy who claims he's our father so you and Mom and Stephanie won't be in danger anymore."

"We don't need you to get to him," Lenny said. "In fact, with Greg's help, the police should be able to handle that."

"That's right, Rafe," Greg agreed. "You go back if you need to. We'll take care of things here."

Rafe shook his head. "Dad, you and Mom and Stephanie can't stay here with that man in the area. Why don't you take a trip, a real vacation. Go somewhere that this guy can't possibly guess at or follow you, and spend a few days. When he's in custody, then you can go home. I'll see you when you get there."

Lenny was thoughtful for a moment, then he turned to his wife and daughter. The look in their eyes was all it took to convince him that Rafe was right, that they needed to go somewhere safe, for they were both frightened. Lenny said, "We'll do like Rafe has suggested. Let's get on the road and just drive."

"But what about Greg?" Stephanie asked. "We can't just leave him here."

"I'll be fine," Greg said with an affectionate grin. "And sometime, after everything has calmed down, I'll visit Utah."

"Really?" Stephanie asked, wide-eyed.

"Yes, really. And that's a promise. It's not every day a guy finds himself a whole new family."

* * *

Melly was waiting in the bank's break room for Lindsay to finish her shift. She'd thumbed through a couple of magazines, but the waiting was terribly boring. At the same time, she was nervous. She knew that when they left the bank, the stalker could easily be out there watching them. And she didn't know what he might try to do next. Thirsty, Melly opened her purse to find some change so she could buy a can of pop and some candy from a row of vending machines.

She took her wallet out of her purse, laid the purse on the table, and snapped the wallet open. She cried out in horror. Melly kept four pictures in the wallet. One was of a guy she was writing to on his mission. The second was of her family. The third was of Cybil. The fourth was gone! Someone had taken her picture of Lindsay right out of her wallet.

* * *

The picture was too small. He wanted something larger, something he could hang on the wall. He left his dingy little apartment and pedaled to town. There he made an enlargement of Lindsay's photo on a copy machine. He blew it clear up to regular page size. It was grainy, but it was beautiful. He made three more copies, paid for them, and pedaled home. With thumb tacks, he hung one of the enlarged photos in each room of his apartment. Then he walked from room to room examining his handiwork. Wherever he went—the bedroom, the living room, the tiny kitchen, even the bathroom— Lindsay smiled at him from the wall.

He smiled back and promised her that it would not be long before she could join him in person. He turned on the TV and watched it absently for a little while, looking up frequently at the picture on the wall. That picture instilled in him a longing that was almost more than he could bear. He shut off the TV, rose to his feet, and again left the apartment. Outside, he got on his bike and pedaled back to Lindsay's neighborhood.

He didn't get a good look at Lindsay when she parked the car in front of the apartment because he was watching the cop car that had pulled in right behind her. A flush of anger rushed through him. *What was she thinking?* he asked himself. *Didn't she realize that it could be dangerous for her to involve the cops?*

He got a little better look at Lindsay when she came out carrying a pair of matching suitcases a few minutes later. But his anger was growing as he watched all three girls loading suitcases, two in Lindsay's car, one in Cybil's car. When they all drove off together, followed by the officers, he pounded his fist into the tree that he was hiding behind. Then he jumped on his bike and pedaled in furious frustration after them. But it was to no avail. They were soon out of sight.

Back at his apartment, he stared at the pictures of Lindsay that graced his walls and promised himself that the next time he saw her, he would be ready to bring her home. But he had to make preparations. First there was the matter of disposing of his Jeep Wagoneer and getting a different car. He was afraid to pick her up in the Jeep, since it had been seen. But he definitely needed a vehicle of some sort, for it would be impossible to bring her home on the bike.

* * *

Harley was angry. He and Deke had crawled through the woods for over two hours in order to get close to the house. At his age, that was not a pleasant thing to do, especially in the cold rain that had been falling for the past hour. Besides, he and Deke shouldn't even be here. He really became agitated when they got close enough to see that someone was waiting for them near the house.

Cops!

The cops thought they were hidden, and he supposed they were if he and Deke had driven in. They'd apparently expected them to try to do that.

Fools, he thought.

He and Deke whispered angrily back and forth, arguing over their next move. Harley wanted to wait, hoping that the cops would leave after a while. The crawl back to the Bronco was almost more than he could bear to think about. He was already chilled clear through. His thin old body was shaking, and he felt his chest constricting. But Deke insisted that they return to the Bronco. They could hide out that day, and try again the following night, he suggested.

"They'll leave at daybreak, if not before," Harley insisted. "We'll wait here. When they go, we can get warm in the house."

"We'll leave and come back," Deke said in a dark, dangerous tone, one that he'd learned from Harley in Harley's younger years. Hearing it now directed at him, it made Harley shiver more violently. And he felt something he'd never felt before when in the presence of his son; he felt fear.

He said nothing more, and they began the long, cold crawl back to the hidden Bronco. By the time he and Deke finally got in and got the engine going, Harley was suffering. Cold, scratched and bruised, head throbbing, chest feeling like it would explode—he was in a sour mood. "Yer a dang fool," he told his son in foolish anger and frustration.

Deke looked over at him. "Just keep yer yap shut," he told Harley. "You may be one foot from yer grave, but me, I got a lot a years left. And they ain't gonna find what's in that orchard before I do."

"Yer crazy, boy. Let's run. Leave the country. I can't crawl back there again," Harley insisted.

"Then I'll go by myself tomorrow night," his son said darkly. "I don't need yer help no more."

Once again, Harley wondered if he'd said too much to the son that was just like him, the son he'd taught too well.

* * *

Greg and Rafe's biological father hadn't survived this many years on the wrong side of the law by being stupid. He did what he'd always done when he felt like things were closing in on him. He backed away from what he was doing and rethought his course of action. For hours he'd sat alone thinking in a roadside rest area well beyond the eastern side of the city. The cops were with his boys, or rather, his boys were with the cops. There had to be a reason, and whatever it was, there was no way it could be good. Regardless of what that reason was, he wasn't about to risk a run-in with the law. That was especially true while he was driving a stolen car.

He spent the night in his car, then drove back to the city in the wee hours of the morning. He stayed clear of Greg's neighborhood. He also didn't give in to the urge to call Greg and again demand money. Instead, he drove to a café and ordered breakfast. There was a

TV blaring away about twenty feet from his table. He didn't pay any attention to it until he heard someone say, "Greg Ralston."

He jerked his head up and looked at the screen. Displayed there was a picture of Greg. "According to the district attorney's office, a witness turned up yesterday that clearly places Ralston in a location nowhere near the scene of the murder. The police are now reexamining their evidence and hope to make another arrest in the case soon," a newscaster was saying.

The story had his full attention. "Numerous attempts to contact the young point guard have failed," the newscaster continued. "The Dallas Mavericks responded to our call for their reaction to the news. They issued a short statement indicating that the future of Greg Ralston with their organization was not certain. They refused to say what that meant. His agent, Jim Hanks, was also contacted. Hanks promised to talk with Ralston and then get back to us with a statement as soon as possible."

The newscast went on to another story, and the father of the man they were talking about mulled over what he'd just heard. He cursed silently to himself as he wondered if Greg's career was already over. His source of riches might already have dried up. All the risks he'd taken might be for nothing. But he wouldn't give up just yet, he decided as his anger slowly dissipated. There were ways to get a little money here and there. His son would surely play ball with someone, sometime. Then he could renew his quest for the financial help his sons owed him.

He headed back toward Utah in the stolen Toyota with the intent of stopping in the city where he'd left his pickup. He wanted the green Cadillac back. It had been his home for many years. But first he thought maybe he'd see if his F-150 was still in the mall where he'd left it. If it was, he'd take it back to Utah and trade it for the Cadillac.

* * *

Rafe pulled into the driveway of the little house he rented. Two other cars were parked there. He recognized them both. One was Lindsay's, the other Cybil's. He glanced at his watch. It was almost eight in the morning. He was a little tired, but had somehow managed to sleep soundly on the entire flight up from Dallas. What he wished he could do now was to sleep for another four or five hours. Unfortunately, he suspected he wouldn't have the luxury.

After carefully scanning the neighborhood, he finally approached his door, pulled a key from his pocket and then hesitated. Was it proper to just walk in? he wondered. It was his house. But there were three young ladies staying in there, and it seemed to him that he should ring the doorbell. But would they dare answer it? he next asked himself.

Not knowing the answer to that question, he pressed on his doorbell and waited. He could hear some scrambling around inside. Then a voice, soft and sounding frightened, asked through the door, "Who's there?"

"Your landlord," he answered. He paused. Nothing happened. "It's me, Rafe Collings," he said a little louder.

With that the door swung wide, and he found himself in the arms of his secretary. "Oh, Rafe," she cried. "It's all so horrible. Thank goodness you're back. Now you can take care of things. You can protect me . . . I mean, us."

"Thanks for taking care of the office, Cybil," he said as he untangled himself from her arms and stepped past her, into the living room. "How's Thorn?"

"No better," she said. "His wife is really worried."

Lindsay was standing very quietly in front of his sofa. Their eyes met. There was a sadness there that puzzled him. He hadn't noticed it the evening they went to dinner. Conscious of Cybil trailing close behind him, he moved quickly across the room. His eyes never left Lindsay's, nor did hers leave his until he stopped in front of her. Then she dropped her gaze to the floor. He reached out and touched her arm, wanting to do much more than that, wanting to take her in his arms and hold her close and whisper something tender in her ear. He ached to tell her that she was on his mind almost constantly.

But he did none of those things. He said softly, "Lindsay, are you okay?"

Slowly she lifted her eyes and again met his steady gaze. Her eyes were dark brown, and when he looked into them at such close proximity, they seemed so deep he felt like he could fall into them. He almost wished he could. Her lips moved ever so slightly, but the movement created a very tiny smile, and his heart nearly burst at the beauty of it.

She finally broke that wonderful little smile and said, "Thanks for coming back, Rafe. We've all been so scared. And thanks for letting us stay here last night."

"Yeah, we appreciate it," Cybil broke in from beside him.

He looked from Lindsay to Cybil and back again. Each girl, in her own way, was attractive, but it was Lindsay's face that he felt like he could look at for the rest of his life. But he made himself look again at Cybil. He suddenly felt very awkward, and so he said, "There are three of you, aren't there?"

"Yes," Cybil said. "Melly's here, but she isn't moving too fast. Her ankle is hurting her a lot. She's in your spare bedroom. She'll be out in a minute and you can meet her."

"Great. Well, I hope you make yourselves at home. I know I don't have much food around, but what I do have you're welcome to," he said, even as a very worrisome thought popped into his head.

He could be a target. And if he was a target, his home and office could be targets too. The girls were safe at his place insofar as the stalker was concerned, but not from his mother's killer or the tall man, or even from Deke and Harley Tuft, for that matter.

"Rafe, what is it?" Lindsay asked. "Something's bothering you, isn't it?"

He nodded, still sorting things out in his mind. The girls would have to go somewhere else this morning, he decided, but he didn't know how to tell them. He didn't want to make them think he was kicking them out and hurt their feelings.

"You need your house back," Lindsay said. "But you don't know how to tell us that." Her brief statement of fact was accompanied by that very modest smile, that smile that he would love to look at for an eternity.

He was amazed at how quickly she'd picked up on his thoughts. It was like she could read his mind, at least to a degree. He smiled at her and she smiled back. "It's not that, exactly," he began.

Cybil spoke up. "Is it that you don't feel comfortable sharing your house with three women?" she asked.

"That's not the problem," he said. "I could sleep at the office for a few days if need be."

"Or you could use our place. We could just trade until you catch the stalker," Cybil suggested.

"Yes, that would work, except for one thing," he said.

Lindsay was nodding her head. Rafe's eyes met hers again.

"You're afraid that the guy that killed your mother might have seen that picture you and Mr. Stanbury had made, and that he might come here in the middle of the night sometime," she said. It wasn't a question at all. She was speaking what Rafe hadn't known how to say.

Cybil gasped as Lindsay's simple declaration sunk in. "Oh, my! What can we do?" Her hand came to her mouth.

"Actually, it's unlikely that he would see his picture. It was only distributed to police departments around the country, and I can't see that guy frequenting police stations." He tried to sound positive, but he felt anything but that. "But while the police and I try to locate the guy that broke into your apartment, we've got to make sure you're all staying in a safe place."

Lindsay, whose eyes were on Rafe most of the time, turned at the sound of a door opening and said, "Oh, hi, Melly. Come meet Cybil's boss."

Cybil's boss? Rafe thought. *How about "my good friend?"* He'd like that better. He looked toward the girl who was now hobbling down the hall and then turned in her direction and walked across the room to meet her.

Melly smiled at Rafe and said, "It's good to meet you. I've heard a lot about you already."

Rafe took her hand and shook it. "Sorry about your ankle," he said, "and about all the other problems."

"Oh, it's okay," Melly said, still smiling at him. She had deep dimples on both cheeks when she smiled. Her hair, a medium brown color, was cut short and curled softly over her forehead. "My, you are tall," she murmured. "It'll be okay now that you're here."

Rafe felt suddenly overwhelmed. These three young women had put a lot of stock in his return, and he wasn't sure he could solve their problem. He could just hope and pray that he'd luck out again, like he did when he located Benny the cabbie so easily and cleared his brother. But Rafe wasn't so self-assured that he took the credit for that success. He'd just been lucky, or, more likely, had been blessed by the Lord. It would take that again.

CHAPTER 19

Dempsey leaned his bike against a tree and slipped silently past several houses until he had a good view of Lindsay's apartment. Disappointment settled over him when he saw that her car was not there. He'd hoped she would come back this morning. Oh, well, he decided; he knew where she worked. He had several hours to buy a car, and then he could follow her to wherever she was staying. It was about time to take her home. She was forcing his hand by being so stubborn and suspicious.

* * *

Bob Staw, Lindsay's would-be boyfriend, had been trying to call Lindsay. But when no one answered her phone after he'd called several times, he decided to go to her apartment. There was a new movie that would be in the local theaters in a couple of days, and he wanted her to go see it with him. But when he drove into the parking area, he noticed a man who seemed to be watching the apartment where Lindsay and her roommates lived. He parked and watched the other man for several minutes. The guy was acting really secretive, and he kept fidgeting nervously with the ball cap that he wore backward on his head.

Bob, as always, had his camera in the car. Since he was very young, Bob had loved photography. He never went anywhere without his camera. As a result, he'd actually made a little money selling pictures to magazines that no one else had been prepared to take. He took his camera from its case and put a different lens on it, a strong zoom lens. Then he quietly snapped several pictures of the guy. Finally the fellow got on a bike and pedaled off. Bob watched until he was out of sight and then glanced again at Lindsay's apartment. Surely that guy wasn't watching for Lindsay or one of her roommates, he told himself.

He sat there for another minute or two, thinking. Finally, he got out of his car, walked to the door and knocked. There was no answer. He looked for Lindsay's car, but it wasn't in the parking lot.

Bob thought about Lindsay as he drove back to his apartment. He knew she didn't share his feelings, but he hoped that in time she would. He'd known Lindsay only briefly, but he'd always remembered her from years previous. The impression the dark-haired girl at the basketball game had made on him when they both lived in Pocatello was lasting, and when he saw her in one of his classes at BYU, he decided to ask her out. He'd actually been surprised when she'd agreed to go out with him. He wanted to spend more time with her, but he felt lucky just to be able to date her at all. To his knowledge, she wasn't dating anyone else, so he'd begun to actually hope that maybe sometime she would begin to feel toward him the way he felt toward her. And the more he was around her, the better he liked her. She was one in a million as far as he was concerned.

* * *

Rafe spent part of the day helping Lindsay, Cybil, and Melly get settled into a new apartment across town from their old one. They had each insisted that they live on at least the second story so that windows would be less accessible to potential intruders. They moved in with what little they'd taken the previous day to Rafe's house.

The decision had been unanimous that they not go back to get the rest of their things until the stalker was behind bars. They didn't want to take the risk of leading him to their new apartment. However, they all recognized that this alone didn't assure them of him not tracking them down. He knew where Lindsay worked and where she went to her classes on the BYU campus. "I'll quit my job," she announced. "And I'll skip my classes. I can always get notes from someone for what I missed."

"Good. Now, let me talk to your boss at the bank. Maybe we can get him to save your job for you," he suggested.

"You'd do that for me?" she asked.

"Of course I would," he responded. And since then he'd been thinking that there wasn't much he wouldn't do for her if given the chance.

Rafe was headed for the bank now. Lindsay had called in and told them she couldn't make it to work that day, but it was Rafe's intention to explain exactly what was happening and see if they would hold the job for her for a few days. He arrived in the area of the bank about the time she would have reported to work that afternoon. He did so intentionally, for he wanted to look for the stalker, to see if he was near the bank watching for Lindsay.

He drove through the neighboring streets, looking for the Jeep Wagoneer, although he had a feeling the stalker wouldn't be using it anymore. He also watched for other suspicious cars, for pedestrians who resembled the stalker, and for anyone on a bicycle or motorcycle. As he searched the area for the stalker, he also kept his eyes peeled for anyone who might present a danger to himself. Only when he was reasonably confident that the area was safe did he enter the bank.

The branch manager was very understanding when Rafe explained Lindsay's plight. "It will run us a little short," he said, "but Lindsay's a very good employee. I'll keep her job open for a few days."

"Thanks," Rafe said. "I'll let her know."

As Rafe rose to leave, the manager said, "Let me know what happens. If this goes on too long, I'll have to look for other help."

"And Lindsay will have to consider moving to another city," Rafe said dryly. "I hope we can get this guy in the next few days."

Rafe again scanned the area when he left the bank, but he didn't see anything that seemed suspicious. He next drove to the hospital to see Thorn. The burly investigator had improved a little, but his wife told Rafe that she hoped he could keep the office running without Thorn for a few weeks, since it would be quite a while before he could go back to work. "His doctor says he's got to have four heart bypasses," she informed Rafe.

Rafe felt like the weight of the world was on his shoulders as he drove back to the office after leaving the hospital. He found Cybil there hard at work. She gave him a big smile when he walked in and said, "Any luck on finding the stalker?"

"Not yet," he said. "And for now, I'm going to have to work on that stack of messages I see piled on my desk. I just came from the hospital, and it looks like the boss will be off for a while."

"Then I guess it's just me and you," Cybil said brightly. "Let me go through that stack on your desk with you. Maybe we can figure out which needs to be handled first."

Once the messages were laid out in what Rafe and Cybil together had decided was their order of importance, Cybil went back to her own desk and Rafe picked up the phone. After making several calls, he agreed to meet one very important client of Thorn's the next morning, then he got up from his desk and told Cybil that he would be out of the office for a little while. She stood, seeming hesitant about something, then blurted, "Rafe, I'd like to buy you dinner tonight."

Taken aback a little he stopped and looked at her. Her face was red but hopeful. If Cybil, as Lindsay's roommate, was asking him out, he had to assume one of two things: either Lindsay had told Cybil she no longer cared for Rafe, or she didn't bother to tell Cybil that she had ever cared for him in the past. Either way, it didn't bode well for him. As he tried to decide how to respond, his heart was breaking into a million pieces. He guessed he had to eat, and it was nice of Cybil to ask. But he didn't want to give her the wrong impression. "I have a better idea," he said. "Let's go fifty-fifty."

"Sure," she said. "What time?"

Rafe looked at his watch. He had several things to follow up on and the afternoon was wearing on. "Seven okay?" he asked.

"Great," Cybil said, grinning broadly.

"Then it's a deal," he said. "I can just meet you here if you like."

"Oh no," she said, quickly, "I look awful. I'll need to freshen up and change. Can you meet me at my new apartment?"

I wish it was Lindsay I was picking up there, Rafe thought. But he said, "That'll be fine. Have a place picked out when I get there."

* * *

It had taken a lot longer to get a car than Dempsey had planned. By the time he drove out of a used car dealership behind the wheel of a suitable means of transportation, Lindsay's normal arrival time for work at the bank had long passed. Not to worry, he told himself. He'd simply be there when she got off.

What a surprise he had planned for Lindsay. He hoped she'd like it. Actually, she'd have no choice but to like it.

* * *

Kerry Sundolf was approaching the Utah border in the blue Nissan Maxima he had rented in Reno. Once in Utah he'd have to be very careful. He didn't want to spend any more time there than he had to. He also didn't want to speak to more people in Provo than was absolutely necessary to enable him to find Rafe Collings. It was critical to his future that he not leave a trail behind that could lead the police to his door in Portland.

Not that it should be too difficult. Rafe was working for a private investigator now, and he should be able to find his business address. That might be all he'd need. He hoped he could take care of business there and get out of town.

* * *

Rafe ran into problems on one of Thorn's cases, and he could see that there was no way he could pick Cybil up on time. So he called her and explained, asking her to meet him at whatever restaurant she'd decided on at seven thirty. He got the distinct impression that Cybil was not happy about that, but she named a restaurant. He was relieved, since he felt uncomfortable picking her up right in front of Lindsay. He wished he'd never agreed to go out at all.

If Cybil was angry with him, it didn't show when he met her in the foyer of the restaurant. She was positively radiant. He couldn't help but be impressed, and he told her so. That made her smile even brighter. Cybil chattered almost nonstop through the evening. Rafe learned more about her in that hour than he'd learned in all the days since she'd come to work for the agency.

Despite the fact that he kept thinking of Lindsay, he had a great time. When they'd finished eating, he was feeling so relaxed that he hated for the evening to end. He hadn't been able to relax for days.

Cybil apparently didn't want the evening to end either, and when she suggested that it didn't have to, he didn't argue. He followed her to a theater where they enjoyed a late movie together.

It was almost eleven when he finally escorted her to her car, helped her in, and said, "Why don't I follow you home?" He felt responsible for her and wanted to make sure she was safely in her new apartment before he went back to his.

She smiled at him and agreed that it would be nice if he did. The lights were off in the girls' new apartment when the two of them pulled up outside. Rafe helped Cybil from her car and walked her up the stairs and to the door. They lingered for a moment. He got the impression that she wanted a kiss, but he wasn't about to do that. So the two of them shook hands. She looked disappointed, and he said, "I'll see you at the office tomorrow. Thanks for a great evening. I needed it."

* * *

Lindsay wiped her eyes and wondered if she'd be able to sleep at all that night. She had heard Cybil come in after eleven. Obviously they hadn't just gone to dinner. She was glad she'd already turned her light off, or Cybil would be wanting to share how the evening went. When Cybil had told her that she would be meeting Rafe for dinner instead of him picking her up at their new apartment, Lindsay had been relieved because she hadn't wanted to see Rafe admiring Cybil and leading her through the door. The very thought was almost unbearable.

She had tried very hard to control her thoughts and the feelings of her heart, but from the moment she'd seen Rafe outside the bank the previous week, she had been able to think of no one else. The feelings that had developed for him before his mission had come rushing back to her in that instant, and seeing him as a mature and very handsome man had only intensified those feelings. She was afraid that she'd upset him when she stopped writing him on his mission. She hadn't wanted to, since she always looked forward to his letters, but she was afraid that she might be a distraction, and so she'd done what she felt was right at the time. And now he said he never received the letter she sent after his mission. All this time she had assumed he was no longer interested, so naturally she had thought he was just lying to her now in order not to hurt her feelings. But what if he was telling the truth? How could she let him date Cybil?

Cybil had every right to date Rafe. And anyone he chose to take out was his right. But even though she reasoned it out in her head, it didn't change the feelings in her heart.

For the next hour Lindsay tossed in her bed and wondered how she could make herself be happy for her good friend Cybil and the man she was falling in love with. She didn't want to hurt Cybil, but she also didn't want to lose Rafe now that she'd found him. She finally drifted off to sleep without having found a solution to the problem.

* * *

Despite his stubborn statements to the contrary, Harley had accompanied his son on foot back to their yard again that night. To his dismay, there were still cops there. "Looks like we'll have to try again later," Deke said.

"No!" Harley objected. "We've tried already, and now we need to do like I said and get out of Texas. I ain't going to prison. I got a lot a good years left, and I ain't spending them behind bars."

"Come on, old man," Deke said. "Let's get out of here."

"Not yet. I need a rest first," Harley said. He was tired, and the thought of the difficult trek through the thick trees and brush in the dark was almost more than he could stand.

"We're going now," Deke said, and he grabbed his pa by the arm and pulled him along behind him.

Harley was angry, and he didn't feel well. He broke his arm free and said, "I'm a coming, but I can't go as fast as you can, Deke."

"Just don't lag too far behind," Deke said with disgust, and he set off ahead.

Harley tried to keep up. But he hadn't gone another hundred feet before a sharp pain seized his chest. He sat down with a groan, hunched over and grimacing. For a moment the pain let up, but then it struck again, even worse, and Harley Tuft rolled onto his side in the tall grass and rocked back and forth in agony. He wondered now if he was wrong about having a lot of years left. And he cursed loudly at his rotten luck. Then he lay still.

Deke didn't realize how far ahead of his father he'd gotten until he heard the old man curse. That stopped him cold in his tracks. He couldn't imagine what had happened, but it made him angry that the old man would shout out like that with cops only a few hundred feet away. He figured that he had to get his pa and drag him back to the Bronco as fast as he could. He started back but had only gone a short distance when he was again stopped cold.

"Over here, Pete," a voice called out. "I think it's old Harley Tuft himself."

"I'll be right there," another voice shouted.

"You better call the captain," the first voice called again. "He's going to want to come out."

Deke had heard all he dared to. It sounded like his father had been caught. He was on his own now. Moving as quietly and yet as quickly as he dared, Deke headed toward the Bronco.

* * *

Rafe awoke to the ringing of his telephone. He groaned and looked at his alarm clock. It was only six, and he was still dog tired. He picked up the phone without checking the caller ID. He couldn't imagine who would be calling him at this time of day.

"Rafe, that you?" a familiar-sounding voice asked as soon as Rafe had spoken his groggy hello into the phone.

"Yes, it's me," he answered.

"Good. Did I wake you up?"

"You sure did. Who is this, anyway?"

"Captain Stevens. I've got some news for you."

Rafe, suddenly very alert, swung his feet out of bed and asked, "Good news or bad?"

"Depends on how you look at it. Harley Tuft is dead," Captain Stevens said.

Rafe felt like he'd been punched. He'd wanted the old man brought to justice, and he'd hoped to find out what had happened to the man's wife, but knowing as he now did that he carried their genes, he didn't want the old man dead. "What happened to him?" Rafe asked, expecting to hear that he'd been killed in a shootout somewhere.

"Heart attack," the captain said. "He and Deke had tramped through some of the same woods you went through to get back to their farm without us knowing it. Don't know how long they'd been there, but I had officers waiting. Of course, we expected that if they came back, they'd drive. I was wrong about that. Looks like the strain of all the walking was too much for old Harley."

"So he died?" Rafe asked for lack of anything else coming to mind.

"Yes, but not before he solved the mystery of your grandma for us, Rafe. One of my men found Harley. The old man was getting delirious and he mistook the officer for Deke, and he said, 'Gotta get Ma out of the orchard. Throw her in the swamp. They'll get us fer killing her if we don't.'"

"So he must have murdered her," Rafe said sadly.

"He and Deke. I've got men heading out there now. We'll see if we can find her remains," Captain Stevens promised.

"Thanks. What about Deke?" Rafe asked. "Any idea where he is?"

"On the run," the captain said. "We set up roadblocks as soon as we discovered Harley. A couple of my men stopped Deke, but he opened up with a shotgun, cut them both down. They'll live, but Deke got away."

"I suppose he's being looked for?" Rafe said.

"Oh yeah. And eventually we'll get him. But I thought you and your brother should know," the captain went on. "I don't think he'll come after you two now, but you should be alert just in case. You can't ever predict for sure what men like him will do."

"Thanks, I'll keep an eye out," Rafe said. "Have you talked to Greg yet?"

"I tried. There's no answer at his apartment in Dallas, and his cell phone goes right to voice mail. I'll keep trying, though."

"Thanks. I will too," Rafe said. "I appreciate your call."

After hanging up the phone, Rafe got up from the bed. He was still tired, but after that call, he knew he couldn't go back to sleep, so he decided not to try. Instead, he headed for the shower. A few minutes later, he ate a quick breakfast and decided to drive down to the office. He had just as well get some work done, he decided, since he was up anyway.

CHAPTER 20

Greg had a surprise for his brother. After the cops had failed to lure the man who claimed to be their father into a trap, they'd come to the conclusion that he'd left the area. Thinking that the tall man probably headed back to Utah, Greg decided to do the same. Before leaving home for an early morning flight he checked the previous day's messages on the phone in his apartment. Jim Hanks had called repeatedly and left messages for Greg to call him. He must have called at least ten times. Greg had no intention of talking to Jim. He was sure his former agent wanted to tell him that he'd like to be his agent again, but Greg didn't want him back. The man had let him down when he was needed most. He wasn't going to give him a second chance, even though Jim said on every message he left that he had nearly convinced the Mavericks to keep him on and to let him play.

There had been no other messages of importance, so Greg deleted them all, packed a suitcase, and headed for his car. He found his cell phone, which he'd accidentally left in the car the last time he'd used it, and found more messages waiting from Jim Hanks. Disgusted, he shut the phone off. He'd have to turn it off on the plane anyway. And when he got to Utah, he could always turn it on again, he told himself.

After an uneventful flight, Greg picked up a rental car and got a map and directions. He pulled into Provo shortly before noon. He decided to check Rafe's place first and see if he was home before he did anything else.

There were no vehicles parked in Rafe's driveway or in the street in front of it. He knocked on his door anyway, but he got no answer. He felt grimy and in need of a shower after the long trip, so he found a hotel and checked in. He showered, shaved, and put on some clean clothes. He was anxious to let Rafe know he was in town, but the last few days had been fatiguing, and sleep was dragging heavily at his eyes. Greg decided he'd surprise Rafe later. He was in need of some rest. He plopped down on the bed and closed his eyes.

* * *

The tall man drove the pickup into the used car lot where he'd traded the Cadillac a few days earlier. He'd been lucky. The pickup had still been parked in the mall parking lot where he'd left it. He'd parked the stolen Toyota beside it in the middle of the night and then moved his belongings back into the truck, including the bags of nitrogen fertilizer, the basic item he needed for a very effective bomb. Then he wiped the Toyota clean of fingerprints and left it there, driving off in the truck.

The same salesman that had sold him the truck and taken the Cadillac in trade met him in the sales lot. "Is the truck running okay?" the salesman asked.

"It is, but I've decided I don't like driving a truck. I've come to trade it back for the Cadillac," he said. "I miss the old girl."

* * *

When Greg opened his eyes again, he looked at his watch. It was three in the afternoon. He jumped up and headed for the door. It was time to see if Rafe was at his office.

His cell phone lay on the seat beside him as he pulled onto the street. He looked at it and wondered how many times Jim Hanks had tried to call. He turned it on and saw he had voice mail, but decided it could wait. After all, he had more important things to take care of. Like surprising his brother, he thought with a grin. He laid it back on the seat, still turned on.

* * *

Rafe had tried to call Greg a dozen times during the day. He couldn't imagine why his brother wasn't answering either of his phones. He'd left a message both on the cell phone and at his apartment. With all that had been going on the past few days, he couldn't help but worry about Greg. He'd also like to know if anything had happened with the tall man. Surely if it had, Greg would have contacted him and let him know.

It had been a busy day. Rafe's friend at the police department had called him and said that they'd found the brown Jeep Wagoneer. At least, they were quite certain it was the one the stalker had been driving. It had been abandoned at the University Mall parking lot in Orem. There were no plates on it. The vehicle identification number had been removed, and when they tried to lift some fingerprints, they couldn't find any. Both the interior and exterior had been thoroughly wiped clean. Rafe had driven to the Orem Police Department's impound yard where the Wagoneer had been towed and looked it over himself, hoping to find anything at all that would lead him to the identity of the stalker. But there was nothing to be found. The stalker had been very careful.

After leaving Orem, Rafe had driven back to Lindsay's old apartment in Provo. After looking around the area for any sign of the stalker and finding none, he entered the apartment with Lindsay's key. As far as he could tell, nothing had been disturbed. It wouldn't have surprised him if the stalker had been there again. But his inspection convinced him that he hadn't.

Rafe left the apartment and drove east. He did a double take when he spotted in his rearview mirror what could only be the green Cadillac the man who claimed to be his father usually drove. He couldn't believe it. All he needed was to have to worry about him again. He was grateful that his family had decided to stay away for a few days, to take a vacation. At least they were where the guy couldn't hurt them. Rafe sped up, just to see if the vehicle would follow him. It did. Rafe made a couple of quick turns, but the Cadillac was still back there. It never got close, but it also never fell too far back.

Suddenly angry, Rafe jammed on his breaks and pulled to the side of the road. Maybe the best way to solve the problem of this man who claimed to be his father was to confront him. The Cadillac also stopped. Rafe waited while a couple of cars passed, then made an illegal turn. His intent was to pull right up to the green Cadillac and try to get out and up to the driver's door before the tall man could get away.

But when he completed the turn, there was no longer a green Cadillac anywhere in sight. Angry and frustrated, Rafe sped up and down several streets, but the car had vanished. Now he'd have to once again keep a close watch for the tall man as well as for his mother's killer, and maybe even for Deke Tuft.

Frustrated and not sure what else he could do right now, Rafe headed back toward his office, which was at the opposite end of town.

* * *

There had been a note on Cybil's desk when she came in that afternoon. Rafe had outlined some things that needed to be done. He told her that he was going to see if he could find the stalker and didn't know where that would lead him. She'd thought a lot about last evening, and she'd been disappointed when Rafe wasn't there.

She'd worked for a couple of hours and had things pretty well caught up when she heard a car drive up out front. She stepped to the window and peered out. There was a car out there, but it wasn't a pickup. Probably a prospective client, she thought with disappointment. She and Rafe already had more than they could do.

A minute later the door opened. She looked up and was surprised to see Rafe walk through dressed like she'd never seen him dressed before. The western cut jacket and jeans had been replaced with a light blue sports jacket, a yellow polo shirt and tan slacks. And for the first time since she'd met him, he wasn't wearing boots. She smiled. "New clothes," she said. "They look good."

He grinned at her. "You look good too," he said. "Is Rafe around?"

She eyed him closely. "Aren't you Rafe?"

"No, I'm Greg Ralston, Rafe's brother. And you are?" the visitor asked.

Cybil felt herself blush deeply. "I'm Cybil," she said. "I'm sorry. I thought—"

"That I was Rafe," Greg interrupted. "I take that as a compliment. And I take it he isn't here."

"No, uh, he's not. He's, uh, working," she stammered.

"When will he be back?" Greg asked.

Cybil knew she was staring, but she couldn't help it. "He didn't . . . " she finally responded. "He didn't mention you were in town."

Greg's easy grin made her heart beat faster. "He doesn't know," he said. "Thought I'd surprise him. So you don't know when he'll be back?"

"Actually, I . . . I haven't seen Rafe today. He was in this morning and he left me a note." She was starting to gain control. "He's really busy right now. Our boss is very ill and won't be able to work for a while. Rafe's trying to get as much work done as he can."

"Do you mind if I wait here for him to come back?" Greg asked.

Cybil didn't mind at all. In fact, she thought it would be great. "Have a seat," she said, pointing to a small leather sofa across the room from her desk.

"Thanks. Don't let me interrupt your work. I'll just look at one of these magazines," Greg said.

"Oh, sure, that would be fine," Cybil agreed.

For a minute or two, Greg thumbed through the magazine and Cybil tried to concentrate on her work, but she was failing miserably. She kept her head down, pretending to work, knowing that she'd blush again if he looked up from his magazine and caught her staring at him.

"You must be Lindsay's roommate," Greg said a minute later.

Grateful for the excuse, Cybil looked up and smiled at Greg. "Rafe's told you about Lindsay, has he?"

"Oh yeah." He grinned. "He won't admit it, but he's smitten. From what he says, she must be a really pretty girl."

"She is," Cybil said, and was surprised that she didn't feel jealous.

"Must be rough on him," Greg said.

"What do you mean?" Cybil asked, puzzled.

"Working with someone as pretty as you are and falling for someone as pretty as Lindsay. Sounds like he's got it pretty rough," he said with a twinkle in his blue eyes.

Cybil smiled. She really liked Rafe's brother. And, like Rafe, he was really cute. "He hardly knows I exist," she said.

"I don't believe that," Greg responded.

"No, I'm serious. I sort of talked him into going to dinner last night, but he had me meet him at the restaurant, and we split the bill fifty-fifty. I think I got the message. We had fun, but you're right. It's Lindsay he has eyes for," she confessed, both to Greg, and, more importantly, to herself. And suddenly she realized that Lindsay felt the same about Rafe. Cybil berated herself for missing all the nonverbal cues. *How could I have been so blind?* she wondered.

"I'm sorry, I'm keeping you from your work," Greg said. "I'll try to concentrate on this magazine."

"That's fine," Cybil said.

Again it was silent in the room. But after a couple more minutes, Greg spoke again. "I can't concentrate."

"I'm sorry," Cybil said. "Maybe you'd rather wait in Rafe's office. It's right—"

"Actually, I'm enjoying sitting right here. It's just that I can't concentrate with someone so attractive in the room with me."

She blushed deeply again. He was smiling at her and looking directly into her eyes. Greg put the magazine down and stood up. "I haven't eaten for hours. Maybe I could go get a bite somewhere and come back a little later. Could you tell me a good place to get a sandwich?"

Cybil also stood up. She was rattled. Nobody, not even Rafe, had ever rattled her like Greg did. "Uh, well, there's . . ." she paused. "What kind of sandwich did you have in mind?"

"I'm not fussy. Just tell me where to go," he said. "Or, better yet, if you have a minute, you could come with me."

Cybil made a sudden and rather rash decision. "I can make up my work later. I'd be happy to show you a place."

"On one condition though."

"What's that?"

"You have to let me buy you something too," Greg said.

"Okay, I'd like that," she said. "I'll leave a note for Rafe in case he comes while we're gone. Then I'll get my coat."

"Don't tell him I'm here," he said.

"Oh no, I won't," she promised as she sat back down, wrote a short note, then left it on Rafe's desk. She grabbed her coat from a coat rack near her desk.

"Let me help you with that," Greg said, and he took the coat from her and helped her put it on.

* * *

Bob Staw knew that Lindsay worked at a bank, but not once had she mentioned which bank. He did, however, know that Cybil, her roommate, worked for a private investigator by the name of Thorndike Stanbury. Why he remembered such a strange detail was beyond him. Still, thinking that Cybil could help him get hold of Lindsay, he looked up the agency and drove there.

Once he got near the investigator's office, he began to have doubts. He really didn't know Cybil. He'd met her at Lindsay's apartment a few times, but that was all. He suddenly felt awkward as he thought about approaching her. It's not like it was an emergency or anything. He just wanted to ask Lindsay to the movie opening soon, and to offer her his notes for their class she'd missed today. He pulled up and stopped a hundred yards or so from the nearest car, a blue one, that was parked directly across the street from the office where Lindsay's roommate worked.

In a state of indecision, he instinctively picked up his camera from the seat beside him. When he wanted to relax, he did it by shooting pictures. Just the day before, he'd spent an hour taking pictures of the scenery in Provo Canyon. His camera still had a powerful zoom lens attached. He brought it up and peered through the lens at the office of Stanbury Investigations. Then he swung it over to the blue car that was parked across the street from the office. It was a Nissan Maxima, and there was a man in the front seat. The guy was looking across the street at the investigator's office. He seemed to be watching it very intently.

He wondered if the guy was looking for someone to do some investigating for him. Intrigued by the hard intensity of his face, he snapped a couple of pictures. Feeling more calm now, he was about to put the camera down when he saw something very strange. The man lifted a pistol with a silencer screwed onto the barrel and poked it through the window. Instinctively, Bob snapped a picture, then another, and one more. The pistol disappeared, but Bob was intrigued now and he continued to watch the man in the Nissan. When the pistol came within his view again, Bob snapped another picture and then turned toward the office, expertly adjusting the lens as he moved.

The office door had just opened and Cybil stepped out, followed by a tall young man with blond hair. Bob snapped a couple of pictures of the couple as he wondered who Cybil was with. He watched them as they walked away from the building, knowing that he might have missed his chance to find out where Lindsay had disappeared to.

Suddenly the blond man stumbled forward, and a fraction of a second later there was a soft sound that could have been a stick striking a bag of laundry. At that exact moment, a crimson circle formed in the light blue material of the blond guy's jacket. Horrified, Bob continued to snap pictures as the blond man's fall changed directions—instead of continuing his forward stumble, he flew backward. Bob knew what had happened, and he turned quickly back to the Nissan, automatically adjusting the lens and clicking pictures even as he swung the camera. The silenced barrel, a wisp of smoke curling from the end, was being pulled back inside the car.

He swept the camera back the opposite way once more. The blond man was on the ground now, and Cybil was screaming and had dropped to her knees beside him. Still taking pictures, Bob again swung back to the blue Nissan Maxima. He took several shots of it as it sped up the street, rounded a corner, and disappeared.

Bob was stunned. For a moment, he hesitated, thinking that he didn't want to get involved. He was a witness to what was probably a murder, and he knew that could be a dangerous thing. On the other hand, could he live with himself if he didn't try to help? Besides, what would Lindsay think of him if he ran like a coward? He knew what she'd think, and he was sure she wouldn't have any more to do with him. With that thought, he pulled his car up to within a few feet of where the Nissan had been parked. He shut off his engine and hurried across the street.

"Cybil," he said with a trembling voice as he stepped up to where she now was holding the blond man cradled in her arms. "I saw what just happened. Can I do something?"

"Get an ambulance," she cried. "Go inside and call 911."

He did as he was asked, wishing that he'd never come here in the first place.

CHAPTER 21

A siren screamed behind him somewhere, and Rafe looked in his mirror. Flashing red lights were coming up on him fast. Along with other traffic, he pulled to the side of the road. An ambulance sped by, and he pulled back onto the roadway, only to hear more sirens. Once again there were flashing lights behind him. They were of the blue variety this time, interspersed with red.

Police cars.

He again pulled over. Two marked police units streaked past him. Something very serious was happening up ahead somewhere, he decided. There was probably a bad traffic accident. He wondered if it might be blocking his route to the office. But as he continued on he didn't come upon an accident. With his window rolled down he could hear more sirens wailing in the distance. The sound made him nervous. This was more than an accident, he concluded. It wasn't until he turned and headed west on the last block before the one his office was on that he saw the flashing lights in front of the little building that served as the office of Stanbury Investigations. There were cop cars, an ambulance, and even a fire truck blocking the street. Something had happened right in front of his office, and it frightened him. A cop waved him down a half block before he got there, signaling him to turn back.

The sheer terror at the thought of what might have happened filled both his mind and his body with terrible foreboding. He began to tremble, and when he stopped for the officer, it was hard for him to speak. He waited while the officer said, "This area is closed. You'll need to turn and find another route to wherever you're headed."

"But I'm going to my office. That's it right there where all the cars are parked," he choked out in broken syllables. "You've got to let me past."

"Sorry, there's been a shooting there, and I've been told that no one goes beyond this point," he was told.

"Someone's been shot? Our secretary is working there! She was alone! I've got to—" he began almost hysterically.

"It's not your secretary," the officer said. "The victim is a man."

"A man?" Rafe asked. "Was he just walking past or something?" He was trying to instill hope within himself that whatever had occurred up ahead had nothing to do with him and the enemies he had.

"Hey, mister, I don't know who you are, but you really do need to turn around," the officer said impatiently.

Rafe was successfully beating back both the terror and the hysteria. He forced himself to take a deep breath and then speak calmly. "Officer, you really don't understand. My name is Rafe Collings, and I work for Detective Thorndike Stanbury." He pulled out his ID and showed it to the officer.

The officer inspected it closely, handed it back, then said, "My orders are still my orders."

"Then get a change of orders. That place up there is where I work, and I've got to get through." He spoke with both anger and determination this time. It was hard to stay calm under the circumstances.

The officer looked at him with disgust, then used his radio to make a call. "Sergeant, there's a man here who claims to work for the owner of the business where the shooting took place. He insists that I let him through."

"Is it Rafe Collings?"

"Yes. He showed me his ID."

"Then let him through, but tell him not to touch anything. Make sure that's clear with him. We may need some information from him. I'll be there myself in less than two minutes," the sergeant said.

"Yes sir," the officer replied. He turned to Rafe. "You can go on through, but—"

Rafe cut him off. "I know. I heard him. I won't touch a thing."

The officer then stepped back and Rafe drove on, wondering who had been shot, suspecting that it might have been a client. He had to park across the street behind several other cars. When he approached the huddle of paramedics and cops that surrounded someone who was lying on the sidewalk in front of his office, another officer stopped him. "No sightseers," the officer announced.

"I work here. I've got to see who got shot," Rafe said.

The officer was suddenly looking at Rafe like he'd seen a ghost. "But . . . but . . ." he stammered. "You are . . . I mean, you look just like the victim."

Greg! Rafe thought in renewed panic. What was he doing here?

Rafe broke past the officer and shoved his way to where he could see his brother lying on his back on the ground. His face was waxy white, and the paramedics were feverishly working on him. There was blood all around. Greg looked like he was dead. Tears filled Rafe's eyes, and he choked up. "Greg," he cried in a mumbled outburst. "Oh, Greg. I'm so sorry."

The officer had grabbed Rafe by the arm and was holding him back. "You can't do anything for him," he was told. "You've got to stay back and let the paramedics do their work. They need room."

Rafe looked at the officer and said, "He's my brother. Is he dead?"

"No, but he's hurt awfully bad. You need to let the paramedics work on him. They're trying to stabilize him enough that they can transport him to the hospital."

"I'm a Mormon elder," Rafe said. "I've got to give him a blessing."

The officer looked at Rafe with a great deal of sympathy. "Just a moment, Mr. Collings. Don't try to get any closer, and I'll check with the paramedics."

Just then Rafe heard a strangled cry, and Cybil burst from the office, her blouse and pants covered with blood. "Rafe. Oh, Rafe!" she cried. "They shot him! They shot Greg! Why would anyone shoot Greg?"

Before he could respond, she threw herself into his arms and he held her as she sobbed uncontrollably. He thought he knew the answer to her question, and it was a terrible one for him to have to acknowledge. Greg had been shot because someone, probably his mother's killer or someone hired by that killer, had mistaken Greg for him. As Rafe held his sobbing secretary, he was also watching his brother. For some reason, Greg had secretly come to Utah.

The officer tapped Rafe on the shoulder and said, "Mr. Collings, they said that if you want to give him a blessing, it would be okay, but to hurry. They're almost ready to put him on a stretcher."

"I'll help if you'd like. I'm an elder too," someone said from right behind him.

"Oh, Bob, thanks," Cybil said.

Rafe looked at the fellow. He hadn't even noticed the guy until now. He was of medium height and medium build, with light brown hair and eyes. "I'm Bob Staw," the man said.

* * *

Lindsay and Melly were both in their apartment when the phone rang. Lindsay looked at the caller ID and when she saw that the call was coming from the Utah Valley Regional Medical Center, she felt a tremor of fear wash over her. She answered the phone with dread, thinking that something must have happened to Rafe. She had been so worried these past few days that something terrible would happen to him that it seemed a logical conclusion.

"Hello," she said tentatively.

"Lindsay, it's Cybil," Cybil began, then she broke down and all Lindsay could hear were racking sobs of anguish, giving Lindsay cause to believe that her worst fears had been realized.

"Cybil, what is it? What's the matter? Did something happen to Rafe?" she asked.

"No," Cybil managed to say between sobs.

Lindsay felt a great weight lifted from her. Whatever had happened must be bad, but at least Rafe was okay, she was thinking. "Cybil, you've got to calm down. Are you hurt?" she asked, thinking that since Cybil worked for Rafe, she could also be targeted by his enemies.

"No, it's Greg that's hurt. He might die," Cybil cried.

"Greg? Greg who?" she asked. But before Cybil could compose herself enough to answer, Lindsay figured it out for herself. "Oh no!" she moaned. "Not Greg Ralston?"

"Yes," Cybil said.

"What happened to him?" Lindsay demanded, shouting into the phone in an attempt to make Cybil settle down and talk to her.

It helped, and Cybil said, "He's been shot and he might die. Rafe thinks he was mistaken for him."

Lindsay could believe that, but what she couldn't understand was what Greg was doing in Provo. Surely Rafe would have told her and her roommates if he knew that Greg was coming up from Texas? "So what's happening now?" Lindsay asked.

"I'm at Utah Valley Medical Center. He's in surgery right now," Cybil said.

"Where's Rafe?" Lindsay asked.

"He's here. This is just killing him," Cybil said. "He said it should have been him, not his brother."

"Rafe would say that," Lindsay agreed. And furthermore, he'd mean it.

"Lindsay, I know you shouldn't come down here with that stalker out there and all, but Rafe needs someone right now. I think you might be able to help keep him from being so depressed," Cybil said.

"Can't you? You're—" Lindsay began, but she never got to finish whatever she was about to say, and she honestly wasn't sure what that would have been, had Cybil not tearfully interrupted her.

"Look, I'm through kidding myself," Cybil said. "Unless I'm totally blind, Rafe is in love with you, Lindsay. And I'm willing to bet you're in love with him too. It's his brother . . . it's his brother . . ." Cybil was crying uncontrollably again and said nothing more.

"Cybil, I'm coming," Lindsay said. "I'll be there in a few minutes."

"Not without me," Melly cried.

* * *

Dempsey smiled secretly. He'd found where Lindsay and her roommates had moved to. It hadn't been all that hard. He was sitting in the used car he'd bought to replace the Jeep Wagoneer. He was watching Lindsay's apartment through a pair of binoculars when she suddenly ran out, followed by her short roommate, the one whose name he'd learned was Melly. He cursed his luck. If she'd been alone, he would have gone after her right then, for it was time now. But he wasn't prepared to deal with Melly. So he started his car and began to follow them. He was determined to be patient and wait until Lindsay was alone, then he could figure out what he needed to do to get her home to *their* place—where she belonged.

* * *

The tall man had been turned away from the street where Rafe's office was located. But he knew that something had happened right near it and that someone was going to be taken to the hospital, for an ambulance was among the emergency vehicles he could see in front of the place where his son worked. He'd parked a couple of blocks away, walked through an alley, and stopped within a block of the office. He waited until they had loaded the victim onto a stretcher and then hurried back to his car. He followed the ambulance at a discreet distance until he was sure where it was going. Then he began to cruise the streets around the hospital.

He was in a sour mood, and the thought that something might have happened to Rafe didn't help that mood. Anything that would make it harder for him to get some money from Greg made him grumpy. And the car that he was driving also made him out of sorts. It was *not* the car he had wanted. Anyone who didn't want trouble today better stay out of his road, he told himself. He was in the mood to fight, and he didn't particularly care with whom.

* * *

Bob Staw was terribly upset. And it wasn't because of all the questions the police had asked him about what he'd seen. He'd truthfully and fully answered every question. It also wasn't over the fact that he'd had to turn over to the officers the roll of film that had been in his camera, the one that had the shooting on it, though he hated losing control of his film; he loved to develop it himself. But he was told that it would be a great help to them in solving the shooting. "We'll see that you are reimbursed for your expense," he was told.

No, what had really upset Bob was what he'd heard Cybil tell the man whose brother had been shot, the man who he'd helped in giving the victim a blessing. He now knew that his name was Rafe Collings. Cybil had told him his name and that he worked as an apprentice investigator for her boss, Thorndike Stanbury. That was all okay. What wasn't okay was when she told Rafe, as they were loading his brother into an ambulance, that she would call Lindsay and have her come to the hospital.

Her next words had stung like a bee. "Rafe, I know Lindsay loves you. She'll want to be here with you."

Lindsay loves you.

All his hopes and dreams for a future with Lindsay Diamond had vanished like smoke in the wind when Cybil said that. The expression on Rafe's face had proven to him that Lindsay's love was not unrequited.

He'd gone back to his apartment and stewed for a few minutes. He looked at the picture of Lindsay that he'd taken of her on their second date. It was one of several he'd taken that evening, and he'd given a copy of it, along with several others, to her. But this one was his favorite. He'd framed it and put it on his dresser. She was the most lovely girl he'd ever known. But now he knew that he'd lost her. He cried over the picture. Then he got on his knees and asked God for the courage to go on living without her, and to not hate Rafe Collings. Finally, he prayed that God would spare the life of Greg Ralston.

When Bob finally got up from his knees, he felt better. Now what he had to do, he told himself, was to go over to the hospital, face Lindsay, face Rafe, and tell them he hoped Greg would live. After he'd done that, just to satisfy his own curiosity, he'd ask them why Greg and Rafe were brothers but had different names.

Then he took the portrait of Lindsay and carried it outside to the garbage. But when he went to drop it in, he couldn't do it. So instead, he put it in his car and headed for the Utah Valley Regional Medical Center.

He hadn't driven more than a mile before it came to him. He remembered who Greg Ralston was. He'd played high school basketball in Pocatello. He shook his head at the strangeness of it all.

* * *

Gleeful would be a good way to describe the way Dempsey felt right now. He had just followed Lindsay's car into the large parking area of the hospital. He watched her park, watched her and Melly get out of the car, and watched them hurry into the hospital. Then he sat back and waited. Maybe Lindsay would come out alone. And if she did, he'd pick her up, and Lindsay would be taking the place of the yellow stuffed kitten tonight. He wouldn't be needing photographs of her on his wall anymore, for he would have her. He'd take them down after they got home that night. And then she could wear the silky yellow nightgown he'd been keeping for her, the one he'd borrowed from her room.

* * *

Cybil suddenly sprang to her feet when she saw her roommates. "Oh, Lindsay, Melly, this is so horrible. I didn't know anything could be so bad."

The three young women rushed into each other's arms, crying unashamedly and hugging each other. But after a moment, Lindsay extracted herself from the other two and looked toward where she saw Rafe sitting. He was seated at the far end of the waiting room, and his head was hanging down. He seemed to be staring at his boots. She walked slowly in his direction, her heart breaking for him. Never had she felt such an urge to comfort someone as she felt now. In this case, she wanted to take Rafe in her arms and hold him tightly and tell him that things would get better.

He lifted his head and saw her approaching. He got to his feet like an old man—it looked painful and he moved very slowly. She stopped when she was about three feet from him and held out her hands. He reached out and touched them with his. She looked into his eyes. They were red and swollen. His cheeks were drawn and his lips quivered. Her heart seemed suddenly to burst, and great sobs began to shake her body.

Rafe gently pulled her toward him. Then he enfolded his long arms around her and held her tightly against his body. "It'll be okay, Lindsay," he said, his voice breaking. "Somehow the Lord will help him through it."

She couldn't speak, for her sobs were growing in intensity. And it wasn't just because of the life-threatening injury Rafe's twin brother had sustained, nor was it because of the terrible hurt that Rafe must be suffering inside, but it was because she'd come here to see if she could comfort him in his grief, and instead he was comforting her.

For a long time the two of them stood there, their arms folded comfortingly around one another. Lindsay had no desire to ever break free of Rafe's embrace. It seemed like she was where she belonged, in the arms of a man she had to admit she loved. But in a little while she became aware of her roommates standing near them, and she reluctantly began to pull back. Then he removed his arms from around her, and he said, "I wonder how the surgery is going."

"I hope he's going to be okay. What exactly happened to him, anyway?" Melly asked.

There was a touch of bitterness in Rafe's voice when he said, "Greg took a bullet that was meant for me. Only it wouldn't have hurt me. I'm wearing a bulletproof vest." He slammed a fist angrily against his chest as he spoke. "It should have been me."

"Greg had come to the office looking for Rafe," Cybil said. "No one knew he was even in Utah. He said he wanted to surprise Rafe. He waited around the office for a while. But when Rafe didn't come, he asked me if I'd have a late lunch with him while he waited."

"Is that where you were going when it happened?" Melly asked.

"Yes. I wrote Rafe a note telling him where we'd gone and what time I'd be back to the office. Then we just headed outside together. I should have been thinking about the danger," Cybil said.

She turned to Rafe. "You've warned me enough, Rafe. It's my fault. But Greg was so nice, and he kept complimenting me, and, well, I just wasn't thinking," she admitted. She addressed her roommates again. "We'd started walking down the sidewalk, and Greg suddenly said, 'Look out!' and he began to duck and at the same time shove me aside."

"You didn't mention that to me," Rafe said suddenly. "Do you think he saw the gunman?"

"Yes, now that I can think clearly. I'm sure he did," Cybil responded. "I didn't even hear the shot."

"The cops figure he had a silencer on his gun," Rafe explained.

"Oh. Anyway, he hadn't any more than told me to duck, which I didn't do, when he suddenly flew backward and fell down. I was stunned for a moment, but when I looked down at him, his jacket was all bloody, and he looked like he was . . ." She couldn't go on.

Rafe was thoughtful for a moment. "Ducking like he did might have been the reason he wasn't killed right then. If he lives, it will be because of that."

"And because of the blessing Rafe and Bob gave him," Cybil added. "It didn't even occur to me that he could have a blessing right then." She looked at Rafe. "I don't know if you even knew what you said, but you promised him that he'd live. I didn't think you knew what you were saying at the time, but I've got this peaceful feeling now that you're right." She paused and her eyes shifted to Lindsay. "Maybe it's because I want it to be that way."

"Maybe," Lindsay said. "And maybe you have more faith than you give yourself credit for."

"Rafe Collings?" a voice said from behind them.

"I'm Rafe," he said as he turned.

"I'm Doctor Hartwell," a man clothed in light green hospital garb said. "I just finished operating on your brother."

"How is he?" Rafe asked, even as Lindsay's heart seemed to stand still with the suspense. She closed her eyes and offered a quick and silent prayer.

"He's going to make it. The bullet didn't hit any of his vital organs. He's one lucky man. A quarter of an inch one way or the other and he wouldn't be on his way to the recovery room right now. When he wakes up, someone will come get you and you can go see him."

Lindsay watched Rafe as new life seemed to seep back into his face. "Thank you, Doctor," he said.

"You don't need to thank me," Dr. Hartwell said. "Thank God. Believe me, that's who saved his life."

Lindsay took hold of Rafe's hand and he smiled at her. "I'll be just a minute," he said as the doctor disappeared through the door he'd entered from. "Would you gals excuse me? There's something I need to do."

"Sure," Lindsay said. "But are you okay?"

"Yes, I'm fine now. I just need a minute alone somewhere."

"Why?" Melly asked.

"I need to do what the doctor just suggested," he said.

"Oh," Melly responded.

Lindsay simply squeezed his hand tightly for a moment and then released it. She was too choked up to say anything right then.

* * *

The tall man saw something in the parking lot of the hospital that captured his full attention. Without hesitation, he drove his car to where what he wanted was waiting.

CHAPTER 22

Bob pulled into the parking lot and shut his car off. This was the hardest thing he'd ever done in his life. It was all he could do to keep from getting back in his car and driving away. Lindsay's red Stratus was parked a short distance away. His heart ached.

He shut the door to his car, then remembered the framed portrait of Lindsay he'd dropped on the seat. Suddenly he knew why he hadn't thrown it away. That would be such a waste. Instead, he thought, he'd present it to Rafe. Symbolically, to him at least, it would be a physical and final way of giving Lindsay to the man she'd chosen over him.

After getting it and once again closing the door to his car, Bob held the picture in front of him and just stared at it for a moment. Then he began to lower it. Over the top of the picture, he saw something that made him freeze. A man was sitting in a green Cadillac, and he was staring in the direction of Lindsay's red Stratus. He instantly remembered where he'd seen that man before, and a combination of anger and fear began to stir his blood.

Bob sat the portrait of Lindsay on the roof of his car, once again opened the door, and grabbed his camera from the seat. Quickly he loaded a new roll of film then swung his camera toward the dark green Cadillac. The man had gotten back inside the car, but the powerful lens pulled his image so close that he might have been only three or four feet away. Bob began to take pictures.

* * *

The man knocking on Dempsey's window was very tall. And Dempsey didn't like the look of anger on his face. He couldn't imagine what he'd done to upset the stranger.

"Roll the window down," the stranger shouted. "I need to talk to you."

Torn between doing as he was asked and starting the car and trying to get away, Dempsey debated with himself for a minute. He finally decided to roll the window down a few inches and see what the man wanted, for if he drove away like he was thinking of doing, he might miss Lindsay when she came out of the hospital.

So he cranked the window down about three inches and asked, "What do you want?"

The man's answer was not anything he might have imagined. "I want you to sell me this car," the tall stranger said. "And I mean right now."

"But I just bought it. It's not for sale," he said. "I need a car."

"You don't need this one as much as I do," Dempsey was told.

"But I do," he protested, wondering what was going on.

The tall man stood up and walked one time around the green Cadillac, looking it over very closely. When he came back to the window, he said, "Looks to be in as good a condition as when I saw it last. How much did you pay for it?"

"That's not your business."

"I just made it my business. How much did you pay for it?"

"Twelve hundred dollars," he answered, deciding that this might not be someone he wanted to make angry.

"I'm in a generous mood today. I'll trade you straight across," the tall man offered.

"But I don't know if I want to trade. Now leave me alone. I have things to do," Dempsey said, trying to sound tough.

The look on the stranger's face when he said that made him feel anything but tough. "Would you rather go to jail?" the tall man asked menacingly.

"I haven't done anything wrong," he said defensively, remembering his conclusion from a moment ago that he probably shouldn't make this man mad.

"Well, let me see, the last time I heard, possession of cocaine was a crime," the tall man said thoughtfully.

"But I don't have any cocaine. I don't use it," Dempsey defended himself.

The tall man's angry face softened, but a villainous smile curled his lips. "Actually, you do have some. It's hidden in this car."

"Then I'll find it and throw it away," he said through the three-inch opening at the top of his window.

"You'll never find it, but when I call the cops, they'll find it. You see, they'll know where to look."

"How do you know there's coke in here?" Dempsey challenged the tall man, even though he had the feeling that it wasn't a wise thing to do.

"This used to be my car. I hid it in there," he was told. "Now, there's a solution to this. We can just trade titles and trade cars, or I can tell the cops where to find the drugs."

Afraid that he was trapped, Dempsey finally said, "Okay, but I can't see why I should."

The tall man was thoughtful for a moment, then he said, "Good. Now get out and let's get this trade done. I've been looking all over for my green Cadillac."

Reluctantly, Dempsey got out. "I like this car," he whined.

"Not as much as I do. I've driven it for years. Do you have the title with you?"

Dempsey nodded.

"Good, get it and I'll get mine. We can have this little deal completed in no time," the tall man told him.

The anger was gone and the tall man seemed now to be in a very good mood. Dempsey decided that the yellow Buick the tall man was trading him looked like an okay car. In fact, it was newer than the Cadillac. It all seemed very strange, but he guessed it would be better to trade than to anger the man again.

* * *

"Bob, how nice of you to come," Lindsay said as Bob walked into the lobby.

"I'm so sorry about Greg," Bob said, both to Lindsay and to Rafe. He was holding the portrait against his stomach with the back side facing out. He couldn't help but notice Lindsay's dark eyes drop to it and then lift again. He also couldn't help but admit that she and Rafe made a handsome couple. Maybe they'd let him take their picture sometime.

"The doctor says he'll probably live," Lindsay said.

Bob suspected that Lindsay was feeling every bit as awkward as he was. "I'm glad," he said. "I was so worried. I've never seen anything as awful as what happened there."

"Thanks for what you did," Rafe said. "Cybil told me that you're the one who called 911. And thanks for helping me give him a blessing."

"It's the least I could do," Bob said. He didn't know quite how to go about the next thing he wanted to do, but he suddenly felt it would be less awkward if he didn't do it in front of Lindsay. So he addressed Rafe. "Hey, could I have a word with you, alone?" he asked.

"Sure," Rafe said as he and Lindsay exchanged puzzled glances.

The two men walked together to the far side of the lobby. "I'm not sure quite how to say this," Bob said, feeling foolish and embarrassed. "So I guess I'll just give you this." He handed the portrait to Rafe.

"Wow, Bob, this is beautiful," Rafe said as he gazed adoringly at Lindsay's picture.

"I thought you might like it."

"Yeah, I really do."

"Good. Oh, and there's one more thing, Rafe. There's this guy I think Lindsay should know about," he began.

Rafe suddenly perked up. "What guy?" he asked anxiously.

"Well, I don't know his name, and I may be all wrong, but I just thought she should know that I think he might be sort of . . . well . . . watching Lindsay."

"Does he have long red hair?" Rafe asked.

"Yeah. So you know about him?"

"The cops are looking for him. He's a stalker, and we think a dangerous one," Rafe said, his blue eyes narrow and his face suddenly very hard.

"He was outside when I came in," Bob said.

"In the parking lot?" Rafe asked.

"Yeah. He was parked pretty close to Lindsay's Stratus."

Rafe looked around for a public phone. "Hold this," he said, handing the portrait back to Bob. "I need to get the cops on the line." He ran to the phone, lifted the receiver, and began punching in some numbers. As he did so, he asked, "What was he driving?"

"Well, this is strange. He was in a dark green Cadillac when I first saw him, but as I started taking pictures, he—"

"He was in a green Cadillac?" Rafe asked.

"Yes, but some tall guy, maybe a little taller than you, traded him cars, then the Cadillac left."

At that moment, Rafe, who looked extremely puzzled, started talking to the police. Bob listened while Rafe repeated what Bob had just told him. Then he said, "Just a moment," into the phone. "Bob, what did the tall man trade him for the Cadillac?"

"A yellow Buick. It was a little newer than the Cadillac."

Rafe repeated that to the officers, then he said to Bob, "What was that about pictures?"

"I took pictures of the guy with the baseball cap. And I have pictures of both cars. I'm a photographer," he added by way of explanation.

"I'm glad you are," Rafe told him. "I hope you'll let me have these photos. This is very important." Rafe ended his call and was now walking rapidly toward the hospital entrance. Bob was following him. "Let's see if he's still out there," Rafe said to Bob. "Lindsay, stay here," Rafe shouted. "We'll be right back."

"The cops have the film I took of the guy who shot Greg," Bob said. "But you can have the roll I just took."

Bob couldn't believe he was agreeing to give up his second roll of film in one day. But Rafe was appreciative. "Wow. I hadn't heard you had photos of that. I've got to see them. I owe you big time, Bob. You see, the guy who shot Greg was probably either the same man that murdered my mother when I was a little boy or someone who's been hired by him."

Bob's head was swimming as he and Rafe burst into the parking lot. "It was over there," Bob said helpfully. He could see his car, he could see Lindsay's car, but he couldn't see the yellow Buick. "It's gone," he said. "But it was here just a few minutes ago."

* * *

Dempsey had reluctantly left the hospital parking lot like the stranger had told him to after they'd traded cars. But he'd circled back as soon as he dared. He hoped he hadn't already missed Lindsay. He drove through the parking area, looking for her car, but in the space it had occupied when he'd been there earlier there was now a large black SUV. Then he saw someone running toward him. He recognized him as the blond man Lindsay had left the bank with a few nights ago. Anger surged through him.

I'll run over him! Dempsey said to himself as he spun the car around, hitting a parked car with his rear fender. But as soon as he got the Buick straightened out, he saw that the man had stopped and that he was holding a gun. *What's he doing with a gun?* he wondered in shock. He didn't know the answer to that question, but the presence of the gun did drive some sense back into his head and he recklessly turned his car again, damaging two others this time, and fled from the parking lot and onto the street.

A siren wailed in the distance. He increased his speed. Two blocks later, a cop car pulled up behind him. A moment later, one approached him from straight ahead. He shoved the accelerator to the floor and sped away. Both cop cars were following him when he blew through a red light three blocks later. Their lights were flashing, and they followed him through it. He fled for several more blocks before he got a lucky break. He barely beat a semi truck through another red light. He had no way of knowing if the lead cop car crashed into the truck or if it was able to stop in time, and he didn't care. But he did know that neither police car made it through the intersection. That's all that mattered to him. He gunned his car, intent on getting far away from those cops as quickly as he could.

Dempsey thought he was in the clear when he saw another set of flashing lights coming his way. They were within three blocks of him and moving fast. He was afraid then that every cop in the county must have the description of his car. So Dempsey did the only thing he could think of to avoid being arrested. He turned into an alley, abandoned the car, and left on foot. It would be a long walk home, but it was better than being in jail.

He would just have to claim his prize another day.

* * *

The tall man saw the yellow Buick fly by, followed by two cop cars. He couldn't believe what he was seeing. He'd told that wimpy fellow with the ball cap on backward to get lost after he'd gotten his Cadillac back. And he'd left the hospital himself, but he hadn't gone far when he'd realized that he'd left the makings for his bomb in the trunk of the Buick. He'd forgotten to move them to the Cadillac when he traded cars.

He'd gone back to the hospital in the hopes that the young fellow hadn't listened to him and would return to the hospital even though he'd told him not to. And he knew now that he had, but he obviously hadn't stayed. For a few minutes he attempted to follow the cops as they chased the yellow car. But the chase ended when the Buick beat the cops through an intersection. One of the cops even plowed into the side of a large truck before he was able to get his sliding cruiser to stop.

So much for his fertilizer. The tall man had still considered using it if the opportunity presented itself. Now he'd have to buy some more; and he couldn't do that until he found a way to get more money. He was almost broke now. He had enough for another meal or two and some gas, but that was all.

The tall man flipped on the radio in the Cadillac as he drove dejectedly around the city. He guessed he'd have to steal some money somewhere, and he began looking for a likely house to break into that night. The local news came on the radio, and he about ran off the road when he heard the names of both his sons mentioned. He pulled over and stopped, his old heart hammering in his chest. He couldn't believe what he was hearing.

Greg had been shot and was very seriously wounded. The man who did it was driving a blue Nissan and had not yet been found. It had all happened in front of the place where Rafe worked.

If Greg died, the tall man thought with mounting frustration, he'd never get any money from him, and he'd be stuck living as he had for so many years, working the occasional odd job, shoplifting, and burglarizing homes and businesses. He was pushing fifty, too old for all that, he thought as he leaned over his steering wheel and cursed his luck.

* * *

Rafe had wanted to stay at the hospital, but Lindsay had insisted he go home. He hadn't slept well at first, but then sheer fatigue kicked in, and he didn't wake up until his phone rang the next morning. Cybil was at the hospital already. And Greg was awake. Rafe walked into Greg's room twenty minutes later. "I'm sorry, Rafe," Greg said weakly. "It seemed so unlikely that the guy who killed your mom would ever see his picture. I just didn't think there was any real danger up here."

"What's done is done," Rafe said. "You can't worry about it now. Just get well."

"I will," he said and closed his eyes.

Rafe could see that Greg was very weak. So he didn't try to talk to him. He just stood for a long time beside his bed. When Greg opened his eyes again, there was the briefest flicker of a smile on his face. "That's a great secretary you've got, Rafe," he said. Then again he closed his eyes. It had taken all the energy he could muster to say those few words.

"Hang in there, brother. I've some things I need to do. The doctor tells me you're going to be okay. So if you don't mind, I think I'll let someone else come in and keep you company for a while. I'll come back later, though."

Greg's eyelids flickered. Rafe took that as an acknowledgment, and he walked out and found Cybil. "Why don't you go in. I think he'd like some company for a few minutes," Rafe said.

"Are you sure?" she asked.

"Yes, I'm sure," he said with as much of a grin as he could muster.

"Rafe, I feel like this is all my fault," Cybil said.

"Your fault? No, this is all my fault. Now I've got something I've got to do," he said. "Keep an eye on my brother for a little while, if you don't mind."

* * *

Rafe returned to his office with the keys to Greg's car in his pocket. He loaded Greg's suitcase and briefcase into his truck so he could take them back to his house. Then he checked Greg's rental car for anything else his brother might not want left in it while he was laid up. He spotted Greg's cell phone. He was surprised to see that Greg had left it in his car.

Rafe decided to see if Greg had missed any calls that might be important. He could see that several messages had been left on Greg's voice mail. Without the password, he couldn't access those. But he also noted the numbers that were listed as missed calls. Besides his own number and Captain Stevens's, there were two others. He decided to call both numbers, but to do so from his office phone where he could record the conversations. It might not be important, but then again, it could be.

Even though he was almost certain that Greg had been mistaken for himself by the shooter, he couldn't rule out the possibility that it was someone who was after Greg. Deke Tuft had somehow slipped through the noose set for him in Texas. He could be anywhere. So Rafe made the first call.

The phone was answered, "Jim Hanks speaking."

Rafe was surprised at that, recalling the conversation with Greg about Jim Hanks abruptly resigning as Greg's agent. He wondered if Jim was wanting to be hired again now that Greg had been cleared of the murder charges. If so, he was not impressed.

"Hello, Jim. I'm surprised," Rafe said as he started his recording system running.

Before he could go on, Jim answered, "It's about time. I've been trying to call you forever. Where are you? I've got good news."

Realizing that Jim had mistaken his voice for his brother's, Rafe decided to play along for a minute. Greg might enjoy hearing this conversation later, when he was feeling a lot better. "What kind of good news?" Rafe asked.

"The Mavericks will be giving you some playing time. But they need to have you report right away," Jim said.

"Oh, really?" Rafe asked. "Why didn't they call directly? That seems like the proper thing to do."

"They tried, but because I'm your agent, they called me when they couldn't reach you," Jim said.

"I wasn't aware that you were my agent," Rafe said coldly as he remembered how angry Greg had been over the way Jim had treated him.

"Oh, that," Jim said with a laugh. "You didn't think I was serious, did you? I was only joking. Now, let's get down to business. They'd like you to report—"

Rafe cut him off, having heard enough. "Jim, I'm afraid that won't be happening. This is not Greg Ralston. This is Rafe Collings and—"

It was Rafe's turn to get interrupted. "Mr. Collings, are you the brother that works for that detective agency in Utah?"

"I am," Rafe said.

"I see. Well, I don't know what you think you're playing at, calling me and pretending to be your brother, but I don't find any humor in it."

"Mr. Hanks," Rafe shot back, "if you'll think for a moment, I never said I was Greg. You assumed it, and you were wrong. I was just calling to find out who had been trying to call Greg on his cell phone. Now I know. I think this concludes our business."

"Not so fast, Mr. Collings," Jim said. "What are you doing with Greg's cell phone?"

"Just helping him out," Rafe said. "Now I really need to go. Sorry to have bothered you."

"Mr. Collings. Ah, Rafe, is it? I'm sorry that I mistook you for Greg. But I really do need to talk to him. If you could get a message to him, I'd appreciate it."

Damage control, Rafe thought. Jim definitely wanted Greg back as a client. But at this point, Rafe wondered if Greg would ever be playing basketball for anyone. "I'll tell Greg you called," he told Jim.

"Thanks, and have him call me right away," Jim said.

"I'm sorry, but I'm afraid that won't be possible," Rafe said. "But I will give him your message. Good-bye."

"Not so fast, Rafe," Jim said.

Rafe disconnected. He suspected whose number the other one on Greg's phone might be. He recognized the area code. He debated making the call, then decided to do so. The call connected Rafe to the Maverick's general manager himself. Rafe briefly explained who he was, that Greg had been seriously injured, and that he'd be in touch with them as soon as he could. He didn't go into any detail as to how Greg had been injured or how long he might be laid up. Instead he said that he'd let Greg explain all that to him later.

Rafe next took the roll of film that had been given to him by Lindsay's friend Bob to a one-hour photo. His highest priority right now was to find the stalker, and that film would help, so they could circulate photos of him. The police had lost him, but they'd found the yellow Buick. They'd made no further progress, but were continuing to look for him.

While waiting for his film, Rafe checked with the police to see what progress, if any, had been made in the search for Greg's assailant. They showed Rafe the pictures Bob had taken, and any lingering doubt Rafe had about who the shooter was had been erased. He felt a familiar but painful twist in his stomach as he looked at the face of the man who'd killed his mother. He also marveled at how close the likeness of the pictures Tom had drawn were to the face in the photos. The killer sported a short, neatly trimmed beard and short, graying hair.

He'd been driving a blue Nissan Maxima, which proved to be a rental car with Nevada license plates. The description of the man, the rental car he was driving, and the plate numbers had been broadcast throughout the western states and was entered nationwide on NCIC, the National Crime Index Computer.

Rafe told them about the roll of film that Bob had given him. "I'm getting it developed right now. I'll bring the pictures over in a few minutes. We should know what the stalker looks like after I pick them up," he said.

He was just pulling into the parking area behind the photo shop a few minutes later when his cell phone rang. He looked at it, noted a Texas number, and answered.

"Rafe, this is Captain Stevens. We've found something I think you need to know about."

"What's that?" Rafe asked.

"We found a grave in the old orchard behind the Tufts' house," the captain said.

"Is it . . . is it Harley Tuft's wife?" he asked.

"We think so. It's much too early to be certain, since it's mostly just a skeleton now. But it looks like it's a woman. It had with it a pair of women's shoes that had not completely rotted away."

"Was she murdered, or can you tell that yet?" Rafe asked.

"She was shot. Of that we're certain. We're sending the remains to the medical examiner. We're hoping to be able to identify her positively through dental records, which we have already obtained for Helen Tuft," the captain explained.

Rafe took a deep breath. Even though this death was old history, and he'd never known Harley's wife or anything about her until recently, she was almost certainly his biological grandmother, and that instilled in him a sadness that left him feeling empty and shaken. "Thanks for calling," Rafe said softly.

"I'm sorry, Rafe, but I thought you and Greg should know. Speaking of Greg, I still can't reach him on his cell phone."

"I know. He can't use it right now."

"Why not? Do you know where he is?" the captain asked.

"In the hospital."

"What happened?" the captain asked. "And what hospital is he in? I could go see him if its anywhere in this part of the state, and I'd be glad to do so."

"He's in Utah, and he was shot," Rafe replied. "He took a bullet that was meant for me." Rafe choked up then and couldn't go on.

"Rafe, I'm sorry. I wish there was something I could do," the captain said. "How bad are his injuries?"

"They think . . . he'll live," Rafe choked out after a long pause.

"I'm sorry about Greg. Tell him I called. I'll call again when I know more of the situation down here," the captain said.

Rafe picked up the pictures he'd left to be developed after finishing his conversation with Captain Stevens. Then he delivered some copies to the police. The photos had all been fantastic. He wondered if Bob would be willing to do some paid work for the agency in the future.

As he drove back to the hospital, Rafe called his father's cell phone. His family was in New Orleans, and they were having a reasonably good time. When he told them about Greg, they reacted like a member of their family had come to grief, and he loved them for it. His dad was also worried about the farm.

"I'll drive down there tomorrow and check things out," Rafe promised.

Back at the hospital, he found Greg asleep, heavily sedated. He gave some pictures of the stalker to Cybil and asked her to give them to Lindsay. "I know she's seen him before and knows what he looks like, but these might help to keep his face fresh in her mind."

"Melly and I need to know what he looks like too. Thanks," Cybil said. "By the way, I checked on Thorn a few minutes ago. He's looking a lot better after the surgery yesterday."

The doctors had performed quadruple bypass surgery on Thorn's heart the day before and had told his wife that he should make a full recovery.

"I'll check with him later," Rafe said. "Right now, I think I'll just stay here with Greg for a while."

CHAPTER 23

Dempsey was watching when Lindsay's roommate left the hospital. He pedaled his bike as fast as he could, trying to keep her car in sight, but after just three blocks, he lost track of her. Lindsay hadn't come back to her new apartment after leaving it yesterday. He wished she wouldn't play these hide-and-seek games. Disappointed, he pedaled slowly home, determined that by the following day he'd have another car—even if he had to steal one. And then he'd watch the hospital again. He was certain that he would find Lindsay soon, and when he did . . .

He smiled as he thought about it. At home a few minutes later, he looked at himself in the mirror. There was one more thing he needed to do, Dempsey concluded. He had already switched from wearing a hat to a bandana, but he needed to drastically change his appearance. He would get a good haircut, shave, find some new clothes, and maybe even dye his hair. He couldn't take a chance on anyone recognizing him.

* * *

Rafe sat beside his brother's bed for thirty minutes. When Greg hadn't stirred in that time, he decided to go see his boss. The surgery had already made a difference. Thorn was feeling a lot better that evening. It took over an hour for Rafe to fill him in on all that had been happening. When he spoke of his mother's killer, Thorn gave him a sobering word of warning. "Rafe, you've got to be more cautious than ever at this point. Don't think he's going to immediately return to wherever it is he's living now. He could easily decide to come back just to make sure you're dead, or he might even hear on the news that he shot the wrong man. That would almost certainly bring him back. It would be a mistake to underestimate him at this point."

"Thanks, Thorn," Rafe said. "I appreciate the advice. And I am wearing a bulletproof vest."

"Good, but that's not any guarantee that you can't get hurt," Thorn cautioned.

"Gee, Thorn, I wish you were better already. I really don't know what I'm doing."

"Actually, my boy, you've already proven my instincts right. When I decided to hire you despite your lack of experience, I had a feeling you'd do well. You've done that and more."

"Thanks, Thorn. But I'm sure not keeping up with your clients. If I could just—"

His boss cut him off. "They'll just have to wait," Thorn said. "You need to find your enemies right now. Then you can get back to work on our cases. And I won't be long getting back to work myself. They aren't going to be able to keep me in this place much longer."

Thorn then made some suggestions to Rafe on looking for the stalker. When Rafe got up to leave, he again said, "Rafe, you watch your back every second now. Got that?"

"I've got it," Rafe said. "And you get well. I'm only the hired help here."

* * *

The tall man was already in Ephraim. He'd sacrificed eating and had bought some more nitrogen fertilizer and a few other items he needed to go with it. He was now busy rigging a bomb. If he couldn't get the money he wanted from Greg, maybe he could get some from Rafe's father. The cows, horses, sheep, and land that he owned had to be worth something. When Rafe's family got home, they would have a nasty surprise awaiting them. And Rafe would surely see to it that at least a hundred thousand dollars would be made available to him, knowing that if it weren't, there would be more surprises.

* * *

"Jim Hanks is never getting another call from me," Greg said hotly. "And I don't know if I want to talk to anyone at the Mavericks head office, either. Who knows, after this I may never be able to play ball again anyway."

Rafe smiled at him. "You're pretty feisty. I can't believe you're feeling this much better this quickly," he said. "You were out like a light when I was here yesterday."

He'd been truly amazed to find Greg both awake and quite animated. He'd come in early that morning, shortly after seven o'clock, because he wanted to get to Ephraim fairly soon. As it was, having found Greg much improved, he'd spent the past hour with him. They discussed the fate of their biological grandmother, and, like Rafe, Greg was saddened over the news—not so much at the fact that she was dead, but more because of how she must have died, and all the violence that must have occurred in the family they came from.

Rafe explained to Greg everything that was happening in the search for the man who'd shot him. He also talked about the tall man and the stalker. "I'm going to go to Ephraim and check on the farm for my dad, then I'll come back and do everything I can to find the stalker."

The door to Greg's room opened. They both looked up to see Lindsay, Melly, and Cybil coming in, three bright smiles on three attractive faces. Rafe couldn't believe how it made him feel just to see Lindsay. His heart raced as he looked at her. But after they'd all said hi to each other and the girls had asked Greg how he was doing, Lindsay's face fell.

"I don't suppose the police have found the stalker," she said. "It scares me to go anywhere. I mean, the hotel I'm staying at now is nice, but I just know he'll find us. If nothing else, he'll watch for me here and follow me from the hospital."

"I have an idea," Rafe said. "I've got to drive to Ephraim and check on the ranch for Dad. Why don't you come with me?"

Lindsay's eyes brightened. "Are you sure?"

"Positive," he said. "Please come."

"Yeah, go with him," Cybil said. "At least then you'll know you're safe."

From the stalker, Rafe thought bitterly, but there was still so much danger out there he hated to think about it. He hoped he wasn't putting Lindsay in worse danger by taking her with him. But he knew he'd be a nervous wreck worrying about her until he got back, so he was relieved when she said, "I'd love to go with you."

* * *

The tall man had finished his work. The bomb was set. In exactly one hour it would go off and the Collingses' house would be leveled. No one would be hurt, and he was sure the family could collect insurance, but when he contacted Rafe again, by mail from a long ways away, he suspected that he'd get some money—not the kind of dollars he might have eventually gotten from his other son, but certainly something substantial.

The tall man had left the Cadillac about a mile away, well hidden, after unloading the fertilizer. He'd walked back to get everything set up for the explosion. He returned on foot to where he'd hidden it. Back at the car, the tall man realized that he was very hungry and without money. He got in his car and ate the only remaining item of food he possessed. It was a candy bar that he'd shoplifted earlier, if that could be called food. It barely took the edge off his hunger. He needed real food. He needed money if he were to get real food. He couldn't wait much longer to find a way to get some.

He slapped his head. What was he thinking? Surely he could find something of value in the Collingses' house that he could steal and then pawn when he reached Nevada. Or, better yet, maybe they'd left some cash lying around. And there had to be food there. They would never miss it, since the house was about to be destroyed, he told himself. In fact, it would be a waste to leave it there. He'd been so busy setting the bomb that he hadn't even thought about those things. He truly was getting too old for this type of activity. He looked at his watch. There were still thirty-five minutes to go before the bomb went off. It would take too long if he walked back to the house from here. He needed time to search it and take whatever he decided he wanted. Anyway, he couldn't carry very much clear back here. So he drove back to their yard in the Cadillac. He parked it beside the barn where it was out of sight of anyone who might happen to pull into the yard, not that he expected anyone to. Rafe's family was clearly out of the area, his threat having scared them away.

His first priority was food. He grabbed some bread and ate it. Then the tall man rapidly filled his arms with canned goods and carried them to his car. He checked his watch. It was down to twenty minutes before the house blew up. He only dared to use fifteen minutes of that time. The first thing he looked for was jewelry. He found a couple of watches, some necklaces and earrings, and a few other items in the master bedroom. He couldn't find any money. In the girl's room he found more jewelry, but he doubted it would be of much value. He grabbed a hunting rifle, a shotgun, and a portable CD player and made another trip to the car.

There was time for one more trip into the house. But it had to be a fast one, then he knew he'd better go. He shut the car door and started back around the barn when he heard a car pull into the yard. Swearing softly, he pressed himself against the barn. A car door opened out in the yard, then closed. A moment later another opened. It too closed. The tall man slipped forward until he could see around the corner of the barn. He nearly fainted when he saw Rafe's pickup truck parked in the yard.

Rafe and a young woman were walking up the walk toward the house. In ten minutes it would blow up. No one was supposed to be hurt or killed. He'd done lots of bad things in his life, and they'd never bothered his conscience much, but he'd never killed anyone or even attempted to. They reached the door and Rafe fumbled with a key. The tall man was in a state of near panic. He looked at the young couple. Then he looked back at his car.

* * *

"I'm sure glad you came with me, Lindsay," Rafe said as he inserted the key into the lock.

"Thanks for inviting me," she said with a smile.

"It's been nice just talking," Rafe said as he turned the key. "Hey, this door's already unlocked. I know Dad said they locked everything up when they left." As he spoke, he felt a tingle of fear rush through him. *What if there's somebody in there?* he thought. *I can't let anyone hurt Lindsay.*

"Maybe we shouldn't go in," Lindsay said.

"Don't go in the house, Rafe!" someone shouted. "It's going to blow up."

He turned to see the tall man standing beside the corner of the barn. "Lindsay, run!" Rafe shouted as he grabbed her hand and dragged her down the walk beside him. The tall man disappeared.

He must have a car back there beside the barn, Rafe thought. He handed Lindsay the keys to his truck. "Drive to the county road," he said. "I've got to catch him."

"Rafe, you can't," she cried. "You could get hurt."

But he was already running in full stride toward the barn, and he barely heard her anguished cry. He dashed around the corner just as the tall man was getting into the green Cadillac. Without hesitating, Rafe lunged toward the car. The tall man slammed the door shut and started the engine. Rafe reached into his boot and pulled out his pistol. As the tall man gunned the engine, Rafe calmly fired a shot into a tire, and then he jumped aside, pointing the gun at the man's head.

The car stopped, and Rafe jerked the door open and pulled the tall man out. "When is it going to blow up?" Rafe demanded, shoving his pistol barrel roughly in the tall man's rib cage.

"In about eight minutes."

"Then that gives you time to save the house," Rafe said. "You can stop that bomb, can't you?"

"Piece of cake," the tall man said, his face pale.

"Then let's go," Rafe insisted.

He expected the tall man to resist, but his shoulders slumped and, to Rafe's amazement, tears filled his eyes. "I couldn't let it kill you," he said. "You're my son. I almost killed my own son." The man rubbed at the corners of his eyes.

"We better hurry," Rafe said.

The tall man ran, Rafe at his side. The crude fertilizer bomb was in the coat closet just inside the front door. "You wait outside, way back," Rafe was told as the older man dropped to his knees while pulling a pair of pliers and a pocketknife from his pocket. "I can't guarantee it won't blow. And I don't want you getting hurt."

"You said it was a piece of cake," Rafe protested.

"So I lied," the tall man said without looking up. "What did you expect?"

"Then let's get out of here," Rafe said. "I can't let it kill you."

"No, you go," the tall man said as he began opening a small box with wires running out of it that sat on the bags of fertilizer.

Rafe stood frozen. The tall man shouted, "Get out of here, kid. Please. I've hurt you way too much already."

"We're both getting out of here if it's that dangerous," Rafe insisted, grabbing the tall man by the shoulder.

"Don't jerk on me! You'll make it go off for sure."

"Then come with me," Rafe pleaded. "The house isn't worth your life."

"No. Run. Get away, Rafe."

Rafe let go of the tall man's shoulder and backed slowly away. At the door he tried once more. "Please, don't get yourself killed. My folks can build another house."

"Get out of here, kid!" the man who claimed to be his biological father shouted.

Rafe ran to where Lindsay, contrary to his instructions, still stood beside the truck, the keys dangling from her fingers and tears running down her face.

* * *

Lenny Collings answered his cell phone as soon as he saw it was Rafe calling. "Hello, Rafe? How are things at the ranch?"

"The tall man won't hurt us now. I think you should come back as soon as you can, Dad," Rafe said, unable to completely mask his emotions. "You're never going to believe what's happened."

* * *

The wild shopping spree through the trendiest department stores in Portland had been exhilarating at first, but the evil look that Mina had seen in her husband's eyes began to haunt her after a few hours.

She'd returned to the mansion she now lived in feeling strangely empty. Her husband had promised that they'd have a lot of good times when he'd proposed to her. They'd do things together, he'd committed. And yet he'd refused to let her go with him on his trip.

Mina didn't even know where he'd planned to go, and every time she'd tried to call him the day following his departure, his cell phone had been out of service. She couldn't even talk to him! But she suspected that if she had been able to, he'd have refused to tell her anything about what he was doing. He was clearly trying to hide something.

Was that what a marriage was supposed to be like?

She didn't think so. If it was, she wasn't so sure she wanted it anymore. Money wasn't everything. Even though she'd bought some very nice things during her shopping spree, she hadn't touched any of them after she'd put them away. They didn't seem important to her anymore. All she could focus on now was that frightening image Kerry had portrayed when she'd begged to go with him, the look of something terrible on his face and in his eyes that she couldn't define.

Mina had seen evil depicted in movies and on TV, but that short glimpse of viciousness she'd seen on Kerry's face and in his eyes was worse than anything even the best of actors could portray. The more she thought about it, the more concerned and frightened she was. She admitted to herself that she barely knew her husband. He'd refused to talk about his past. And he'd told her several times that he wasn't interested in hers. His explanation was that the past didn't matter. They had the future, the rest of their lives, to look forward to. It was them together, he'd said, that mattered. He didn't want to be reminded of what it was like before she'd come into his life, he'd told her. That had satisfied her before, but it made her curious now and added to her trepidation.

She'd waited until the maid had gone that afternoon, then she began to look for something that might give her a glimpse into her husband's past. So she began to search, and it wasn't a random search. She began in his private office, the place he did most of his work when he wasn't at his office downtown. It was also the place he'd told her she didn't need to be concerned about, for it had nothing to do with her. Again, that had seemed logical enough before, but now it made her wonder.

After an hour of methodically going through files and desk drawers, Mina began to doubt that she would find anything other than papers and correspondence, all of which seemed to have to do with his business here in Portland. She was about to abandon her search when she discovered something that piqued her interest. The bottom of the large drawer of her husband's oak desk didn't seem to be as deep as the drawer looked like it should be from the outside. She carefully pulled everything out and placed it in order on the floor so that she could replace everything in the same order as she'd found it. Then she tapped on the bottom of the drawer. As she'd suspected, it sounded hollow. She checked the bottom piece of wood and found that it wasn't tight. She discovered a tiny groove at the back of the drawer. Using a knife, she pried, and what proved to be a false bottom came up quite easily.

There were several large manila envelopes hidden in that secret spot, and each was stuffed with papers. What she found in those envelopes, as she had suspected, had nothing to do with normal business dealings. There was a record of bank accounts in foreign countries in one envelope. There were staggering sums in each account.

Another envelope contained pictures of men. They were tough-looking, evil men, and the photos looked like they'd been taken without the men's knowledge, like with a secret camera. On the back of each picture there was a name, a first name only. And below the name was a phone number. There were twenty pictures in all, and Mina instinctively knew that she didn't want to ever meet any of those men. It also made her doubts about her husband that much stronger. After a quick study of the area codes, she realized that the men must be from various locations across the country.

She returned the pictures to their envelope and opened another one. It was full of newspaper stories; some were actual clippings, others were taken off the Internet. She scanned through them. They were all accounts of crimes that had been committed in various places across the country. There were no pictures, only text. Many of the crimes had been violent, and there was nothing to indicate any of them had been solved. She had the uneasy feeling that she knew who had committed those terrible crimes.

More of the manila envelopes were filled with articles. The next to the last one she opened was all about one crime. This series of articles differed from the rest—it seemed to chronicle an ongoing story. It contained pictures of a young man by the name of Rafe Collings from Ephraim, Utah. Several of the articles were about Rafe when he was only six. She was sickened when she read about this little boy finding his mother murdered in a bank, the victim of an armed robbery.

Further articles were about the young man at later stages in his life. Each was accompanied by at least one picture. From everything she read, it appeared that Rafe was an exceptional young man. It didn't take Mina long to figure out that she was only a couple of years older than him.

Although there was nothing to identify the papers the articles came from, she thought most of them must be from a local paper. It made Mina wonder how Kerry got the articles. It also made her wonder why. It was like Kerry was following the boy's life. Mina was more disturbed than ever when she read the final article about Rafe Collings. It said that he was working as an apprentice to a private investigator in Utah. The picture that accompanied the article had been drawn on. In the very center of Rafe's forehead, someone, almost certainly her husband, had drawn a small target. And next to the picture in what she recognized as Kerry's handwriting was written, "You're dead, Rafe."

Mina shuddered in horror. She'd married a monster! It was almost more than she could fathom. He had deceived her. His money had blinded her. At that moment, she began to plot her escape from his mansion and her marriage. Even as she did so, she opened the final manila envelope. It contained several forms of identification in a host of different names. The only common detail on each one was the picture. It was of her husband, Kerry Sundolf.

After carefully putting everything back in the envelopes and returning them to the secret compartment in her husband's desk, and then restoring the files in the drawer itself exactly as she'd removed them, she hurried to her bedroom. She rapidly packed a suitcase, taking only clothes she didn't think her husband had ever seen her wear. She wanted to be gone before her husband returned and she didn't want him to immediately figure out that she'd left him, for she wanted a good head start on him. As she worked, she found herself listening with growing apprehension for the sound of the door opening, of Kerry's voice calling her, or of his footsteps on the marble floors.

Once she was packed, she laid her cell phone on the bed, making sure it was turned on. She hoped he'd see it and think she'd forgotten it and would be back. She hurriedly lugged her suitcase to the gold-colored Mercedes her husband had given her as a wedding gift. She got in the car and started the ignition, then she suddenly had an idea and jumped out. There was one more thing she needed to do before she left.

She ran to where her husband kept his firearms and opened his gun cabinet. Five minutes later she drove away, determined to be hundreds of miles from Portland before she stopped for the night.

The only stop Mina made before leaving the city was at a bank. She showed her ID there, the new driver's license which identified her as Mina Sundolf. When she left the bank, her purse was stuffed with thousands of dollars in cash. Enough to start a new life elsewhere, someplace where her husband could never find her.

She hoped.

As she drove, she thought about those photos in her husband's secret drawer, those pictures of evil men. She was glad that by getting away from her husband, she would be assured of never having to meet any of them.

* * *

Rafe got a call late that evening from the Provo police just as he and Lindsay were finally getting the chance to settle down for dinner in Ephraim. The blue Nissan Maxima had been found in Salt Lake City, he was told. It was a rental car that had been rented in Reno, Nevada, just two days before the shooting. They had already conducted a search of every rental car company in the city. No one by the name that had been listed as the renter of the Maxima had rented another car in or around Salt Lake. Did he know anyone by the name Alfred Davidson? they wondered.

Of course he didn't. Nor had they expected that he would.

CHAPTER 24

Greg had not attended an LDS church service since he was a young man. Back then he'd only gone a few times with a friend in Pocatello. But when Cybil suggested that she'd come over and take him to the sacrament meeting that was to be held that day in the hospital, he readily agreed. So shortly before eleven that Sunday morning, she pushed his wheelchair slowly down the hallway to the elevator.

* * *

Deke Tuft watched them until the elevator door closed. Then he watched which floor they were going to, and he punched in the same number. They were just disappearing through a door down the hallway when he got off the elevator. He walked down and peered into the room in time to see the attractive young woman help Greg get situated. He turned from the door with disgust when he realized Greg was attending a church service of some kind.

He'd grown increasingly disgusted lately. Things had not gone his way at all. Even his dad had died on him. Now he alone was left to face the penalty for what he had only helped Harley do. He had to find his sister and make sure she didn't ever tell a soul what he and his father had done to his mother. And then he had to make sure that Stella's sons didn't say anything either. After that, he didn't know where he'd go or what he'd do. He wasn't thinking that far ahead.

* * *

"You're welcome to stay and visit for a little while," Greg said after Cybil pushed him back to his room. "It gets lonely in here."

She smiled at him. "I'll come again, Greg. But right now I've got some responsibilities to take care of in my own ward, and our meetings start at one. I'll be late if I don't get going."

"What is it about you Mormons that makes you so devoted to doing your duty?" Greg asked sincerely. He'd noticed it before, and he truly wanted to know what caused such devotion.

Cybil stopped at the doorway. "I guess we just love the Savior," she said. "At least I know that I do. We'll talk more about it sometime if you'd like. Right now, I think you need some rest."

Greg watched as Cybil walked out of the door. He wanted what she had—to be happy, to love life, and to have a strong faith in God. Those things seemed more important to him now than the prospect of the wealth and fame that could come by playing in the NBA. He knew that might never happen now, but if he could have what she had and what his brother had, he'd be happy in a way that he'd never been before.

The door opened, and Greg looked up, expecting to see a nurse. What he saw startled him. A man who could only be Deke Tuft walked in and stopped beside his bed with a yellow-toothed grin. "Didn't expect to see me, did you, Greg? And this time I know you're Greg, not Rafe."

"That's right, and you're Deke Tuft, my birth mother's brother," Greg said, wondering what Deke wanted, but not really sure he desired to find out. He was desperately feeling for the button that would summon a nurse.

"You know it, and I need to find her. She's my sister, and I'd like the chance to talk to her again. It's been a long time," Deke said with sickening sarcasm.

"Is that so?" Greg said as he found and silently pushed the call button. "You just think she knows something that could put you away for the rest of your life."

"And what would that be?" Deke asked with a smirk. "I suppose she told you and Rafe some lie. That was the way she's always been. Your mother is a worthless tramp."

Greg shook his head as he attempted to sit up in the bed. "I don't believe that," Greg said with more boldness than he was feeling. "Actually, I'm afraid we never knew our mother. You see, she died when we were born."

"Sure she did. That don't make no sense," Deke said, but from the look that came into his eyes and the shadow that crossed over his face, Greg thought that he had Deke wondering. "Stella was healthy as a coon," Deke added.

"She died when Rafe and I were born. Apparently they had to do a C-section to get us out. She never lived to even see us."

Deke looked puzzled.

"That's right," Greg went on. "The doctor had to cut her open and take us out," he said. "We couldn't come out naturally, I guess. And then she started bleeding too much. She didn't live but a few minutes after that."

"Where's she buried?" Deke asked skeptically.

"Rafe thinks it's in Richfield, that's a town south of here. Only trouble is, we never knew her name. Nobody knew her name. So she's in a pauper's grave. This might surprise you, but Rafe and I didn't even know about each other until we were sixteen, and then we didn't know for sure that we were brothers," Greg said, wondering why a nurse hadn't responded, and then, thinking of the dangerous man that Deke was, he found himself hoping that one wouldn't come. He prayed that he would get a call on the intercom instead.

His prayer was answered. A nurse called on the intercom. "What can I get you, Greg?" she asked.

"I wondered if I could get something for pain in a few minutes. I'm okay now, but I can feel it coming on. However, I wonder if you would mind calling the cops. I have a visitor who's wanted for murder."

As he said that, to his relief Deke darted out of the room. As soon as he was gone, he said, "The man that just left my room—can you see him?"

"Yes, I see him."

"Don't try to stop him. He's extremely dangerous. Just call the police and have someone follow him outside and see what he's driving. And let the cops know. If he comes back in here, I might not get out alive."

"Are you sure I shouldn't detain him?" she asked.

"Yes, quite sure," Greg said. "I'm lucky he didn't finish me off just now."

* * *

After spending the night at a friend's house, Rafe and Lindsay had attended his family's ward in Ephraim. They hadn't been out of church long before his cell phone rang. "Greg, how are you feeling this morning?" Rafe asked.

"I'm doing fine. I even went downstairs to sacrament meeting with Cybil."

"Great!"

"But that's not why I called," Greg went on. "I just had a visitor."

Rafe felt a shiver run through him at the tone of his brother's voice. "Who?" he asked.

"Our dear old Uncle Deke."

"Greg! Where did he go? Are you sure you're okay?" Rafe asked in alarm.

"He left, that's all. But the hospital staff got a description of his car and a license number. He's not driving the Bronco anymore. But I really am okay. Deke said he wanted to talk to Stella."

"What did you tell him?" Rafe asked.

"The truth. And I think he actually believed me. Hopefully the cops will find him soon," Greg said. Then he asked how things were going in Ephraim.

Rafe told him, leaving nothing out. Greg could hardly believe what he'd just been told and had to wipe some tears from his eyes.

* * *

Greg received a phone call a couple of hours later. "Greg, this is Detective Campbell of the Provo Police Department. We think we just arrested the man who was in your room earlier. You did say his name is Deke Tuft?"

"That's him," Greg said.

"We'll need a positive identification later for court purposes, but for now we just wanted to make sure we had the right guy. He's wanted for murder and much more down in Texas," the officer said. "He'll be held without bail."

"Good," Greg said. "This is a big relief."

"Now if we could just find the man who shot you," Detective Campbell added.

"Yes, that would be nice," Greg said. "But more for my brother than for me."

* * *

Rafe and Lindsay had just pulled into Provo when Greg called him again. "Rafe, they have Deke in custody."

"Good, now if we could just find my mother's killer," Rafe said as he got out of his truck and into the chilly fall air.

"That was what the detective said," Greg responded with a chuckle. "Where are you guys? Are you still in Ephraim?"

"Oh no, we're in Provo again," Rafe said. "I'm trying to figure out what to do to get the stalker in custody."

"What are you going to do?" Greg asked.

"Well, Lindsay and I have been talking. We have an idea."

"Is it risky?" Greg asked.

"Yes, I suppose it is, but Lindsay's willing. It was actually my boss's idea."

"What are you planning?"

Rafe told him, and Greg said, "You guys be careful. And keep an eye out for the guy who shot me."

"You've got my word," Rafe said.

* * *

Rafe kept his word the best he could; a half dozen plainclothes officers assisted him. Lindsay was the bait. She had insisted. Rafe was nearby at the moment—very nearby. The location was the hospital parking area, the one place they figured that the stalker would expect Lindsay to show up. She arrived in her red Dodge Stratus. Both Lindsay and Cybil got out of the car, watched closely by the police who were posted in various vehicles in the area.

Rafe stayed in the Stratus, hidden in the backseat.

Cybil stayed with Greg while Lindsay walked alone back to her car a few minutes later. She was wired, and everything she said or that anyone near her said was transmitted to the officers and to Rafe. She was in sight of at least two officers at any given moment.

She could also hear the officers, thanks to a tiny receiver that was in her ear, worn like a hearing aid and covered by long locks of shiny black hair. Rafe was tense as he listened from his cramped position. "Lindsay," an officer said, "there's a vehicle coming up behind you. It's an old black van with heavily tinted windows. It looks awfully suspicious. Step between some of the parked cars just in case it's him, but try to make it look natural. We don't want to spook him. We're coming your way."

"Okay," Lindsay said, her voice trembling. "I see it."

Rafe waited, wishing he was where he could see her and praying that she'd be okay.

"It went on past," she said a moment later.

"It's parking now," an officer said. "Rafe, it's just a few spaces down from where you're at."

"Did you get a look at the driver, Lindsay?" Rafe asked.

"The windows were dark, so I couldn't see in."

"Can you see your car yet?" he asked next.

"Not yet. I'm still quite a ways away," Lindsay responded.

"Rafe, the driver got out of the black van," one of the officers said. "I've got him in my binoculars. He doesn't fit the description of the guy whose picture we have."

"Remember, he could have changed his appearance," Rafe said.

"Lindsay, there's another car behind you. It's a pickup. Can you see it?" an officer asked.

"Yes," she said. "I'm getting between some cars again."

It was silent for a moment, then into Rafe's earpiece came Lindsay's voice. "It stopped. The driver's getting out."

"I'm coming," Rafe said.

But before he could move, an officer said, "Stay put, Rafe. We've got her covered."

"Does it look like him, Lindsay?" Rafe asked.

"No, it's a woman. She looks old."

"Don't let that fool you; he could be disguised," Rafe cautioned. "Are you guys closing in?"

"We've got it under control, Rafe," an officer assured him calmly. But Rafe wasn't so sure. It was just a feeling he had. If only he could see. "I think I better . . ." he began. But before he'd completed his thought, there was a sharp rap on the passenger-door of the Stratus. It was followed by some scraping sounds, then the door opened.

Rafe caught just a glimpse of the man who had just broken into Lindsay's car as he began slipping into the front seat, his head below the level of the window. Rafe opened the passenger side rear door and scrambled out. The intruder yelped in surprise, and he tried to back out of the car. But Rafe caught him by the back of his shirt collar. The man twisted with surprising quickness, and kicked Rafe in the shin.

"We've got her . . . him . . . whatever," Rafe could hear the cops say in his ear as he winced with pain. The man's coat slipped off and left Rafe holding it as he darted away. Rafe threw the coat aside and tore after him. They were almost to the black van before Rafe tackled him from behind and crashed to the ground on top of him.

"We got the wrong person, Rafe," an officer said. "This really is a lady. She's just getting a book from her daughter's car."

"I've got him," Rafe said between deep gulping breaths as he held his captive to the ground beside the van.

"Where are you?" Lindsay screamed. "I can't see you, Rafe."

"I'm beside the black van," he said and gulped a deep breath. "We're on the ground."

"I'm coming," Lindsay said.

"Stay with an officer," Rafe shouted.

A minute later, two officers arrived to help him. By the time Lindsay and another officer got there, the suspect was on his feet, his hands cuffed behind his back. "Do you know him?" one of the officers asked Lindsay.

Rafe stepped over to her and put an arm protectively around her shoulders. Lindsay's face was pale, and she was staring at the man. "Yes," she said. "Even without his beard I recognize him. I don't know his name, but he's the guy that's been stalking me."

The stalker looked at Rafe through hateful eyes. "She's mine," he said.

"No, I'm afraid you're mistaken," Rafe said as he pulled Lindsay closer. "If she'll have me, she's mine."

"I'll have you," Lindsay said weakly. "I've never wanted anyone else."

* * *

"Well, at least we're down to just one enemy," Cybil said lightly when Lindsay and Rafe joined her in Greg's room a few minutes later.

Rafe nodded his head. "Yeah, but I'm afraid that the one that's left is not going to be as easy to catch as the stalker was," Rafe said. "And as Greg knows, he's not one to tip his hand before he shoots."

"Rafe, why don't you let the cops catch him? I'm so scared for you," Lindsay said. "You've been through so much already. Please, go somewhere safe while they look for him."

It was getting late, but none of the four of them wanted to leave, and of course Greg couldn't. Outside, it had turned cold and windy. According to the TV in Greg's room, a storm was blowing in. It promised rain, wind, and lower temperatures by morning. There was even snow forecast for as low as six thousand feet above sea level.

It was warm in Greg's room, and the four of them were comfortable in each other's company. Outside, in addition to the weather, danger and uncertainty lurked.

* * *

Kerry Sundolf, most recently known in the Portland area as a successful and wealthy businessman, wondered where his young wife was. Her cell phone was lying on the bed. It was turned on, but the charge was low. He was sure she'd forgotten it, for she never went anywhere without it. He couldn't imagine where she could be at this hour. It was too late to be shopping, and he would have thought she had that out of her system by now.

He looked in her closet and couldn't see anything missing at first glance. Even her stack of suitcases was piled near the back. He counted them. She'd had six, of that he was certain. There were five there now. He again looked at her clothes. He couldn't be sure, but he thought there might be a few things gone, a blouse or two, some slacks, maybe a dress.

He went next to the bathroom. She had so much stuff that he had no way of knowing if she'd taken anything, but she could have. She was probably spending the night with a friend, he decided. Maybe she got lonely without him here in their big house. Kerry was tired and didn't have time to worry about it now. He expected that she'd be back the next day. He had enough to think about without worrying about Mina right now. Anyway, the way things were going, he might have to leave her. He'd already reached that conclusion over the past few hours. He hadn't known until he was nearly home that he'd shot the wrong man, that Rafe's twin brother was the one he'd shot, and that he had survived.

But worst of all, he'd also learned that the police had photos of him. It would be devastating if they got into the press. Others would see the pictures and they would identify him, and he'd have to leave his good life and his new wife behind. It all made him very cranky. But he was very tired now, and before he decided how to deal with Rafe and what to do with the rest of his life, he needed a good night's sleep. And he was going to have it. He was safe enough for now. Even if the cops did have pictures, it would take some time, probably days if not weeks before they could trace him to Portland.

But as a precaution, before he went to bed, Kerry made sure all the windows and doors were locked, and he set the burglar alarm. He laid his pistol on the nightstand and leaned a rifle beside the bedroom door. Confident that he was safe, he went to sleep.

* * *

Rafe was almost to Lindsay's apartment before he realized that he'd forgotten to turn his cell phone on after leaving the hospital. He wasn't sure why, but it seemed to be a rule that cell phones couldn't be used in hospitals. He pulled it from his pocket and turned it on. Discovering that he had voice mail, he immediately accessed it.

Lindsay was leaning against his shoulder. He thought she might be asleep, but he wasn't sure. She hadn't said anything for several minutes and he knew how tired she was. He was tired too. There was only one voice mail message waiting for him, but the fatigue fled when Rafe heard a woman's voice saying, "Mr. Collings, I got your number from a nice policeman in Provo. I hope that's okay. You see, I think that I know who killed your mother. I can't tell you how I know, but his name is Kerry Sundolf, and he lives in Portland, Oregon. He's been gone for a few days from his home there, but he will probably be back soon." The voice, that of a woman probably in her twenties, went on to give an address, as well as a description of the man, which gave legitimacy to her assertions. Then she concluded by saying, "There is nothing more I can do, because I'm afraid for my life."

Rafe stopped in front of Lindsay's apartment. She stirred as he shut off the engine. "You're home," he said as he scanned the area from force of habit. Of course where street lights didn't shine there was the darkness that his eyes couldn't penetrate, and that was worrisome. He got out, circled around the truck, and helped Lindsay out. He walked her to the door, kissed her good night, and turned to leave.

"What are you going to do tomorrow?" she asked. "Will I see you?"

Rafe's mind rapidly scanned possible truthful answers. That he was planning to drive straight to Salt Lake from here and catch a plane to Portland, he didn't want to tell her, for he knew she'd be terrified for him. Finally, he said, "I'll be working on finding my mother's killer," he said. "I don't know if I'll be able to see you or not. I want to, that's for sure."

"Be careful, Rafe," she said. "I don't think I could live without you now that I've found you again." She kissed him once more, then clung to him as he wrapped his arms around her. They stood there together for a minute or so.

Finally Rafe said, "I shouldn't be standing here like this. It puts you in danger. I've got to go."

"Promise me you'll be careful," she pleaded.

"You have my word," he said, and then he opened her door and watched her go in. Lindsay Diamond had become the most important person in his life in a very short period of time. He wished he didn't have to do what he had to do, but he was committed. Kerry Sundolf, if his mysterious caller was right about him, was out there somewhere, and Rafe wouldn't be safe until he was stopped.

While driving to Salt Lake, Rafe called the Provo police and eventually was able to talk to Detective Joe Campbell, who had been assigned to lead the investigation of Greg's shooting. After listening to the voice mail, he said, "I'll see what I can do about getting a warrant."

"Thanks, that would be helpful. I'm on my way up there now."

"Shouldn't you wait? Once we have a warrant, I could go, and with the help of the Portland police, it would be much safer trying to arrest him," the detective suggested.

"But he might be gone by then," Rafe said. "I'm hoping we'll get lucky and find him at his house and keep him in sight until he can be arrested."

"Don't do anything crazy, Rafe," Detective Campbell cautioned.

Rafe got lucky and caught a red-eye flight to Portland via San Francisco. He managed to get some sleep on the trip and was reasonably alert when he arrived in Portland. When he got off the plane, it was almost eight o'clock in the morning, Pacific time. He called the local police from the airport and told them who he was and why he was in Portland.

"Do you have a warrant for Mr. Sundolf?" he was asked by a Lieutenant Rob Masters, to whom he'd been referred.

"No, but the police in Provo are working on that now. I just want to keep him under surveillance until the warrant is ready."

"We can't stop you from doing that, I suppose," Lieutenant Masters said, sounding a little hostile to Rafe. "But you will be in trouble if you cause any kind of disturbance. Mr. Sundolf is a very prominent businessman in our city. I'm quite certain that you're barking up the wrong tree here, that you're after the wrong man."

"I don't think so. In fact, if you'd meet me somewhere, I'd be glad to show you the photos of him that were taken by a witness when he shot my brother," Rafe suggested. "You must know what Sundolf looks like if he's such a prominent person."

"Oh yes. His picture has been in the paper a number of times, most recently when he got married," the lieutenant said, beginning to sound less hostile and more interested now. "I'm sure that I can find a picture as well. Then we'll compare them. However, I'll be very surprised if the picture you have turns out to be Mr. Sundolf."

Arrangements were made for an officer to pick Rafe up at the airport. He wasn't sure if it was done out of courtesy or to keep him from striking off on his own. Either way, he was relieved. He hadn't looked forward to a long surveillance. He hoped that once they saw the pictures he had in his pocket that they'd do whatever needed to be done to make sure that Sundolf didn't get away.

Rafe was ushered directly into Lieutenant Masters's office. The officer had a newspaper on his desk, and when Rafe sat down, he opened that paper. The photo of a newly married couple appeared in the upper right-hand corner of the page. Rafe felt his body began to shake as he looked at the happy expression on the face of the man who had murdered his mother.

"That's him," Rafe said, touching a finger to the face he'd never forget. "That's the man who killed my mother."

Lieutenant Masters was watching him closely. "Are you okay, Mr. Collings?" he asked.

"That's him," Rafe repeated as, with shaking hands, he pulled two pictures of the man who shot Greg from his pocket and dropped them on the desk where the lieutenant could see them.

"Whoa, you're right!" the lieutenant exclaimed. "Kerry Sundolf is clearly not what he claims to be."

Twenty minutes later, the faxed copy of an arrest warrant from Provo was in Lieutenant Masters's hands.

* * *

Kerry hadn't meant to sleep so late. He wasn't sure what had woken him up, but it wasn't his alarm clock, for he'd failed to set it. He hurried to the window and looked out. He was nervous. He knew that he should get away from here soon. What he saw in the street behind his house prompted him to utter a string of vulgarities. A cop car was pulling slowly by. *How could they have figured it out so soon?* he asked himself in anger. Still cursing, he ran from his bedroom, grabbing his rifle from beside the door.

He peered through the front window and saw another cop car pull up. It stopped, and a moment later another one joined it, then one more. Kerry worked the bolt, chambering a round in his rifle. The same face he'd seen just days ago was watching the house from over the top of one of the police cars. But he knew it wasn't the same face. This time it was Rafe Collings, not his brother. And this time he wouldn't miss.

Hatred filled his vile heart as he aimed at Rafe's head through the window. He was leaning over the back of a chair to make sure he was steady. He put the crosshairs between Rafe's eyes as an officer called out in a bullhorn for him to surrender, to come out with his arms raised. Ignoring the order, Kerry Sundolf squeezed the trigger. A loud bang filled the house, sending reverberating echoes through its expansive chambers.

* * *

Lindsay had tried to call Rafe a dozen times already. She'd tried his home, she'd tried his office, and she'd tried his cell phone. Deep in her heart, she had the feeling that he'd known something he hadn't told her the night before. She was terribly frightened for him. She got in her car and drove to his house. His truck wasn't there. Next she drove to his office. His truck wasn't there either. Finally, she drove to the hospital where she was once again disappointed. Greg hadn't seen him or heard from him, and neither had Thorn.

In desperation she called the police and asked for Detective Joe Campbell. When he came on the line, he sounded very tired. She explained who she was and that she couldn't reach Rafe. He said, "I guess he didn't want you to know. He's in Portland, Oregon. He found out last night who shot Greg, and he even got an address."

"Last night?" she cried. "But I was with him last night. I would have known if anyone called him unless it was after he left me at my apartment."

"I don't know what time he left you there, but what I do know is that he had a voice mail message on his cell phone. The caller told him who shot Greg. He flew to Portland during the night."

"But he can't go after that guy alone. It's too dangerous," she said as a wave of terror swept over her that was worse than anything she'd experienced before, even in those times when she had been in mortal danger herself. And it was at that moment that she knew that her love for Rafe was greater than she had imagined, that he was more important to her than anyone in the world.

"He's not alone," the detective assured her soothingly. "He's with several officers from Portland. I faxed up a warrant an hour ago. I'm sure he's just fine."

* * *

The face of the man lying at his feet was unrecognizable. Lieutenant Masters, a tough, no-nonsense cop, a veteran of many years who had seen violent death more times than he cared to remember, was sickened at what he saw.

He turned away. To the officer next to him he said, "There'll need to be pictures taken, the scene will need to be processed. You know what to do."

"Mighty ugly, Lieutenant," he said. "But I'll take care of things."

Rafe Collings, who had always said that he'd know the face of the man who murdered his mother when he saw it again, never got to have that experience.

EPILOGUE

About one year later

Lindsay pulled the mail from the box and hurried inside. She thumbed through it, and nearly choked at the return address on one of them. It was from Houston, Texas. With trembling hands she dropped the rest of the mail on the kitchen table and called to her husband, the man she'd married just three months ago. He came in, wiping the remnants of the shaving cream from his face.

"Look at this," she said.

"Oh, my gosh! Open it while I go wash my face and hands," he instructed.

She did as he'd asked and read down through most of it. When her husband came back in, she quit reading and handed the letter to him, wiping the tears from her eyes as she did so.

"Lindsay, what's the matter?" he asked tenderly.

"Read this," she said. "Then you'll know."

He took the letter from her hand.

Dear Son,

I just wanted to write and let you know how much I love you. I just completed the last of my rehabilitation. I've been clean now and have not committed any crimes since I saw you last. Thank you for giving me a chance to start over. I didn't deserve it. And thanks for giving me enough money to get on my way that day. I know you had to sell one of your best horses to cover the cost. I promised you that I'd make it. And I have. I got a real job last week.

I drove to Dallas and visited Greg yesterday. He said you told him what I'd done when you were babies, how I'd taken him from the hospital. But you've got to believe me, Rafe. I intended to raise him myself, but it was harder than I thought it would be. And when I found this couple that was willing to pay for the privilege of raising him, I decided it was not only good for me, but also best for him. He says that he can forgive me.

There's something else I want you to understand, Rafe. I loved your mother. I didn't abandon Stella. It wasn't like it appeared. Yes, I left the car that day when we hit the moose. But I watched from the distance. I knew she'd get better care if the authorities didn't know about me. I even went to the hospital later to check on her. That was when I figured out that she'd given birth to twin boys and then died. I should have just stepped in and claimed both you and your brother, but that's not the way I did things. I was a messed up guy, as you well know.

Please forgive me, my son. And know that I love you. I hope that I can see you again soon. And tell Lindsay that I love her too. You are so lucky to have each other. Tell her she's just as pretty as your mother was. Because it's true.

Rafe had stopped several times to wipe the tears from his eyes while he was reading. Beside him, Lindsay was sniffling and wiping hers as well.

What got to both of them the most, though, was the way Rafe's biological father signed his name at the end of the letter.

It read:

With love,
The Tall Man

Rafe felt a wave of gratitude wash over him. He had so many things to be thankful for. He was grateful to be alive. And he often thought about the woman who had tipped him off about Kerry Sundolf. A woman who had plugged the barrels of her husband's guns, and in doing so had saved Rafe's life.

Rafe rose to his feet, held out his arms, and took into them his greatest blessing of all. Lindsay laid her head against his chest, and contentment filled them both.

CLAIR M. POULSON, who was both born and raised in Duchesne, Utah, spent many years patrolling the highways and enforcing the law as a highway patrolman and deputy sheriff. That followed two years of service in the U.S. Army Military Police Corps. He completed his twenty-year law-enforcement career with eight years as Duchesne County Sheriff.

While sheriff, he served as president of the Utah Sheriff's Association, and as a member of the Governor's Commission on Criminal and Juvenile Justice; the Utah Peace Officer Standards and Training Council; and a national advisory board to the FBI.

For the past fourteen years, Clair has served as a Justice Court Judge in Duchesne County. Along with his service on the bench, he has been involved with the Justice Court Association, serving for several years as a member of the Board of Directors. He is currently representing the Justice Court judges of the state as a member of Utah's Judicial Council.

Clair also does a little farming, his main interest being horses, although he has raised a variety of other livestock, including cattle, pigs, and sheep, for many years. Both Clair and his wife currently help their oldest son run Al's Foodtown.

Clair has always been an avid reader, but his interest in creating fiction found its beginning many years ago when he would tell bedtime stories to his small children. They would beg for just one more "make-up story" before going to sleep. He still practices that hobby with his grandchildren.

Clair uses his life's experiences in the criminal justice system to help him develop plots for his novels. *Mirror Image* is Clair's twelfth published novel.

Service in The Church of Jesus Christ of Latter-day Saints has always taken a lot of Clair's time. He has served in a variety of stake and ward callings, and places a high priority on that service. He has also been involved in various community functions over the years.

Clair met his wife, Ruth, while attending Snow College. They are the parents of five married children. They have eleven grandchildren, with whom they enjoy spending time. Ruth has taught piano for many years and has trained many fine pianists, including all five children; she is now teaching the two oldest grandchildren. She is also a great help to Clair in his writing, as are the members of their family.